THE MAN
WHO INVENTED
THE NEWS

The memoirs of
Marchamont
Nedham

THE MAN WHO INVENTED THE NEWS
The memoirs of Marchamont Nedham

Nigel Hastilow

Published by
Halesowen Press
WR11 7SA

www.themanwhoinventedthe.news
www.halesowenpress.co.uk

Two or three brawny Fellows in a Corner, with meer Ink and Elbow-grease, do more harm than an hundred Systematical Divines with their sweaty Preaching.

Andrew Marvell

I employed what might be called 'journalistic entryism', working as required by my employers while holding polar opposite political views that, were they to have been known, would inevitably have led to me not only being fired but also being unemployable.

Roy Greenslade

former editor of the "Daily Mirror" on his support for the IRA

Mr Greenslade admits that the need to pay his mortgage overrode his desire to speak out. His calculation worked nicely. He now lives in a handsome country house in Co. Donegal, not far from the western borders of Northern Ireland where the IRA often murdered Protestant farmers. He is still alive; those farmers aren't.

Charles Moore

"Daily Telegraph"

CAST OF CHARACTERS

Captain Doctor Marchamont Nedham (sometimes, but not here, spelt Marchmont Needham, pronounced Needham, as in "feed 'em" and "need 'em" not "fed 'em" or "bed 'em"). Lawyer, doctor, author, editor, journalist, bon-viveur.

FAMILY AND FRIENDS

Chastity Dyer, better known as Big Susie, server at The George Inn, Burford.

Glynn, Margery, née Collyer, formerly Nedham, Marchamont's mother.

Glynn, Rev Christopher, Marchamont's step-father, vicar of Burford.

Glynn, Robert, Marchamont's step-brother.

Glynn, Judge John, Marchamont's uncle.

Heylyn, Rev Peter, chaplain to Charles I, former pupil at Burford School.

Heylyn, Edward, gentleman farmer.

Lenthall, William, MP, Commons Speaker, owner of Burford Priory.

Lenthall, Elizabeth, his wife, a friend of Margery Glynn.

Nedham, Lucy, née Collyer, Marchamont's cousin and wife.

ROUNDHEADS

Audley, Captain Thomas, soldier, publisher, licence-holder, spy.

Bradshaw, John, a lawyer.

Cromwell, Oliver, a gentleman of modest means.

Cromwell, Richard, his tumbledown son.

Essex, Earl of, a general.

Fairfax, Thomas, a more important general.

Fiennes, Nathaniel, second son of The Viscount, MP for Banbury.

Fiennes, Elizabeth, wife of James Thompson.

Fleetwood, Major General Charles, a would-be dictator.

French, John, a surgeon.

Lambert, Major General John, a military hero.

Marvell, Andrew, student, MP, poet.

Milton, John, a propagandist.

Monck, Major General George, an illiterate Devonian.

Pride, Colonel Thomas, a drayman.

Prynne, William, a Puritan.

Rich, Colonel Nat, a captain of horse.

Rushworth, John, a clerk.

Saye and Sele, 'The Viscount', Lord Lieutenant of Oxfordshire.

Thompson, James, an ex-soldier. Fiennes family retainer.

Thurloe, John, spymaster.

Vane, Sir Henry the Younger, ex-governor of Massachusetts, a republican.

ROYALISTS

Astley, Bernard, a Royalist spy.

Butler, Godfrey "God", grandson of an Earl.

Charles I, a King.

Charles II, a King.

Elizabeth of Bohemia, the Winter Queen, sister of Charles I.

Henrietta Maria, Charles I's wife. A French Catholic.

Hyde, Edward, adviser to Charles I and Charles II

Lighthorne, Lucy, a comely but dispossessed noblewoman.

Prince Charles Louis, eldest son of Elizabeth of Bohemia.

Prince Rupert of the Rhine, a dashing cavalier, his younger brother.

Oxinden, Henry, an impecunious clergyman.

Washington, Colonel Henry, Governor of Worcester.

NEWSPAPERMEN

Crouch, John, editor of "The Man in the Moon" and "Mercurius Fumigosus or the Smoaking Nocturnall".

Hall, John, Marchamont's assistant, a poet.

Mabbott, Gilbert, editor of "The Moderate".

Muddiman, Henry, Marchamont's apprentice.

Newcomb, Tom, a printer.

Pecke, Sam, editor of "A Perfect Diurnall".

Sheppard, Sam, editor of "Mercurius Dogmaticus".

Robert (Bob) White, a printer.

CHAPTER I

Communicating the affaires of
Great Britaine
For the better Information
of the People

August 1643

'What do we do now?' Audley smashed his fist into the brick wall. It must have hurt.

'We say we did it deliberately. It's a symbol of everything we stand to lose if the nation submits to slavery.'

'Bloody, bloody, bloody printers,' said Audley. He grinned apologetically. 'I know I'm a bloody printer. Even so.'

'What does White say?'

'Haven't pointed it out yet. Tell you the truth, Monty, I didn't even notice. Not 'til you did.'

'Easy to miss,' I said sympathetically, though I didn't really think that.

'Hardly. It's the fucking title of the bloody news-sheet.'

'I know,' I said a little more glumly.

We sat in the Greyhound, one of the low taverns we frequented near the Thames wharves, and contemplated it. The first edition of our eight-page news-sheet. Price one penny. Covering the news for the week Tuesday the 23 of Aug to Tuesday the 29 of Aug 1643. Thin paper, very thin. Print bleeding through the pages did make it a little difficult to read but not impossible. And there was an appetite for news. Everywhere you went, the question was the same, 'What's the news?'

The main story for our first edition? Catholic troops from Ireland landing in Wales to reinforce the King's army while the Earl of Ormond failed to save a castle near Dublin from attack by Catholics who, cruelly, mercilessly, indiscriminately slaughtered good Protestant men, women and children.

I made sure we included the line about Wales 'where to this day many of the inhabitants are ignorant as heathens'. It does no harm to be provocative. If the Welsh were for the King there must be a reason for it and ignorance was as likely as anything. Idiots. Sheep-shaggers. Live in caves. Unspeakable accents.

This was a good first edition. It put Parliament's case to the people. It described the devilish dealings of the Cavaliers. It started to counter the ridiculous nonsense spouted by the "Court Mercury".

And yet... and yet...

Audley and I both knew the only thing that would be remembered about our first edition was the most obvious, disastrous thing of all. The spelling mistake.

Some idiot printer had spelt it "Britanicus" with just one 'n'. We all know it should be 'Britannicus' but somehow we managed to get it wrong and neither Bob White nor George Bishop, the printers, noticed. Nor did Audley. Nor, to tell the truth, did I. We'd all seen the first proofs of the news-sheet and we'd been so excited we didn't really read it properly, if at all. Too busy chattering about how to get it distributed, how many copies we would need to print, whether we could get them into Oxford, how we might catch the messengers to other parts of the country and what we would do for the second edition. We completely missed the most glaring error of them all.

We got our own name wrong.

It wouldn't look good to admit a mistake at the very outset of our new career. Better to pretend we meant it all along. We would brazen it out.

First, though, we had to tell our patrons.

Sir Harry Vane looked up from a pile of papers, frowned and said, 'I'm too busy to bother with details. If we can't do a deal with the Scotch, the only word we'll be spelling is t-r-e-a-s-o-n. I am here trying to save the nation. I am devoting my time, my health, my wealth, my entire being to the cause of the Lord and liberty and you come whining to me with questions of grammar? My dear Nedham, really.'

The Viscount was phlegmatic. 'I doubt if the most part of the population will notice. I confess I did not. Is it even wrong?'

His son Colonel Nat Fiennes was even less concerned. 'I thought you did it deliberately,' he laughed and slapped me on the back, 'To overturn the traditions of the nation. Symbolic, what?'

Back to the printers. Bob White, thin and angry at the best of times, was less accommodating. 'What do you expect?' he demanded. 'Do you suppose we read every word you give us to set and print? Do you see us idly hanging about in this studio day after day with nothing better to do than read, and then re-read, the yards and yards of verbiage and drivel you and your fellow scribblers throw at us on your ink-stained, blotchy pieces of paper? It's bad enough you expect us to decipher your handwriting in the first place. Do you seriously think your pearls of wisdom are so worth the reading we must do it five times over in pursuit of every trifling mistake? Do you, Marchamont, really? And you, Captain Audley, when we have bent over backwards to rescue your prose from itself in the past?'

His partner George Bishop was equally belligerent. For Bishop, attack was the best form of defence. 'And have you sorted out a licence for this thing yet?' he demanded, waving the paper in our faces.

We had not.

'Yet you want to print another 100 copies this week, 850 in all? Well get a licence or we'll all go to jail and I have no intention of being imprisoned because Marchamont Nedham is a lazy good-for-nothing who can't be bothered to read his own news-sheet or take the simple step of keeping the thing within the law.'

It didn't take long for our rivals at the King's court in Oxford to point out our news-sheet couldn't spell its own name.

We retaliated. If we were to establish "Britanicus" as the brightest star in the Parliamentary firmament, there must be no surrender. I told Audley we should insist it was all part of our plan. After all, this was a lawless country and that certainly extended to the way words were spelt. There was no list of words and their correct spelling. Who was to say "Britanicus" was wrong and "Britannicus" was right any more than "Nedham" should be "Needham"? Some people spelt "frenzy" as "phrensie", "kingdom" as "kingdome", "soldiers" as "souldiers" and so on. Even William Shakspere usually spelt his own name incorrectly.

Rather than ignore those who attacked us over our spelling, I decided we should revel in it. In our second edition, I drew the readers' attention to it. I told them the "Court Mercury" was so bereft of news it resorted to slander.

I wrote: 'They are not able to spell one word true there; for they spell the Parliament, Rebels; Popery, the Protestant Religion; Idolatrie and Superstition, Decencie; and many such strange kind of spellings.'

We had a serious purpose – to further Parliament's cause and counter Royalist propaganda – but this was an amusing way to wage war. I liked to imagine the faces of Peter Heylyn and his sidekick John Berkenhead when they saw the next edition of "Britanicus". They would hate what we wrote about their spelling just as they would hate our exposure of the Earl of Northumberland and Sir John Evelyn as Royalist spies, not to mention the news that Parliament's leading general, the Earl of Essex, was on the march to relieve the siege of Gloucester and scatter the Cavaliers.

It made me chuckle to imagine the Royalists' indignation at our mockery. They might take themselves seriously but why should we? 'We must laugh at them whenever possible,' I told Audley. 'There is nothing more damaging to a cause than being laughed at. We must laugh mercilessly.'

So it was that, in the next few weeks, they attacked the Earl of Essex, and we mocked their generals for the dotards they were. They protested there were only 18 Peers left in London and 160 MPs. We pointed out there were even fewer in their so-called Parliament at Oxford. They wrote about Parliament soldiers ransacking a poor woman's house. We described in detail how Cavaliers destroyed a village and raped the women. They complained a Parliamentarian prisoner was caught on the Sabbath when most people were in church, committing buggery on a horse. We explained they had mis-spelled and he was actually committing burglary with a view to fleeing from Shrewsbury on horseback (we both later reported that, bugger or burglar, the man was hanged).

As George Bishop said, we did need a licence. You couldn't be too careful. You never knew which way the wind was blowing. Today, it might be perfectly acceptable to the grandees in Parliament to attack the king and support the Scots; tomorrow it might be the other way round. Equally, it might be fine to argue in favour of religious freedom one week and punishable with imprisonment the next. A licence was a necessary evil.

We marched down to Stationers' Hall in Ave Maria Lane (you'd think the Saints would have changed this Papist name, but no). It was a wasted visit. They said we had to go to the House of Commons and ask for John Rushworth. Audley pointed out his last news-sheet had been given a permit by someone at Stationers' Hall. 'Rules have changed,' said the unhelpful bureaucrat behind his big empty desk.

In Westminster, we found Rushworth in a small office hidden behind piles of documents and a barricade of empty bottles. He was a greasy-faced Puritanical man with thinning black hair and bulging eyes, wearing a stained black suit. It turned out he was deputy clerk of the Commons.

'I do a bit of writing myself,' he told us confidentially. He spoke as if spies were listening to his every word and you couldn't be too careful. 'I can be your correspondent if you like.' He looked over his shoulder at the shelves full of parchments and books as if there might be someone concealed in the shadows.

'How much?' Audley demanded loudly, clearly irritated by this ridiculous secrecy.

'Farthing a line.'

'Farthing a line?' Audley was incredulous. 'Good luck with that.'

'Maybe,' I said. 'It might be helpful to have an informer who sat through all the Parliamentary debates and let us know what was being said. Do you supply anybody else?'

Rushworth grinned a sickly grin. 'It has been known,' he said, shuffling papers and looking up at us slyly.

'Tell you what, you let us have something we can put in our newsbook and we'll see. But only if you don't pass it on to anybody else. We don't want to see the same thing turn up in something like "The Perfect Diurnall" let alone the "Court Mercury".'

'That might cost a little bit more,' Rushworth whispered.

'I know,' I said, 'Let's discuss it with my old friend and neighbour.' He looked at me quizzically. 'I think he might be your boss, the Speaker, Mr Lenthall.'

'I'm sure that won't be necessary,' said Rushworth quickly. 'No, no, not at all, not at all. I am sure we can do business together gentlemen.'

Audley plonked a big fist on Rushworth's desk and lent forward on it, lowering his face to the same level as the weaselly bureaucrat's. 'I'm sure we can,' he said. 'A quarter of a farthing,' he said. 'Sixteen lines to the penny. Only if we use it and it doesn't go anywhere else.'

'Of course, of course,' said Rushworth, standing to usher us out.

It turned out the man was good at obtaining commissions. He even had some sort of job with the colony of Massachusetts. 'Rushworth? Not worth a rush,' said Audley.

Even so, he gave us the licence, a bit of officialdom that would come back to haunt us.

CHAPTER 2

Speciall Passages
and certain
Informations
from several places

December 1641

I was enjoying a quiet drink in Hell when I was accosted by Captain Tom
Audley. They'd arrested the Archbishop and everyone was celebrating
except Andrew Marvell. He was planning to flee abroad.

Hell, I should explain, is one of those basement dives near the Palace
of Westminster. It was turned into a tavern after a couple of hundred
years as a prison for people who owed the King money. It was a useful
place. Not expensive, close to the King's court, Parliament and the law
courts, much-frequented by lawyers among whose number I counted myself at the time. My chambers were way down in the City of London but
it was often necessary to run errands and meet people at Whitehall and,
once there, it was often necessary to obtain a drink in one of the cheaper
taverns. And it was often necessary to meet one's friends and catch up
with the news.

'And where,' growled Audley, leaning towards Marvell and banging the bowl of his pipe on the table for emphasis, 'Where, sir, do you
consider safety to be found? In the Americas? The Indies? France? The
Netherlands?'

'He's got a point, Andy,' I added, 'You can't possibly think of going to
the West Indies can you?'

'Good Lord, no. A tour of Europe. Improve the mind. Visit sites of
antiquity. Learn more of ancient Rome and ancient Greece.'

'Good luck with that,' growled Audley, draining the rest of his beer,
slamming down his tankard and calling for another.

'I'm sorry, Marchamont,' said Marvell with a frown, 'But self-preservation is nature's first great law. All nature's creatures observe it except one – man. We ignore this law at our peril.'

'Spoken like a true coward,' declared Audley, standing over poor Marvell and glaring down belligerently at the young man.

'No, no, Audley,' I said, 'Not everyone has the stomach for a fight like you do. Marvell's a poet, aren't you, Andy? He prefers to meditate on apples and vegetables, bai gum. Come on, sit down Audley.'

'Must you, Monty? Most people say I lost my accent at Cambridge.'

'Most people are mostly wrong most of the time, Marv-Hell.'

'Anyway, who is this fellow?' he asked, indicating Audley, who slumped back in his seat and warmed his hands in the fireplace where a small pile of wood created the illusion of warmth. It was December 18 and winds were blowing raw from the East. It looked as if the Thames would freeze over completely. It wasn't safe to walk across yet but ice was forming. It might be solid by Christmas Day.

'Tommy, allow me to introduce my young friend Andrew Marv-Hell. Marvel, meet Tom Audley, printer and newsbook-writer of this parish.'

'Not printer any longer,' Audley said, looking at Marvell, 'Don't have time. Have to use White and Bishop.'

'That's how we met,' I explained to Marvell. 'Bob White's from Witney.'

Marvell looked at me blankly.

'Robert White, printer. Remember? Didn't he produce your little Latin effulgence?'

'George Bishop and Robert White,' Marvell answered, recognition dawning across his chubby face.

Tom Audley was a good ten years older than Marvell and me. He said he'd taken part in the European wars, fighting for the Dutch, and he certainly had a scar on his left cheek which he would indicate in support of the assertion. I couldn't be sure he was telling the truth. Audley was rarely straightforward. I've heard him explain his scar as the result of an encounter with the Spanish in Belgium, the unfortunate consequence of a skirmish in Breda or even arising from his heroic defence of the life and person of Elizabeth Stuart, sister of King Charles and known as the Winter Queen, from an alleged assassination attempt for which he was rewarded and acclaimed a hero of the Protestant cause.

Audley was a bull of a man. Squat, stocky, fierce to look at with a fat, round – albeit scarred – face and huge shoulders.

We met when I called on Bob White one day at his print-shop off Warwick Lane, round the back of the Inns of Court, to see how he was doing and there was Audley groaning and complaining about the difficulty of completing that week's newsbook.

Turned out it was only the second one he'd made and he'd already been forced to move printer. The first edition was produced on his father's press and it was quite successful, selling almost 200 copies at a penny each. Then his father, Sampson, read it and refused to allow his press to be used again. Sampson Audley said he was damned if he would allow his press to be used against the King.

Audley's was one of several news-sheets on the market. Many had the word Mercury in the title. Mercury, after all, was Roman God of eloquence, messages and communication, though critics liked to point out he was also God of financial gain, trickery and thieves. At a penny each, a man who sold 200 a week could make a reasonable living. I did a rough calculation: 200 pennies is 16 shillings and eightpence. Printing costs, say, five shillings and the Mercury women who sell it get another five between them, that still leaves Audley with six and eightpence. Most people don't earn five shillings a week so I reckoned he was doing better than the average even if it wasn't making him rich.

'The hard part's filling eight pages,' Audley moaned. 'I've managed it so far but really, where is all the news to come from? There must be some news from the Inns of Court, Marchamont? What about the latest cases? Or what is said in Parliament?'

'You know it's illegal to report Parliamentary debates,' I reminded him. 'Still, I do know one or two Members of Parliament,' I said slowly. 'And there's definitely stirrings in the city. I might be able to let you have some intelligence from time to time.'

'Marchamont? Don't be rash,' counselled Marvell, 'Prostituting your art.'

'I have no art, Andy, and what's wrong with a little light prostitution? We all sell ourselves for something. When it's not for money, nobody objects. And ever at my back I hear the cursing bloody bailiffs hurrying near.'

Audley slapped his palm down on the table. 'Enough,' he cried at Marvell. 'If you want to run away to Rome with your Popish friends, then go. Meanwhile, Marchamont, there are a couple of people I want you to meet.'

A few days later, Audley led me across squares and courts, round corners and up flights of stairs as we made our cold way round the abbey, past St Margaret's Church and into the rambling old Palace of Westminster with its new Banqueting House.

We ended up in a room overlooking the Thames. It was mercifully warm, with logs blazing in a huge fireplace, tapestries on the walls and wine and Venetian glasses on a long table.

There was nobody in the room but we were clearly early for an important meeting. Audley had washed, trimmed his beard and tried to tidy his hair. There was not much ink on his fingers, though I suspect he never could clean it off entirely. 'People like me are born with printer's ink in our blood,' he once said, waving his fat, blackened fingers at me with a grin made lop-sided by the scar across his face. He wore a thick greatcoat over his clean black jacket and trousers, leather gauntlet gloves and an ugly sheepskin hat.

We waited.

Eventually a door was flung open and two servants ceremoniously led three gentlemen into the room. The first limped a little and waved a vague hand in Audley's direction before slumping down in a chair near the fire, groaning and calling for wine. The second, the youngest and tallest of the trio, walked purposefully towards the windows and gazed out across the now-frozen river in the grey December half-light while the third strode over to me, hand outstretched in greeting with a broad smile on his face.

'Marchamont,' this one declared as if I were his oldest and dearest friend. 'You were at Oxford with a friend of mine, were you not? John French. I'm Nat Fiennes.'

Fiennes was, I guessed, at least 30. He wore his hair long with pearl ear-rings and a pearl necklace at his collar. His jacket was yellow silk, his cheeks were pink from cold and his smile was as wide as the fireplace.

'Mr Fiennes, a pleasure,' I said. I was on my best behaviour. 'Yes, I know Frenchie. How are you two acquainted?'

'Our Mister French is one of our leading medical men,' said Fiennes, adding, 'His father's our steward at Broughton, you know?' before turning to greet Audley with even greater friendliness and enthusiasm.

The man at the window turned towards me. 'Vane,' he said, nodding. I nodded back but couldn't place him. Audley and Fiennes were loudly discussing the treacherous Scots. Vane looked on.

'We're both Oxford men, Nedham,' said this Vane character, 'Though why they ever had Laud as chancellor I can't imagine.'

I looked more closely. Audley told me we were only meeting Viscount Saye and Sele. I gawped at Vane a bit stupidly until the penny dropped. Vane. Sir Henry Vane. The Younger. Oh my God. The man who sealed Strafford's fate. Tax-gatherer. Treasurer of the Royal Navy. Just back from fighting the Scots on behalf of the King. What do you say when you meet someone you really ought to recognise and fail to? It's all a bit embarrassing. There's only one thing for it – put them at a disadvantage.

'Sir Henry, of course. I didn't recognise you. I do apologise. Now tell me, Sir Henry, is it true what they say? About the title?'

This was a dangerous question but I didn't take to the man. He looked severe and argumentative, as if everything he saw was wrong. I felt I had to needle him a little. He turned to look at me with intense, dark eyes and severe frown. 'No,' he said, 'It is not.'

Gossip said Sir Henry's father, another Sir Henry, had caused Strafford's downfall not because of the failure of the war with the Scotch nor because Strafford threatened to use Irish Catholic troops to invade England and put down dissent against the King.

Gossip said the real reason for animosity between Strafford and the Vanes came when the King's favourite adviser was made an Earl and chose, as his secondary title, to call himself Baron Raby. This infuriated the Vanes because the Raby in question was a castle in County Durham which belonged to them. The Vanes had bought Raby Castle and nearby Barnards Castle off King Charles 15 years earlier. The Vanes thought if anyone was to be Baron Raby, it should be one of them. They thought Strafford was deliberately mocking them when he took it for himself.

If it's true Strafford chose the title to upset old Sir Henry, the joke blew up spectacularly in his face. The Earl was eventually put to death thanks to evidence supposedly stolen by the younger Vane and passed to that awful man John Pym, who was leading opposition to the King in Parliament. This so-called evidence, probably invented by the Vanes, was enough to convince the Commons to pass a law condemning Strafford to death. It had to be a law because all attempts at an ordinary fair trial had failed.

King Charles was left with little choice but to sign Strafford's death warrant, even though he had promised his trusted friend he would never do such a thing. As the Bible says, 'Put not your trust in princes.'

Still, the Vanes didn't do themselves any favours with the King. He never forgave himself for condemning Strafford to death or the Vanes for forcing him into it. As a result, after they'd finished negotiating with the Scots on the King's behalf, Charles sacked both father and son from Government jobs.

This was not something the Vanes could take lying down.

Even so, referring to all this on my first encounter with Sir Henry the Younger was not exactly tactful.

Luckily, Nat Fiennes came to my rescue and introduced me to his father, Viscount Saye and Sele.

'Stupid name,' his Lordship mumbled. 'Just call me William.'

Viscount Saye and Sele had always been a cantankerous man. Wherever there was trouble, you could find William Fiennes staring intently at documents, commenting pithily on affairs and organising his family and friends to do his bidding not just in England but far away in America where he was setting up righteous settlements.

Now he called everyone to the table, quietly asked one of the servants to pour wine and invited me to sit opposite him. His son Nat and Sir Henry Vane sat either side of the Viscount while Audley remained standing in front of the fire.

The Viscount was all business. 'Mr Nedham, I am told you are presently working at the Inns of Court as a lawyer. Is that right?'

'It is, sir. I have been at Gray's Inn for a couple of years now.'

'You were a schoolteacher?'

'I was, sir. Under-master at the Merchant Taylors' School for three years.'

'But you left...'

'I did, sir.' The Viscount raised an eyebrow. I went on, 'Whipping boys at a penny a week...' Nathaniel Fiennes laughed. Vane stared at the table-top. The Viscount pursed his lips.

'You were at Oxford?'

'All Souls, sir, I obtained my BA in '37.'

'When you were 17?'

'Yes, sir.'

'And you were a chorister?'

'You are well-informed, sir,' I said lightly.

'It is my business to be, Mr Nedham,' the Viscount said humourlessly. 'High Church? Laudian?'

'No, sir. It was a scholarship. It saved my parents money.'

'Ah now, your parents. Your father is the Reverend Christopher Glynn, vicar of Burford and head of Burford Grammar School. Correct?'

'Step-father, sir, yes.'

'I know a Glynn,' said Vane, looking up as if emerging from a trance. 'John Glynn, the judge.'

'My uncle, sir,' I said with some satisfaction.

'He went to my old school, Westminster. He's a Member of Parliament. He prosecuted Strafford.'

'Yes, that's the one,' I said.

Vane grimaced, which I took to be the nearest he could get to a smile. The Viscount went on, 'So your family is of our persuasion, I take it?' I tried to look non-committal and quizzical though I may have come across as a bit simple. 'Anyway,' the Viscount went on, 'Not a Laudian. Not a Papist. A presbyterian. A follower of Calvin.'

'Or Luther,' I said optimistically. I really did not want to get bogged down in discussions about predestination, free will and all the rest of it. 'The truth, Your Lordship, is that I believe people should be free to worship as they choose without constraints imposed on them by the King, the State, the Archbishop of Canterbury or, for that matter, by the Scotch Kirk.'

There was a long silence. Vane was studying the table-top again. Fiennes was looking closely at me, which I found slightly disconcerting. The Viscount was examining the piece of paper in front of him on the table.

Fiennes broke the silence. 'Our good friend Captain Audley here suggested we might like to meet you, Mr Nedham. He says you are a promising young man from a good family, well-connected, well-educated, studying the law and interested in the world around him.'

'That is true,' I confessed.

Vane added, 'These are strange days, Nedham. Strange days indeed.'

The Viscount sighed. 'We need information, Mr Nedham. And we believe you can help us gather it. Or should I say help Mr Audley gather it?'

'Information?'

'Things are changing, Mr Nedham. The King can no longer rule without the Parliament. The Church must be reformed. No more bishops. Taxes cannot be levied on the whim of the Privy Council or a few corrupt advisers. We are on the cusp of creating a new England, sir, a new England.'

'But this is not achieved easily,' put in Nathaniel Fiennes. 'There will be argument, disagreement, dissent... We need to know the whos, the whats, the wheres, the whens, the hows and – above all – the whys and the wherefores. Captain Audley is drawing all that information together on our behalf. Little snippets get into his newsbook. But the newsbook is only a cover for intelligence-gathering. He meets me once a week to impart the latest news – or more often if there's something urgent.'

'And Audley thinks you could help him in his endeavours,' the Viscount said. 'Tell us what they are saying in the Inns of Court, in the City. What do the merchants think? What's the Lord Mayor up to? What about the apprentices?'

'A spy,' I said, not sure whether this was a frightening or an exciting prospect. Getting involved with a political faction when the country was on the brink of falling apart might be exhilarating. A seat close to the centre of things, close enough to see how they played out? Tempting. 'But would it involve breaking confidences?'

I was 21 years old. I'd spent three impoverished years in the City of London trying to teach Latin and Greek to smelly schoolboys at my stepfather's old school while studying medicine at the same time. I'd given up teaching for the law but it would still be some time before I might be called to the bar and, in the meantime, I wasn't much better off than I had been at the Merchant Taylors'. London was expensive. And here were three prominent men offering me interesting work.

Vane stood, placing the tips of his long fingers on the table and leaning towards me. 'You are impertinent, sir. You will do very nicely for what we have in mind. Audley will see to the details. I must go.'

He nodded briefly all round and stalked from the room. The Viscount struggled to his feet and groaned. 'The world is about to be turned upside-down, Mr Nedham.'

He hobbled from the room on the arm of his son Nat. 'You need a drink,' said Audley.

'Not a newsbook then?' I said.

'Disappointed?' he asked.

'I don't know. Maybe. They're the coming thing, you know.'

'I know. And some of what you supply me with may find its way into "True Daily Occurrences".'

'It's a boring title,' I told him.

'They all are,' said Audley. 'Anyway, are you happy?'

'What exactly am I to do and how much will I be paid?'

'Two shillings a week,' Audley said. 'Deliver a letter into my hands at Hell every Wednesday around mid-day with all the news you've gleaned during the past seven days from around the Inns of Court and the City of London. In case of urgent news, commission messengers. All expenses paid, of course.'

I hesitated. 'Two shillings?'

'Two shillings and sixpence,' said Audley and we shook hands.

I spent the rest of the day wondering if I should have held out for more.

CHAPTER 3

A Trve Relation of Certaine
Speciall and Remarkable
Passages from both Houses
of Parliament

1642

It wasn't many days before I was busy on the Viscount's behalf.

On a freezing cold afternoon, as Parliament was debating its own privileges and the liberty of the subject, proceedings were rudely interrupted by the King himself. Charles, backed by his nephew Prince Rupert and about 300 armed men – courtiers, ruffian Cavaliers and mercenaries – marched into the debating hall to arrest five MPs they called traitors. To the King's fury and embarrassment, he found his birds had flown. As Charles was marching in through the main entrance, the quintet – John Pym, John Hampden, Arthur Haselrig, Denzil Holles and William Strode – were slipping away to a waiting wherry that whisked them downstream, not to the confines of the Tower of London but the freedom of the city.

It was this incident which did so much to make the career of our near-neighbour in Burford, William Lenthall, the Speaker. When the King demanded to know where the fleeing five might be, Lenthall declared he wasn't allowed to answer any question without permission of Parliament. For this little speech, Lenthall was awarded an astonishing £6,000 though that wasn't enough to stop him complaining how politics prevented him earning a decent living.

Back at Gray's Inn, we didn't know any of this as it was happening. But by the time Pym and the others reached the city, word had spread and a crowd gathered to welcome them. Naturally, we at Gray's Inn wanted to enjoy the spectacle – after all, these heroes were all lawyers apart from Haselrig. They'd all been through the Inns of Court, were old comrades at the bar, and staunch Puritans.

At half past six, long after darkness descended and the night turned cold, the militia was summoned. Troops were called to arms at Grey's Inn, Lincoln's Inn, Middle Temple and Inner Temple. Would we have fought His Majesty through the streets of the city? I don't know. We assembled on the green with our muskets – we were thought too feeble and bookish to be pikemen – and waited in our ranks as our cold breath froze in the air.

We didn't stand on parade for long, but we were told to stay at the ready. I was able to send regular messages to Audley in Westminster keeping him up to date with developments: 7pm trained bands assembling, inns of court militia at the ready; 8pm trained bands stationed around St Paul's, outside the Tower, at the entrances to the Guildhall and at other strategic locations; 9pm fugitives in St Stephen's Church, close to the Guildhall; 10pm a great crowd gathering near the Guildhall calling out 'privilege, privilege' which is what MPs cried at the King when he retreated from Parliament.

I wasn't sure this was the sort of information Viscount Saye and Sele and the others wanted. But it was exciting to be chronicling the day's events as they developed, issuing bulletins hour by hour, and there was no shortage of messengers happy to barge their way through the crowds to find Audley in Hell or one of the other taverns or seek out the Nathaniel Fiennes who lived close to the Palace.

The gossip grew increasingly interesting. How did Pym and the others know the King was on his way to arrest them for treason? Someone must have warned them before the King marched into the House. Someone at court, close to the Monarch, must sympathise with Parliament. The gossip I passed back to Audley, was that the information came from Lucy Hay, Countess of Carlisle. Everyone lusted after Lucy. They even published poems about her:

> *I was undoing all she wore,*
> *And had she walked but one turn more,*
> *Eve in her first state had not been*
> *More naked or more plainly seen.*

The widow Hay was 43 but the daughter of the Earl of Northumberland was still attractive. She'd been Strafford's mistress until he was executed but Lucy had stayed at court and remained Queen Henrietta Maria's closest confidante. She had since become the mistress of one of the King's fiercest and cleverest critics, none other than John Pym. She was sitting astride two horses at the same time.

If anyone knew in advance of the King's plan to march on Parliament, it would have been Lucy Hay. She might easily have sent a warning to Pym. Or – and this was a more devious suggestion – was it possible Pym used Lucy to incite the Queen, who in turn forced the King into his invasion of Parliament in order to provoke a crisis?

It was no surprise four of the MPs were lawyers. The war began at the Inns of Court. In those days everyone who was anyone began his career at the Bar. Gray's Inn alone claimed no fewer than five dukes, three marquises, 29 earls, five viscounts and 39 barons. School, Oxford or Cambridge, Inns of Court. It's worked for two hundred years and will doubtless continue for centuries to come.

By the time I arrived at Gray's Inn, the legal profession was in trouble. Teaching was in decline. Barristers didn't waste time on students any more. Training cases, known as moots, held by the four Inns of Court, weren't taking place so students did not get to improve their advocacy skills. Many people thought new technology was so good old-fashioned notions such as lectures were not worth bothering with. Why go to a lecture when you can read a book instead?

This was a spiral of decline. I did learn a little law and the art of debate. I continued to study medicine as well. I pursued my duties as a clerk, carrying documents, getting papers signed, taking notes in court – I learned shorthand – running errands and so on. Mostly I found myself thinking about my commission from Captain Audley, the Viscount, Fiennes and Vane.

I noted chance remarks of my colleagues, especially lawyer MPs of my acquaintance. Who was for the King, who was for Parliament? They'd want to know who might be more or less of the same opinion as them. People like John Bradshaw, a Northern lawyer who moved to London and was friends with the Puritan propagandist John Milton.

The more I heard the word of God from his chosen ones, the less convinced I became. What I do know is that everyone at the Inns of Court, in common with my friends at university, not to mention the teachers at the Merchant Taylors' School, hated Catholics.

It was easy to see why so many London lawyers were suspicious of Queen Henrietta Maria. She was French, she was Catholic, she had Catholic courtiers and friends and too much power over the King. There was very little to be said in her favour.

Even before the King's invasion of Parliament, I'd written a note to Audley telling him the talk at Gray's Inn was for impeaching the Queen. They'd done for Strafford. They were working on Laud. The Queen was the logical next step.

It wasn't the King, it was his evil advisers. None closer nor more evil than his Catholic Queen.

The day after the fugitives fled Parliament, Charles himself turned up in a carriage and had a herald proclaim the need for the Lord Mayor of London to turn over the five traitors. They were to be found, surrounded by a protective crowd, declaiming from the balcony of the Guildhall on the evils of the King's advisers.

The Mayor, Sir Richard Gurney, was run out of town after trying to call up the militia for the King – a dangerous thing to do when trained bands of apprentices were swarming through the streets chanting 'freedom, liberty, privilege' and building barricades.

Charles was allowed as far as the Guildhall, with a small company of men. But it seemed everyone in the city had taken to the streets jeering and shouting at him. Some lads started rocking the King's carriage. They were beaten off but it was enough to make Charles aware he wasn't welcome. He turned tail and ran back to Whitehall.

There was turmoil. People were on the streets day and night. Preachers set themselves up outside St Paul's and other churches to denounce Papists, berate the King and prophesy the Beginning of The End. One or two were clearly mad. A few were women. They preached for hours on end and, in some cases, their audiences blocked the streets to the annoyance of anyone trying to go about his usual business.

The courts were not really functioning. Indeed, the law itself seemed to have been suspended. In its place was argument, speculation, chaos and a cacophony of preaching aided and abetted by an outbreak of newsbooks.

I sent messages to Audley and eventually got one back telling me to keep them coming. His newsbook, "True Daily Occurrences", announced the King's invasion of Parliament and Mr Speaker Lenthall's famous words. There was a little bit at the end about the King's failed attempt to arrest the five MPs by marching on the city itself but it was very hard to read, being printed in tiny type.

The trouble was newsbooks, and Audley's was no different, were composed over several days. The front carried the oldest news and subsequent events were added over the following pages. By the time the typesetters reached the last page, or sometimes even the penultimate one, they had to judge whether there were enough words to fit the space available. If they were short of news, the typeface on the last couple of pages would be increased to fill the space. If there was too much news, they would use smaller letters to fit it all in. They never used more paper than necessary, nor would they think of deleting words they had prepared earlier. The result, I am sorry to say, was that some newsbooks, even my own at times, were not pleasing to look at nor, indeed, easy to read. Sometimes even the sharpest-eyed reader might have to resort to bright light and magnifying glass.

News, though, is not predictable. Sometimes there is an abundance; at others, a drought. One newsbook sometimes left a page blank and declared there was not enough news to fill it. That was nonsense but if you must fill eight pages once a week, it is difficult to judge on the first day how much news there will be by the seventh.

Especially as the whole idea of news was new.

As Government fell apart, censorship laws fell with it. No authority was willing to enforce the ban on reporting events in Parliament – mainly because Parliament wanted these events reported.

In theory there was a licensing system. Printers and writers could be hauled before a court, or Parliament, to answer for anything that gave offence. But it was hard to judge what might be risky when newsbooks were encouraged to be offensive and – better still – likely to sell more copies if they reflected the views of their more trenchant readers. This was no time for politeness.

At the start, a few newsbooks pretended they were impartial. They weren't and neutrality didn't last long. In 1642, everybody had to take sides or at least pretend to.

The next edition of "True Daily Occurrences" reported that the King and court had left London entirely. 'Fled' London, the newsbook said.

When the fugitives Pym, Hampden, Haselrig, Holles and Strode returned in triumph to Westminster, it was like a regatta on the Thames. The five heroes were rowed in a large barge, each wearing a scarlet cloak. Bands played. Cannons saluted. Militia lined both river-banks. Crowds gathered all along the route from the Tower upstream to Westminster where they were greeted with special ceremony by the Speaker, Mr Lenthall, and those members of the House of Lords who had not fled with the King.

There were only about 30 Peers left and more than 100 of the 650 or so MPs also followed the King to Windsor.

Nobody, at that stage, thought the King himself might be tried and executed but Henrietta Maria – French, Catholic, a meddling woman – was not liked. Several lawyers were working up charges against her. One of them was John Bradshaw, a determined and plain-speaking barrister from Cheshire who took me on as his clerk soon after he arrived at Gray's Inn.

Bradshaw's chambers were up a narrow, ill-lit stairway to a small landing with three doors. One led to his office, the second to an office shared by two clerks and the third led to John Cook's chambers. Cook was a pious man; Bradshaw was a serious one. There's a difference. Both believed the powers of the King and the Church had to be reformed but, whereas Bradshaw believed it was for the betterment of the nation, Cook believed he was doing God's work. This made Cook much more difficult to work for because every discussion, decision or delay required the approval of the Lord whereas Bradshaw could assess a case, decide and move on. My fellow clerk Nat Rich worked for Cook; I worked for Bradshaw. I had the better of the arrangement.

Bradshaw was a determined and ambitious man. I helped fix his election as Judge of the Sheriff's Court in London. I persuaded Audley to get the Viscount, Nat Fiennes and Sir Henry Vane to use their City contacts on Bradshaw's behalf.

The electors were the 100 members of London's Court of Common Council. They were mainly merchants, with a few lawyers, a soldier or two, a pair of clergymen, a couple of shopkeepers. I compiled lists, I made visits, I bought drinks, I had little chats. As often as not, I prayed with them. The council men were persuaded of Bradshaw's merits over his rival, Richard Proctor. It was an easy win but Proctor was a bad loser. He went off to Boston in the Massachusetts Bay Colony and wrote letters of complaint against Bradshaw for as long as he lived.

It was a well-paid job which gave Bradshaw power over civil, as well as criminal, cases which came up in the city. His hearings took place in a courtroom next to the Fleet Prison. It was an efficient system.

'It's a power-base,' Bradshaw explained. 'If we're going to change the country, we must take control of the instruments of power. Your uncle, John Glynn, is Recorder of Westminster. We are making progress though I'm not sure everyone in Westminster is with us yet even if the King has fled with his sycophants and catamites.'

Bradshaw was elected only a couple of weeks after war was officially declared. The King raised his standard in Nottingham and on the same day Prince Rupert's cavaliers won a small victory over Parliament's army at Powick Bridge near Worcester. Bradshaw was not ungrateful for the many long hours I put in on his behalf while the country continued to fall apart and I scribbled weekly – sometimes daily – notes to Audley. He started to insert them unaltered into "True Daily Occurrences". It was exciting to see my words in print.

That September my fellow clerk Nat Rich abandoned the Inns of Court to join the Earl of Essex's lifeguards as a captain. He tried to persuade me to go with him. But I thought, why get yourself killed when you can have more fun and make more money by staying well away from the firing line?

CHAPTER 4

Communicating the
Intelligence and
affaires of the Court, to
the rest of the KINGDOME

1643

I first met John Milton in John Bradshaw's chambers. Milton was there partly to discuss freedom of speech, one of his hobby-horses at the time, but also to pick Bradshaw's brains on the question of divorce. Bradshaw was happily married, by which I mean he had a wife and son tucked away in Cheshire and seemed content to live near the Inns of Court without the distraction of female company.

As for Milton, he was full of mad ideas, completely out of touch with reality. Lived life with his head in the clouds. Paid no attention to anything. Thought we should be on our knees praying all day, especially on Sundays.

Milton thought the attractions of a day of prayer were more enticing for the common man than a day spent drinking and playing football. He thought King James's "Book of Sports" was a work of the anti-Christ. All the King had done was remind everyone it was acceptable to enjoy archery, dancing, leaping, vaulting, May games, Morris dances, Whitsun-ales and football on the Sabbath. This was too much for poor, pious Milton who thought Sundays should be spent on our knees begging forgiveness for the sins of the world.

Pasty-faced Milton was 33 years old – the same age, I couldn't resist pointing out, as Christ when he died. Milton was not amused. He'd recently married a woman called Mary. She was only 17 and it all went horribly wrong. She hated London. She hated the way Milton beat the nephews he was tutoring. She hated Parliament and Puritans. When her father urged her to seek refuge with the King in Oxford after the Battle of Edgehill and before the road from London was closed, she fled.

'It's like being chained to a corpse,' puffy-eyed Milton complained. Milton had been crying. He went on in his dreary monotone, 'No man conspires to his own ruin and God cannot have decreed a man and a woman must live in perpetual misery with one another. My proposal, which I shall be publishing soon, is that where a man cannot live with a woman except in a state of perpetual war, he shall have the right in law to divorce himself from her.'

Bradshaw smiled. 'John Milton the libertine,' he said. 'How about that, Marchamont? Our poet is a debauched cavalier.'

Milton pursed his lips primly and peered at us through the half-light of another winter afternoon.

I didn't understand why Bradshaw treated Milton with such respect. The man had published a few poems but had no other occupation. It turned out Bradshaw and Milton were working together on a second, maybe a third, tract against the appointment of bishops. 'I can't write poetry now,' Milton complained. 'I blame it on my wife's desertion to the King. She was like Eve, tempting man to his ruin.'

Everything was falling apart. Soldiers – urged on by Sir Harry Vane – were smashing up churches, besieging towns, stripping the countryside of food while politicians huddled together worrying how to end what they had started. Bradshaw said there was no choice but to bring the King to heel. If the King regained real power, his enemies would be hung, drawn and quartered. The Parliamentarians had gone too far to back down without a deal which secured not just religious freedom – no more bishops – but asserted the authority of the Commons, its right to make laws and raise taxes. And the King would have to agree not just an amnesty for so-called rebels, he'd have to condemn some of his least trustworthy advisers to well-deserved deaths.

Milton, for one, was adamant that Archbishop Laud had already lived too long.

Mind you, all this talk of divorce was a little off-putting for me. I hadn't told anyone yet but I was about to marry.

If I knew then what I know now, I might not have been so keen on the idea. Three wives and nine children later, I realise it is a greater undertaking than even John Milton thought. Marriage is not to be entered into lightly; especially if, by some mischance, you're in danger of being married to more than one woman at a time.

I can admit this now because I shall be dead before these words see the light of day but, when I first contemplated marriage, I had no thought for the consequences. It was just that I liked my little cousin Lucy Collier, she always admired me and would be, I was quite sure, grateful to become my wife. I had been home briefly at Christmas, skirting Oxford to avoid the Parliamentary blockade, and spent time with my family. We'd celebrated more or less in the traditional manner, though my stepfather was circumspect with Church services and we avoided decorations around the parsonage. Puritans were quick to take offence and persecute those who did not adopt the correct attitude towards religion.

Lucy and her widowed mother, my Aunt Lucy, were with us. Lucy was lively, charming and helpful. She was pretty, rosy-cheeked and laughed but not too often and not too loudly. She was serious but not excessively so. She was firm of flesh and smiled happily at the occasional stolen kiss.

I decided to make Lucy my wife. A man could not remain single all his life and, especially in a time of upheaval, there was something to be said for a little of the normality and stability a wife might provide.

I consulted my mother. She almost swooned with delight, clapped her hands, gave me a kiss on the forehead and said I should get on with it, she didn't know how long she could keep such momentous news a secret.

I consulted my father, who was less enthusiastic. In his vicarly style, he held his hands clasped in front of him and asked, 'Are you sure, Marchamont? This is not the best time to be taking a wife. What will you do for money? Can you afford servants and a roof over your head? There is a war on, you know. Do you think it's wise to be starting a family?'

I consulted Big Susie, when we were in bed in her garret at The George celebrating Christmas. Susie, who only recently lost her husband Makepeace at the Battle of Edgehill fighting for Parliament, laughed at me. Susie knew Lucy. 'She's difficult, Monty. You do know that, don't you?' she said.

'Difficult? What do you mean difficult?'

'She may look like butter wouldn't melt in her mouth but she can be a right cow. A proper bitch. You should see the way she talks to us servants.'

'She won't talk to her husband like that.'

'Oh won't she?' said Susie laughing.

That's why all Milton's talk about two carcasses chained unnaturally together, and a man tyrannised by his wife was a little disconcerting, especially as my Lucy was 17, the same age as Mrs Milton. The difference, though, was that I was ten years younger than Milton and I wasn't a permanently-angry Puritan.

Sir Henry Vane was turning into one of the leading lights in the rebellion. Though in theory the revolt was being run by Parliament, it wasn't practical for 500 MPs to take day-to-day decisions. They set up a Committee of Safety which took over from the King's Privy Council and was responsible for waging the war, raising money, maintaining law and order and so on. It was also responsible for trying to find some sort of religious settlement.

Sir Henry joined the Viscount and Nat Fiennes on the committee. Others included my uncle, Judge John Glynn, as well as John Hampden and John Pym, the devious, lawyerly brains behind the whole thing.

I was working for three members of the committee running the country and related to another. This had to be useful.

'Well, Audley,' I asked, 'Have you tippled drink finer than mine host's Canary wine or are fruits of paradise sweeter than these dainty pies of venison?'

'What are you on about?' he demanded, the scar on his face becoming a little more livid as he leaned his great bulk towards me. 'And since when has venison pie been "dainty"?'

'It was just a passing rhyme,' I said.

'It doesn't bloody rhyme,' Audley growled. 'Here, look at this,' he said and waved a news-sheet in front of my face. 'Look.'

'Another newsbook. So what? They come and they go but "True Daily Occurrences" goes on forever.'

'No, Nedham, no. It doesn't. Can't make money out of it. Losing money all the time. If it weren't for the Viscount's subsidies, we'd have to knock it on the head. And now there's this. "Mercurius Aulicus".'

'Aulicus? "The Court Mercury".'

'I know what Aulicus means,' Audley snapped, though I was pretty sure he didn't. 'Look. Pure propaganda. The first edition's all about how Sir John Byron fought off Parliament troops at Burford, of all places, and transported two cart-loads of ammunition to Lord Hartford at Stow.'

'Not much of interest there,' I mumbled. 'And Burford? Why Burford of all places?'

Audley wasn't made for quiet conversation. His voice carried across the inn. Other ears turned to listen. A stranger came over, sat down and inquired, 'A new newsbook? Let's have a look.'

'Can you read?' Audley growled threateningly.

The man, who might have been a builder working on one of the many repairs always being undertaken around the Palace of Westminster, looked towards his drinking companions, three other well-built young men of threatening demeanour.

'Here, here,' I said hurriedly, 'Take a look.'

The man, slightly appeased, cast an eye over the eight badly-printed pages of "Mercurius Aulicus" and pronounced it 'interesting – good to read something from the King's point of view. We're not all rebels and traitors you know.'

Audley slouched back in his chair. 'I'd watch what you say if I were you,' he told the builder quietly. 'You'd be surprised what happens to people who speak ill of the cause of liberty and freedom.'

'Ah,' said the builder, now actively spoiling for a fight, 'The cause of liberty and freedom is so precious we don't have the liberty or freedom to criticise it, is that it?'

Audley grabbed the man's coat at the throat and hissed in his face, 'Yes, that's just about it. And if you don't like it, you can fuck off to Oxford and fight for the King and his Papist doxy.'

I must admit at this point I was afraid the builder might produce a knife from his overalls and plunge it into Audley's well-fed stomach. The man's three mates came over and stood menacingly behind him where he sat on a stool at our table. One of them said, 'Alright Will?'

Will, the man on the stool, said, 'Here, look at this. The King's got his own newsbook' and handed it over to the others.

'What's it say?' one of them asked.

'Dunno,' said another.

'Ah so you can't read,' announced Audley in triumph, releasing his grip on the young man and returning to his wine.

'I can,' said Will, dusting himself down. 'These boys can't.'

'Read it then,' one of them said to Audley.

'Yeah, go on,' said another.

There was a general clamour among the drinkers, with several others now paying attention. It looked as if most of them wanted to know what the news-sheet said. Will handed the pages back to Audley who snorted and shoved them over in my direction. 'Go on then, Nedham, you're the Oxford man and this came from the King in Oxford.'

'It's probably illegal,' I said rather feebly but, as a small group of drinkers gathered round, I thought it politic to do as I was asked though I prefaced my remarks by making it clear this was what the enemy was saying and we should not take it seriously.

I stood warily and began to read out the words of the first edition of the "Court Mercury": 'The world hath long enough beene abused with falsehoods: And there's a weekly cheat put out to nourish the abuse amongst the people, and make them pay for their seducement...'

The report ended with one of the wounded Parliamentarian officers telling Sir John Byron he was dying and likely to be damned for fighting against the King. As I read this long article about a negligible little skirmish around the pubs of Burford, the atmosphere became more and more subdued. It had a surprisingly sobering effect on these drinkers. Most of them may well have been out on the streets in the recent past protesting in favour of Parliament and against bishops and Papists. Yet this story about the Roundheads' apparent setback in Burford, which included dramatic sword-fights, men being shot dead or fleeing into the darkness pursued by cavalry, seemed to reduce the drinkers into contemplative silence.

When I finished, Will and his friends withdrew to their own corner where they engaged in quiet conversation about whether the story represented God's judgment on the rebels and what this might mean. Others, too, were impressed by this news.

'This is nothing,' I said quietly to Audley, who was staring at the papers I had been reading. 'I mean, the news is nothing. This story is trivial compared with some of what's been going on in the last few months. Imagine if this news-sheet had been around at the time of Edgehill. What a triumph for the King it would have been then. What a victory. Instead of the bloody stalemate it actually was. I had no idea anything like this had happened at Burford and I have actually visited the place since the incident recounted here. They had soldiers from both sides in the town but I doubt if there's much truth in this.'

'What does it matter if it's true or not?' Audley asked angrily. 'They obviously believe every word of it,' he said, waving vaguely in the direction of Will and the others. 'I think this changes things, Marchamont.'

Lucy and I married at Easter. The day was chilly but the daffodils were out and the sun shone. The River Windrush bustled down the valley towards the Thames. My step-father conducted the service. My mother cried a little; so did Lucy's mother. Lucy was dry-eyed and frowned. My step-brother Robert was best man. He was only a year older than Lucy and it did look as if his tongue was hanging out. The service was plain and short. The women were soberly dressed. There were no flowers; there was no music. Afterwards there was a little wine. Lucy and I repaired to The George for the night, which was awkward because Big Susie was asleep upstairs.

Lucy insisted the first thing we did was get on our knees and pray to God to bless our union. This we did at tedious length before eventually falling into each other's arms and the night proceeded in the customary fashion. For all her piety, Lucy enjoyed herself immensely, as I knew she would. She was in expert hands.

I am not, I confess, a particularly handsome man. Even at 23, I was not strikingly attractive. I had, even then, a plump stomach and a roundish face in which two brownish eyes sat a little frog-like between a short but slightly bulbous nose. My ears protruded a little, as if they had been damaged in a fight, and my black hair was long but already growing thin on the ground. I was not a tall man though I knew, long before I met him,

I had at least an inch and a half over King Charles in our stocking feet. Like he did, I tended to wear boots with heels.

It was not my outward appearance that made me attractive, either to men or women. What they like is my wit, charm and sophistication. Add to that my mastery of the techniques of love and my power to give excessive pleasure to any woman and it's no surprise my wedding night was an unmitigated success.

I received tutoring in the art of love from a Frenchwoman, Madame Clemence, during my time at Oxford. Madame Clemence, who drifted over to England in the train of Henrietta Maria when the Princess married King Charles, devoted herself to the education of young Englishmen as assiduously as any Professor of Greek. She would say the trouble with most Englishmen was they had no interest in the needs of a woman. This was why any woman of spirit sought her pleasures with Frenchmen. Madame Clemence was an Anglophile and believed it was her duty to bring this country's men to the same understanding of these things as a Frenchman took for granted.

It was my fortune to fall into the hands of Madame Clemence at an impressionable age and, thanks to a willingness to be guided by her professional expertise, I developed, though I say it myself, into something of a master in the art of love-making.

Lucy certainly thought so.

After such ecstasy, it was, perhaps, not surprising Lucy found the journey to London arduous and the accommodation, when we arrived, disappointing. Three low-ceiling rooms, one elderly maidservant and a yard shared with three other households wasn't much to boast of. Worse still, she thought I'd misled her both about where we would live and how much money we would have. I explained the need to be frugal. This was not something Lucy wanted to hear.

CHAPTER 5

A True Catalogue, Or
An Account
of the Several Places
and most Eminent Persons

August 1643

'We have to take this seriously. We have to fight back,' said the Viscount in his quiet, calm voice.

'We are fighting back,' replied the excitable Sir Henry Vane.

'With words as well as deeds,' said the Viscount.

His son, Nat Fiennes, now a colonel in Parliament's army, sat at the far end of the table rubbing his hands together obsessively and staring out of the window at the constantly-falling rain.

'We're fucked,' said Audley, never a man to worry about the nation-wide ban on swearing, despite his Puritanical outlook.

'What?' I asked mildly.

'We're fucked,' he said again, slapping the palm of his hand down on the big oak table.

Audley and I had been summoned to Viscount Saye and Sele's quarters in Westminster which we last visited more than a year ago. This time, circumstances were very different.

Sir Henry was now one of Parliament's leaders. He'd spent most of the summer trying to win over the Scottish. When he got back from outer darkness, that is to say, from Edinburgh, he was immediately imprisoned in his own house by a mob from Kent protesting against... nobody was quite sure what they were protesting against, though they claimed to be supporters of the King. They wanted peace. They weren't the only ones. Across London there were demands for peace, especially from women complaining about the absence of their husbands at the wars and the price of bread.

Even basic provisions were becoming expensive. Parliament had imposed taxes on everyday essentials: beer, wine, tobacco, sugar, even leather. Audley complained, 'Buggers only began fighting the King because of taxes and now look at them.'

The theatres and bear gardens were shut. The doxies of Drury Lane were being regularly rounded up and whipped (not for fun or, at least, that's what they would have us believe) by the Puritans. The only entertainments left were a few hangings, from time to time a parade of dejected Royalist prisoners of war or occasionally a book-burning in Cheapside.

These didn't appease the mob. They wanted peace and prosperity.

The Viscount looked at Audley through his spectacles. His face was long and lean, his eyes big and sad. He did not like to hear a man swear but he said nothing, just pursed his lips, grimaced and said, 'Sir Henry?'

'It's not over yet, my lord, not by a long way,' said Sir Henry. 'We now have the Scotch on board. They will be marching south before the year is out. The tables will be turned.'

As he spoke, I wondered if Sir Henry was entirely convinced the Scotch would change the course of the war and, if they did so, at what price.

'Nat?' said the Viscount after Sir Henry had gone on about his negotiations at tedious length while the rest of us listened to the hammering rain.

Fiennes seemed miles away. Now he sat up straight, tried to smile, took a sip of wine, cleared his throat, said, 'Yes, yes, well, erm', paused, stood, marched to the window, stared out at the rain on the river and announced, 'You know they want to put me on trial, father, don't you?'

The Viscount sighed heavily. 'I know Prynne wants to and that other fanatic, what's his name?'

'Clement Walker,' said Fiennes, turning back into the room and, somehow reinvigorated, resuming his seat a changed man. 'We shall fight them, father, gentlemen. We shall fight them as we must fight the King. How dare they? They are demanding I be put on trial for treachery and cowardice.'

'It's been such a bad year, they need a scapegoat,' I said. They looked at me with curiosity. Who, they seemed to be asking themselves, was this nobody summing up the situation so wisely, so pithily?

'Yes,' nodded the old Viscount.

'Indeed,' said Sir Henry, 'A scapegoat. Everybody needs a scapegoat.'

'And do you think,' continued the Viscount quietly, looking straight at me with his tired eyes, his voice even and smooth, 'Do you think we are doing ourselves any favours in pursuing a case like Nathaniel's when there is a war to be won?'

It was like taking to the stage. I had their attention. Even Audley was listening. I said, 'Sir, we must not be in the business of tearing one another apart when we have such an important objective before us, namely the liberty of the people and the freedom of the nation. This is our cause, liberty and the rule of law. We fight tyranny, usurpers of our ancient rights, foreign interference, we fight slavery. We must not fight each other.'

Sir Henry murmured, as if in prayer, 'And I will set the Egyptians against the Egyptians; and they shall fight every one against his brother and every one against his neighbour, city against city, and kingdom against kingdom.'

'Yes, quite,' said the Viscount, who was not given to Biblical quotations.

'And what are we going to do about it?' demanded Fiennes. 'I thought we were here for a reason.'

'We are, we are,' said the Viscount calmly. 'Audley, you know why we are here. Perhaps you should explain our proposals to Sir Henry and Mr Nedham.'

Audley stood up and looked down the length of the table to where Nat Fiennes was sitting at the far end. The lashing rain seemed to redouble its efforts.

'A pamphlet, a weekly mercury, a newsbook,' he said. 'I've made some headway with my "Daily Occurrences" but not enough. We need better organisation, better distribution, better intelligence. And better writing, gentlemen. I am a blunt soldier. I do my best but my best isn't good enough if we are to make war with words as we make war with swords. The King has the "Court Mercury". It is undermining faith in our cause. It only costs one penny but copies are changing hands for as much as two shillings and sixpence, it's in such demand. It gloats at our failures. It pokes fun at our leaders. It exaggerates the King's successes. It undermines morale. It is full of lies but it is highly effective.'

'How do they get it into London from Oxford?' asked Fiennes.

'Under women's skirts,' said Audley. 'Hidden in barrels. Under wagon-loads of grain. It is smuggled in with ease and sold around Saint Paul's by the Mercury women. It out-sells all the other newsbooks put together. It travels all round the country as well and there's a suggestion it's also printed here, in London somewhere, as well as in Oxford.'

'Then we must root it out,' said Sir Henry angrily.

'If we can,' the Viscount murmured.

'The proposal,' Audley concluded, 'The Viscount's proposal, is that we should set up a publication specifically to rival, contradict and oppose this "Court Mercury". Nedham has more information about it, gentlemen. Marchamont?'

It was my turn. This was one of those meetings where everything was agreed in advance but everyone had to play his part anyway for the sake of propriety. I launched into what my sleuthing had uncovered.

'The King's "Court Mercury", gentlemen. They call it "Mercurius Aulicus" to give it some sort of standing with the hoi-polloi but the English name will do for us. Anyway, its first edition was devoted entirely to a small affray in Burford. As I said to Audley, there was so much going on at the time there had to be a reason why this affair was the only item thought worth a mention. It could hardly be said to communicate anything about the affairs of the Court. An obscure knight saw off a small troop of Parliament men in a town most people have never heard of. Except, I suppose, for Mr Speaker Lenthall. That, perhaps, was the point. Maybe they wanted to intimidate Mr Lenthall, let him know his home town was not safe for his wife and family. But if the Cavaliers knew the Lenthalls lived at Burford Priory, wouldn't they have ransacked the place?

'Anyway, it turns out the explanation is that the pamphlet is written by someone I know a little, a cleric called Peter Heylyn. He's from Burford and we went to the same school. He is now with the King in Oxford. Heylyn is one of the King's own chaplains. A great friend and supporter of Archbishop Laud...'

'Ex-Archbishop,' insisted Sir Henry.

'The ex-Archbishop,' I corrected. 'Anyway, Peter has been a notorious controversialist for years. He even wrote a "History of the Sabbath" which claims there is no religious reason not to enjoy sports and recreations on the Lord's Day.'

Sir Henry spat wine onto the table in indignation. The Viscount grimaced. Nat Fiennes frowned. Audley smiled and said, 'You see what we are up against, gentlemen.'

'We have concluded Captain Audley cannot undertake this task alone, Mr Nedham,' said the Viscount smoothly. 'He needs a writer. We have seen your intelligence reports. They are lively and well-informed. We are aware you have contributed to Captain Audley's own newsbook. Now we wish you to contribute to ours.'

'We are fighting a war, sir,' said Nat Fiennes, 'And it will not be won on the battlefield alone. It will be won and lost in the hearts and minds of the people. We must take up the gauntlet thrown down by the "Court Mercury" and accept its challenge.'

Despite the rain, Audley and I loitered in New Palace Yard discussing what had been agreed and – more importantly for me – what I should be paid. Was I to abandon my legal studies and give up medicine? Was I to devote myself fully to the war of words? If so, were the Viscount and his friends going to make it worth my while?

How much was Audley getting? He wouldn't say.

Were we supposed to make a profit from our newsbook and pay ourselves out of that or were our patrons footing all the bills? If the latter, what happened to the money we did get from selling our news? Who would be responsible for printing and distribution? Could we get the thing into Oxford, to provoke the Cavaliers with it?

'Ha! Boys!' Nat Fiennes slapped a hand on each shoulder and pulled us to him. 'You know Vane is now the second man in Parliament, don't you? Since John Hampden died, Vane has become Pym's lieutenant-general.'

'So why is he allowing Prynne to pursue you?' I asked.

'Good question,' said Nat. 'Vane is not entirely reliable, you know.'

'Is he selling us out to the Scotch?' asked Audley.

'Another good question. He has what he calls his solemn league and covenant. If you read it carefully it doesn't promise to impose Calvinism on England. It just says we'll study the best Protestant churches and copy them, or words to that effect.'

'Constructive ambiguity,' I said.

'Indeed,' said Fiennes.

The death of John Hampden, one of the original five MPs who the King tried to arrest, killed in battle, was just one more setback during a terrible summer for Parliament. I was surprised by Nat's good humour. After all, he was facing trial for his life.

My questions would have to wait. Nat was going to buy us both a drink.

Settled in a back-room of Purgatory, a tavern like Hell just outside Westminster Hall, with jugs of heavy beer, I asked Colonel Fiennes why he was so optimistic.

'The Lord is with us,' he said, with a beatific smile. 'The Lord will guide us. The Lord will save us.'

Audley grunted. The two men both had considerable faith in God but their faiths weren't the same. Audley's view was that the Lord helped those who helped themselves; Fiennes seemed to think the Lord would come to the aid of his chosen people simply because he loved them and they had been selected for salvation.

'I wish I had your faith,' I said, though I didn't really wish it.

Fiennes was eager to talk. He changed the subject. 'You know Essex has gone mad, don't you?' he said in a hushed voice, looking over his shoulder to make sure we weren't being overheard. 'He thinks the war should be solved through Trial by Combat as if we were all Knights of the Round Table. He says each side should have an army of the same size, agree on a battleground and fight it out. The winner would prove he had God on his side and the whole country would be saved the pain of further conflict. Unbelievable.'

'What if it's taken seriously?' I asked.

'It won't be,' growled Audley waving a newsbook in our faces. 'It's already being lampooned by "The Scout". It's one of White and Bishop's.' Fiennes looked puzzled. 'Printers,' Audley explained. 'They'll be doing ours.'

I looked at my companions. Audley seemed grim and purposeful, a man on a crusade. Fiennes, however, was remarkably cheerful. 'You don't seem concerned about Prynne and this treason trial, Colonel Fiennes,' I said. 'Perhaps it's God's will for you to be convicted.'

'Perhaps it is,' said Fiennes, 'Just as it was His will for us to surrender up Bristol to the Cavaliers. We cannot know the Lord's designs; we can only play our part as best we can.'

Not wishing to become embroiled in a philosophical debate, I changed the subject. 'So, gentlemen, what are we going to call our new publication?'

The prospect of working on a new Parliamentary newsbook should have excited me yet I was dejected. This had nothing to do with the war, politics or my new job – my marriage was heading into a war zone of its own.

Lucy said she was bored. Actually, she didn't say that. She said, 'Marcahmont, thou knowest slothfulness casteth into a deep sleep, and an idle soul shall suffer hunger.'

Lucy had taken to quoting the Scriptures. It was a disconcerting habit. I said a woman who was bored of London was bored of life. I pointed out the whole city was at her disposal. She said we did not have enough money to make much of the place and complained I was hardly ever at home. She protested she had no friends. She pouted. I kissed her tenderly. She said she would make the best of it.

Unfortunately, that meant spending her days at meetings where preachers droned on about why God's remarkable goodness meant He had a great need for vengeance on His many enemies.

I told Lucy about the plans for a newsbook. She was scornful. 'These newsbooks are abominations, Marchamont. They are concatenations of falsehoods, full of the venom of the snake. Dost thou not know lying lips are an abomination to the Lord?'

Then I told her the good news. I was to be paid £3 a week. This was decent money. Not riches, admittedly, but ten times the pay of the men who would print it. 'We will move to better lodgings,' I promised Lucy.

'We'll get you another servant.'

She smiled a little but it was not an encouraging smile. It was a sorrowful smile. We were in our bedroom. Lucy was in a long night-dress with her hair loose about her and looking remarkably pretty in the soft candlelight. She came over to where I was sitting on the edge of the bed and held my head between her hands, though she did not clutch me to her or encourage further intimacy. Instead, she sighed and whispered, 'For what shall it profit a man, if he shall gain the whole world, and lose his own soul? We must pray for thee, Marchamont, before it is too late to save thy soul.'

I retaliated with one of the few lines from the Bible I do know. 'My dear, a newsbook dedicated to the truth – what could be more Godly than that? Does not the Good Book tell us, "And ye shall know the truth, and the truth shall make you free"?'

CHAPTER 6

A check to the
checker of Britanicus

December 1643

I haven't been strictly honest.

The truth is, my marriage to Lucy Collier did not proceed in the prescribed manner. That is to say – it is a little awkward to confess this but I feel I must if these, my memoirs, are to remain faithful to the truth – the marriage ceremony which I earlier said took place at Easter in fact occurred a couple of months later, at Whitsuntide. Well, early in June to be precise.

By then, my new wife was beginning to betray the state of things. She was not big, but she was big enough for observant feminine eyes to register suspicion. The masculine mind would not have noticed but my mother and Lucy's mother (not to mention Big Susie when I took my leave of her the night before the matrimonial ceremony) were all aware of my new wife's delicate condition.

The previous Christmas, Lucy and I made time for each other. At Easter we made more time for each other. Lucy then wrote to me in London explaining the situation and requiring a response before she threw herself on the mercy of my parents. Things were made more difficult because, by the time she sent her letter, Lucy had been Saved. There was a little faction of strict Puritans in Burford and they had their claws into my little Lucy. She repented mightily for the sin of fornication but it was, apparently, God's will that I did the proper thing.

Nobody spoke of Lucy's condition on the day of our wedding, though my brother made a few lewd remarks and chuckled once or twice at embarrassing moments.

Still, Lucy was a pretty girl.

In early December, a year after she and I became more than just cousins, there was the usual screaming and agony, the long, hand-wringing wait, the brandy and consoling support of Captain Thomas Audley while my wife was upstairs in the hands of three elderly crones who said they knew what they were doing. As a medical man, I could have been in attendance as well – perhaps I should have been. My medical experience of childbirth was entirely theoretical. I might one day be required to perform the offices of doctor in such a delicate situation. Perhaps I should have taken the opportunity to observe proceedings from close quarters or even play a hands-on part in the process. I am not squeamish. Yet something persuaded me this was one confinement best avoided.

Lucy gave birth soon enough. The child appeared to be healthy and three days later we had it Christened. We were not obliged to wait for it to achieve adulthood before baptism, as some fanatics urged. We named it Lucy, after her mother. Lucy was a popular name in those days: Everybody thought of Lucy Hay, the turncoat trollop; the most beautiful woman in the country, according to Nat Fiennes, among others.

The Christening at our parish church, St Andrew by the Wardrobe, was plain and simple. There were no Godparents, Lucy decreeing them Popish encumbrances. We took the child to church, walked home past Baynard's Castle with snow descending in mouthfuls and Lucy announced, 'I shall withdraw with Lucy to my mother's as soon as it is practicable to do so, husband.'

I decided to assert myself as a husband and as a man. 'Are you asking my permission, woman?'

'It is neither desirable nor Godly for our child to be raised in this Godless city, as thou knowest. It is a den of iniquity, a Sodom and Gomorrah. The Lord hath called upon me to withdraw. My mother will take us in but I shall ever be thy true and faithful wife.'

I was being abandoned by my wife just like poor Milton. 'This is a bleak prospect, Lucy,' I said, taking her pretty red cheeks in my gloved hands.

'Thou hast little enough time for me, husband, what with news-mongering and drinking.'

'It is drinking for a purpose, Lu-Lu,' I said, 'I have to gather intelligence, meet informants, cultivate contacts. How can I know what's going on in the world if I do not get out and about? But I need someone at home to care for me and for whom I care, my dear girl.'

She would not be persuaded but the weather got worse and worse and the opportunity for my two Lucys to escape to Burford was a long time in coming.

It was a bleak winter as '43 turned into '44. It had rained all summer and most of the autumn. Now snow fell, ice gripped, the Thames froze over again and the country plunged into a hard frost.

John Pym died in agony – stomach cancer. It was said at his funeral he was the greatest Member of Parliament who ever lived. After King Charles fled London when he failed to arrest the five MPs, their leader was generally, but not affectionately, known as King Pym.

Pym was one of the saints. His sober determination and ability to manipulate the rules lay behind all the changes: asserting Parliament's 'inalienable' rights, reforming the Church, getting rid of bishops, demanding the King respect 'ancient liberties'. Pym was the brains of the whole thing. He wrote the manifestos, led Parliament, planned the strategy and won over the common people. According to Audley, it was Pym's suggestion to the Viscount that led to the establishment of "Britanicus". You could say I owed him my career. Without him, the cause started to flounder.

Naturally the "Court Mercury" gloated unmercifully. Peter Heylyn claimed Pym was a traitor who died of skin disease. It wasn't true but that didn't stop people believing Pym left behind what Heylyn called 'a most loathsome and foul carcass'. Heylyn, being a priest, portrayed Pym's death as the disgusting demise of demagogue caused by the justifiable wrath of God. If Heylyn were to be believed, the Almighty was punishing rebels for their abominable assault on His anointed King and every traitor should expect a similarly horrible death.

This worked well with the common people whose credulity can never be over-estimated. In the taverns you could hear them debate whether Pym's death was a judgment from God. Many people, not just women, thought it was.

I wrote an elegy, 36 lines of rhyming couplets, blaming his death on his heavy burden of care. I shall not re-print them here. Time has moved on and Master Pym is not remembered today as he was at the time of his death when thousands turned out for his funeral and his body was laid to rest at Westminster. His lover Lady Lucy Hay wasn't one of the mourners. She had already moved on.

Heylyn gloated in the "Court Mercury" that no sooner had Pym died than his cause was collapsing. Colonel Fiennes, though the son of a Viscount and despite the family's devotion to Parliament's cause, was facing court martial in Saint Albans, a small town outside London, where he was put on trial for surrendering the city of Bristol.

The case was brought by that nasty little man William Prynne and his partner in excessive holiness, Clement Walker. They forced a Commons vote on Nat Fiennes' impeachment and had the gall to publish their accusations against him in a newsbook.

They really laid it on thick. They accused Nat of surrendering, after four days, when he'd said he could hold Bristol for at least two months. They said: 'Contrary to his former trust, promises, duty, and the honour of a soldier, he most dishonourably, cowardly, and traitorously delivered up the City and Castle.' The charge sheet went on and on. Anyone would think Nat Fiennes was the only soldier ever to wave a white flag.

They wanted him to lose his estates and his life.

I made a winter's journey to Saint Albans for the trial. Audley went all the way to Bristol where he managed to infiltrate the city, even though it was in Royalist hands. He was investigating Prynne and Walker's affairs.

The trial dragged on for ten days, which gave me every opportunity to see the dull, dreary, obsessive William Prynne doing his worst. I sat at the back of the chapel courtroom observing. Prynne was sure of his own righteousness. When he spoke, flecks of foam appeared round his mouth. Spittle flew here and there. I was glad to be out of range.

He was one of those Puritans who thought it vanity to appear well-kempt. The neglect of his person was exaggerated. He wanted you to note his worn coat, his ill-cut and ragged grey beard, his terrible breath and missing teeth, not to mention, of course, the missing ears. It was the lack of ears, cut off on the order of Archbishop Laud many years ago, which conferred on Prynne the authority and dignity of a martyr.

As I watched him make his case against Nat Fiennes, it was difficult to think badly of Archbishop Laud. Laud may have wanted bishops and tithes and altar rails and choirs and vestments and all the rest of it. But at least he saw through William Prynne.

Audley discovered Prynne and Clement Walker owned two ships and two warehouses captured by Prince Rupert when Bristol fell to the Royalists. Their loss cost both men hundreds of pounds. Rather than accept the fortunes of war, like so many others were forced to do as houses were burned and looted, crops and cattle stolen and women ravished, Prynne was looking for someone to blame. If he got Nat Fiennes convicted, he could claim compensation from Parliament.

'This case is all about Prynne's money,' Audley declared. 'Nothing more.'

Nat Fiennes wasn't so sure. 'It's not just money. He doesn't trust us.'

'Us?' asked Audley.

'My father and our friends. We think everybody should be free to worship God according to their own ways of thinking.'

'Not the Catholics?' interrupted Audley, appalled.

'No, obviously not the Catholics, Captain. But every good Protestant whatever his chosen path to Heaven. We are all brothers and sisters in the sight of the Lord and we cannot dictate to each other the road to salvation.'

Nat went on a lot longer. We had touched on one of his favourite subjects, religious toleration. We had to accept some people really did believe in predestination. Others really did think we had to get back to nature. Some truly believed polygamists were doing the Lord's will.

I did say, 'One wife is enough for any man' but it didn't staunch his flow.

At the end of it all we agreed a plan. I should write to the Earl of Essex setting out the real reasons behind the prosecution of Nat Fiennes over the loss of the city of Bristol. I should explain the true reason for Prynne's desire to condemn Colonel Fiennes. I should add that the prosecution gave comfort to Parliament's enemies without any benefit. Lastly, I should say Colonel Fiennes pledged his constancy in Parliament's cause and threw himself on the General's mercy. I should add that the gratitude of the now best-selling newsbook "Mercurius Britanicus" went without saying and that this weekly journal was at His Lordship's disposal should he find himself requiring its services at any point.

Essex was, of course, on the Government's ruling committee along with the Viscount and both Sir Henry Vanes, father and son, so we were pushing at an open door.

The verdict of the court martial was a foregone conclusion. Prynne had already won an Act of Parliament impeaching Colonel Fiennes. He'd staged the trial in Saint Albans with his friend Isaac Dorislaus as Judge. There was no jury.

Dorislaus was a fanatical Calvinist who'd made a name for himself in England with his vocal opposition to the King. After all the evidence from various suborned witnesses, it still took Judge Dorislaus a week to deliver his verdict.

When the court finally re-convened, Prynne was agog, his frog eyes bulging under his Puritan cap. His sidekick Clement Walker had wisely retreated to London after the trial ended on December 23. The rest of us, Audley, Fiennes and I, lodged at the White Hart, a dismal inn with lazy servants, not much to eat or drink and very cold. I wrote to Lucy to explain I would not be home but received only a brief note saying she no longer marked Christmas with frivolity and idolatry so it was no great matter.

Judge Dorislaus, in his strange Dutch accent, announced Colonel Nathaniel Fiennes was guilty of traitorously surrendering Bristol and should be hanged.

At that point, as previously arranged, a messenger who had been loitering outside, marched into the courtroom – actually a chapel on the side of the cathedral – and presented the judge with a pardon signed by the Earl of Essex.

Judge Dorislaus read it quietly to himself for several minutes. Eventually, as everyone watched and waited, he said, 'I have received the following notification from the Lord General: "I give and grant unto the said Colonel a free and full pardon of all manner of offences, errors, and oversights committed in the surrender of the City and Castle of Bristol, discharging hereby the said Colonel from the execution of the capital punishment, imprisonment, restraint, and likewise from all further impeachment, and prosecution concerning the said surrender." It would appear, Colonel, that you are free to go.'

The guards who had taken hold of Nat released him and we left to celebrate in the White Hart. As we did so, Prynne was ripping up papers in indignation and Judge Dorislaus was unhappily reading and re-reading Essex's pardon.

It was a moment of triumph though Nat told us later at the inn, 'I'll have to go abroad. Prynne has dragged my name through the mud. I'll never get over the shame of it.'

Prynne was a bad loser. Within weeks he was trying to overturn the pardon. He could not direct his wrath at the Earl of Essex so instead he had a go at "Mercurius Britanicus", that is to say, at me.

We reported Nat Fiennes' trial and the pardon granted by the Earl. But the truth wasn't good enough for William Prynne. He claimed I'd been bribed by Nat to write positive things about him. Prynne knew Nat was the Viscount's son and an ally of the Vanes. He knew they were financing "Britanicus". So, in attacking me, he was taking them all on.

And he wasn't giving up without a fight.

He launched his counter-attack in a pamphlet with the long and dreary title of "A check to Britanicus, for his palpable flattery in justifying condemned Nat Fiennes".

As you would expect from Master Prynne, it was tedious in the extreme. Verbose, dreary, beside the point, occasionally very odd indeed, religiose, exceptionally unfunny. The slimy fellow made several ridiculous jokes about Nat losing his head but they all fell flat.

He went on at length about the surrender of Bristol. He pointed out that, during his Governorship of the city, Nat hanged two men accused of trying to bring about its surrender to the Royalists and asked, if they deserved to be hanged, why the Colonel in charge of preventing such a thing should escape alive.

He did have a point there, as he did when he added that several other Parliamentarian commanders had been executed for surrendering far less important towns to the enemy.

But he went too far when he accused Nat of lining his own pockets, secretly working for the King and re-stocking Bristol before its surrender to ensure the Cavaliers took over a well-supplied city.

Prynne gave the game away, though. He complained that he, William Prynne, had been dropped as an auditor of the Accounts of the Kingdom and protested that the House of Lords shouldn't be able to appoint their own auditors.

This had nothing to do with the surrender of Bristol. This was about money and power. Prynne wanted both and his enemies in Westminster were manoeuvring to deny him.

It was my pleasure to help them by publishing my own pamphlet replying to his ridiculous accusations and empty whinings. My pleasure and my profit. Nat did defray a few of my expenses though, as I liked him anyway, it was no great hardship for me to publish a 32-page refutation of Prynne's drivel.

It was not my job to offer a fair and balanced view of the circumstances surrounding the surrender of Bristol to Prince Rupert. It was my job to make a case, pursue an argument, take on an opponent and win.

One of the strange aspects of the publishing business is that some readers seem to think the writer is obliged to present the truth, the whole truth and nothing but the truth. How can he be expected to do that? The very people who demand 'the truth' from a news writer are those who insist their version of the Protestant faith is 'the truth' and everyone else's is not just wrong but the spawn of Satan.

Prynne made a couple of good points, about the people Nat executed and the execution of other commanders who surrendered castles to the enemy. So what?

Prynne, in my book, was a malignant and Jesuitical spirit fomenting divisions and stirring up disputes between allies in his own interests. I insinuated we knew about his financial dealings in Bristol and the money he lost. I condemned him for questioning the right of the House of Lords to appoint their own auditors. I even accused him of taking bribes from the Royalists to attack Nat Fiennes and my newsbook.

My patrons were highly satisfied with the work, even though it meant we missed an edition of "Britanicus" to get it written.

But Nat did go into exile. Back to study Calvinism in Switzerland and lick his wounds. I asked him, 'Won't the voters of Banbury miss their Member of Parliament?' He said there were only 14 of them, he was related to seven and he didn't think it would be an issue.

February's floods made travel almost impossible but Lucy departed for Burford with the baby. She took our one female servant and a hired groom as her male escort, despite my furious protests. They were caught in a storm near Kingston, delayed by troop movements near Reading and almost drowned crossing the Thames near Lechlade.

By the time they reached Burford, the baby had a chill and within two days she was dead. She was buried by my father, her grandfather. I wasn't told until weeks later.

CHAPTER 7

Thou art an underling pimpe to the whore of Babylon

Spring 1644

I wasn't terribly upset about the baby's demise, to be honest. I should have been, I suppose, but these things happen. Parents can't expect more than half their children to reach adulthood. The odds are not good. Lack of food or bad food. Lack of hygiene. The virtual absence of medicines. Old wives' tales and witches' potions. The apothecaries' long-standing cure-alls which never succeed. Doctors' bleedings. The plague. I sometimes think the most astonishing thing is that any of us live to be fully-grown. Just as it's astonishing when a man dies a natural death, on his sick-bed, surrounded by his grieving family.

"Britanicus" was doing well. We were up to 1,000 copies a week which, sold at one penny each, brought in just over £4. A quarter of that went to the Mercury women, who touted their wares around St Paul's and elsewhere. Another quarter went to White and Bishop, the printers. The rest, £2 a week, went to Captain Audley and me, though we did pay a few shillings to greasy John Rushworth to keep the whole thing legal.

Our earnings were, of course, on top of the £3 a week paid to me by the Viscount and our other patrons. I imagine Audley got more but he told me to mind my own business whenever I brought the subject up, which was often. There is nothing worse than not knowing something when you know someone you know knows something you don't know.

Anyway, there were other ways to make money. One or two of Parliament's less successful generals were happy for us to enhance their reputations by making the most of small skirmishes and little victories.

We explained such positive publicity did not come cheap. If someone like Sir Billy Balfour wanted to turn a brief encounter with Prince Rupert into 'The Bloody Battle of Aylesbury', who was I to stop him – for a small consideration? It was good for the Parliamentary cause and if the "Court Mercury" retaliated by questioning Sir Billy's heroism, we could simply say they were lying to hide the truth that their cause was on the run, even in Aylesbury.

Early in the morning of a windy March day, a messenger arrived at my lonely quarters near Lincoln's Inn with a summons to present myself to the Earl of Essex at 10 am prompt that very morning.

Essex? Son of Queen Elizabeth's favourite who was executed for treason? General commanding the entire Parliamentarian war effort? The man who recently responded to my investigation into William Prynne's financial affairs and issued a complete pardon for Nat Fiennes? The man who wanted to settle the entire dispute through trial by combat? That Essex.

I threw on a colourful cloak, a Parliamentary-yellow silk sash and made sure to wear my pearl droplet ear-rings. Everybody knew about Essex and it did no harm to look one's best for a man who spent most of his time on battlefields or marching across filthy countryside strewn with corpses. Essex liked fashionable young men.

It wasn't far to Essex House, the big ugly castle of a place between The Strand and the Thames. The place was heavily guarded and I had to state my business to three different retainers, two in uniform, one in Puritanical black, before yet another servant ushered me into an ante-room and told me to wait.

There was nowhere to sit in the dark, oak-panelled lobby. There was no view, no fire, no candle. Plain wooden floorboards. A wooden cross on a wall. It was like being in the most austere of chapels.

After a few minutes, the man himself appeared at the open door. The first thing you noticed was his confidence. The Earl had the slightly indifferent look of a man accustomed to command, not used to being questioned and impervious to criticism. His manner suggested he didn't care what anyone thought; he knew his own mind and that was enough.

Tall, thin, gaunt, with a fierce moustache and scowling eyes, the Earl did not strike me as a man who preferred men to women and boys to girls. Two failed marriages – one wife a virgin throughout, the second perhaps giving birth to Essex's child, perhaps to someone else's – had done nothing to dampen the gossip. Today he looked strictly Puritanical, Godly and efficient.

'Nedham,' he bellowed as if addressing a troop of soldiers on a parade ground. Essex's hearing had been damaged by exposure to canon-fire. 'Your news-sheet.'

'Your lordship?'

'Speak up man.'

I raised my voice. '"Mercurius Britanicus", my lord?'

'Of course "Britanicus", that's what I said.'

I wasn't sure what to say so I waited as the Earl advanced across the room and stood just a pace away from me. I could smell something sweet on his breath. Perhaps an apple. 'We're winning, you know,' he said, 'We're going to win.'

'Of course, my lord. God is on our side.'

'He is. And so are the Scotch. We have an army of Scotsmen marching south. You know they're at Newcastle?'

'Are they?' This was news. I felt a rush of excitement. Here was something to report. 'Can I use that?'

'Of course,' said Essex, as if he were dispensing an honour to a loyal retainer. It turned out he was. 'After all, I am now your proprietor,' he said, smiling and turning his back on me. 'Follow me.'

He led me into a parlour illuminated by dull light from high windows. A fire burned fitfully. Essex poured two glasses and handed one to me. 'Rhenish,' he said. 'Good Protestant wine.'

It was early, even for me, but I was hardly likely to refuse the most powerful man in the country, especially as he seemed to want me to like him.

'Thing is, Nedham, I have acquired your licence. I am now your licenser.'

'My lord.' I didn't know what to make of this. What had happened to the Viscount and Sir Henry?

'Your pamphlet. Very popular,' said Essex. 'Army reads it. Officers. Men. Good for morale.'

'I am delighted to hear it, my lord. Thank you.'

Essex did not look delighted. Indeed, he frowned. 'Politics, Nedham. Everything is politics.'

'Indeed, my lord.' Was it? I wasn't sure but I wasn't going to argue.

'Your patrons. Independents. Not sure about that. Has to be some conformity in religion. Chaos otherwise. No?'

Was he asking for my opinion? If so, what did he want my opinion to be? The same as his, I supposed. 'Up to a point, my lord,' I said. 'Up to a point.'

'Sir Henry's solemn league and covenant. Now there's a thing. Conformity in all things. Us and the Scottish together. Together, Nedham, one Church. United.'

'Yes, indeed, your lordship,' I said. I wasn't in the market for contradicting him.

'Now Henry Vane,' he said, 'Younger Henry. Strong supporter. Good man. No wish to tread on his toes. Henry is not committed to his own treaty, is he, Nedham? Too much ambiguity. Room for manoeuvre. We can't afford to upset our allies, see?'

'No, your lordship. I mean yes, your lordship. I mean, we cannot afford to upset the Jockies, sir, yes.'

'Not "Jockies", Nedham.'

'No, sir.'

Essex put down his wine, stood, crossed the room to where I was sitting, his boots echoing across the wooden floor. He stood over me with a hand on the hilt of the sword at his side and a grim smile on his face. 'We can't afford to go around upsetting our allies, Nedham. Do I make myself clear? As your licenser? Licensers have the power to withdraw a licence at any time. You know that, I suppose, don't you?'

'I do, your lordship.'

'I shall not interfere, Nedham. Your arrangements with Vane and Lord Saye are a matter for you and your fellow newsmonger, what's his name? Audley. But remember. The King is the enemy, not the Scotch.'

'And they are poised to take Newcastle, my lord?'

'So General Leslie tells me.'

'May I see his letter? Use it in the next edition?'

'You may. One of my secretaries will bring it to you. I must go. But remember, Nedham. You have a great deal of freedom but it is not infinite. Difficult times. Tread carefully.'

Later that day I met John Bradshaw, my old boss at Lincoln's Inn. He had taken over larger chambers vacated by one of those Royalist lawyers who'd run off to Oxford at the outbreak of war. Bradshaw was still moving in. There were piles of books and legal briefings, a couple of clerks in an outer room trying to sort things out and the man himself poring over a witness statement.

'Nedham, good to see you,' he said, looking up, alert and vigorous like a spaniel on a hunt. 'Find somewhere to sit, if you can.' Books were piled on the three available chairs so I took those on the one closest to the fire – there was a bitterly cold wind – and put them on the floor.

'John,' I said, 'Licensing of newsbooks.'

'What about it?'

'Is there anything we can do?'

'Do?'

I explained "Britanicus" was now beholden to the Earl of Essex. Bradshaw couldn't see the problem.

'He says we can't say anything unpleasant about the Jocks,' I complained.

At that moment, John Milton sidled into Bradshaw's office. 'Ah, the divorcer,' said Bradshaw in a jocular fashion. Milton winced as if he'd been slapped. He was clutching a pile of papers which he deposited clumsily on Bradshaw's desk.

'Another effusion, John?' said Bradshaw.

'I couldn't help overhearing your conversation as I came in about licensing newsbooks, Nedham. You might like to peruse this once Bradshaw has read it.'

'What is it, Milton?'

'I'm going to call it "Areopagitica".'

'You would,' said Bradshaw in his flat and cynical Lancastrian accent.

'What does that mean?'

'It's the hill in ancient Athens where Saint Paul gave his sermon about ignorant worship. My thesis is that we must bring an end to censorship.'

Bradshaw picked up the papers and started to flick through them. 'You're working this up into another jeremiad then, are you Milton?'

'I am. How can people make free choices when they do not have free speech and remain in ignorance? Before the war, the King tried to suppress new ideas; now we are in power, what do we do? Suppress them too?'

Milton had a point but was he willing to have a complete free-for-all? 'What about Papists, Milton? Will they be free to publish their tracts?'

'Papists were the first to burn books. I do not extend this freedom to Popery and other superstitions. They would wish to extirpate all other speech. Toleration has its limits. You cannot tolerate the intolerant.'

'And what if some newsbook like "The Court Mercury" or, heaven forfend, "Britanicus" itself, took advantage of your freedom to publish some gross libel?'

'Ah,' said Milton, his pink face aglow with zeal, 'Let it be published but if it is then found to be mischievous or libellous, the publication should be burned and the author executed.'

'So we should be free to say whatever we like but if we cross the line in some way then the law can still hang us, is that it?' I asked.

'Just so,' said Milton with a satisfied smile, 'Just so.'

I looked at Bradshaw. 'Sorry, John, I was wrong to complain earlier. I think I prefer the licensing system we have at the moment if the alternative is execution. At least the Earl of Essex isn't likely to be quite that drastic. Still, Milton, when your tract is published, let me know and I'll give it publicity in "Britanicus". It will definitely help your sales.'

'Sales?' said Milton, insulted by the very word, 'This is aimed at those who understand these things and have the power to change them. Sales are the last thing on my mind.'

I didn't believe him and I was right not to because, in time, Milton's printer happily paid money to advertise the great radical's pamphlets in my newsbook.

One of the most annoying things is discovering important information after everybody else. Not only was I ignorant of Tom Audley's pay, I was equally in the dark about what he got up to half the time. Then, one day as we were visiting the printers in Warwick Court, Audley announced, 'I'm taking on another couple of news-sheets, Marchamont. Bob's asked me to.'

Audley indicated Bob White, who at that moment was leaning over one of his three presses trying to adjust the ratcheting on a tray of type which had somehow become jammed when an apprentice tried to run off copies of one of their other publications.

White's partner George Bishop had walked out and was threatening to set up his own rival news-sheets from a workshop down near the river somewhere. Audley said, 'Bishop's left Bob in the lurch. I said I'd help him out for a while.'

'You might have told me,' I complained.

'I'm telling you now,' retorted Audley with a grunt which implied the conversation was at an end. He gave one of those smiles that isn't a smile but a smirk, a gesture of defiance. It made his scar look particularly livid, as if he might possibly have come by it in combat after all. 'You'll just have to do more work,' he added.

'Bob,' I called across the print-shop. 'You've got a new apprentice I hear.'

'Marchamont,' he said, 'You'll need to get "Britanicus" done by Sunday night next week. It's going to have to be printed for Monday morning not Tuesday in future. We've got too much on.'

I looked at Audley, who shrugged. They'd planned this in advance. A two-pronged attack – Audley takes a back seat and "Britanicus" gives way to White's other rags, the "Kingdome's Weekly Intelligencer" and the "Parliament Scout".

'Seriously?' I demanded, slamming a mallet down on a wooden table hard, but not hard enough to do any damage. I was peeved at being kept in ignorance but I wasn't really angry because here was my opportunity to take on "Britanicus" alone. Audley wouldn't be paying much attention; he'd be too busy dealing with Richard Collings and John Dillingham.

Collings and Dillingham were responsible for the "Intelligencer" and the "Scout" respectively. I quite liked Collings's newsbook because it included pictures. There wasn't much to say in favour of the "Scout" especially as Dillingham was a fat little tailor with fingers in too many pies to be trustworthy.

It occurred to me that, by coming out on a Monday, I would be able to take advantage of the news in the weekend post and distribute it before anybody else. I'd beat the "Intelligencer" and the "Scout" along with all the other rags in London. But I wasn't telling Audley and White this. They needed to know I was angry.

'Oh and Sir Henry wants to see you,' Audley added casually.

After we'd put "Britanicus" to bed, I traipsed across town to Westminster and sought out Sir Henry at his town house in the abbey sanctuary yard. There were several large houses there, converted from the monastery 100 years ago. Sir Henry moved into one of the Royalists' properties confiscated by Parliament. They called these Royalists 'delinquents', seized their homes and goods, sold off anything valuable, supposedly to finance the war, and rented out properties to their friends at rock-bottom rates. Or they simply appropriated them and moved in. Our Parliamentarians were very generous in the re-distribution of large country estates and big town houses.

Sir Henry, whose family was not short of money, was one such beneficiary. His place, once quarters for the abbot of Westminster, was fitted out with furnishings taken from the King's palace down the road at Whitehall and he retained a large staff.

The evening was mild with a scent of spring from the budding plane trees. It was late, after dark, and the yard was ill-lit. There were too many drunks wandering around to feel safe. I was glad to be ushered into a large, well-lit hall where Sir Henry was finishing a late supper with several of his friends. I recognised Judge John Glynn immediately.

'Uncle,' I said, bowing to him.

John looked up from the remains of his quince cheese with a smile. 'Marchamont, dear boy. How are you? Sir Henry told me you were on the way.'

I joined them at the table and was given some quince cheese and a cup of a novelty drink.

'Coffee, my lad?' asked Uncle John Glynn. 'Vane's is the first place I've encountered it. They say it has medicinal qualities and the power to cure drunkards.'

As well as Uncle John and Sir Henry, there were three others at the table. Bradshaw was there with Sir Oliver St John, the Solicitor General, and a younger man, John Thurloe. He watched and listened without saying a word.

Sir Henry asked, 'You know they've been attacking you in my old colony of Massachusetts, do you Nedham? The "Court Mercury" says you have been outraging the Puritans there.'

'If it's in that Royalist rag we can be sure it's untrue,' I laughed, 'Though if there were to be any truth in it, then I am delighted our readership is now so widespread. We must be doing something right.'

'They're attacking Essex,' said St John.

'Thing is,' cut in Uncle John Glynn, 'Essex isn't really on top of his game is he?'

Vane looked up from his coffee and scowled. 'You've been rather kind about Essex, haven't you, Nedham?'

'He is our licence-holder,' I pointed out.

'Even so, Nedham,' said Vane, waving an old copy of "Britanicus" and read, '"We shall never pitch upon a general of more notable resolution, courage and fidelity to this cause than his excellency the Earl of Essex. An excellent pattern of fidelity and resolution who had rather purchase peace at any price than with the ruin of the country." We can do without that kind of eulogy, thank you very much.'

Rather more kindly, Uncle John Glynn explained, 'Seems to me, Marchamont my boy, you rather hit the nail on the head. Essex does want peace. At any price, as you say. He doesn't want to crush the King and the Court. He is one of them after all.'

St John demanded, 'If he brought the King to the negotiating table, what would peace look like? We would have to insist on executions. Prince Rupert, Prince Maurice, Hyde, Goring, Ormonde, Henry Howard. Newcastle. Others.'

'That bastard Byron,' suggested Bradshaw.

'The King would never agree to all that, surely,' I said.

'He gave us Strafford,' said St John with some satisfaction.

'Didn't have any choice,' said Uncle John.

The two men glanced at each other with complicit smiles. They had both been involved in the execution of the King's great minister. Indeed, it had made their names. St John believed in execution without a trial. He said huntsmen had no qualms about killing foxes so why should anybody care that Strafford was knocked on the head without the benefit of a legal conviction. He hadn't changed his views as far as getting rid of his enemies was concerned.

'Even so,' I said. 'I can't see him giving up his own nephew, can you uncle?'

To his credit, the judge laughed and shook his head. 'Good point, Marchamont,' he said. 'But we all know this King is not a man of fixed opinions or strong affections.'

'Except for the generalissima,' I pointed out.

'Ah yes, the French Catholic. She'll have to go, of course,' said St John. 'And if they will not make peace at any price, what is the logical conclusion we all must come to?'

There was silence around the table.

'Getting back to Essex,' I said, 'The Earl won't give up his position without a fight.'

'Maybe,' answered Sir Henry, signalling to a servant for more coffee, 'Maybe. But he won't have the guaranteed support of "Britanicus" any longer. We've wrested the licence out of his control. If you apply to Rushworth at the Commons tomorrow, Nedham, he'll provide you with the paperwork.'

Not long afterwards, Sir Henry handed me the first great scoop of my career.

CHAPTER 8

Lead, when moulded into
Bullets, is not so mortal
as when founded
into Letters

Summer 1644

Someone – Essex himself perhaps, maybe Fairfax, possibly Cromwell, someone important anyway – anyway, someone intercepted and copied a letter sent by the King to Prince Rupert while the latter was rampaging round Lancashire. That letter found its way to Sir Henry Vane just before he was due to leave London for Yorkshire. Sir Henry summoned me to his office and handed me a copy.

As I read it, I found myself trembling with excitement. I could hardly wait the 48 hours until Monday for the news to appear in print. I rushed back to the workshop near St Paul's and started scribbling. I wouldn't let Audley see what I was up to, which gave me additional satisfaction. I wasn't going to give his other newsbooks a head start.

I decided to print the whole letter and then add a commentary explaining why this story was so significant and what it told us about the state of the Royalists.

Obviously, the simple fact that it had fallen into our hands would be enough to cause fury in Oxford. I could imagine the reaction of the King and his courtiers when the next edition of "Britanicus" reached them.

There would be no time for the King to retract his orders or force Prince Rupert into some other course. Thanks to "Britanicus", the world would know the truth. The King told his nephew to relieve the siege of York, capital city of the North of England, as soon as possible, take on and defeat Parliament's armies in the North then hurry south to relieve Oxford.

The killer line was where the King told Prince Rupert if he failed to relieve York and beat Parliament's armies 'all the successes you can afterwards have must infallibly be useless to me'.

What an admission. Win one battle or we are completely lost.

This letter suggested that, even though the Royalists had been having the best of the fighting for months, they were in a more precarious position than we thought. If the King was afraid defeat at York would destroy his cause, it made the next battle all the more significant.

Given the chance, the Royalists would have put a different gloss on all this. They would have complained the King's confidential messages should never be made public and threatened to execute those responsible for revealing Royal secrets including, no doubt, the reporter of such news. They might have claimed the interpretation placed on the King's words was the work of scurrilous lying hacks with an axe to grind. They would have said I misquoted the King, took his words out of context, disregarded the circumstances. They might have blamed a secretary for some mistake in transcription. They would have found any excuse they could think of to deny the importance of the letter and pretend it was a mere bagatelle.

They never got the chance.

This was news. I had to get it into the hands of my readers as soon as possible and in sufficient quantities to meet demand. I told Audley I wanted to double the print run to 2,000 copies. He said he would not agree without knowing what the fuss was about. We argued. Bob White sided with his new partner.

'Be reasonable, Marchamont. How do we know if we're likely to sell all those news-sheets if you won't tell us what the story is?'

'It'll change the course of the war,' I said.

'All the more reason to tell us,' growled Audley. 'Come on, Marchamont, we're all friends here. I can go to Vane myself if I have to.'

'Good luck with that,' I said, 'He's half way to York by now.'

Eventually, of course, I would have to hand over my manuscript to the printers so, after a long-enough delay, I told Audley and White about the letter. By then, I'd stolen a march on the other papers in White's print shop as well as my rivals elsewhere. Everybody would know the story broke in "Mercurius Britanicus". Everybody would know it was broken by Marchamont Nedham.

What a shame I had nobody to celebrate my triumph with.

The King's letter sent Prince Rupert hurrying to York where he rescued the Duke of Newcastle's little army. But instead of consolidating the Royalists' position, Rupert took the letter to mean he must tackle the enemy head-on. That is, face three separate armies commanded by the Earl of Manchester, Sir Thomas Fairfax and Lord Leven, the Scottish commander.

What Rupert didn't know, because the news didn't reach him on time, is that the King had destroyed a Parliamentary army at Cropredy, near Banbury in Oxfordshire. It made the King's letter redundant and meant there was no urgent need for Rupert to hurry south to protect the cavaliers' capital at Oxford.

If Rupert had known, would he have avoided confrontation at Marston Moor? Probably not. He was always eager for battle. Anyway, it's idle to speculate. Rupert fought and lost.

Sir Henry Vane sent long and detailed descriptions of the battle and its aftermath which were only available to Audley and me. As a result, the three newsbooks in Bob White's print-shop were the only ones to reveal full accounts of the battle.

For instance, we told our readers Prince Rupert hid in a field to escape capture and relied on the gallantry of his horse, which surpassed the rest of his followers in the swiftness of his flight away from the battlefield.

Even better was the story about Rupert's poodle, Boye. The superstitious called Boye 'the Prince's Devilish familiar' and claimed he could deflect bullets. The dog was put to death by a preacher skilled in art of necromancy. Or at least the dog-killer was a preacher skilled in necromancy by the time the death was reported in our newsbooks. Boye's death was a symbol of the triumph of the Godly over the Satanic. Obviously, that required a skilled necromancer which we felt it necessary to provide for our readers.

Vane went to York to meet the generals. They debated removing the King from the throne altogether. Quite how they thought they'd do this was not clear but Vane had an alternative candidate, Prince Rupert's elder brother Louis. He'd already moved into Whitehall Palace.

I took this as encouragement to become more critical of the King himself rather than simply complain about his advisers and his terrible wife.

The Royalists' defeat at Marston Moor gave me plenty of opportunity to question the King's wisdom. I pointed out he was beholden to an army of mercenaries, from the German brothers Prince Rupert and Prince Maurice down. His Irish soldiers were worse than Turks. He had French, Walloons and Welshmen in his army. His greatest support came from Cornwall which is, as we all know, the very arse of Christendom.

I said the King was led by his petticoat army. He was hen-pecked — readers hardly needed reminding (but they were reminded, often) that Henrietta Maria had goaded Charles and called him a coward before he tried to arrest the five MPs.

I reminded my army of readers it was Charles who provoked war by levying the Ship Money tax without Parliament's permission. I asked what he had done with the money and gave the answer: squandered it on masques which encouraged the court doxies to dress up as shepherd-esses and gambol across the stage flaunting their bodies in diaphanous dresses, the whole gaudy pantomime set against theatrical backdrops created at vast expense by Inigo Jones. How could the court have been so decadent?

It was also necessary to remind readers of the King's Popish sym-pathies – how could he not lean towards Rome when his Queen and all her closest friends were defiant Papists?

Worse still, the King couldn't be trusted. I was particularly proud of my line: 'Never did any great tennis-ball of passion and fortune roll about more than he has done.'

This war was the King's fault, I said. His white coronation robes were dyed red in the blood of his subjects. The miseries and terrors were caused by Charles.

These attacks were mounted week after week with Sir Henry Vane's approval and support. It was challenging to come up with a new angle every time but I succeeded and readers lapped it up. "Britanicus" was selling well.

All this made me terribly popular in some quarters and even more unpopular in others. Never mind the corridors of power, what about the halls of commerce and the streets of poverty? More and more often, I was accosted by ordinary people going about their daily business, as far as that was possible when everything was disrupted by war. They would stare at me, berate me, slap me on the back, threaten to clap me in irons, drag me to Tyburn and set light to a pyre with Marchamont Nedham at its summit. Mostly this was done with a certain amount of good humour but from time to time a fanatic would threaten to knife me and I found myself planning my progress across the city with an idea of where to run for safety.

It surprised me ignorant peasants were capable of reading and I told them so. This did not help but it was as good as a fist in the face for some of them, they looked quite downcast.

It didn't happen often that I was assailed by a Royalist because such people, if caught, were liable to fines, imprisonment or worse. What I did note, though, was how many people who supported Parliament drew the line at denigrating the King. For them, he was still God's anointed. For them, attacking the King was as bad as attacking God. I sometimes argued there was a difference between the position and the person but they weren't having it. The King was the King and his position and power came from God Himself.

In early September, Audley and I went for our usual lunchtime pint of wine to The Fleece in Covent Garden. 'I'm going to have to give it up, Marchamont,' Audley said. 'Can't manage to produce stuff for the "Brit" when I'm doing the other two. You'll have to do "Brit" on your own.'

'I've been doing that for months – and without any recompense,' I pointed out.

Audley said, 'You can take all the revenue. You'll be much better off. But a word of advice, Monty. This war is all about religion, God, faith. I sometimes think you don't really understand that.'

'I know that's what people say, Audley. But God's an excuse. Everyone, most of all the sanctimonious, Jesuitical Presbyterians, are only really interested in power and money.'

Audley laughed. 'You'll be saying they're only interested in women next.'

'Well, Oliver Cromwell is marrying off his daughters to his allies. Does he know something we don't?'

'Yes,' said Audley with the satisfaction of someone who is about to demolish his opponent's arguments, 'Oliver Cromwell does know something we don't. He knows God is on his side. With knowledge like that, you can do anything.'

Bradshaw invited me to his chambers to discuss his lucrative job as legal adviser to the sequestrations committee. He was in charge of assessing appeals by the families of delinquent Royalists against Parliament's decision to seize their money and goods and sell them off. The victims of this policy included the wives and children. Parliament, in its mercy, thought dependants who were not, themselves, waging war against it should be allowed to keep enough money to live off, usually one-fifth of the value of an estate.

Bradshaw had to wade through the submissions in each appeal to the committee and offer an opinion. Occasionally, he told me with a smile, that opinion could be influenced. Money might change hands. Or, more rarely but nonetheless sometimes, the persuasive power of a pretty face and a pert demeanour had more effect.

I remember distinctly the occasion in October when Bradshaw handed me a copy of Milton's new pamphlet calling for freedom of the press. It was still in my pocket when a messenger arrived at the print-shop as I was putting together the early pages of the following week's "Britanicus" (I tended to complete the first four pages three days before publication then add the latest news in the remaining four pages at the last minute) with a note. It demanded my immediate presence in the Painted Chamber at Westminster. It was signed Oliver Cromwell.

Cromwell was certainly the coming man but nobody would have given him much chance of becoming the next King of England, Scotland and Ireland, the Lord Protector, the great dictator.

He was a sturdy fellow, hefty, built like a cart-horse rather than a thoroughbred. He was of medium height but his heavy build lent him a threatening presence. His voice was unimpressive and carried something of the yokel in it. He frowned most of the time. His eyes bulged a little. He was a devout believer, if not in God, then at least in God's servant Oliver Cromwell.

He was not a man to be trifled with.

The Painted Chamber, in between the Lords and Commons, is a big place for one man. Cromwell had commandeered a desk and placed it at one end of the long, narrow building. A guard stood at each corner and two were stationed at each of the three entrances but, for all practical purposes, Cromwell was alone. I arrived as the autumn afternoon was declining in a glint of russet and gold. The chamber was ill-lit. It must have been difficult for the MP for Huntingdon to read the paperwork he was ploughing through.

'Nedham, good to meet you,' he said without getting up. 'Have a seat.'

There were chairs lined against the walls but none opposite Cromwell's desk. I took one and carried it over. 'There are some things you need to know,' he told me, business-like and straight to the point.

'My lord?'

He ignored me and looked up at the tapestries on the wall. 'We need to get rid of these,' he said, making a note. 'Now, Nedham, thank you for coming.'

'Not at all, sir.'

'Your fame goes before you.'

'Fame?'

'Infamy, should I say? I've rarely come across someone so hated.' I think this was a blunt man's attempt to break the ice.

'I could say much the same of you, sir.'

Cromwell smiled. I looked at his ugly face with its big, bulbous nose and prominent warts. His hair was dark and thin but there was a red fervour in his hazel-coloured eyes, a hint of fanaticism, perhaps, or did I just see what I wanted to see? Is that how he really was or am I looking back and seeing what he became? I'm not sure. What I do remember, though, was his certainty. He didn't hope or believe, he knew.

I placed my copy of Milton's new tract on his desk. 'I thought you might be interested in this, sir. Hot off the press. It's a call for freedom of speech, by John Milton,' I explained.

Cromwell picked it up and read, '"For the liberty of unlicensed printing". An interesting idea. Not sure it'll catch on. It's hard enough getting people to agree as it is. Far more difficult when we have scribblers whipping up indignation and conflict at every turn. Writers do have some power but they must use it responsibly. Milton is a bit of a radical, isn't he?'

'Not like John Lilburne and the others who want to bring everybody down to the same level.'

'No, not that bad. Milton's a Godly man, I know. I shall have a look at this later. But the reason you're here, Nedham, is we need to prepare people,' Cromwell announced. 'Things are going to change and we must have their support. You will prepare the way.'

'Like John the Baptist,' I quipped.

He didn't take kindly to that. He frowned and twisted his fat, calloused hands together as if he was having difficulty trying to stop them from strangling me. 'This winter,' Cromwell continued, ignoring my comment, 'I will be taking the best men from the best regiments and moulding them into the best-trained, best-disciplined and best-equipped army this country has ever known. There will be an entirely new way of doing things. We won't appoint officers just because they're landowners and aristocrats. I'd rather have a plain, russet-coated captain that knows what he fights for and loves what he knows than what they call a gentleman who is nothing else.'

Here was news. 'May I take some notes?' I asked and Cromwell pushed a quill and paper across the desk. I moved closer.

'We won't have men who don't believe in our cause. We won't have men who don't believe, with fervour and passion, in the true faith. Truly, I think he fights best that prays best. We will have 20,000 men in 11 regiments. And they will be paid, properly, in full and on time.'

'That'll be a first,' I laughed.

He frowned. 'It will be, I agree. Gentlemen in Parliament must understand the need to treat their army with the respect due to the men who put their lives in danger every day on behalf of the liberty of its members.'

'Are the grandees happy with these plans?' I asked, innocently enough. Gossip said Cromwell was falling out with some of his better-bred companions-in-arms.

'Manchester, the Earl, you know, Manchester says we can beat the King as often as we like yet he is still King. I say, if that is true, what was the point of taking up arms in the first place?'

'But what is the logical conclusion from that, my lord?' I asked. 'The Elector Palatine's son, his nephew?'

'He is a Protestant at least,' said Cromwell not answering the question. 'One more thing, Nedham. Next year, we're going to get rid of all the politicians in the army. Nobody will be allowed to have a seat in Parliament and a command in the military, not even the navy. The Ironsides, as Prince Rupert calls us, will be a far more formidable force by the next campaign season.'

'A new model completely,' I said. 'A new model army.'

'Precisely,' Cromwell replied with satisfaction as he waved me away and I retreated with another "Britanicus" exclusive.

When the most important people of the day treat you as if you are of equal importance, it's not surprising you start to have delusions of grandeur. As I swaggered back down the Strand to the city, I reflected on my place in the new order. I was rather pleased with myself – I had money, position, even a degree of power. And all without risking my neck in even the most modest of skirmishes.

It doesn't take much to bring you back down to earth.

I hadn't seen my wife for almost a year. We had not mourned baby Lucy together. We exchanged a few peremptory letters but it hardly constituted a marriage. It was as bad as Milton's.

In early December, in the cold and dark, I set out on a back-roads trudge to Burford. I needed to see Lucy and my parents. It was almost Christmas and I wanted somebody to share my good news with. Success is all very well but, without friends or loved ones to appreciate it, what's the point?

I had a pass, signed by Sir Henry Vane, which should protect me from most marauders. But the country was filled with hungry and neglected men roaming in bands, looking for food, money and trouble. There wasn't much food about and most towns and villages had been stripped of anything worth taking. What could be had was too expensive for most people. Travellers were fair game.

I went via Windsor, where the castle-barracks sheltered hundreds of men. For miles around, their depredations could be seen in burnt-out buildings, ransacked homes, denuded farms and beggars on the streets, in doorways, shuffling along icy lanes in search of succour. There wasn't much I could do except spur on my horse and keep my head down.

Reading had been wasted. Abingdon was in Parliament's hands. There were six bodies hanging from scaffolds in the market square where the ancient cross had been demolished. The town was teeming with soldiers, too small to hold so many. I got away as quickly as possible, skirting to the south of Royalist-held Oxford and on to Witney where I decided to pay a visit to Minster Lovell, home of the Heylyns. Now I was near Burford, I would take any excuse to delay my arrival and the inevitable interview with my wife, not to mention cross-questioning by my mother.

They were an odd lot, the Heylyns. Peter may be chaplain to the King and responsible for the "Court Mercury" but his elder brother Edward was a gruff gentleman farmer whose main aim in life was to avoid involvement in the civil war on either side. A third brother, Henry, was fighting for Parliament.

Only Edward was at home and his obsession was the same as ever. He had been caught up in a long and involved libel case brought by Henry Chaloner, son of Sir Humphrey Chaloner. They fell out over money. Edward wrote to Henry's wife Ursula calling him a cowardly, blustering, giddy-headed fool. The case went to court. Edward lost. There were more disputes. Eventually the war brought an end to their arguments and the Heylyns repossessed the house in Minster Lovell where Henry Chaloner had been living without paying rent. Edward had not given up the battle.

'I'll make the wretch grovel, Marchamont,' he swore almost as soon as he had taken me into the parlour and supplied me with some very sweet

Madeira. 'He had to beg my forgiveness once, you know. The Court of Chivalry.'

'God, is that thing still going?'

'Not really, no. I told Peter I needed a hearing and told him to ask the King but nothing doing.'

'You've survived the war so far, then?'

Edward pointed to a pair of huge, ugly hounds lying by the door. 'They tend to keep most people out,' he said with some satisfaction.

'How is Peter? And Henry?'

'Henry's somewhere in the West Country last I heard. Could be dead for all I know. Peter's with the King. Eyesight's going, you know.'

'Not good for a man producing a newsbook.'

'Oh you know about that, do you? See it in London?'

'We do. I'm making a newsbook as well.'

Edward stared into the fire where the flames were burning briskly. 'Can't be doing with any of it myself,' he said. 'Can't understand why anybody's bothered with all that rubbish. Peter comes over waving his pamphlets in my face. Soon as he's gone I throw 'em on the fire. This whole bloody war is just bloody isn't it, Marchamont? Just bloody.'

I stayed the night with Edward but I could put it off no longer. Next morning, I made the short ride along the River Windrush into Burford. It was cold. The village was hidden in a wintry mist. There were icicles on the river. The water flowed moodily. A few leaves were frosted on the bough, most crunched underfoot. The day was dead, sound was muffled, everything was gloom. I went first to the rectory where, as I was dismounting, my step-father Christopher emerged on his way to school. 'Here you are, my boy,' he said, greeting me with a friendly handshake. 'We expected you yesterday. Your mother is looking forward to seeing you. I'm not sure I can say the same for your wife.'

'You look well, sir. How is the school?'

'The school is well enough though some of the boys are being kept at home. Either we are too Royalist or too Puritan, it depends on the family. Luckily, we enjoy the patronage of the Lenthalls. It gives us some protection. The Earl of Essex was here in the summer. His idiot men tore down the flags and pennants over the monument in church. They were worse than the Cavaliers. The King's army came through not long before Essex but they were no trouble. The King stayed at The George with his son Charles and the Earl of Lindsey. The Earl and the King slept in the same bed you know.' My step-father chuckled.

'Did you see Peter?' I asked.

'Heylyn? Yes, he called in to pay his respects. He said you'd been goading him but he seemed more amused than angry.' My step-father smiled. 'I have seen a couple of copies of your newsbook, Marchamont. Very provocative.'

I shrugged and grinned. 'It pays well.'

'Does it indeed? Glad to hear it. I shall see you at supper but for now I must go to school. They'll be wondering where I've got to.'

My mother was delighted to see me, said I looked too thin, gave me food and then sent me up the hill to find my wife.

Lucy was in her mother's parlour reading the Bible. 'Husband,' she greeted me, 'At last. Hast thou devoured thy living with harlots?'

I recognised her reference to the parable of the prodigal son so I answered, 'And shall you kill the fatted calf then Lucy?' She looked up with a wary half-smile and I thought, perhaps I still had charm enough to make things right with her.

CHAPTER 9

Good Newes from all
Quarters of the Kingdome

Winter 1644-5

We got over the death of baby Lucy. My wife was philosophical, accepting the will of God; I was forgiving, even though she exposed the baby to a perilous journey in treacherous weather.

It was harder to suffer Lucy's religious fervour. The brethren met in a house at the top of the hill with a preacher who called himself Salvation Jones and enjoyed regular visions of the Holy Ghost. He said England wasn't repentant and deserved the cruelties of civil war which would purge the nation and force everyone onto their knees in sorrow. When Lucy started going on about how 'God commands all men to repent' and how 'there are times for repentance, weeping and mourning', I stared out of the window and tried to count the sheep being driven down the hill.

Lucy no longer attended my father's church. She preferred meetings with Salvation Jones who, until his great conversion, had been a cobbler in Witney. At least these militants did not try to disrupt my father's services.

'Thou art mine husband, Marchamont. I am thy dutiful wife,' Lucy told me, 'But mine eyes have been opened to the glory of the Lord and the truth of his revelations.' She really did believe in her duty as a wife and in the glory of the Lord, as revealed by Salvation Jones. There was no point in arguing. There were disputes enough in the country without bringing them into our home.

Lucy was far from happy with the state of the nation. She did not think Parliament was going far enough in its war with the King. She was furious Charles had stayed at The George which was, in her eyes, the family home.

'Essex too,' I reminded her.

'Yes, the Earl. I met him,' Lucy said, sounding very pleased with herself. I considered pointing out pride was a sin but thought better of it.

'The King and the Earl were pursuing one another across the downs,' she said, 'Or seemed to be.'

'And the town escaped unscathed?'

'Nowhere is safe from cavaliers,' she said. Her pretty face creased into angry frowns, like a baby about to burst into tears.

'And Fairfax's saints were saints indeed, were they my dear?'

'They tore down Papist flummery in your father's church and we joined them in prayer.'

'Marvellous.'

Later I visited The George on my way to the rectory. Lucy would not accompany me. She was in a sewing circle darning socks for Parliament's soldiers.

The George was quiet and I was able to become reacquainted with Big Susie. 'Chastity,' I called with a laugh as she was crossing the inner courtyard with a pail of water.

'Well, if it isn't the doctor. Or is it the lawyer? Or the news-monger? Or the married man? What is it today, my lord? The Puritan? The cavalier?' she said, chuckling as she accidentally-on-purpose dropped her bucket, spilling water over my boots.

'A good afternoon to you too, Mistress Chastity. Still living up to your noble name?'

It turned out she was not and, after further insults and after re-filling the pail, which, let it be noted, I carried for her, Big Susie and I crept up the back stairs to her attic room for a while.

Later I asked, 'How are Humility and Fear-not?'

'I still think of mother and father as Mary and Edward. But now they are in New England, I don't think of them very often. Anyway, your Lucy comes up to me in the market one day and starts demanding I repent my evil ways. My evil ways! "What do you mean by that?" I ask her. "We all know, Chastity Dyer," she says. "We all know. You are at the Devil's work. Repent," she says, "Repent." And then she says, "You know the witch-finders are about, do you not? Repent your sins, mend your ways, you would not want to attract the attention of the witch-finders, would you Chastity Dyer?"'

My mother told me Lucy's sect was not popular around Burford. 'They attract the misfits, Marchamont,' she said. 'Labourers, beggars, stupid women, one or two of the better sort but not many. That man Salvation Jones, nothing but a charlatan. Somebody taught him to read, more's the pity. He quotes the scriptures at random. Sometimes you'll find him outside The George preaching to nobody but his most devoted disciples of whom, I'm sorry to say, your Lucy seems to be one.'

'Please keep an eye on her while I am in London, mother. She frightens me with her fervour. She's been talking about witches.' I laughed.

My mother drew in her breath and held it. 'No more, Marchamont,' she hissed. 'You must not make light of these things.'

'Mother?'

'Nobody is safe, Marchamont. It only requires someone to make a denunciation.'

'But surely there's nothing like that going on, mother.'

'Not round here, not yet. But Jones and his acolytes take this sort of thing seriously. Give them an inch and they'll be hanging innocent women or ducking them in the river. And there are always rumours about the villages.' My mother's voice trailed off.

'I'd better get her back to London where she can do no harm.'

'Do no harm?' my mother said incredulously. 'London is where all the harm in the country is being done. And you're one of those responsible, Marchamont. You and your scurrilous news-sheet, what's it called? "Britanicus". How can you attack your monarch? The King was appointed by God himself.'

I'd been expecting this. Mother felt things strongly and her belief in the divine right of kings was not to be shaken by the likes of Sir Henry Vane or the Earl of Essex let alone Oliver Cromwell. Even now, she couldn't mention Pym's name without fury nor the Earl of Strafford's without a tear. She was also vehement about the fate of Archbishop Laud.'

'Mother, it pays the bills,' I said.

'Pays the bills,' she said scornfully. 'That is no excuse for betraying your King, Marchamont.'

'This is dangerous talk, mother.'

'Elizabeth agrees with me,' she said with an air of triumph, as if that settled things.

'Elizabeth?'

'Lenthall, the Speaker's wife. She thinks things have gone far enough and it's time for the Parliament to make peace. I agree. You have some influence with your little pamphlet, Marchamont. If you must carry on that line of work, why can't you use it to promote peace? Everybody wants peace now. The war has gone on far too long as it is. How can you support these traitors?'

I escaped back to London. It felt safer there.

Little did I know.

There was a newsbook to get out. I'd prepared much of it in advance. The edition was devoted to debate about Cromwell's plans. I unveiled my phrase, 'the New Model Army', and floated Cromwell's proposal that members of the Lords and Commons should be banned from holding rank in Parliament's army.

The Viscount and Sir Henry supported the idea. The Earls of Essex and Manchester were furious. What, I wondered, did that mean for Cromwell himself? A General and an MP, he too would have to give up one role or the other.

This was the year Parliament officially banned Christmas and early in January William Laud, the old and spiteful Archbishop of Canterbury, was finally beheaded. It did not go down well among Londoners any more than the executions of Sir John Hotham and his son did. The two men refused to hand over Hull to the King at the start of the war but transferred their allegiance to the Royalists and paid the ultimate price. Nobody came out of that episode very well and Londoners, cold, hungry, looking for an end to the war, were not excited by, or even interested in, these executions. If anything, they suggested nobody was safe, even people who served Parliament loyally and well.

It wasn't the executions that alarmed me, it was the arrest of the fat little tailor John Dillingham. He had fingers in several pies but he was arrested over his newsbook "Parliamentary Scout", one of the three printed by White and Audley.

I knew Dillingham because we bumped into each other at White's print shop. He was short, tubby and sweaty. His main occupation was tailoring which should have kept him busy as he was under contract to make hundreds of red coats for the New Model Army. The worrying thing was that, if a man so close to the Government could be thrown in the Fleet Prison, no newsbook writer was safe.

Audley was alarmed. 'Dillingham had a go at the Earl of Essex, claiming the army would be better off without him,' he explained. 'Dillingham was set up by Cromwell.'

'Cromwell?' I said, thinking back to my own encounter with him only a few weeks earlier.

'Yes, Cromwell and Dillingham dined together before Christmas,' said Audley, 'He told Dillingham that Essex was on his way out, a man with no friends and no power and the "Scout" would be doing history a favour if it prepared the way for Essex's downfall.'

'Rumours of his death appear to be much exaggerated,' I said. 'As for doing history a favour, what does that mean?'

'I think it means anticipating events and nudging them along a bit,' said Audley. 'Turns out Essex has more friends than Cromwell and Dillingham bargained for. Dillingham's very unhappy. Thinks Cromwell set him up. We'll have to abandon the "Scout" altogether and suspend the "Intelligencer" as well.'

'What about "Britanicus"?'

'That's up to you,' said Audley unhelpfully. 'It's all yours. But be careful, Marchamont, be careful. Your friend Milton might want a free press but there's no such thing and I have no intention of going to jail if I can avoid it.'

Talk about famous last words...

CHAPTER 10

We cannot say, that
this Fellow writes,
but vomits

Spring 1645

Cromwell was as slippery as any other politician. Dillingham's arrest proved it. Cromwell set up Dillingham to undermine the Earl of Essex. The reaction allowed Cromwell to assess the strength of the Earl's political support. The fact that the tubby tailor ended up in prison was, in Cromwell's world, a small price to pay for discovering Essex still had powerful allies.

I went to see Sir Henry.

He was in the Treasury, where he collecting taxed taxes to pay for the navy. Ironically, Sir Henry was once responsible for the Ship Money tax which caused half the trouble in the first place. He wasn't paying much attention to the collection of taxes though. He was angry. You could tell by the way he stared sightlessly at a tapestry of a unicorn and nymphs.

'Essex has had Dillingham arrested and closed "The Scout",' I told Sir Henry without any preamble. It was no time for politeness.

'I know. Dillingham is to give up scribbling and stick to his needle,' said Sir Henry, never taking his eyes off the unicorn.

This was disturbing. If Parliament could close the book on Dillingham so easily, what did the next chapter look like for Marchamont Nedham?

'That man Essex,' Vane spat, 'You need to understand, Nedham. They're saying I've turned my back on the Scotch. They say I've used them to acquire power and now I'm abandoning them. That's not true and Essex knows it. The truth, and you need to make sure our readers understand this, the truth is that I will not, I cannot, in all conscience

I dare not, impose one form of religious worship on the whole nation. Where is the liberty and freedom in that? Where is the toleration? No, I shall not do it. The Viscount agrees with me. Damn it all, even the King agrees with me.'

'The King, Sir Henry?'

'Yes of course the King. You know we've been talking to him do you not?'

'Up to a point, Sir Henry, but I know little about your progress.'

'You are not at liberty to report this, Nedham. We are close to a settlement though I do not think the King will agree to the impeachments.'

'Executions?'

'Quite.' Sir Henry looked away from the unicorn and down at his hands, which were wrestling with each other on his desk. 'The impeachments are a stumbling block. Not insurmountable, I trust, but even so. Which is why we must show a united front. We can't have Essex and his faction threatening our liberty and imposing Calvinist conformity on England. We won't stand for it and Essex should know better.'

'And Dillingham?'

Sir Henry went on, 'You needn't worry about him, Nedham. And as long as the Viscount commands a majority in the Lords, you'll be fine.'

It turned out the Viscount's majority wasn't as secure as Sir Henry thought.

The few remaining members of the House of Lords were not happy. In early '45, the Commons was pressing ahead with plans to ban Members of Parliament from the army and – more horrifying for the average Earl – proposing to abolish the House of Lords altogether. This was the kind of thing John Lilburne and his fellow Levellers wanted, though only as a first step.

I helped Lilburne, an intense man with a permanently-furrowed brow and not much sense of humour, write a couple of pamphlets. He wanted regular elections, a turnover of men in power to stamp out corruption, he wanted equal-sized constituencies and the vote for all free men (not servants or Catholics obviously). This was dangerously radical. I gave his campaign the right sort of spin and Londoners started wearing green ribbons in their hats to show support for Lilburne's cause.

As "Britanicus" was still doing well – especially now one of its rivals had been shut down – I wrote to Lucy commanding her to come back to London. I pointed out she'd promised before God to obey me and, as a further incentive, I said we'd get a new house and another servant or two. The news business was booming.

I even told her I missed her. I added terms of endearment and a few Godly phrases. And, because it would cheer her up, I included a description of the execution of Archbishop Laud.

I wanted her back. I was afraid if I left her in Burford she'd denounce Big Susie for a witch. That would embarrass my parents, outrage Susie, threaten her life and liberty and it would, above all, embarrass me. What kind of man had a mad witch-hunting harridan for a wife? I needed her back with me so I could calm her down and guide her in the ways of the unrighteous.

When she eventually, reluctantly and some weeks later, replied that she would be prepared to make the hazardous journey down the Thames Valley when the time was right, I'd almost forgotten I'd asked her. I was far too busy.

There had been a month of talks between the King's men and Parliament in, of all places, Uxbridge, half a day's ride from Westminster on the road to Oxford. Audley was there at Place House, where the negotiations took place, with Sir Henry, and kept me up to date with what was going on but it was clear from the outset there would be no deal.

Parliament required the execution of the King's most loyal supporters, Parliament wanted to impose Scottish Calvinism on the country and demanded control over everything from the army to the education of the King's children.

The talks were doomed to failure, the more so because Charles was still winning on the battlefield. The Marquess of Montrose, for the King, had trounced a rival Scot somewhere nobody in England had ever heard of. Even so, it counted as another victory for Charles.

Then 'Britanicus' was handed another world exclusive. This gave me the chance to expose the King's duplicity, untrustworthiness and tyranny. A second letter from Charles to his nephew Prince Rupert fell into my hands, thanks to Sir Henry. In this letter, the King vowed he would never surrender his crown, his religion or his friends.

If you looked at it objectively, as I said to Audley over a pint of Renish wine, the King's position was not unreasonable. Giving up his friends to execution, handing his children's futures to Parliament and letting the Commons assume power over the army left him with nothing. He would be King in name only. No King would agree to that.

In "Britanicus" I said the King's letter showed he lacked conscience and honesty, that he rejoiced in the ruin of his faithful subjects and it proved he was a tyrant and idolator. I'm not sure that was a fair assessment but it did sales no harm.

CHAPTER II

Send a hue and cry
after the King

June 1645

The Battle of Naseby gave me the scoop that made my name – and made me a marked man. It led to my first imprisonment and turned out to be the beginning of the end of "Britanicus".

Naseby was the first great victory for Cromwell's New Model Army. This was the point when the war was won. The King's army was scattered. Its Irish whores were put to the sword. And Charles himself? There were various rumours.

Readers of "Britanicus" were asked: 'Where is King Charles? What's become of him? It were best to send Hue and Cry after him. If any man can bring any tale or tiding of a wilful King, which hath gone astray these four years from his Parliament, with a guilty Conscience, bloody Hands, a Heart full of broken Vows and Protestations: give notice to Britanicus and you shall be well paid for your pains.'

We had such fun.

After the battle, Cromwell captured the King's carriage which contained a locked cabinet. The contents of this cabinet – a treasure trove of confidential papers and letters – fell into the hands of "Mercurius Britanicus" and I devoted three successive editions to exposing them in all their intimate glory. In the King's own handwriting, I had evidence of his double-dealing; his subjugation to his French, Catholic wife; his dislike of some of his closest advisers like the Marquess of Hertford.

Sir Henry summoned me to his chambers in Westminster to study the letters. They were a gold mine; dung to shower over King and court.

Parliament had to be 'nulled by the sword', he said in one of his letters to the Queen.

I announced in the newsbook: 'I will shew you more Tricks here, than ever Hocus-Pocus did at Bartholomew Faire. It will yield us at least a Month's sport; and I mean to anatomize every Paper, week after week, till I have gone quite through; keeping still to my old Motto, "For the better Information of the People".'

Sales soared. Controversy roared. People slapped me on the back and congratulated me. Others wrote pamphlets against me. It was a triumph.

I'd probably have got away with it completely but for one small mistake. I decided it was time not merely to accuse Charles of tyranny and so on, but to attack the man in person. In doing so, I made a passing reference to his speech impediment.

Everyone knew he had an evil Scotch accent which should have been drummed out of him but stubbornly remained despite all his years in England. Worse, though, was his stammer.

Sometimes it was hardly noticeable. But it was well-known he stumbled over words. In privy council meetings, during royal audiences, even in casual conversation and especially when addressing a group of people, giving a speech to Parliament or a party of ambassadors, for instance, he sometimes took a painfully long time to spit out whatever trite nonsense he was trying to say.

Charles's stammer was notorious.

Unfortunately, it was not notorious enough for a writer of newsbooks to refer to it with impunity.

It's not as if I said anything particularly offensive. All I said was: 'Bid him speak and you will soon know him.'

Admittedly it was obvious what I was referring to. When we were putting the newsbook to bed, Audley, White and I had a good chuckle over it. Audley said, 'Only you, Monty, only you would be so blatant.'

The following day, as the newsbook was being sold around St Paul's, a dozen armed men marched down The Strand, round the back of the cathedral and straight into White and Audley's print shop where the captain and the printer were discussing whether there was any chance of reviving "The Scout". They were arrested, marched off to Westminster and locked in the gatehouse.

The men then came for me but a messenger from Sir Henry Vane reached me first and, rather than surrender immediately, I sought refuge with Judge Bradshaw.

'So much for freedom,' I said to him. 'The House of Lords has arrested Audley and Bob White, the printer, for attacking the King.'

'Did they attack the King?' Bradshaw asked.

'No, I did. Audley is deputy licensor, though, and White is named as the printer.'

'Ah well, can't be helped,' said Bradshaw, without much interest.

'But what about our right to keep people informed, tell them what's going on?'

'You've had a good run for your money, Marchamont. Maybe it's time to call it a day.'

I was astonished. I'd always thought of Bradshaw as a friend and mentor. Now he was dismissing me and my newsbook as of little or no consequence.

'We've won,' said Bradshaw, sitting up straight and rubbing his hands together with satisfaction. 'We have no need for newsbooks any more. The King must surrender. The war is over.'

'Over? I doubt that. Nothing is settled.'

Bradshaw stood and took me to his window overlooking the small square at Lincoln's Inn. It was a hot afternoon but already a few early autumn leaves were falling big and green across the trampled grass, worn away by the marching of the militia. I stood beside him. He put a fatherly arm over my shoulders and said, 'My dear Marchamont, the settlement will come. The King has to give way now. Mark my words. But we don't want to provoke him overmuch or give comfort to our enemies.'

'The Cavaliers?' I asked, naively.

'No, the Levellers, the Puritans, the Calvinists, the Scotch... even the Dutch. We must have a compromise with the King. The alternative is what? There is talk of democracy. Imagine – giving the vote to everyone. There's even talk of holding everything in common – commune-ism. Nobody wants that. We can't have that. Think about it. It overturns the natural order of things. And if that means we must stifle so-called freedom of speech, well, I'm sorry Marchamont but, if I were you, I'd stick to medicine for a while.'

'Medicine, yes,' I said distractedly. I'd been toying with the idea of becoming a physician. The arrest of Dillingham unnerved me; now I was facing arrest myself. 'I'll have to give myself up, I suppose. First, though, I'll send a note to Henry Vane, Lord Saye and Speaker Lenthall asking for help.'

'Don't worry, Marchamont, you won't be locked up for long,' Bradshaw said consolingly. 'But be warned. Until everything is settled, the powers-that-be won't take kindly to freedom of speech. It has never been acceptable in this country and there is no reason to suppose it will be now, whatever our good friend John Milton may think.'

Greasy little John Rushworth was in his gloomy Westminster office, at his desk surrounded by piles of documents, sharpening a quill pen. 'Notes,' he said apologetically, 'Notes of meetings. Notes and notes, meetings and meetings.' Rushworth smiled half-heartedly. He had the look of a poacher caught red-handed, knowing he would hang. It was his natural look. 'And here's one about you, Nedham,' he went on, rummaging for something and then holding up a particular piece of paper with an apologetic grin. 'Here we are. Warrant for your arrest.'

'What now then?' I had a bag with me. Coins, bread and cheese, beer, some particularly rough geneva gin, a couple of books. No clothes. I would send out for them later, I decided.

'Audley and White are in the gatehouse cells.'

'And me?'

'You can visit them if you like.'

'Visit them?'

'Yes, if you like.'

'Where are you going to imprison me?'

'With them if you like.'

'If I like? What do you mean?'

'There's a warrant for the arrest of Marchamont Nedham but not for his imprisonment. Prison is only for the licensor of "Mercurius Britanicus" Captain Thomas Audley and the printer Robert White.'

'You mean they're being punished for something I wrote and I'm off the hook?'

'So it would seem. That's what the Earl wanted, Mr Nedham.'

'Essex?'

'Who else? The Earl does not believe you should be able to libel and slander the King.'

'So why jail Audley and White and not me? It doesn't make sense.' I wasn't sure whether to be relieved to remain at liberty or outraged I was escaping Scot free.

'Perhaps, you know, Essex is hoping you'll return the favour,' said Rushworth with a lizard-like leer. 'Or maybe he just doesn't think you're very important. Hack-writers are ten a penny these days. Every Tom, Dick and Marchamont thinks he's a writer. Isn't that so?'

I did not grace this with a reply. I headed for the gatehouse where I persuaded the bored guards to admit me to Audley and White's cell. I decided to pretend to be arrested and pretend to be imprisoned and spent the next few nights in the discomfort of the lock-up at the gatehouse to the Palace of Westminster listening to the complaints of Bob White and the accusations of Captain Tom while all the time I was actually a free man. I just couldn't bring myself to admit it to them.

To tell the truth, the accommodation wasn't particularly Spartan. There were mattresses and blankets, chairs, candles, a separate privy, food and wine if we were willing to pay extortionate prices for them (we were) and visitors, including the Earl of Essex's men sent to negotiate a public, printed apology.

Then Lucy turned up.

CHAPTER 12

The vomitting out of
poisoned Crocodile teares

Summer 1645

Lucy slapped me. 'Thou hast been cast into prison for sedition?'

'Only for mentioning the King's stammer.'

'The King's stammer?' Lucy was surprised, took a step back, stared at me, smiled a little. 'I knew not the King hath a stammer.'

'He d- d- doth.'

'Terrible stammer,' Audley offered helpfully. 'Takes an age for him to spit out the most m- m- m- mundane sentences.'

Lucy smiled a little more. She looked almost amused.

'And he has the most awful Scottish accent,' Audley added.

'We've been told to apologise,' I said.

Lucy looked at me, then at Audley, then at Bob White, sitting in the corner with his head in a flagon of ale. Bob was miserable. He missed his wife and children and his printing business was on its knees. He needed to get out as quickly as possible. Audley, on the other hand, didn't seem bothered one way or the other. There was something he wasn't telling us, I was sure of it. But as there was something I wasn't telling him, I decided it wasn't politic to challenge him.

'Apologise?' said Lucy indignantly. 'Apologise for what, husband? For telling the truth?'

'That's about it but don't you worry your pretty little head,' I said, kissing her on the forehead and ushering her towards the door. 'You go home and make it habitable and I shall be home before you know it. And thank you for coming back, my dear.'

'I did not return to a man who surrenders at the first difficulty, Marchamont. The righteous are bold as a lion. Shalt thou not endure the trials the Lord hath prepared for thee?' Her little face was screwed up angrily.

'Are you telling me not to apologise, my dear?' I asked.

'Indeed I am, Marchamont.'

'Would you have me a martyr?'

'Indeed I would, Marchamont. Watch ye, stand fast in the faith, quit you like a man. Be strong.'

I hurried her off home. I was not in the market for martyrdom.

We fobbed off Essex's men with grovelling words of apology. They complained the article had been 'saucy and uncivil' to the King and I was to humble myself in print. I had to say, 'I have overshot myself.' The Royalists had great fun, accusing me of vomiting poisoned crocodile tears.

The thing is, I wasn't humbled or humiliated. On the contrary, the fact that Essex and his faction made such a song and dance about my 'hue and cry' convinced me I was doing a good job. I was making my name and I didn't care if I upset a few powerful men. What was the point of a newsbook if it didn't humble the great from time to time?

As far as Lucy was concerned, I blamed our surrender on Audley and White. Bob wanted to get home and I told Lucy that Captain Tom was unwell.

In fact, Audley didn't even complain when the Lords announced he was no longer allowed to licence "Mercurius Britanicus" or any other publication for that matter.

After we agreed the wording of the apology and White fled home fearing the wrath of his wife, Audley and I retired to Purgatory where, over a flagon of Madeira, I asked what was going on.

He leaned back, hands clasped behind his head, a smile of satisfaction on his scarred face. 'Wouldn't you like to know, dear boy?' he said patronisingly. 'I know they didn't jail you. I know they only issued a warrant for your arrest. I know you didn't have to spend three days locked up with me and Bob. I know, Monty. I also know the way the wind is blowing. Essex has served his purpose. He's yesterday's man. We needn't worry about

Essex much longer, believe me.'

'You don't mind they've withdrawn your licence and given it to what's his name?'

'Mabbott. Gilbert Mabbott.'

'Yes, the cobbler's son. Doesn't it bother you?'

'He's a friend of Rushworth. They're both friends of Cromwell.' Audley was enjoying himself. He was playing me like a fish. I was caught and he was taking his time to reel me in. He drank some wine. He looked round the room, which was quiet this August afternoon. It was raining outside but the air was hot and close. There must be thunder somewhere.

Audley leaned forward and spoke confidentially, 'General Cromwell. He's the future, Monty. Essex is out. Fairfax and Cromwell are in. The war's over. The King has nowhere to go. The army will be in charge soon. Those prigs in Parliament, they don't know it yet but their time is coming to an end. Essex is thrashing about trying to assert his rights but he's on the slide. A noble lineage counts for nothing on a battlefield.'

'Audley,' I was truly shocked, 'You sound like a Leveller.'

'No, Monty, it's just that it pays to be on the winning side. Fairfax and Cromwell, the Vanes and their friends, they are the winners, mark my words. And I must tell you, Monty, my involvement in newsbooks is reaching a full stop.'

'Have you told poor Bob?'

'He'll survive. Demand for the printed word has never been greater. They're queuing up to see what libel Marchamont Nedham's guilty of this week. Mind you, Monty, you must realise, it won't be long before newsbooks have served their purpose.'

This sounded like a warning. Audley had always been a man of dark corridors and secret passageways. Then it occurred to me. He wasn't a soldier or a newsbook man. He was a spy. 'Served their purpose?' I demanded, 'What do you mean?'

'No Government will tolerate a free-for-all, Monty. You must realise that, surely. At the moment, it's fine – within reason – to let all these newsbooks scribble their slanders, twist the truth, distort the facts and take sides with any charlatan or mountebank who takes their fancy. But when everything is settled...'

'Settled?'

'When we have a single Godly Government in power, when everything is resolved and there is peace again, all these newsbooks will have to go. You can't run a country with all these dissenting voices shouting from the sidelines. The truth is the impertinence of newsbooks, especially "Britanicus", can't be tolerated indefinitely. They hate it.'

'They?'

'Our rulers. Our Parliament men. Our lords and masters. They hate newsbooks. Who wouldn't? Nobody wants to be answerable to the rabble. Newsmongers like Monty Nedham think the powerful must give an account of themselves or face the consequences. Look what you said about the King. No King could tolerate that, could he? It's not surprising Essex and his friends objected. They don't want to overturn the old order. If that happened, they'd lose their own power and privilege. They think things have already gone too far.'

I was stunned. I stared at my friend. I realised I'd never really known him at all. 'But you started it, Tom. You led the charge. You fired the first paper bullets.'

'I did, Monty, that's true. But that was then. Times have changed.'

I must be slow-witted. It was only then it dawned on me. 'You've been working towards this all along, haven't you?'

'Not suppression of newsbooks as such but the establishment of a strong, free, firm Government. It takes time,' said Audley with a smile. 'And while you may be a good newsbook man, Marchamont, you've got a lot to learn about politics. You trained in medicine, didn't you, when you were up at Oxford? If I were you, I'd be sharpening my scalpels and bottling up my leeches.'

Lucy prepared a welcome for me. She was delighted I was responsible for highlighting the King's stutter. 'At last, Monty,' she said, 'Thou and I art on the side of the Saints together.'

As usual, I wasn't sure what she was on about but she was being friendly in a way she hadn't been since the death of poor baby Lucy. We were trying again and my wife threw herself into the endeavour with gratifying alacrity. I was not inclined to dissuade her from doing what she decided must be God's work. Lucy wanted another baby.

Afterwards, she was keen to discuss the state of the nation. This was dangerous territory. Lucy was dogmatic, inflexible and – like most women – not given to rational thought. She had fixed opinions based on zeal and prejudice. I had no desire to upset our new-found domestic tranquillity by disputing with her. She had been reading Levellers' tracts. I did not confess I'd had a hand in writing some of them; she might mistakenly think I agreed with all that rubbish.

Lucy was sure we had to do away with the King and his entire family. I wasn't convinced. Who would run the country, if not a King? Parliament, she insisted. It was an argument people were taking up all over London. It filled our natural rulers like the Earl of Essex with horror. What was this monster 'democracy' they had unleashed on the land?

For a newsbook, it was all to the good. One of the pleasures was the ability to point out the failings of the King and his party. It wasn't necessary to propose alternatives; it was enough to remind people of his many flaws as man and Monarch.

'Charles needs to be conquered as he can't conquer himself, being subject to his own passions, other men's ambitions and flattery,' I wrote.

I did enjoy myself. What was most satisfying, I think, was the knowledge that my arrows were hitting their targets in Oxford where the King was increasingly under siege.

Then, at the end of '45, the "Court Mercury" ceased to be. Ran out of money owing their printers more than £60. Bob White told me that. Apparently, he and the "Court Mercury" printer were acquainted and continued to communicate even though they were working for opposite sides.

The newsbook's demise was a symbol: The Royalist cause was dying. Cavalier strongholds fell day after day. Chester surrendered. Basing House, the impregnable fortress of Royalism in Hampshire, gave up the ghost. When Cromwell and Fairfax re-took Bristol so easily the King sacked his own nephew, Prince Rupert, his most feared general, "Britanicus" indulged in a little pot-stirring. We speculated that the King sacked Rupert because he feared his nephew was a traitor and Rupert had done a deal with Fairfax and Cromwell to put him on the Throne in his uncle's place.

If other newsbooks chose to pour scorn on our claims, so much the better. All notoriety was good notoriety – and how could they be sure we were wrong?

The coup story probably wasn't true. There was no evidence the King really did suspect Rupert of being a traitor. It was still worth speculating. Even if Rupert denied planning a coup and the King denied mistrusting his nephew, nobody would believe them. And, for some in the King's Court, there would be the constant suspicion that it was true and a coup was being plotted. Where would that leave the King, the Queen, their children and closest allies? Were their lives at risk?

They couldn't win.

I rubbed my hands together with glee when I imagined the Cavaliers reacting with horror and impotent fury at what they would probably call an inverted pyramid of piffle.

CHAPTER 13

The poets are dead,
beggared, or run away

Spring 1646

Sir Henry stared at a point in the air about six feet ahead of him, half way between his desk and the window overlooking the Thames. I stood nodding and trying to understand his monologue. His voice was slightly harsh, with its northern accent making it hard to catch the words. It was harder still to follow his sweeps of logic. He seemed to omit important facts. I couldn't tell whether this was because of the quickness of his mind and his assumption other people could keep up with him or whether it was a sign that his ideas were flawed.

Either way, I listened intently. Sir Henry thought he might become a Kingmaker.

'Lewis,' he said, 'In the Palace across the way. Sound young man. Good judgment. Experienced. Staunch Protestant – damn it all, the family's lost everything because of their faith. Older than Rupert and that child-soldier what's his name? Maurice. The King? Good question. Good question. Shot his bolt. Exile, I suppose.'

Sir Henry rambled on. It seemed he was plotting to replace King Charles with his nephew Prince Charles Louis.

Louis had no kingdom. His Protestant father had lost it to the Catholic Holy Roman Emperor. His mother, Elizabeth – known as the Winter Queen because that's what she had been for one winter only – was King Charles's sister. In those days, she lived in exile in Holland with a petty court. Louis' brothers, Prince Rupert and Prince Maurice, were fighting for their uncle against Parliament. Despite being sacked after the surrender of Bristol, Rupert was still in the country trying to revive the King's cause and win back his place in the Royalist army.

'But Lewis is a German,' I said. 'The people of England will never accept a German King. Does he even speak English?'

'The people of England will accept what they are told to accept,' said Sir Henry with glassy-eyed certainty. 'What business is it of theirs?'

'The Levellers think the people should have a role in deciding who governs them,' I ventured bravely.

Sir Henry laughed humourlessly. 'The Levellers? Those shabby, greedy know-nothings? Ha! You can forget about the Levellers. We can handle them. The real question is what to do with the King's children. The Prince of Wales? Can we exile him too? Would he accept his cousin's supremacy? Doubt it, doubt it. God's will, though. Question is, what is God's will? Is it His will to hand the Throne to Lewis? He is a Godly good man. Speculate, Nedham. Speculate.'

I was happy to float these ideas in "Britanicus" even if they were nothing more than products of Sir Henry's fevered imagination. He was the architect of the alliance with the Scots. He was at the centre of power. If he was thinking of replacing the King with his nephew it was news even if nothing came of it. It would also be interesting to see how Prince Charles Louis reacted. Would he deny any ambition? Would he strut around a little more assertively? What, if anything, would he say to his uncle the King or his cousin the Prince of Wales if they were to meet? Charles was already suspicious of Rupert. Could the King trust Rupert and Maurice not to betray him if their brother was being lined up for the Crown?

It was all good fun but the world of politics was getting more and more complicated.

In April, the King, hair hacked, beard shorn, dressed as a servant, sneaked out of Oxford with only two companions. What he had in mind was anyone's guess. For some weeks, nobody knew where he was.

Turns out he travelled towards London, then East Anglia, staying at inns and sleeping in barns until this bedraggled trio fetched up at Southwell in Nottinghamshire – ironically, close to the castle where Charles first raised his standard to start the war — where he surrendered to the mercies of the Scottish army.

The Calvinists weren't pleased to see him and the King was not impressed to discover they were stabling horses in the cathedral, smashing statues and Holy relics and digging up graves to steal coffin-lead to melt down for shot. They showed deference towards their Monarch but, in reality, they took him prisoner.

It was the end of the war, or so it seemed. The King had lost. Maybe now the country would get back to normal while Charles, the Scots and the Parliamentarians reached some sort of peace agreement.

This was good for the newsbook industry. People wanted peace and prosperity. They wanted to know what was going on. Demand for "Britanicus" was stronger than ever.

Sadly, there was less call for good write-ups about the heroism and courage of Parliamentarian officers, there being so much less fighting, though mopping-up operations went on for months as stubborn men in inaccessible castles held out beyond the bitter end.

On the other hand, MPs wanted positive coverage of their wisdom and perspicacity and paid handsomely for it. My patrons were still in power — indeed Nat Fiennes was on his way back from exile in Switzerland. After Fairfax re-took Bristol so easily, he and Cromwell realised Nat couldn't be blamed for its fall to Prince Rupert and his rehabilitation was complete.

Yet the newsbook business was precarious, if not downright dangerous. Fortune's wheel had a nasty habit of turning with startling speed. Essex and his faction managed to close half the newsbooks in London. "Britanicus" was drinking in the last-chance saloon. As Audley said, nobody in power likes to be criticised or held to account.

Audley himself was backing off. Though he had been restored as licensor a few weeks after his release from prison, he had bigger fish to fry. Manoeuvring over a deal with the King probably. He wouldn't tell me. No matter how many ways I asked my questions, he wouldn't give me a straight answer.

I didn't realise then but Audley had shifted his allegiance. His patrons were no longer Sir Henry Vane and the Viscount, though they thought he was still their man and, no doubt, he was still taking their money. I discovered some years later he was really working for Cromwell, Cromwell's son-in-law Henry Ireton and their lawyer, the sinister John Thurloe.

What I did know was that war might be over but the King was still the King and nobody had any idea what to do now.

A fearless chronicler of the news might defy the men of power and carry on printing the truth, or at least his version of it, no matter who it provoked or dismayed. But a fearless chronicler of the news might quickly end up without money, without liberty, even without life.

I had a wife to keep happy. I had a living to make. I had a household to maintain. I had to think about other ways to make a living.

I'd tried teaching but the pay was terrible. I'd worked at the law but there were too many lawyers and, in any case, the law changed from week to week according to the whims of Parliament. However, when I was at Oxford University, I trained to be a physician. Doctor Nedham it would be from now on, as well as Captain Nedham, the newsbook writer of Lincoln's Inn.

I could do both easily enough.

CHAPTER 14

Tending to the rescue
of mankind from
the tyranny of diseases

Spring 1646

It wasn't difficult to get a licence from the College of Physicians. An Oxford education and a smattering of knowledge of anatomy was all they required. I had been to most of the lectures. I had cut up a corpse. I understood Galen's four humours: black bile, yellow bile, blood and phlegm. I'd applied leeches. I'd tasted urine. There wasn't much to doctoring if you knew your ancient Greek and were willing to expose yourself to death, disease and putrefaction.

My motto was always primum non nocere (first do no harm), a phrase which has since been wrongly attributed to various medical men going back to the Ancient Greek, Hippocrates. I was the first physician to use it, though others now claim the credit.

The great thing about this philosophy is that a physician can treat a patient, receive praise and reward for a successful outcome, and do little or nothing. For instance, far more men have been killed after being treated for gout than have died of the disease itself. Prescribing a little laudanum will make the patient feel much better and do no harm to his long-term health. It will not cure his gout but it will improve his frame of mind. This counts as a singular medical success and enhances the physician's reputation.

It also helps to listen to what a patient tells you. That may sound obvious but it is tempting to assume an illness conforms to some previously-diagnosed condition and requires the usual cure. I remember visiting a man who was in a pitiful state. He had been ill for days. His body had evacuated all it consumed and more. He was almost hysterical. I was called in on a friend's recommendation after his usual physician declared there was nothing more he could do for the patient and committed him to the mercy of the Lord.

The bleedings had done him terrible harm. The man was exhausted and emaciated. I prescribed a good roast chicken and a pint of canary. When I called the following day, he was sitting up in bed looking quite cheerful. He declared himself much improved and we agreed he should undergo the same agreeable regime until he was up and about again. He was not unhappy about paying my fee.

In the medical world, as elsewhere, a war was taking place. Old-fashioned views were being challenged. Diseases identified by the Ancient Greeks and cures prescribed in those far-off days were still the basis for medical practice. The Ancients' theory and practice were taught at university and carried out by most physicians.

Yet war and plague gave us the chance to observe illness at close quarters on large numbers of people. We – that is to say, more progressive doctors interested in modern methods – offered our services at little or no charge to the poorest people in return for the chance to practise innovative solutions for their diseases. Sometimes these didn't work and the patient died. Still, that was a price worth paying for our increased knowledge. And the patient would, like as not, have died anyway, so we were doing no harm.

In those baleful days, everyone wanted a physician.

Plague stalked the steamy, shit-caked streets and stews of muddy London year after year. Since the Great Plague of '25, when Charles became King – was that a sign from God, his enemies asked? – there were regular outbreaks. Nobody was safe.

Looking back after the worse plague of '65 and the fire that followed, we were let off quite lightly in the '40s but it didn't seem like it at the time. With starvation and war accounting for even more bodies, it's not surprising so many people turned to extreme religion. It seemed the Lord was turning his wrath on the country even if every warring party, from the Levellers to the King, said God was on their side.

The plague is always worse in the summer and it wasn't long before the death rate started to rise in the City. It may well be caused by the filthy miasma of thick, foetid air which hangs over London in the heat of July and August.

Lucy and I decamped towards Westminster, at first renting a house just off the Strand. It was a decent size. We had three servants. She invited her mother. Happily, the invitation was turned down – Mrs Collyer was wary of the plague and who could blame her?

Lucy was content enough, though. She was still determined to do her Godly duty and procreate. I encouraged her diligence. Unfortunately, when I was away from home, she held prayer meetings of her Puritan brethren. Some of them, I'm sorry to say, were Levellers. But as plague swirled around London, she put a stop to meetings and rarely left the house.

Plague did provide a budding physician with an opportunity to establish his practice. One popular preventative medicine was a combination of turmeric, mustard oil and the liver of three chickens taken with plentiful quantities of small beer. I found it most efficacious. Few of those who took this consistently were visited with the plague, which was a cause of great satisfaction to both patient and physician. I myself did not try it nor did I suggest it to Lucy. Still, it may have helped.

It was useful that, in the course of my newsbook activities, I came across influential men who were either themselves in need of medical attention or whose wives, mistresses, friends, children or parents required the services of a well-spoken Oxford-educated medical man proficient in the most recent techniques and willing to look beyond the ancient nostrums and quack doctoring which pervaded the profession. I even subscribed to the new theory that blood circulated round the whole body, even if the idea was first proposed by the King's physician.

When the Speaker, William Lenthall, fell ill, my practice really took off. I happened to be in Westminster discussing the political situation with Sir Henry when William walked into the room to have a word and collapsed in front of us.

It was a warm day in May but the Speaker was excessively hot. His cheeks were flushed and his heart was racing. The poor man could scarcely breathe. It looked like the ague. I immediately took charge. I loosened his jacket and untied his shirt, had the windows thrown open to cool the air and made him sip a little brandy. I told his attendants there was no time to summon his usual doctor.

I had him carried to his house overlooking the river and ordered servants to prepare a healthy broth. Was the poor man afflicted by the muggy air of London or was it just exhaustion? I concluded he was tired from overwork not struck down by the malign smog off the Thames.

I dismissed everyone from his bedroom and told him, 'You must go home for the summer, sir. Rest is the only cure I can prescribe for you. I do not believe it to be what the Italians call mal airia but it may be, so take some opium and wine. But rest is the main requirement.'

Lenthall gave me a wan smile. 'How will they manage without me? I cannot leave them.'

'Prorogue Parliament,' I said, 'Why not? Give everyone a break. The Committee of the Two Kingdoms will carry on anyway. A little less Parliament would not be such a bad thing, especially now the King has surrendered.'

'Oh Marchamont, that's just the trouble. Who is in charge? The King? Parliament? The army? The Scotch, God forbid?'

I made him lie back and rest. I told him he must eat but not stir for the rest of the day. 'Aren't you going to bleed me?' he asked.

'I am not, sir,' I said.

'Then how can you call yourself a physician?'

Lenthall looked a little better when I returned in the evening. He lay in a cool, airy room, pale but no longer feverish. He smiled faintly. He looked every one of his 55 years, his beard grey and straggly, his hair thin but unruly. I thought, doctors see the mighty when they are fallen.

'You were kind to John when you were both at school,' Lenthall said quietly. His usually-strong voice was weak and croaky.

'Was I?'

The patient was subdued, as if he thought he might have been close to death. He hadn't been. 'You helped him with his Latin,' said Lenthall.

'He wasn't very good at it.'

I remembered. John Lenthall, four years younger than me, a weedy little fellow. He deserved to be hit regularly. I ignored him mostly but I do remember explaining the second declension to him several times and shooing away a couple of local bullies. Perhaps, in the way of young boys, he came to hero-worship me. I shouldn't be surprised, several of his classmates did.

'I worry about him,' Lenthall said.

'We were at Lincoln's Inn together for a while,' I said.

'Before you went into the news business,' Lenthall laughed. 'Now here you are a medical man.' He slumped back on his pillows exhausted.

'You really do need a rest, sir. A long rest away from Westminster. Back in Burford with your family.'

'John's here somewhere,' he said with a groan.

'I've seen him around. MP for Gloucester, isn't he?'

'He is,' sighed Lenthall. 'I'm afraid for him. Too many factions, too many arguments, too much danger.'

'Burford, sir,' I said again. 'For the summer.' Lenthall nodded acquiescence. 'Doctor's orders.'

He smiled a weary smile, closed his eyes and slept.

William Lenthall may have retired to Burford but he was in constant contact with politicians and soldiers in London and throughout the country. He was even in correspondence with several Royalists. He took the opportunity to praise his medical treatment at the hands of Marchamont Nedham and it wasn't long before I had built up quite a considerable practice. My methods were simple: do as little as possible, prescribe the least harmful substances I could and let nature take its course. Some patients died; that happens. Those who recovered – the greater number, let me say – were delighted with the sympathetic treatment they received. Admittedly they were less pleased with the bill but, as I continue to tell them, you can't put a price on good health.

It was wise to switch to medicine. As the spring of '46 progressed, the political divisions in the 'victorious' party grew deeper and more bitter. Essex and the Puritans were one faction; the 'independents' under Cromwell, who wanted religious freedom and toleration, were another; the Scottish, who wanted our money, were a third; Levellers like my wife were another noisy group demanding new rights. There was nobody in charge but King Charles, and he was a prisoner.

Sir Henry Vane fell ill. There was a fear he had contracted the plague. He isolated himself in Raby Castle where the Vanes were reinforcing the defences thanks to a £16,000 grant from Parliament. It made the £8,000 given to Speaker Lenthall, when he complained about how much money he was losing by devoting all his time to the House of Commons and none to his legal practice, look almost modest.

Then overnight the Viscount lost control of the House of Lords and I lost my protection.

CHAPTER 15

Mercurius Britanicus His
Welcome to Hell
With the Deuill's Blessing.

May 1646

They didn't bother to knock. They broke down the front door, clattered through the parlour, brushed aside Mercy the serving girl, clomped up the stairs and smashed open my bedroom door. They could have just lifted the latch.

There were seven of them. Six fearsome, stupid Roundheads in their unnecessary helmets and a little officer with a grin on his idiotic face.

'Marchamont Nedham, you are under arrest. Get up, get dressed. You've got to come with me,' he said as two of his goons stood beside our bed and threatened to pull me out from under the sheets.

It was very early. I guessed half past five. I could hear birds chirping their morning chorus.

Lucy was kneeling beside the bed praying, as she did every morning, though I was rarely awake to witness it. Still in her night-dress, her hair hanging loose about her, she leaped to her feet and whirled round to glare at the intruder. 'Dost thou dare disturb a woman at prayer?' she demanded. 'What hath he done that deserves this vile intrusion?'

As I struggled into my breeches, the officer told her, 'I have a warrant for Master Nedham's arrest signed by the Earl of Essex.'

'On what charges?' Lucy was magnificent in her rage. She stood all of four feet nine inches tall and beautifully indignant. 'What right hast thou? Whither wilt thou take him? Husband, be strong. And who art thou, anyway, to be arresting your betters?'

'Captain Pride,' he said, 'Officer in the Earl's regiment.'

'With what is my husband charged, sir? I demand to know.'

'Sedition, madam. Seditious libel, to be precise.'

He offered Lucy a rolled-up paper. I took the paper from his hand and read it quickly. I was being arrested, it seemed, for reporting the news. Nothing to do with insults against the King or speculation about whether Prince Lewis might take the Throne but for 'publishing divers passages between the two Houses of Parliament and other scandalous particulars not fit to be tolerated'.

I was being arrested for reporting the debates in Parliament. Officially, this was still illegal but, as every newsbook had been covering Parliament's proceedings for the past six years, the law had quite fallen into disuse. The grounds for my arrest were bogus. I was being silenced because I was on the wrong side in the struggle between Essex and his Presbyterian fundamentalists and Cromwell and his more liberal religious independents.

The warrant was signed by Essex's lackey John Rushworth, the Parliamentary licenser.

As they led me away, Lucy called after us, 'Fear none of those things which thou shalt suffer. Behold, the devil shall cast you into prison, that ye may be tried, and ye shall have tribulation ten days. Be thou faithful unto death, and I will give thee a crown of Life. Ten days, husband. Ten days.'

That Spring, "Britanicus" had been serialising more exclusive material in the form of letters to and from that ridiculous man George Digby, Earl of Bristol.

I say ridiculous with the benefit of hindsight. At the time I knew little about him other than his reputation as one of the most handsome and clever men in England, a protégée of Peter Heylyn, the former editor of the Royalist rag, the "Court Mercury".

Anyway, Digby's letters once again proved the King's duplicity. Even as the King surrendered to the Scots, he was plotting to bring over an army of Irish Catholics. He was also expecting a Royalist army to advance into England from Scotland. Worst of all, he was negotiating for help from the French.

I also got hold of letters the King sent to his brother-in-law, the King of France, 20 years earlier complaining about his then-new wife. Charles moaned in his letters that Henrietta Maria snubbed him in public. He complained she quarrelled with him over who should ride in the King's carriage. He protested she thought it an indignity to follow the example of previous Queens of England. He claimed she surrounded herself with priests and Jesuits and even made public penance, tactlessly demonstrating she was a devoted Catholic to the whole of Protestant London.

It was extraordinary our King should write such letters to another Monarch complaining about the behaviour of his own wife. What kind of a man did it make Charles? I said he was 'supine and careless, nothing being done but by Her consent to the manifest ruin of our religion and nation', called her a petticoat Machiavelli and asked what the Scotch would do with their prisoner, the King. I called him a tyrant who was planning to set the Scotch against the English, divide and rule. He could not be trusted.

These attacks on the King were too much for people like Essex. They may have been at war with Charles for the past four years but they were Royalists at heart. They could not imagine a country without a Monarch. Whatever blood was shed in Parliament's cause, they still believed in hierarchy. If England lost its King, what would happen to its aristocracy? They did not want to see their King abused and mocked. They could not imagine a world without a King and a hierarchy which kept them at the very pinnacle with all the wealth and privilege their dynasties had enjoyed for centuries.

Even Sir Henry Vane, while he might envisage putting Prince Lewis on the throne, could not contemplate something as dangerous and vulgar as a republic.

I had gone too far.

My second imprisonment and the end of "Britanicus" was all the fault of an extremely old man. Edmund Sheffield, the first Earl of Mulgrave, was 82-years-old and not of sound mind. He was so old he must have been the last man left alive to have commanded a ship against the Spanish Armada in Queen Elizabeth's day.

More to the point, he was one of only 20 members of the House of Lords still at their posts after most of the so-called aristocracy fled to Oxford and held pretend Parliamentary debates in the King's pretend Parliament there.

The Earl was a sick man. He rarely left Butterwick House, his mansion in Hammersmith. He was too old and infirm to take an active part in proceedings but, since the King quit London in '42, Mulgrave's vote in the Lords had been granted by proxy to Viscount Saye and Sele. With this vote in his pocket and supported by nine like-minded independent peers, the Viscount commanded a majority in most divisions. His party controlled the upper house.

Then Mulgrave's grandson and heir, Edmund Sheffield, got at him. Sheffield talked the old man into signing papers handing his proxy vote to Essex. Edmund was a staunch Presbyterian, one of the intolerant chosen people who could not abide the idea of more than one method of worshipping God. It would have been easy for this zealot to undermine the Viscount, especially with Sir Henry Vane out of the way.

The net result was that, within 24 hours of power in the Lords shifting from the Viscount to the Earl of Essex, Marchamont Nedham, Captain Thomas Audley and printer Bob White were all once again behind bars.

This time it wasn't the relative comfort of the gatehouse to the Palace of Westminster, it was the notorious Fleet prison, probably the most overcrowded and noisome jail in the whole of London. It was set beside the foul ditch called the Fleet River. In summer, the stench was almost unbearable. It was a source of the bad airs which caused so many agues, especially when the water level was low and the insects were prospering in the heat of the day.

The Fleet was a curious place. Most of its clientele were debtors. Live beyond your means and run up an enormous bill and you end up at the Fleet. Lose your inheritance gambling and the Fleet became your home.

Owe money to your social superior and he might consign you to the jail if you could not repay the money on demand.

You might not be a criminal as such, just someone with no money and no access to any. That put you at a disadvantage in the Fleet because prisoners had to pay their way – you had to pay for food, accommodation, favours such as a better room or, if you were feeling flush, the 'freedom of the Fleet' which meant not even staying in the jail itself but renting an expensive, run-down apartment nearby.

For the average bankrupt debtor, it was impossible unless their friends stumped up the money. Some did. Most were consigned to the cellars below ground level which were the most damp, crowded and disgusting of the lot.

It wasn't so bad during the day when prisoners more or less had the run of the place and queued up at the two grates opening onto the street so they could hold their hands out to passers-by and beg for alms. Most passers-by passed by on the other side though occasionally a Good Samaritan parted with a copper coin.

The second group of prisoners included Tom Audley, Bob White and me. Financially, we were well-off compared to the majority. Politically, we were at the distinct disadvantage. We had been jailed for political crimes. Several inmates fell foul of the Committee for Safety. Others offended the House of Commons. The "Britanicus Three", as I liked to call us, were there on the orders of the House of Lords.

Most prisoners could escape by simply paying off their debts. Political prisoners, by contrast, were often unsure what they had done to merit arrest. Many were indignant that preaching a sermon, for instance, declaring support for the King, or criticising some aspect of Parliamentary procedure was a cause for incarceration. The wrong prayer at the wrong time in the wrong place might be enough. Or speaking out on behalf of the Levellers. Many prisoners had been denounced to the authorities and spent days on end speculating over who had betrayed them and why. In some cases, the reason was not political or religious but financial. A tradesman or merchant behind bars was one less competitor for those in his line of work.

Audley, White and I wasted no time doing a deal with our captors. We were allowed to rent a small apartment on the second floor of an ancient house in a narrow little street round the corner from the main entrance to the Fleet. We had two rooms. Audley and I shared the larger bed; White the small one.

I couldn't stop myself reciting a new ditty I had composed:
General Essex may be an Earl
But he prefers the lowly churl.
It is a vice he cannot hide
Which leaves his wives unsatisfied.

White was far from happy. 'That's not funny, you arrogant, self-centred little shit,' he growled. 'Think you're immune, don't you? Think you're above it all? Think you're something special, don't you? Now look at us. This time it's worse than before, Nedham. You and your big mouth. What makes you think you can get away with hurling abuse at the King and the court when nobody else can? As far as I'm concerned, you're finished. If I even have a business left after all this.'

Bob White was reduced to tears of frustration and anger. I turned away. Audley glowered. 'This is inconvenient, you know, Monty,' he said.

'Oh you think I wanted this to happen to us, do you? Really? Don't be ridiculous. But who knows what you are allowed to write these days and what you aren't? Can we not ask questions of the men in power?'

'Of course not, Monty,' said Audley. 'You can't just write whatever comes into your head. You have to think of the consequences. You know Essex and his faction are at loggerheads with the Viscount and Cromwell and the rest. Essex has the upper hand and he wants to shut you up.'

'Can you blame him?' interrupted White bitterly. 'No control, no restraint, no decorum. That's your problem Nedham. No common sense.'

It got no better three days later when Audley and I were hauled before a committee of the House of Lords. There were only five of them but they were uniformly hostile and, moreover, not one of them had a sense of humour. I have always said newsbooks need an element of jocularity. They should be fun as well as informative. These Peers were glum, serious and hard-faced. They were not tolerant men. They could not be amused. They were, of course, doing God's work and I was, if anything, one of the Devil's disciples.

Essex himself was at the centre of the tribunal, brooding and fiddling with his sharp moustache. With him were the Earl of Manchester, the Earl of Northumberland, the Earl of Denbigh and the Earl of Stamford.

They immediately dismissed Audley, releasing him from the Fleet along with Bob White, on the basis that neither of them had written for "Britanicus" in any of the last 80 editions at least. I remained.

'I am honoured, gentlemen, to appear before such a noble tribunal,' I said, bowing low. This did not go down well. Perhaps I smirked a little.

Manchester, an enemy of Oliver Cromwell and once his superior officer, looked especially unimpressed. 'You, sir, are an outrage to common decency and to Godly endeavours. Your newsbook poisons the minds of the common people against His Majesty, vilifies his Ministers, disturbs the public peace and is a scandal to all good government.'

Stamford, a coward who had surrendered without a fight a few years ago and had no money, spoke next but so quietly I could scarcely make out what he said. 'Your news-rag seems to require no historical knowledge, no judgement, no sound mind, and not even a decent grasp of our mother tongue.'

Manchester resumed the attack. 'Your so-called "Britanicus", is riding with the scum of the people. You make weekly sport by railing at all that is noble. You endeavour to sacrifice the fame of some Lord or person of quality – nay the King himself – to the beast with many heads.'

'Your Lordship,' I protested, 'I am fighting a war on behalf of Parliament no less than the men with pikes and muskets.'

Essex laughed bitterly and slammed his palm down on the table. 'You call yourself Captain, is that not true, Nedham?'

'It has been known, my Lord.'

'Yet when did you last face the musket or pike? When did Captain Nedham last resist a charge by Prince Rupert's cavaliers?'

There was silence. Was this a rhetorical question or did Essex sincerely expect an answer? He knew I had never been in battle.

'Instead of fighting on behalf of the Parliamentary cause you say you support,' Essex resumed after a long and embarrassing silence, 'You indulge yourself, sir. You indulge yourself. Plant rumours. Publish gossip and tittle-tattle. Destroy reputations. Make fun of your betters for the amusement of the common people and the destruction of rank. You are a Leveller, sir, and a commune-man. Not a man of God. A democrat. A democrat.' Essex spat this out with derision. 'The very idea of democracy. Do you not see how destructive it is, this silly fashion? And as for deriding the King… Well.'

He had gone red in the face with anger. Manchester soothed him with some wine and a few quiet words before turning to me. 'You, sir, will be returned to the Fleet prison.'

'But your Lordships…' I started but two of Colonel Pride's idiots seized me by the arms and marched me out of the chamber and back to my lodgings at the Fleet, already vacated by Audley and White.

Lucy was livid. She brought me dinner – a meat pie, probably mutton though it was hard to be sure. 'Thou art an innocent man. Thou shouldst remain incarcerated like good John Lilburne. Ten days, husband, and no longer.'

I wrote to the Earl of Denbigh, who had asked no questions at my hearing and seemed to be reasonably sympathetic. I asked him – no, I probably begged him – anyway, I implored him to present a statement to the House of Lords declaring that whatever errors may have fallen from my pen, neither the desires of my friends nor the temptations of others could ever make me swerve from my loyalty to his Right Honourable House.

It seemed grovelling enough. Lucy thought I'd gone too far but I think she wanted me to become a martyr. There were those who thought I should, at the very least, have my hands and ears cut off. Lucy may have been among them for she would then be married to someone who had truly suffered for the cause, whatever that cause might be.

What I said to Bradshaw and Milton when they condescended to visit was that I thought the 'cause' was an end to tyranny yet the House of Lords had set itself up as judge and jury in my case without any sort of trial or legal justification for its high-handedness.

Bradshaw said, 'To right wrongs it is necessary sometimes to commit wrongs in order to do right.' Milton looked puzzled.

'It is the law of the sword,' I complained. 'And there was I thinking we were fighting for freedom. The King himself was no worse. Nobody is safe if Parliament behaves like this. Nobody.'

Lucy was wrong. It was 12 days before they let me out but only after they delivered a bitter blow. I was freed on condition I wrote no more newsbooks or pamphlets without the approval of the House of Lords. I also had to lodge £200 as a guarantee of my good behaviour with that reptile John Rushworth.

'When do I see the money again?' I snapped.

He smiled his slippery smile, pawed the coins, poured them into a strongbox and wrote out a receipt. 'Bound over to keep the peace, it seems, Monty. What a shame.'

'When do I see the money again?'

'Who knows?' he said with a shrug. 'And that's the end of "Britanicus" then. Your readers will be disappointed. Where will they go for their weekly dose of lies, sarcasm and vituperation?'

'Just because we stopped paying you,' I said dejectedly. 'But you never supplied us with news.'

'Too busy,' said Rushworth. Then he added, 'You know, do you, that Oxford has surrendered?'

'Oxford?' This really was news. The King's headquarters finally opened its gates and handed over control to Parliament. All those dispossessed Royalists would become prisoners or petitioners. This was proof they had lost.

For a moment I felt the surge of excitement that hits whenever a significant piece of news falls into my hands and I must rush to publish ahead of any rivals. I thanked Rushworth for this intelligence and hurried from his office.

It was only on the steps outside I realised – I no longer had a newsbook to publish it in.

CHAPTER 16

Here lies Britanicus,
Hell's barking cur

1646-7

"Britanicus" was dead. Bob White was reduced to printing other people's pamphlets. Tom Audley tried another newsbook for a few weeks but it came to nothing. I, meanwhile, was busily building up my medical practice.

I think I mis-diagnosed William Lenthall's collapse. I said it was exhaustion. In fact, it probably was the ague. Luckily my prescription of rest in Burford didn't kill him but nobody knew how to cure the ague anyway. It carries off plenty of people. Most of those who recover do so despite, not because of, medical intervention. They say the Spanish may have found a cure somewhere in South America but I've not seen it nor has any physician I know.

I set up a surgery at my house in Westminster and acquired patients. My reputation as a news-monger was so widespread some people sought me out to catch up on the political gossip more than to discuss their ailments. Patients who knew of my writing would turn up with very little wrong with them. They would consult me not just about their bad teeth, foul breath and aching heads, their rotten feet and severed limbs. Once we dealt with their maladies, they would consult me on the issues of the day. There was always something to discuss and, in the absence of "Britanicus", no reliable source of information. Indeed, there were few sources of news of any sort, reliable or not. The Lords had cracked down on newsbooks and enforced their prohibitions with jail sentences, fines, even floggings.

I gave them the benefit of my knowledge and understanding. My patients went away thinking their shilling was well-spent.

The Earl of Essex died in September. Heart attack, apparently. I wasn't sorry. It gave the Viscount and his faction more power in the House of Lords but that didn't bring back "Britanicus". Sir Henry Vane was busy buying the King back from the Scots and trying to negotiate with Charles. Not even the return to power of the Viscount's son, Nat Fiennes, helped me but with so much going on, it was impossible to keep my head down and concentrate on medicine. There was a lot to be said and it was increasingly clear to me very few people were saying the right things in the right way.

Milton might put out a pamphlet, half of it in Latin. It would be read by a few of his intellectual friends and nobody else. Others issued newssheets purporting to tell the truth but really interested only in the hunt for witches, tales of magic and ghost stories about apparitions appearing in the fields of Warwickshire after the Battle of Edgehill.

There were big issues at stake but few people capable of setting them out to appeal to a wide readership. It was frustrating being denied a platform for my wit and wisdom. It was necessary instead to address specific issues in longer pamphlets.

The Leveller John Lilburne asked me to help. Lucy told me I had to agree. I argued, on Lilburne's behalf, that no man should be thrown in jail except for a capital crime such as treason, murder, robbery or burglary. Imprisoning Lilburne for arguing in favour of freedom, justice and power-for-the-people was wrong even if you disagreed with what he was saying. Damn it all, they threw me in jail for the same offence and I was no traitor. Mind you, it did seem that arguing over the importance of Magna Carta, a document signed more than 400 years ago, was beside the point. Nobody cared. I tried to persuade Lilburne of this but he would have none of it.

'Our fundamental freedoms are enshrined in it,' he insisted – and he was prepared to go to prison to prove it.

Freeborn John was one of those dishevelled, obsessive individuals who paid no heed to their own comfort. If his wife Elizabeth hadn't forced him to eat, he would have starved to death. His clothes were always stained with ink or gravy, his beard was unkempt and his hair would often stand on end for want of a brush.

Yet his pamphlets were widely read, especially among the rank-and-file soldiers he commanded until he fell out with the Earl of Manchester. Lilburne had already done time in the Tower for branding the Earl a traitor who sympathised with the King.

The real problem was the fanatics. The struggle between the tolerant and the intolerant took place on every street corner, in every pulpit, in legal and illegal publications, between black-suited Parliamentarians and steel-helmeted Ironsides.

It also took place in my own parlour where, increasingly, Lucy sided with the intolerant and fanatical. I tried discussing it with her once when we were taking a break from the almost-daily attempts to conceive a child. 'Why not let people believe what they want to believe as long as they aren't Papists and believe in God,' I asked. Innocently enough, I thought.

Lucy was arranging sweet peas in a vase at the time. They grew in our patch of garden at the back of our house near Covent Garden. She looked up from under her linen cap and scowled, reached for the Bible, which stood on its own small table, and said, 'Wait while I find the answer.' After riffling through the pages for a while she announced, 'There is only one way to worship God. Deuteronomy tells us so. If someone tries to lead you astray, "thou shalt not consent unto him, nor hearken unto him; neither shall thine eye pity him, neither shalt thou spare, neither shalt thou conceal him but thou shalt surely kill him; thine hand shall be first upon him to put him to death, and afterwards the hand of all the people. And thou shalt stone him with stones, that he die". No, husband, thou art mistaken if thou think'st there is more than one way to Heaven. "Strait is the gate, and narrow is the way, which leadeth unto life, and few there be that find it".'

I would have disputed with her but thought better of it. My wife was being amenable, even affectionate, and I was not inclined to upset the apple-cart for a debate I knew I could not win. Lucy was by no means the only God-fearing individual with a clear view of the Pit of Damnation. They were everywhere, including a majority in the House of Commons even if the balance of power in the Lords had swung back in favour of the Viscount and his more liberal peers.

It was another ice-cold winter with snow on the ground from early December until mid-March. There were many illnesses, which was all to the good as far as I was concerned. Many physicians fled London to avoid the plague and decided not to return because of the volatile political situation. The economics were clear – demand for medical attention was growing while the supply of physicians was reduced. It was a lucrative time to practice. I stuck to my principles and did as little damage as I could. Some patients were indignant when I refused to bleed them or apply leeches but most were grateful. Generally, they got better and, when they did, they were generous in their praise for my skill and care. Like all good doctors, I buried my mistakes.

I was still writing tracts. I even wrote one calling for all parties to reach an agreement, pointing out how dangerous more warfare would be for independents, Presbyterians, Royalists and the merchants of London. I was reading Niccolò Machiavelli, an Italian. As far as he was concerned, most people were selfish and motivated only by self-interest. It was in the interests of all parties to reach a peaceful settlement; it made no sense to prolong their disputes.

I did not show this to Lucy. She would have objected. And I did not ask the House of Lords for permission to publish it. It seemed to me the King and the independents – the Viscount, Sir Henry, Cromwell and the rest – had enough in common to be reconciled. After all, none of them wanted the rigid Presbyterians to come out on top.

In February, Sir Henry bought the King from the Scots for £400,000 and Charles was taken to at Holdenby Palace in Northamptonshire. When he arrived he was cheered by crowds of people. An optimist might think Charles was about to be restored to his throne.

My pamphlet was re-printed twice in as many months. It was a best-seller, especially among Royalists who thought I was lighting the way to peace and reconciliation.

In the summer of '47, we visited Burford. Lucy would see her mother, I would see my parents – a few weeks in the fresh air, out of the city, enjoying the peace and tranquillity.

The journey had become easier. There were fewer armies stalking the high roads, fewer marauding bandits and not so many highwaymen. Most soldiers were in camps, debating what to do, demanding pay, searching for food and setting up committees.

My step-father's brother, Judge John Glynn, was in Burford visiting both his family and Mr Speaker Lenthall. Uncle John had been MP for Westminster for seven years. He was now Recorder of Westminster and he'd joined the new Committee of Safety which was supposed to be reconciling Parliament and the army. Nat Fiennes was another member, though I had not seen him since his return from Switzerland.

Uncle John had a lawyer's mind. He could speak at length on any topic and when he had finished it was difficult to sum up what point he had actually made. Even so, people listened to him in the courtroom, the Commons or the Government committee.

At a dinner in Burford Abbey thrown by William and Elizabeth Lenthall, Judge Glynn declared, 'Peace. We want peace. Cromwell and Ireton have offered it. The King must accept it.'

Lenthall agreed, 'The sooner this business is over, the sooner we can all get back to normal.'

'We have to do something about Lilburne's Levellers,' said the Judge. 'They accuse Cromwell and Sir Henry of wanting to keep the poor in everlasting slavery. Do these people not understand the natural order of things?'

'But peace must be the aim,' said Lenthall.

Lucy looked as if she would speak. I glared at her. My mother smiled, 'Lucy, my dear? Do you have an opinion?'

The gentlemen looked at her, my pretty little wife with her dogmatic opinions and innocent smile. 'Peace, you say, gentlemen,' she began and

I feared the worst. 'How did Abraham bring peace to the cities of the plain? Through the slaughter of the Kings.'

'Lucy!' I cried indignantly.

'Lucy?' said my mother questioningly.

'Lucy,' said my step-father patronisingly, with a slight smile.

The Judge and the Speaker said nothing and changed the subject.

After the King was sold to Parliament and treated as a guest at Holdenby Palace for a few months, the army seized him. A troop of 500 men turned up and rode away with him. They say the kidnapping was completely the initiative of the man in charge, George Joyce. But Joyce was a mere cornet, the lowest officer rank in the army and a tailor by trade. Everyone knew the brains behind the King's arrest were Cromwell, Fairfax and Ireton.

With this move, the balance of power shifted, from the Puritans to the independents and from Parliament to the army. Cromwell immediately offered the King a deal – religious freedom, the return of Bishops, new elections to Parliament, a general amnesty – nobody would be executed, not even the King's most loyal and most hated friends.

The King was re-united with his children at a public house in Maidenhead. Cromwell cried to see their joyful reunion.

I did manage a brief visit to Big Susie during our stay in Burford but she now had a more permanent admirer and was unable to give me the attention I was accustomed to. 'What can you expect?' she demanded indignantly.

I also looked in on my old friend Edward Heylyn, who was happy to curse all sides in the conflagration. He wanted to be left alone to do a little farming and a great deal of hunting. He had escaped the worst depredations of the two armies, which were prone to descending on substantial estates and stripping them bare while offering worthless pieces of paper as payment. Edward had provided a roof over the heads of three Parliamentarian officers for some months but they left after the fall of Oxford.

In their place was his brother Peter, one-time editor of the "Court Mercury", my former newsbook rival. Still nominally a chaplain to the King, Peter was a sorry figure. Thin and wasted by the privations suffered during the siege of Oxford, his plight was made worse by the rapid loss of his eyesight.

'I can still see a little, I can see shapes, objects and people but not who or what they may be,' he said. 'Nowadays Edward has to read to me and I have a secretary to write my letters.'

He sat, glassy-eyed, at the dining table groping for his cup as we drank wine together. Peter was still a vehement man. 'I forgive you, Marchamont,' he said, 'For that is what the Lord requires me to do. Forgive my enemies. But you were my enemy, you know. Every time we saw your dreadful rag we knew we were in more trouble. You couldn't resist it, could you, attacking everything sacred and profound? Not just the King but the true Church of England, bishops, Peers of the Realm, all that's greatest about this country. There was Marchamont Nedham pouring vitriol over it. How could you, Marchamont?' Peter looked genuinely puzzled. He didn't seem angry; just disappointed and curious.

'A glib facility for words,' I answered glibly.

'But you helped to plunge the country into lawlessness and anarchy. Is that really what you wanted?'

'I'm not sure it's my fault,' I said. 'But I did see an opportunity for some sport.'

Heylyn closed his almost-sightless eyes as if in prayer. His mouth pursed and shrivelled. His hands lay in his lap as if in contemplation. 'You saw the opportunity for some sport.'

'Come on, Peter. Nobody takes newsbooks seriously.'

'You know as well as I do that's not true. Why did your patrons pay for you to set up "Britanicus" in the first place? To counter our newsbook. They realised we were swaying opinion in the King's favour and needed someone – some facile, glib mercenary – to swing it back in their favour. They knew – and you know as well, Marchamont – that newsbooks do indeed carry great influence among the people. They read them and they believe them. You know that as well as I do.'

I felt like a schoolboy being ticked-off by the headmaster. 'True, up to a point, I suppose,' I conceded. 'But people have the right to know what's being done in their name, do they not?'

'Do they?' Peter said quietly. 'Do they? I wonder.'

After a pause, I asked, 'Anyway, what happened to your newsbook, Peter?'

'Simple. Ran out of money.'

'Did you not secure a patron?'

'Of course. The King among others. They ran out of money. Everyone did.'

'What now, Peter. What will the King agree to?'

'The King will agree to no demands from any of the parties now warring over him. He is the King, answerable only to God. He will not bend the knee to Fairfax or Cromwell or Sir Henry Vane or any of that pack of wolves.'

'Oh dear,' I said.

CHAPTER 17

Here lyes Ambition,
Envy, Pride
and Lust

August 1647

I left Lucy with her mother. She was, at last, with child again, affording me some rest in London while I went about my doctoring. Then a curious letter arrived from none other than Peter Heylyn.

He invited me to attend a meeting with two friends of his at a bar in Wapping two days hence. Heylyn wouldn't be there. The men would know me. They were anxious to meet me, he said. No reply was necessary; the two men would wait for me at the Red Cow next to Execution Dock in the early evening.

Wapping? At night? I wasn't at all sure I wanted to go. The docks were dangerous at the best of times and this was the worst of times – there had been riots against the army and now the army was occupying the city. That ought to make the streets safer but it didn't feel like it. The whole place was under martial law. Admittedly the New Model Army behaved surprisingly well – no robberies, no rapes, not much unnecessary violence. People were saying if this was the only way to restore law and order then perhaps being ruled by the army was better than being governed by a dwindling band of greedy and fanatical Puritan incompetents in Parliament.

It didn't make Wapping any more attractive, though. But curiosity got the better of me. Peter Heylyn wouldn't deliberately lure me into a trap. Would he?

I approached Wapping warily. Its filthy main street, its malign alleyways, its ramshackle tenements and filthy shacks do not welcome visitors.

At least in the early evening you might see trouble coming before it was too late. The place was filled with criminals and sailors. Mutineers were tied to posts at Execution Dock and drowned at high tide. Mercifully, there were no corpses rotting on the ebb tide tonight.

Trapped between river and marsh, Wapping was an unhealthy place. I walked tentatively. It was hot. The roadway was caked with mud and dung; dusty but passable. The Red Cow was a dull, lowering building with its back to the river, three small, crowded, smoky rooms. That early, the drinkers were still stocking up on the evening's quota of ale and spirits. It was too early for serious fighting but the atmosphere was already tense. As I entered, several men stared at me; one spat on the floor; another sucked his clay pipe in serious contemplation. One said, 'Oh ho, a cavalier.' There was some laughter.

I perched on the end of a bench and nodded to the others sitting nearby. I ordered a brandy, a mistake as it was so fierce I could scarcely sip it without choking and spluttering, much to the amusement of the assembled company.

I sniffed the brandy. I waited a half hour. I ordered a second brandy, with water this time, and waited another half hour.

After an hour I grew tired of waiting and got up to leave. A leering sailor with two prominent fangs in an otherwise toothless mouth, grinned in my face. 'Cavalier, is it?' he said. 'A toast to the King then.'

Several men took up the chorus. 'The King.' They drank and stared at me.

'God bless him,' I said.

'God bless him?' asked the sailor, staring aggressively. 'The man has blood on his hands. We want no King's-men here.'

He pushed me into another man, who pushed me into a third, who returned me to the first. I was being softened up. They meant violence.

The first man drew a knife, pushed me up against a wooden pillar, hissed into my face, 'King? Parliament? Army? Which is it? Are you a Papist?'

I was terrified. Whatever answer I gave would be wrong. My throat could be cut. I'd be a dead man.

The two-fanged man with the knife and his two companions grabbed me and marched me from the room. The others turned back to their drinks. They had seen it all before. My fate was no business of theirs.

The knifeman steered me onto the main street, down an alleyway, left into a second, right into a third and then into one of the tenements, up rotten steps, into a room on the first floor. I didn't resist. I thought it was safer that way.

'Sit,' two-fangs ordered, indicating one of two chairs. He and his companions withdrew. The door was locked.

The room was plainly furnished, illuminated by three freshly-lit candles. There was a table with a bottle of Madeira and two expensive-looking glasses, an empty fireplace with a metal guard, a couple of small portraits on the wall. Also on the table was a copy of the last edition of "Britanicus". Perhaps I was expected. I began to feel a little less apprehensive.

I picked up my old newsbook and began to flick through its eight pages. It was more than a year old; I was surprised anyone had kept it that long.

The lock turned, the door opened, a tall man stooped and let himself into the room. 'Miss it?' he asked, indicating the newsbook.

He sat opposite me. He was dressed plainly, in shabby Puritan garb. His boots, though plain, were new and, apart from a little dust, remarkably clean.

'Wine?' he said. 'Help yourself. I apologise for the inconvenience but it is for your own protection.'

His voice betrayed him. This was a King's-man. I was not in the mood to be easily befriended. 'Who are you? What do you want? Is Heylyn responsible for this?'

'The Rector? Ah yes, he did suggest we talk to you.'

'Did he?'

'He did.'

The cavalier poured us both some wine, drank off his glass at one draught and refilled it. 'Very good,' he said, 'Go on, try some.'

'No thank you, I have already endured two glasses of disgusting brandy waiting, I must now suppose, for this meeting. I shall take my leave. It is late and I must return home.' I know I sounded unusually pompous but I had my dignity to think of.

I got up to leave and threw "Britanicus" back on the table. 'You miss it, don't you?' my host said. 'How can you not? The world is falling apart, there are riots in London, the King is being marched from one prison to another, the Puritans are imposing themselves on everyone, food is scarce, people are starving. There is much to write about. Yet where is our leading news-man? Where is Marchamont Nedham when his country needs him?'

The cavalier poured himself a third glass. I turned back. He stood, held out his hand. 'Let me introduce myself. Henry Washington,' he said.

I took his hand. Washington had an open, friendly face, though a little flushed thanks to his three swift glasses of Madeira. 'Sit, Captain Nedham, sit, please.'

I sat, poured some wine, drank it off and poured some more. 'Yes, I do miss it,' I confessed. 'Why?'

Washington brushed imaginary dust from his clean but elderly trousers. 'Borrow those from a servant?' I asked.

'Ha!' he smiled but looked seriously at me. 'The tide is turning, Nedham. Your friends Lenthall, Vane, Viscount Saye, Nat Fiennes, they've all fled to the army. Your uncle Judge Glynn and ten other MPs of the so-called Peace Party have run away, to France of all places. The King is back at Hampton Court.'

'Yes, I am aware of my uncle's exile. And who doesn't want peace? Why won't the King just agree to Cromwell's terms. He did lose the war, you know.'

Washington smiled. 'True, the fighting did not go entirely His Majesty's way. Yet he is still King and he knows with absolute certainty that God will not suffer rebels and traitors to prosper. It follows it is not possible for the King to reach an accommodation with such men. God will not permit it.'

'God,' I said, 'May not permit it but when the army takes control of the streets of London and the Palace of Westminster, where is your God then? God is on the side of the big battalions. Sword-law not God's law.'

Washington laughed briefly. 'Exactly, exactly. That is why we need you, Doctor Nedham.'

CHAPTER 18

Fetters are th' onely
favors now

September 1647

I knelt. I kissed the rings on his left hand. Big rings on small hands perfumed with lavender. The carpet was red velvet, the tapestries depicted vivid hunting scenes, the throne was gold. There were three courtiers and a couple of bejewelled women. The guards wore the uniform of the New Model Army. Cromwell and Ireton had been there the previous day, playing bowls with the King.

It was almost as if Charles were back on the Throne and back in power.

He was at the Royal Palace of Hampton Court. He was attended by a retinue of servants and staff almost as numerous as in his heyday. His wife was in France and his children were dispersed around the country or with their mother abroad. But he had his chaplains, including Peter Heylyn, and a few close companions.

The King was a good two inches shorter than me, despite the heels on his elegant shoes. He sat on his throne in velvet and silk, colourful and dandyish despite his 46 years. He was greying and his eyes looked tired, haunted, sad. His voice did indeed carry the tang of Scots in it, not to mention the stammer which, in our brief interview, occurred on only two occasions. His hair and beard were freshly trimmed; he did not look like the refugee who turned up in Southwell and handed himself to the Scottish army trusting, mistakenly, to their honour.

I confess I felt a little sorry for him. He tried to maintain his dignity and majesty but it was a crumbling façade. His eyes had dark rings round them, his forehead was care-worn, his cheeks sunken, his brief smile full of hesitancy and suspicion as if he knew there was nobody left he could trust. The King was in daily fear of assassination. He kept getting letters warning him of an attempt on his life.

Now he was placing his trust in Marchamont Nedham.

The King's supporters wanted a new newsbook. Of course they did. Who wouldn't?

I had been briefed by Henry Washington. The Royalist cause was more popular than ever – how could anyone doubt it? Witness the outpouring of love for the King on his Royal progresses or the riots in London in support of the King and only put down by the strong-arm tactics of the New Model Army. Where, though, was a mouthpiece for all that support? Several Royalists since Heylyn and Sir John Berkenhead had tried producing newsbooks but they weren't widely read. The Royalists concluded the man who made such a success of "Mercurius Britanicus" was the only one capable of achieving the same feat again, this time in support of the King and the Royalist cause.

Washington introduced me to Bernard Astley, another courtier, who had survived the war, gone into exile and returned on the quiet. Astley said he was authorised to offer me employment and provide money to ensure the success of our enterprise. I explained I was no longer a newsbook man but a doctor. He said that was ideal cover because I would be working without a licence; I could hardly expect the House of Lords to sanction my activities.

'We still have friends, Captain Nedham,' said Astley. 'We can find a friendly printer. We know how to distribute newsbooks, don't worry about that. But we need someone to write them. Of course, no-one will know it's you. You will have to be anonymous for your own sake. They'd arrest you if they got a sniff of your involvement. You will need to work alone. No associates. No taking anyone into your confidence – not your friend the Speaker, not your friend John Bradshaw, not your uncle Judge Glynn and certainly not your wife.'

'Washington has done his spying well,' I said, somewhat resentfully. I disliked the idea the King's men had trawled through my private life and discovered who my friends were and what my wife's opinions might be.

The question I really wanted to ask was, 'How much?' But I thought that might seem a little mercenary.

Money was not the only issue, of course. They were appealing to my professional pride. There are few things more flattering than to be asked, nay begged, to exercise one's literary skills in pursuit of a cause. Was it a good cause? Was it reasonable for me to write in support of a King I had mocked only a few months earlier? A King with his people's blood on his hands? A hen-pecked, vacillating, pompous, untrustworthy man whose salvation lay in his own slippery and unreliable hands?

Was this not as shameful as some of those 'warriors' who switched from the losing side to the winning side in the heat of the battle? Was I a turncoat?

I told myself I had been scrupulous not to take sides throughout the war. I had reported the facts and interpreted them as reasonably as I could. I might have been disparaging of the King but only because his behaviour invited it. I might have written in support of Parliament or the army or the abolition of bishops or the execution of Archbishop Laud. That did not mean I had to remain consistent and single-minded to the point of obsessiveness or stupidity. When the facts change, my opinion is liable to change as well. That was the pragmatic approach, surely.

And why turn down an opportunity like this? They didn't come along every day. Money, power, influence, a sort of fame or notoriety (it would not be long before the world became aware whose sharp and witty pen was responsible for this new publication – readers would soon recognise my unique style) not to mention excitement. It was, after all, exciting to be at the centre of affairs, shaping people's opinions and leading them in the right direction.

'It is a sovereign's duty to forgive his m-m-m-misguided subjects as I trust in the forgiveness of sins by the Lord God Himself.'

That's what the King said to me after I had kneeled and kissed his hand.

He gave an odd little smile which said he did not trust me but thought I might prove useful. 'They tell me I must forgive you and ask for your assistance, Doctor Nedham.'

'Your Majesty does me too much honour,' I grovelled, head bowed, still on both knees.

'That,' the King said slowly, 'Is certainly true. Yet my chaplain speaks highly of you.'

'Majesty.'

'The hue and cry. That was you, wasn't it? Most diverting. "A great tennis-ball of passion and fortune?" Yours as well, I think. "Bloody hands, a heart full of broken vows and protestations." "He cannot conquer himself being subject to his own passions, other men's ambitions and flattery." "More tricks than Hocus-Pocus at Bartholomew Fair." Shall I go on?'

'Your Majesty.' I looked up briefly. He seemed genuinely hurt, like a stage actor whose performance had been criticised, as if his skin were too thin for such barbarity. What was I to say? Contrition wouldn't do. I tried a different tactic. 'Your Majesty.' I stood up and took a couple of steps back. 'I am flattered, delighted. I think you have proved to yourself the value of my pen. You have read and remembered what I have written in the past. You will remember what I write in the future and you can be sure it will be directed at others – the Puritans in particular, the democrats, the Levellers.'

'Cromwell? Ireton? Fairfax?'

'Indeed, Your Majesty.'

'Her Majesty the Queen will not be well-disposed towards the man who called her – now, what was it? – the p-p-p-petticoat Machiavelli.'

'My own dear wife will not be pleased with this arrangement either, if that is any consolation, Your Majesty.'

The terrible truth is, I liked him. The King had a sense of humour. He was cultivated and cultured. He was intelligent and defeated. He had my sympathy. It must have been hard for him, brought up to believe he was anointed by God Himself, to discover his whims and wishes were now questioned by his own subjects. It was woeful to see such majesty cornered like a hunted fox, fearful he will be torn apart by ravening hounds.

'Your Majesty's commission is a sacred commission which I do not undertake lightly,' I said with as much humility as I could muster. 'I shall be faithful to your cause while maintaining the same approach as always – news must be intermingled with levity and memorable phrases if it is to capture the attention of the reader.' I was getting carried away now. 'I shall introduce each edition with some lines of poetry of my own composition.'

The King looked quizzical.

'Light verse to introduce the reader to the topic of the moment, Your Majesty. And I shall call it "Mercurius Pragmaticus", my lord.'

'"Pragmaticus?"' the King looked sceptical.

'Pragmatic, practical, realistic, dealing with reality as it is, not as we would wish it to be,' I explained, 'But above all, from the Greek – πραγματικός – reality, truth. The Real Truth, sire, The Real Truth.'

CHAPTER 19

Divers scandals Libels,
and treasonous Pamphlets

Autumn 1647

Over the next few months, the beagles of the State tried to sniff out
our printing presses but we were always one step ahead and in a new
lair before they tracked us down. On one occasion, I waited on horseback as they swarmed and barked around a farm out in the direction of
Marybourne before returning to barracks empty-handed. They'd got the
wrong house.

We did lose one press, a few weeks after the enterprise began. It was
set up at a farm in Goodman's Fields, beyond Aldgate. The farm sold
milk and ale – three pints for a halfpenny – and was busy. People came
and went all the time. Sadly the beagles raided the place and arrested
Joe Huntley, our printer. I don't recall what became of Huntley though,
somehow, Washington managed to buy back the presses without much
difficulty. Money is a powerful argument.

I now wore black Puritanical weeds. I removed my pearl ear-rings. My
guise as a sober gentleman let me make my way unobtrusively round the
city, from patient to patient, collecting gossip as I went. They included
John Bradshaw and Mr Speaker Lenthall. I kept in touch with my uncle, Judge John Glynn, still in France after the latest purge, while Henry
Washington introduced me to a few Royalists.

Washington and I did not meet in the same place twice. Taverns were
the usual venues, the seedier and more down-at-heel the better. Washington had sworn not to take up arms against Parliament after he surrendered the City of Worcester, where he'd been the governor. His oath said

nothing about newsbooks, however, and he was convinced the power of the press could turn the tide of war.

I did my best. After all, there was plenty to go at. The news continued to flood into the city from across the country, none of it good for the King yet little of it good for the country either.

The King's enemies still paid lip-service to the idea he had a say in the future. It was obvious – and I pointed it out week after week – that the army was after the King's blood. The army wanted to murder the Monarch. Even the Levellers, Puritans and Parliamentary aristocrats were opposed to the idea. Even the Viscount and Sir Henry Vane, both Cromwell's political allies, were reluctant to go that far.

Talks with the King dragged on while the rank-and-file soldiers set about trying to persuade their officers there should be a Government which gave fighting men a say, not to mention pay for all the work they'd done defending the liberties of the nation against the tyranny of the King. As if the tyranny of the army – which included imprisonment without trial, excessive taxes, arbitrary confiscation of land, property and money, an end to liberties of speech and religion not to mention widespread starvation and misery – were somehow preferable.

I pointed all this out regularly in "Pragmaticus", or "Prag" as it was popularly known by the growing army of readers who queued outside bookshops, bought it in taverns, surreptitiously slipped a penny to the women touting it around St Paul's and the gentlemen who placed regular orders with their own trusted sources.

By the autumn of '47, it's reasonable to say nine people in ten thought it was time to restore the King, call elections to Parliament, disband the army and stop all the nonsense from destroying the country and ruining its prosperity. People needed a voice for this. "Prag" gave them a voice.

Other illicit newsbooks sprang up from time to time. They didn't last. They were not well-funded. They did not have the backing of Royalists at home and abroad. They did not have access to presses which could be packed up and moved, if not at a moment's notice then at least without too much difficulty.

This incurred the envy of lesser men. One was a supposed poet called Samuel Sheppard, who turned out a paper called "The Dogmatic Mercury". Another was a madman called John Crouch who put out a rag called

"The Man in the Moon", full of fantasy and bad jokes. Some people loved it.

My job, which these fly-by-nights did nothing to help, was to point out the divisions among the King's enemies. Cromwell was not having it all his own way. The unruly army was trying to impose democracy; Old Nol preferred his friends in the aristocracy.

It was amusing to bait the great General and provoke the people who cringed before him, notably members of the House of Commons. 'Mr Cromwell hath Parliament in the Mill, grind they must, seeing that they are at his Beck who holds a Whip and a Bell over their guilty Heads,' I said, and, 'When he hath used them long enough under the name of Parliament, then (perhaps) they shall be disbanded several ways, that the Sword-men may stand for ever.'

We had fun at the expense of people like the not-very-Reverend Alderman Atkins. He claimed to be a Puritan but it was well known this stupid, greedy hypocrite had been a prostitute's pimp before his miraculous conversion. The fact he became an Alderman was testament to the turbulent times. He became notorious for shitting his breeches when he had to make a speech to the Mayor of London. Atkins was one of the dregs who allied themselves to Parliament in the early years of the war and were terrified of losing what they had won by foul means.

I had a roster of insults for Cromwell, of course. He was vulgar, bloodthirsty, hypocritical, power-mad and ugly. He was the Brewer, the Town Bull of Ely, Crum-Hell, King Cromwell, The Grand Signior, Nose Almighty, Copper Nose. He was personally responsible for the decline of every trade in the country except preaching. He was selling seats in Parliament – an egg merchant bough a seat for £60 and voted as ordered by Cromwell when the House divided 57 to 57.

I boasted I had inside information from Westminster and from Derby House.

It was no idle boast.

I visited the Speaker regularly. As his physician, it was important for the sake of Mr Lenthall's health and the health of the nation that he was cared for after his debilitating ague. What could be more natural than for patient and physician to discuss affairs of State which were such a burden to so distinguished a politician? Of course, the Speaker did not know of my Royalist activities. He saw me as his friend. Indeed, I was his friend. There was no harm in relating to a wider audience some of the information he imparted to me during my frequent examinations. He also paid well for this medical attention. My fee, ten shillings a visit, was paid from Parliament's funds not his own pocket, though how Parliament could afford it was a matter of speculation when it owed its own army no less than £3 million.

As for the Derby House Committee, the country's ruling body consisted of seven Peers and 14 MPs, I had several sources. One was Judge John Glynn except he'd fled abroad. But Sir Henry Vane was a member. So were the Viscount and his son. I made a point of becoming re-acquainted with Nat Fiennes; he was delighted.

'I see you are becoming a sober citizen at last, Marchamont,' was his first comment when we met at the Blue Boar's Head near Derby House in Westminster. Puritans kept trying to close it but it survived and prospered. It served expensive meat pies. The landlord blamed the price on the times we were living in but they had always been costly.

Nat was grinning. 'You must come to Broughton, Monty,' he said. 'We're rebuilding the place now bloody Prince Rupert's fled the country. You really must visit. After what that man did to it, there's a lot of repairing to take place but it makes a change for a castle to be restored these days, what with Parliament ordering most of them to be knocked down.'

'I shall,' I promised, 'As soon as I can get away. But my patients you know…' I said airily, waving an arm about as if to demonstrate how much in demand I was.

'Have you seen this new newsbook "Pragmaticus"? Quite like the old days, except it's on the wrong side. Must say, though, the committee's very fed up about it. They say it's far too accurate in its reports on the proceedings in Parliament. MPs will completely lose the freedom and privacy of our debates. I think the source is one of our own clerks, that one Brownlow, a drunken, debauched fellow with a red face. Can't prove it though. Not yet, anyway.'

'Rack him,' I said.

'The rack?' Nat looked shocked. 'We don't go in for that sort of thing, Monty. We are a civilised nation and God-fearing folk.'

'I was joking, Nat.'

He smiled and seemed embarrassed to have taken me seriously. 'Of course, of course.'

I was delighted when he started quoting "Prag" back to me, though. 'That paper says the army might demand a full and free Parliament' – he took it from his pocket and started quoting – "wherein the high-shoes, Reverend Cobblers and Kettle-menders must all come gossiping" – amusing.'

'But is he right, Nat?' I innocently asked.

'I suppose so,' he conceded. 'I'm not sure anybody seriously wants the great unwashed to have a say in how the country is run. Not even Lilburne and his Levellers quite want that, do they?'

A few days after our meeting, the King fled Hampton Court going nobody knew where. He fetched up on the Isle of Wight and surrendered to the governor Robert Hammond. That seemed a safe enough move. Hammond's grandfather was King James I's physician and his uncle was one of King Charles's chaplains.

Charles's safe haven of Carisbrook Castle quickly turned into a prison. Hammond, instead of being the King's friend, became his jailer.

Christmas was spent in Burford where it turned out my wife was heavily pregnant. I think she had written to tell me but I confess I'd forgotten. Lucy was pleased to see me. She said she was tired of Burford and accompanied me back to London.

One of the problems of a regular publication is it's difficult to take time off and with Lucy back home I couldn't write there any longer. If she saw what I was doing, she might well betray me. I like to think Lucy loved me, in her own way, but she loved her version of God more and she loathed the King, the cavaliers and all their works. They were all, in her view, Papists. If she knew I was working for them, I think she would have actively sought my imprisonment.

I was forced to work secretly in a garret off Fleet Street which Washington found; two rooms, candles, a desk, quills, pen-knife, ink, sand to dry it, and reams of paper. The copy was delivered by messenger to a safe house in Chiswick then returned by a separate messenger to the printer, whose name and location were not known to me. Washington wanted everything kept in separate compartments. He said it was safer that way. The beagles would find it harder to sniff us out. Few people knew what I was up to. Apart from Washington and Bernard Astley, only John Crouch and Sam Sheppard suspected I was responsible for the country's most successful Royalist newsbook.

Lucy was not well. Her confinement was long and painful, if her cries of distress were anything to go by. We named the child Theodosia and baptised her according to the new rites at St Dunstan-in-the-West, on Fleet Street.

We buried Theodosia there three weeks later, on February 12, a bone-chilling day as bleak as any I can remember.

CHAPTER 20

They have blown away Popery
and Protestantisme to
make way for that grand
Idolatry Covetousnes

Spring 1648

I am not a religious man. Indeed, the more I hear of the Lord's plans and punishments for mankind, the less convinced I become that He either knows or cares about us. However, I am not entirely an unbeliever.

I have often thought a woman's shapely, well-rounded, luscious breasts are one of the proofs there really is a God. The God who gave us women's breasts is, indeed, a good God, a kind God, a generous God, a loving God. I couldn't say any of this to my wife, of course, though her own breasts were truly manifestations of the divine. However, London in the '40s was rarely a place to savour this great gift from Heaven above.

Rarely, but not never.

I was on a visit to John Bradshaw when I first met Lucy. Not the Lucy I was married to; the Lucy I would be married to. My tragic, beautiful little Lucy. Royalist Lucy, dispossessed Lucy, penniless Lucy. She was sitting on the steps leading to Bradshaw's offices crying her eyes out.

It was late April. I'd gone to see Bradshaw to discuss the Lords' decision to close half the newsbooks in London. Bradshaw was involved in this censorship and I was curious to know what he thought, though obviously I wasn't about to disclose I was still involved in the trade.

Before I reached the Judge's offices, I stumbled on Lucy sobbing mightily and sniffing, wiping her nose on the sleeve of her blue cotton frock, her face blotchy and red. Maybe it was her dimples. Maybe it was her thick, curling hair. Probably it was her cleavage. Whatever it was, I stopped and asked if I could be of service.

She sat, knees up to her chin, face to the ground, and shook her head. Her raven-black hair shone in the spring sun. She carried with her a scent of something fresh and attractive, possibly apples. It made a change from the usual London stink.

She looked up with big, green, watery eyes and shook her head. She wiped her nose on her sleeve. I offered my kerchief which she accepted with good grace and blew her nose with no ladylike delicacy.

I asked her again if I could be of help.

She appraised me for the first time. I'm not sure she liked what she saw but I tried to appear friendly. 'Madam,' I smiled, 'Dr Marchamont Nedham, at your service.'

'Doctor? Not of divinity I trust.'

'A medical practitioner, madam.'

'Can you cure a stony heart?'

'Not yours, surely?'

'No, that man in there. Judge Bradshaw. The commissioner for the sequestrations committee. Can you cure his stony heart?'

'What has he done, madam?'

She then launched into a tale of woe. I didn't take it all in at the time because she spoke so fast and vehemently, interspersed with tears and expressions of rage. Her father had been killed in the war, her mother died of grief, her brother was imprisoned and transported to the West Indies as a slave, her fiancée fled to France and abandoned her while the sequestration committee confiscated all the family's money leaving her alone in the world without a penny and with nowhere to live.

The sequestration committee was in charge of seizing Royalist houses, land and money and handing it to the Government. Bradshaw was legal adviser to the committee. His job was to hear appeals from distraught Royalists, consider the paperwork and recommend whether they should be deprived of their money.

Few Cavalier families got it all back. In some cases they could buy the return of their estates by appealing to the Committee for Compounding with Delinquents, in return for a hefty sum of money up front. Parliament's constant need for cash allowed the committee and Judge Bradshaw to do deals with less ardent Royalists if there was enough ready money to be had – but that was a lot of ready money because the committee demanded three times an estate's annual income and if you'd just had all your property confiscated, it was hard to raise the needful.

Payments did not just go to the State, of course. This was a lucrative trade. Committeemen were willing to see things from the victim's point of view – for a reasonable consideration. It was understood. That's why they sat for hours on end listening to the weeping and wailing of miserable mothers and deprived daughters.

Bradshaw told me, 'You can't be too careful. These Countesses and Viscountesses pretend they had nothing to do with their husbands' behaviour but then you hear from witnesses the women were more rabid in their hatred of Parliament than the men. They deserve to be cast adrift without a penny.'

The committee was doing God's work. Apparently, He wanted to enrich his faithful at the expense of the King's supporters. Officially, the committeemen were not allowed to profit from their work. But when your job is to confiscate lucrative estates from delinquent Royalists, sell them and pass the proceeds on to Parliament, it is hardly surprising some of the pious saw the spiritual necessity of rewarding themselves and their friends by picking up country houses, estates, land and rents at knock-down prices. Was it their fault the market for palaces, manors, castles, halls, granges and the like had slumped and prices were at an all-time low? It was a damned nuisance if the only man who wanted to occupy some former abbey recently owned by one of Charles's loyal followers happened to be their wife's brother.

The Saints, from Cromwell down, were enjoying the fruits of their Holy War. King Crum, once an impecunious member of the lesser gentry, was coining at least £10,000 a year. He'd been handed Royalists' estates in East Anglia, Hampshire, Gloucestershire and South Wales. Admittedly he'd killed a lot of people to acquire such wealth but he did so under a cloak of legitimacy thanks to his sequestration committee.

True, Royalist castles were not simply taken over, they were pulled down. Corfe, Kenilworth, Newark and about 100 others were made uninhabitable to punish their owners. Other strongholds had been destroyed in the fighting. Some were burned to the ground by one side to prevent them falling into the other's hands. Destruction was everywhere.

Even so, land is wealth and what was once a Cavalier's miraculously became a Roundhead's.

However, our ever-merciful Parliament decreed wives and children who were not guilty of fighting with the King should not starve. They could have one-fifth of their family wealth restored to them if their appeal was successful.

This Lucy, sitting outside Bradshaw's offices gnashing her teeth, complained he would not even discuss her case. She spat at the door in fury. 'Tyrants. These people call His Majesty a tyrant but they're the oppressors. They're the thieves. They're the ungodly.'

'Be careful what you say, madam,' I warned and glanced around. There were no guards in earshot, just a preacher crossing the lawn with a Bible tucked under his arm like a sword. 'Tell me your name. I'm visiting Judge Bradshaw, perhaps I can intercede.'

She looked me up and down and sneered contemptuously, 'I don't need your help. You're one of them. A damned fanatic.'

'I assure you I am not, madam. I am a physician.'

Why I was bantering with this doxy I cannot say. Perhaps it was because I was compassionate and sympathised with her plight. Perhaps it was because she was spirited, not to say attractive. I don't think I had baser motives but maybe I did. I can't remember now. In any case, I took her to a tavern and bought her a meat pie and some madeira. She wolfed them down as if she'd never seen food before. I ordered another pie. It was supposedly lamb though it was hard to be sure. My guest did not care.

Eventually satisfied, she told me her name and more of her plight. She was Lucy Lighthorne. Her family owned an estate not far from the Viscount's castle at Broughton. Father Sir John fought and died at Edgehill. Mother died after the Roundheads sacked the family home, Lighthorne Hall, taking away just about all their possessions. Her brother was captured at Naseby and, by all accounts, he had been transported with other officers and men to the West Indies to work as a slave on the Spanish plantations. The Lighthornes were condemned as delinquents. Some months after Lighthorne Hall was raided, commissioners threw Lucy out and commandeered the estate.

As for her fiancée, he was a poet. He'd been imprisoned in '43 for writing something scurrilous about the Earl of Essex. Then he went to France to raise money for the Royalist cause. He got no further than Calais, where he fought a duel. He may have died; he may still be alive. Miss Lighthorne had not heard from him or any of their friends. She tried to contact his parents but they were on their estate in Scotland and communication was more or less impossible, still less travel to some far-flung part of that benighted country.

For a time, she had been given comfort and shelter by an aunt in the West Country. They defended her aunt's castle from siege but surrendered eventually. The survivors were thrown out. Her aunt, a Lady Grant, fled abroad with her own daughters but Lucy chose to stay in England and fight for the return of the family fortune.

She had been singularly unsuccessful and was now lodging with one of her former servants, a woman called Agnes, in Cripplegate, just about the lowest of all the low places in London. Lucy, at the age of 19, was exhausted, starving, wretched and angry.

I resolved to expose the greed of the Saints in the pages of "Pragmaticus". I also resolved to discuss Lucy Lighthorne's plight with John Bradshaw and I resolved to meet Lucy again in three days' time when I hoped to have news.

She tripped away looking, if not exactly happy, then at least grateful, which was something.

'Rushed off my feet, Marchamont,' said Bradshaw, looking up from a pile of documents but not rising or offering me much more than a brief smile.

He had two assistants poring over documents in the anteroom. 'Lilburne, you know,' Bradshaw said, as if that were explanation enough.

'What now?'

'We got him out of prison. We got him compensation for what they'd stolen from him. But the Lords have jailed him again even though half of London is up in arms in support for the Levellers.'

'Everyone's wearing their green ribbons,' I said, 'Especially the women.'

'Yes, well, the Lords are mad to suppress "freeborn John". The more they try to silence him, the louder his supporters cry his name. Anyway, I'm preparing another appeal on his behalf. And then there's all this committee work….' He indicated piles of documents scattered across his large desk.

'That's what I wanted to talk to you about, John,' I said. 'Specifically, a friend of mine, one Lucy Lighthorne.'

'A friend of yours, Marchamont?' He looked sceptical and half-amused. I think I may have grinned a little as if in acknowledgement of some unspoken understanding between us. Bradshaw nodded decisively. 'Let me see.'

He stood, went to the outer office, had a word with one of his clerks, returned with some documents tied up with red ribbon. He looked carefully at the top paper. 'Yes, well, I dare say we have been a little harsh,' he said, making a few amendments. 'Where we said she should not be allowed more than £20 a year, I think we meant £200. There, that should do it.' Bradshaw added the missing nought to the document, rolled it up, tied the ribbon and returned it to the outer office.

'Case comes up day after tomorrow,' he said. 'Don't expect any difficulty. Now, Nedham, I really must get on.'

We shook hands and parted.

The next time I saw my old boss was the day he sentenced my new boss to death.

CHAPTER 21

In vain doth valour bleed
While Avarice
and Rapine share
the land

Summer and autumn 1648

Can you imagine anything more ridiculous than a sonnet dedicated to a General written half-way through a siege? I couldn't decide if John Milton was mad or some sort of demented genius. Not content with railing against the institution of marriage (his wife came back home and gave him two children so it wasn't all bad) and demanding free speech (he became a censor), he turned his hand to praising Thomas Fairfax. Ambition, I suppose. It can't have been money. He'd been left enough by his father and inherited his father-in-law's estate in Witney, near Oxford, as well. Short of money, Milton was not.

War had broken out again. Cromwell was marching north with another army to give the Scotch a good hiding. Fairfax was camped outside Colchester, poised to reduce the city to ruins as soon as its starving inhabitants finished eating all their cats and dogs.

Milton assumed Fairfax, not Cromwell, was about to become the chief of men. He thought he knew which side his bread was buttered and John Milton was full of praise of the Captain General of the Armies.

I visited Milton at his new home in High Holborn. The garden opened onto Lincolns-Inn Fields. He thought the country air would improve his health while the quiet would let him pursue his studies in peace. But he was worried about his eyesight. It was getting worse. He said his vision was misty and his left eye in particular seemed to be dimming. His head ached most of the time.

'Hmm,' I said, after examining his eyes, which were surprisingly clear.

'Darkness visible, is it?'

I told him to light more candles and spend less time reading and writing. I did consider syphilis but Milton would have recoiled at the very word. I decided it wouldn't be worth the heartache to make even the most tentative suggestion in that direction. He would have been utterly appalled to have the French disease. It might have tipped him completely over the edge. I wondered if it was wrong for a physician not to pursue every possibility. Was it unethical? Neglectful?

I knew Milton was consulting others so, if there was any real risk, someone else could take responsibility for delivering the bad news. And anyway, if he'd got the disease and passed it on to his wife, the damage was done already. Giving him mercury would not, in my professional opinion, improve his health no matter what other quacks might believe.

I offered more practical advice but my patient was a difficult man. Milton was delicate: thin, meticulous, neat, tidy, exacting and sober. He dressed like a pious clergyman and spoke softly. He was never knowingly happy. Yet he was combative in his own way. He wrote like a thuggish Norman warrior or, at the very least, one of Cromwell's most furious Ironsides. I think he saw himself as a Crusader.

He presented me with his little sonnet in praise of General Fairfax. It was tolerable, I suppose. I quoted the last two lines back at him, '"In vain doth Valour bleed while Avarice, & Rapine share the land". What exactly does that mean, Milton?'

'Too many people,' he said quietly, gazing sightlessly at his jar of porter, 'Are exploiting these wars for money. Where is God? Why are they lining their pockets when we must create a new republic?'

'Have you been to Colchester?' I asked.

'That is beside the point, Marchamont. One does not need to make the tedious trip to Colchester to know the General will achieve what he has set out to achieve and give England the truth and liberty we have been fighting for all this time.'

'Truth and liberty is it?' I asked doubtfully.

'Which we shall only achieve by taking the obvious course.'

'Which is?'

'I am writing a book to explain it.'

'To explain what, Milton?'

'The King. He has to go.'

'Into exile?' I asked with feigned innocence.

'Execution,' said Milton. 'I've told Fairfax, I've told Cromwell, and Sir Henry. It has to be done. He cannot be trusted. He intrigues with everybody – the Scots, the Levellers, even officers in the army. He's trying to set us all against each other. Royalists talk about financing an uprising by the Levellers – what kind of a Hell would that be?'

'Better to reign in Hell than serve in Heaven,' I joked but Milton ignored me.

He went on, 'Divide and rule. It's the King's only policy. He has no loyalty; he speaks no truth. He is a traitor to his country. A tyrant.'

'A King,' I reminded Milton. 'A King. God's anointed. God's, Milton, God's.'

'God does not permit traitors to His faith or His country. God is a just God, a vengeful God.'

'Really? I suppose you think you understand God and think you can justify the ways of God to men? Good luck with that.' I think I spoke with a little more vehemence than I intended. In any case, Milton looked shocked.

'Marchamont, I thought you and I were of the same persuasion.'

'But the King, Milton. Executing the King. What law is left if we kill the King? How can it be lawful? The King is the law. Get rid of the King and you're left with chaos and old night – a wild anarchy. In that cursed hour we will see close ambition varnished over with pretended zeal and it will be sword-law through all the country.'

There was a long silence as Milton gazed out towards his garden without seeing much. He sipped his beer and then said quietly, 'I know you, Marchamont.' He smiled regretfully. 'You have a nice turn of phrase.'

I was shocked. Nobody knew my secret. I was a medical man. Why did Milton think otherwise?

'I can still read, you know. And I see well enough to recognise ink stains. You haven't washed them off your hands today.'

Milton thought of himself as the intellectual brains of the revolution.

Would he betray me? How much danger was I in? I couldn't tell but when Washington and I met for oysters at the Angel in King Street, Westminster, I said Milton was aware I was still writing and though he didn't directly accuse me of writing "Pragmaticus", he didn't have to; it was obvious he had worked it out.

It was too dangerous to carry on, I said.

'You can't stop now, Marchamont,' Washington replied. His high forehead was creased with frowns of anxiety. 'We need all the ammunition we can get.'

'You know there is yet another delegation being sent to the Isle of Wight, don't you? My uncle's among them. He's not optimistic. He writes that the King is disputing every point.'

'The people are with the King,' said Washington rather hopelessly.

'Even so, I can't risk carrying on any longer,' I said.

Washington rubbed his chin with a large, calloused hand. It was the sort of hand used to swinging a sword. It was a big, threatening hand. 'I'm not the only one who knows what an invaluable contribution Marchamont Nedham is making to the King's cause, you know.' He sighed. 'If you give up now, some people may not take kindly to it.'

'Is that a threat?' I asked.

'Not at all, Marchamont,' Washington smiled. 'But you know how it is. There are many hot-heads about and few people able to keep them under control. I really could not be answerable for their actions.'

I carried on.

Admittedly there was another reason why I continued to work for the King, apart from loyalty to the Monarch and fear of reprisals if I were to stop.

My new friend Lucy Lighthorne.

My wife Lucy took time to recover from the birth and death of our second child. I consoled her as much as I could but she sought succour from the Lord rather than from her lord and master. She was philosophical. Several times, she told me with bowed head, 'The Lord is nigh unto them that are of a broken heart; and saveth such as be of a contrite spirit.'

She spent more time with her cronies, listening to interminable sermons by semi-literate preachers, studying the Bible with the chosen people and avoiding those not of the same faith. She was derisive about the Royalists who revolted against Parliament and the army. She mocked the starving men and women of Colchester besieged by Fairfax. She took to the streets to welcome the army when its men asserted their superiority over the Presbyterian London militia. She even questioned the Levellers for threatening to come out in support of the King.

For some months after the death of baby Theodosia, we did not share the same bed.

Which was perhaps just as well.

It took time for Lucy Lighthorne to secure the money Bradshaw said she should be allowed. I became her adviser. I helped her find more suitable lodgings. Coincidentally, her rooms were quite near those I was secretly renting to work on "Prag". I lent her money to set herself up, employ a woman and meet the expenses of a lengthy trip up to Warwickshire where she had to talk to the local committee. They were reluctant to carry out the restitution ordered at Bradshaw's recommendation because the spoils had already been distributed among the local Parliamentary squires.

Eventually, though, Lucy got the money she was due. It was enough to allow her to live in comfort provided she was not extravagant.

She came back to London in the early autumn, full of news from the provinces. She claimed support for the King was growing day by day. Even in the Earl of Warwick's own county – the Earl had recently been re-appointed admiral of Parliament's navy – support for the King was marked. There had been riots.

There was more she wanted to tell me. She looked at me with her wide, innocent eyes and said, 'Marchamont, you have saved me, you are my protector, can I trust you?'

'Of course, my dear,' I smiled, taking her hand and stroking it.

She was sitting on the floor and buried her head in my lap, her words muffled as she spoke, as if this might somehow reduce their impact. 'I have a message for Lord Cottington.'

Cottington had been the King's Chancellor of the Exchequer and was now in exile with Prince Charles in Holland.

'Lucy,' I said, 'You know you have only been given this money back because Bradshaw ruled you were not guilty of actively supporting the King, don't you?'

She nodded, head still buried in my lap.

'Yet you carry a message – who from? – to a leading Royalist. Do you know how dangerous that is?'

She nodded again. There may have been a few tears.

'Well, to prove you can trust me, let me tell you a secret of my own. You know that newsbook you like so much, "Mercurius Pragmaticus"?'

She looked up.

'Behold the author.'

She sat up in surprise but before she could respond, I went on, 'Even so, you should not be carrying messages for Royalists. Women have no business involving themselves in such dangerous games.'

'Why should I not?' she demanded indignantly. 'These people have destroyed my life. I will do whatever I can to destroy them and preserve the King. They may call me a traitor but they are the ones who have betrayed their oaths to His Majesty. They are the traitors.'

I had to prevent her raising her voice and being unmasked. The walls were thin enough and there were spies everywhere. No servant could be trusted. 'Shhhh, Lucy, shhh,' I said, kissing her on the lips.

Some time later, as we lay in each other's arms, she made another confession.

She told me she was a Papist. A Catholic.

A servant of Beelzebub and the Whore of Babylon.

What was I to do?

She did look lovely.

CHAPTER 22

Mr Nath. Fines, who demanding
by what power he was
committed, it was answered,
By the power of the sword

December 1648

I was fast asleep, sleeping the sleep of the just.

A hammering at the door on a cold, bleak, before-dawn morning.

I feared the worst.

It didn't seem fair to arrest a man for speaking the truth in a newsbook but that's a risk we run in the noble pursuit of enlightening the masses. It could have been a patient needing urgent attention but, somehow, I thought otherwise. Guilty conscience, perhaps.

The knocking was loud, peremptory, demanding. It woke my wife Lucy, who fell to her knees to begin her morning prayers. Lucy's piety was of no immediate use. I struggled into breeches, shirt and boots aiming to squeeze out of a back window to escape this latest arrest (I'd worked out a route some weeks before). Yet as I emerged from my room our servant Mary came hurrying up the stairs with a piece of paper.

'Message, sir,' she said, 'The gentleman said he could not stay.'

The message was from my old Lincoln's Inn friend Nat Rich. We still bumped into each other from time to time. I wrote up Rich's military heroics in "Britanicus" some time ago and he had not forgotten. It helped his career. He was now captain of a regiment of horse.

The note just said, 'Marchamont, Tell your uncle John Glynn not to attend Parliament this morning. Your friend, Rich.'

I had no idea what was going on but I took the warning seriously enough to rush over to the judge's lodgings near the Palace of Westminster, where he was just dressing.

Judge Glynn had endured an unhappy time. He fled abroad after being excluded from Parliament only to be enticed back by promises that he could speak his mind without fear of arrest. That wasn't true. Soon enough he was jailed in the Tower because he said he did not believe the army should run the country.

He spent all winter in one of the Tower's more comfortable apartments but it was not pleasant. No sooner was he released than he rode West for his brother Thomas's funeral in Caernarvon. Then, in the summer of '48, he was sent by Parliament to negotiate with the King at Carisbrook Castle. The talks got nowhere.

Judge John was no longer a young man. At 46, and somewhat corpulent, these travails were exhausting him. He was pale and shocked when I handed him Rich's note. 'I don't know what's going on,' I said, 'But it's clear the army is up to something. It might be wise to make yourself scarce.'

The Judge took the warning seriously enough to beat a hasty retreat. He left London straight away and headed for my step-father's home in Burford; a convenient place from which to negotiate with Mr Speaker Lenthall for his safety.

I headed down to Parliament. What was going on?

I saw Rich's cavalry lining the streets, backed up by a troop of men looking grim. On the threshold of the House itself stood a little group of soldiers barring entry while one particularly officious officer checked each arrival against a list of names. A few were permitted to pass on into the Chamber. Many more were denied entry and, instead, were marched off by a trooper holding onto his arm.

I recognised the lackey with the list as Thomas Pride, the loathsome drayman who arrested me over the "Britanicus" business. He was now a colonel, it seemed, but that didn't stop him smirking. He was obviously enjoying himself.

Pride was arresting any MP who would not submit to the army's demands. As they marched the excluded MPs away, to be held in the local taverns, including Hell and Heaven, soldiers angrily demanded the pay they were owed. The MPs claimed it had all been pocketed by their commanders. One or two MPs and soldiers came to blows but nobody was killed.

The crisis came after Parliament voted to carry on negotiating with the King. The army ran out of patience. Its commanders decided a more helpful Parliament was needed, a compliant Parliament that would abandon the endless talks.

No fewer than 140 MPs were excluded; 40 were jailed. It left a rump of just 56 MPs willing to do as the army instructed.

Pride's Purge sorted the negotiators from the king-killers.

CHAPTER 23

In came that pure holy Goblin Nol Cromwell,
who brought in along his fellow saint Henry Marten,
who looks thin, as if he had gotten a Scottish clap

December 1648

Toothache is a sore affliction. It especially seems to plague the great men of Huntingdon. Oliver Cromwell was almost conquered by the pain. Where no sword, pike, rifle, musket, arquebus, canon or cavalry charge succeeded, a gum infection was enough to lay low the great general for days on end.

He would have us believe he lay on his sick-bed in his modest little farmhouse with his common little wife and held a clove to the pain.

At most times in a life, a sore tooth might not be of any great significance. We all have difficulties from time to time and seek out a barber or blacksmith to rid us of the offending instrument of torture. Many a head is short of its own teeth and relies on those of dogs or sheep.

Cromwell claimed he was indisposed during Pride's purge. It was a military coup. The regime changed. The army took over. Politicians who did not approve were side-lined. Yet Oliver Cromwell, the army strong man, was nowhere to be seen, because of his terribly painful toothache.

It was the most convenient toothache in history.

Cromwell arrived in London the day after the purge. We were asked to believe the coup had been orchestrated by Henry Ireton without the knowledge, let alone support, of his father-in-law Oliver Cromwell. If Nol had objected to the army take-over, he could have reversed it. He didn't.

Obviously.

Poor old Nat Fiennes was one of the purged. At least they let him leave London. I looked in on him before his departure and promised to visit at Broughton.

Nat was fortunate not to be on the list of those who were to be jailed. It seemed likely Cromwell would order a series of public executions of the supposed traitors in Parliament. I enjoyed speculating in "Prag" about who was for the chop. Some of Parliament's most well-known names, people like William Prynne and even the General Sir William Waller, were likely to have their heads separated from their bodies as the army got down to its bloody work.

I reminded readers that only the restoration of the King could possibly stop this bloodshed. The army was guilty of subverting the fundamental laws and constitution of the nation, demolishing the very foundations of Government.

And I had fun pointing out how convenient Oliver Cromwell's toothache turned out to be. He and Fairfax both claimed complete ignorance of the plot in advance. Fairfax was angry. He refused to have anything to do with what followed, which made his denial credible. Cromwell, on the other hand, took advantage of the coup, which made his denial incredible.

Over the next few weeks I used "Pragmaticus" to argue against the terrible prospect that Cromwell really did intend to execute King Charles. Surely the grandees would not go to such an extreme.

I reported the Earl of Warwick, admiral of the Navy, refused to back the army and believed the peace treaty offered to the King was too onerous for the Monarch to accept. Warwick later insisted this claim was untrue. He would say that, wouldn't he? Just because Warwick denied it was no proof it wasn't true. It is a well-established principle of news-writing that, just because someone important says a claim is untrue, that does not actually make the claim untrue. The real question is how much embarrassment the exposure of his private thoughts might cause the grandee accused of thinking them. If an admiral as important as the Earl of Warwick was exposed as being disloyal to Cromwell and the army, he might well wonder how safe his head was on his shoulders. In that case, he would be keen to express his undying loyalty to the most powerful faction in the country.

So Warwick denied my report. That didn't mean it was untrue. Even if it was mistaken, so what? My job was to sow dissent. The Warwick story certainly did that.

As well as doing my best to expose the hypocrisy, greed and tyranny of Cromwell and his cronies, I warned that if we were to be denied peaceable Government under hereditary Kings, our country faced rebellion after rebellion because no power would ever be legitimate, especially if Government kept changing at the pleasure of the people.

The news wrote itself. The coup was marvellous copy for the country's most successful newsbook. We were selling in record numbers. Everybody wanted to read the news, or have it read to them, and "Prag" had a reputation for hard-hitting editorials coupled with wit, mockery and disdain for the saints and grandees now seizing power.

It wasn't plain sailing. Some of my contacts were arrested, others, like my uncle, fled London. Charles was taken from Carisbrook Castle to some less salubrious place on the mainland and marched back to London under heavy guard. The only surprise was that he had not yet been murdered by one of Cromwell's saints.

The remnants of the Commons passed a resolution demanding the army redouble its efforts to capture and punish the author of "Prag" and any other Royalist rags they might find. But the beagles were always on the wrong scent and my cover was not exposed, not by John Milton or my new friend Lucy Lighthorne. The person most likely to throw me to the wolves was my own dear wife. Luckily, she was busy demonstrating in support of the army.

After not celebrating Christmas and before the start of the New Year, which we were prohibited from marking in any other way than by penance and fasting, it became apparent the grandees really were planning to put the King on trial. Cromwell convened his king-killing committee and appointed none other than John Bradshaw as its chairman.

CHAPTER 24

When God extends himself
to any man, he must doe
whatsoever he would have
of him, though it be to the committing of Adultery

January-April 1649

I couldn't go around openly doctoring any more. My secret life was under investigation. I went into hiding.

Where better than in the loving arms of my new friend Lucy Lighthorne?

My sweet Roman Catholic became my go-between, passing reports and messages to Washington while the grandees convened their supreme court to try the King.

I had to be there. Lucy Lighthorne and I went together, shoving through the crowds as we tried to get a place inside Westminster Hall for the trial itself. People were everywhere, jostling and fighting for a view. Some seats were set aside for the great and good. Lucy pointed out Fairfax's wife Lady Anne, a fearsome-looking woman. Lucy knew her, leaned over a barrier and spoke to her briefly. I kept my distance and curtseyed modestly – if asked, I was Lucy's servant Nancy Yubberton but nobody noticed the bent old woman trailing two steps behind Lucy Lighthorne, whose startlingly good looks and imperious carriage always attracted attention.

Suddenly a blast from six trumpeters startled us all. The trumpeters rode horses into the hall leading a small procession. The court president, John Bradshaw, in a startling scarlet cloak, walked sedately to his throne-like seat and called for order. He then read out a roll-call of his fellow judges starting with the name of General Fairfax. Lady Fairfax cried out so everyone could hear, 'He has more wit than to be here.'

Bradshaw had no idea how to react. He frowned, grinned, smiled, coughed, pulled his sleeves, stood, sat again, banged his gavel, cleared his throat, looked at his clerk for help, stood again, and then continued reading from his list of more than 60 judges.

When most – though not all – of those names had acknowledged their presence, Bradshaw called for the prisoner to be brought in. I studied my friend as we waited for the King's arrival. It was cold. His cloak was tightly wrapped around him. He wore a peculiar-looking, broad-brimmed Puritan hat. Lucy whispered, loudly enough for others to hear and murmur approval, 'That hat is bullet-proof. Bradshaw's afraid he will be killed, not the King.'

When the King was finally brought into the hall, Bradshaw began with a long diatribe explaining to the King why he had been brought to trial. He and the King descended into legal argument. The King wrapped Bradshaw in knots. The King demanded to know by what authority he was being tried. Bradshaw couldn't answer. The debate went round and round until eventually, humiliated, Bradshaw adjourned the hearing, the King was led away and the crowd dispersed.

We didn't go to the later hearings. One was more than enough. There was no legitimacy to their charges of treason nor did Bradshaw and his crew of cut-throats have any right to try a King. The hearings were a sham and it was plain to all observers that Charles had the best of the debates.

The trial lasted from January 20 to January 27. Three days later they executed the King.

Poor Bradshaw. He would never get over the stigma of being the King-killer-in-chief. He was only following Cromwell's orders but he didn't have to take on the task. Partly, I suppose, he believed in the cause of liberty, whatever that might be, but mainly, I fear, he enjoyed Somerhill House in Kent, the mansion he was given, and all the other worldly rewards his treachery earned him.

I sometimes wonder why I stayed on friendly terms with Bradshaw for the next decade.

While they were killing the King, Lucy Lighthorne and I thought it politic to make a tactical withdrawal from London and put "Prag" to one side for a week or two. There was the King's own memoir to work on, for a start. I helped produce and distribute his autobiography "Eikon Basilike", the book that did so much to enhance Charles's reputation and make the country weep over his tragic murder.

I tried to explain to my wife that I was being hunted once again by Parliament and I had no option but to leave London for somewhere more congenial.

'But why, husband?' she asked. 'You are a physician, not a scribbling scandal-monger.'

'Up to a point, my dear, up to a point,' I squirmed. 'Alas...' I was wringing my hands. I held them out like a schoolboy to display my ink-stains.

'So?' she said. 'That comes from mixing your lotions and potions.' She paused, thinking. 'Doesn't it?' she demanded.

'It is ink, my dear.'

Lucy was incredulous. 'Ink? Wherefore?'

I confessed I had still been involved in newsbooks.

'Oh Marchamont, why didn't you say so?' she smiled indulgently and ran a hand down my sleeve. 'Of course.' Obviously, she assumed it was a Parliamentarian rag.

'This is awkward but I do not have time to discuss it, Lucy, I must be gone,' I said, hurrying to throw some clothes into a bag. 'Truth is I've been working for the King. "Mercurius Pragmaticus".'

She looked at me with alarm and shock. I expected fury. I was afraid she might attack me, scratch out my eyes. Instead, she said quietly but clearly, 'Yea, mine own familiar friend in whom I trusted, that ate of my bread, hath lifted up his heel against me.' She turned and walked quickly away.

The other Lucy wanted to get married. We left London with no real idea where to go. We could not head for Oxford or Burford, where I might be recognised, but I wanted somewhere close enough to London to carry on working on "Prag".

We headed for Warwickshire, where Lucy was from. Luckily, she had cash. There was so much poverty and disillusion most people were happy to provide bed and board for ready money without asking questions. A man and his wife travelling in the dead of winter, as news of the King's execution blanketed the country like a sad covering of snow, aroused suspicion but, in those days, everyone minded their own business for fear of attracting unwanted attention.

We rode from lodging house to ale-house to tavern without even a servant. We called ourselves Mr and Mrs York. It was a cold and comfortless time. We said we were trying to find relatives we'd been separated from by the war. Most people accepted this – all over the country, families had been split asunder, bereaved and made homeless by the wars.

Some friends of Lucy gave us the use of a little cottage on the outskirts of a small village called Burton Hastings and we set up home together. They said they could not supply a servant or a cook as the war had impoverished them. We tried to make the best of it.

There was a welcome appearance of spring. The larks were singing. I heard a cuckoo and told Lucy I'd seen a swallow, though she didn't believe me. For a few short weeks, we enjoyed a pastoral idyll.

Lucy taught herself to cook. She said she had seen others doing it in the past and it couldn't be that difficult. Obtaining food was harder. She expected me to go hunting, catch rabbits and hares and skin them. I did try. I managed to stab a rabbit to death. I even skinned it, after a fashion, but so badly there was scarcely any meat left to eat. Lucy laughed and set about the next one herself, determined and undaunted.

We bought milk, eggs, bread, beer and other essentials from suspicious locals who charged high prices and handed over their goods resentfully.

We had been in Burton Hastings several weeks before I could get word back to London and publish the first of the new series of "Mercurius Pragmaticus, For King Charles II". It didn't do to accept the new regime as legitimate, I said, it was usurping the freedoms and liberties of the nation. There was only one legitimate ruler, I said, and that was the

King now in The Hague.

Lucy wrote to friends. Somehow, she managed to procure the services of a Catholic priest. I explained yet again I was already married, to another Lucy in fact. I had not kept that attachment a secret. She laughed and said it was not a real marriage in the eyes of God because it had not been conducted according to the rites of the Roman church. She wished to be my wife and a Catholic ceremony would cement our relationship without breaking any vows I may have made to Lucy Collyer because I was not her husband in the eyes of God.

Who was I to question God?

Father James Roberts was a Scot. He came with news of the latest disaster to befall the King's supporters north of the border. Cromwell had executed the Marquess of Hamilton. It was no great loss. The man was hated by everyone he dealt with. In "Prag", I said it would be hard to tell where Hamilton's soul had gone because:

> 'A Scotch man enters Hell at's birth
> And 'scapes it when he goes to earth
> Assur'd no worse a Hell can come
> Than that which he enjoy'd at home.

Father Roberts told me Cromwell and his savage crew stood nearby scoffing and triumphing at the ruin of Hamilton and two other Peers who were executed at the same time. They watched the grizzly ceremony through binoculars to enjoy a closer view of their bloody deeds. Lucy and I were duly disgusted.

We were married in the Roman way by Father Roberts, in secret, in a secret chapel they knew of. The following day my new wife announced Father Roberts had given her a message for the new King in Holland. She had to leave immediately.

We parted, Lucy for Folkestone, me for Minster Lovell to seek refuge with my old friend Edward Heylyn and his brother Peter.

Which is where I was trapped when Oliver Cromwell came hunting down the Levellers.

CHAPTER 25

A True Relation of the Proceedings in the Business of Burford with other Discourse of public concernment

May 1649

'Christmas was the last straw,' Big Susie told me as we lay in her little garret at The George after we had become reunited in the usual way. 'What's wrong with Christmas, I'd like to know?' She was indignant. 'How dare they cancel Christmas and call me ungodly? What's ungodly about celebrating the birth of Our Saviour? And what's wrong with a few drinks, some food and a bit of fun? I ask you...' Susie sat up in the bed, pulling the sheets around her ample charms. 'These people think there's something Satanish about enjoying yourself. If God hadn't wanted us to enjoy ourselves, he wouldn't have given us strong drink, good food and handsome men.' Susie stroked me affectionately. We hadn't seen each other for two years but she was as welcoming as ever. A good friend.

'And whose side are you on these days, Monty?' she asked with a chuckle. Susie knew my career was not entirely straightforward.

'Well, the truth is, my dear Chastity' – she slapped me on the arm – 'I'm not sure where I stand. I was for Parliament, then I was for the King. Now, though...'

'It's the army for you, Captain Nedham,' she answered and started to hum a marching tune.

We heard a commotion downstairs and the landlord shouting for Susie, Chastity, to come and help. She threw on a shift and apron and scurried away. I took my time to dress while looking out of the garret window. Dozens of soldiers marched haphazardly down the steep main street towards the river. Another troop passing through Burford, I thought.

The George was frequently used by the better sort of traveller to break their journey. I wondered who this lot were and what they wanted. Could I risk descending the stairs to find out? Perhaps this might be something worth recording, not that the world was short of news but a reporter must always keep his eyes open for a good story.

These uniformed yokels wouldn't know who I was, I decided, having studied their aimless wanderings. They were after free quarter. Free quarter was the ruin of many a town. Soldiers turned up, demanding board and lodging, the best food, as much drink as they could manage and, as often as not, the favour of the local wives and daughters – most of it taken by force if not volunteered quickly enough – and then, at best, they issued pieces of paper promising their army would pay for it just as soon as they won the war. They ate everyone out of house and home then roamed the countryside looking for more – chickens, sheep, pigs and cattle were stolen every day, leaving farmers and smallholders in despair.

I slipped outside. The rabble filling the street turned out to be a squadron of Levellers. Poor bastards. All they really wanted was to get paid for the fighting they'd done and go home. But Parliament didn't have money for peasants and Cromwell wanted cannon-fodder for his crusade to rid Ireland of Papists. Several regiments refused to fight unless they were paid up to date and given the freedom to choose between Ireland and home.

Unfortunately, they dressed up these reasonable demands with a load of militant politics. I take some pride in the fact that I was first to name them Levellers in one of my not-infrequent attacks on their Utopianism but no matter how many times I pointed out that levelling up would bring anarchy, they insisted they had God and the Bible on their side. In January, they'd seen the King executed; they thought anything was possible.

I mean, really, can you imagine? A country without a hierarchy, where every man was equal, and nobody was greater than anybody else (except for Catholics and servants)? The first thing they'd want is to get their hands on the land and the money. That's what anybody does when he gets power. But in a world where every man was on the same level, there would never be enough money to go round. We'd all be equally poor, ill-educated and squalid. It's no wonder their philosophy wasn't popular among their superiors – not just Royalists and Dukes but merchants, tradesmen, landowners, anyone with a bit of money.

Chaos arrived in Burford with the Levellers. They were weary, half-starved, badly led and not sure where they were going. Their vague aim was, apparently, to meet dissidents from other regiments before demanding a conference with Cromwell, Fairfax and the rest of the military junta.

They hadn't bargained for the junta preparing to meet them first.

I slipped past Leveller soldiers sitting around swigging beer and arguing about God and found my way to the parsonage. I wanted to pay my respects to my dear mother and step-father.

The Rev Christopher Glynn was not at home. He was outside his church trying to prevent further depredations at the hands of invading Puritans.

My step-father was a good man, the only father I ever knew – Marchamont Nedham the First, my real father, died when I was one. Rev Glynn had been my teacher as well as my parent. He was a friendly, mild-mannered, patient fellow with a calm look and a hesitant half-smile. He could be stern and bad-tempered, when he was teaching at Burford Grammar School, which he ran in addition to his duties at St John the Baptist's. But he was naturally kind. He had no time for the new creeds and faiths springing up all over the country but he thought they should be tolerated. He said most of them would wither and die soon enough.

My mother was in the garden waving her arms vigorously at half a dozen soldiers who were trying to set up camp there. She was supported by her two servants, plump little Mary – grand-daughter of a Papist who must now be in Purgatorio or worse – and pretty Faith, daughter of a farm-hand from Great Milton. The Leveller soldiers were arguing over the garden wall. Marjorie, my mother, gave as good as she got.

'Ah Mrs Glynn, may I be of service?' I asked in a loud enough voice to still all argument as I marched smartly across the lane to the garden.

'These men are demanding free quarter, Captain,' she called back.

It was the use of the word Captain which threw them. Mother knew not to reveal my true identity but she also knew that, from time to time, I was known by the rank of Captain. Whether I was a naval or an army captain was never explained; I was just Captain Nedham sometimes, when it suited, and today, it suited. I was not in uniform but my bearing was noble and my voice had a natural air of authority.

One of the men, a tall, thin youth with one arm in a sling, turned to me. 'We're asking for quarter sir,' he said.

'I can see that. Be off with you. This house has been commandeered by your superiors. What regiment are you, anyway? I may need a word with your commanding officer. Where is he quartered?'

I find most of the time people will take you at your assessment of yourself. If you act like an officer in the army, they will not question you and will react accordingly. Thus, these soldiers, already despondent, were unwilling to risk my wrath. They slinked off muttering and I turned to my mother, arms and grin wide.

I wouldn't say my mother disapproved of me but she preferred not to know what I was up to. She would say ignorance was bliss. If I was safe, she was happy. Then she would ask, with a frown which made her look even older than her 50 years, 'You are safe, now, Marchamont, aren't you and eating properly?' and I would grin and assure her I was.

'Is little Robert here?' I asked.

Robert was my step-brother, aged 17. He was not at home, as I should have realised. He was at university in Oxford. I took my mother by the arm and led her away from the servants, further into the garden, where roses were starting to bud.

Mother, dressed in something like Puritan black with a white apron, a brooch and rings on her fingers, wanted to know where I'd been since the dreadful day of the King's execution. Even now, she couldn't mention it without tears. She sighed and gazed towards the meads of the river in silence, sunlight glinting on the water. The air smelt of spring, fresh-cut grass and sunlight.

'See, the birds still sing,' I said, as if that might cheer her up.

'Oh Marchamont,' she groaned, 'It's such a tragedy. I refuse to believe it is God's will. Your father says it must be but, no, it cannot be God's will for man to commit such a sin, such a crime. Like killing God himself. That cannot be His will.'

'What about these Levellers, then?' I asked, trying to change the subject.

'Poor souls,' she said, waving in the direction of the High Street. 'Cromwell's responsibility, that wicked man. They're starving. They haven't been paid. They have no money. We must find food for them.'

'I wouldn't if I were you, mother.'

'Why ever not, Marchamont? It is our Christian duty?'

'Mother, these men are mutineers. Old Nol won't treat them kindly. And he may not be well-disposed towards those who come to their aid. Think of father. Life's difficult enough for him already. You wouldn't have them in the house,' I reminded her, 'But if you start offering to feed them, you'll never get rid of them. Send them up to the priory.'

My mother clucked with amusement. 'Elizabeth would never forgive me.'

The priory, just up the hill, was the Lenthalls' home. Mr Speaker William Lenthall was the local celebrity. Mother and Mrs Lenthall were friends. They discussed gardening. They worshipped in Church together and my father used to teach their son John. William Lenthall guided my father through the constantly-changing demands placed on vicars so he stayed within the law and secure in his post. It was not a time for outspokenness from the pulpit and the Rev Glynn, never a vehement man, was skilful at ducking the cross-fire over liturgy, ceremony and prejudice.

'You did well to call me Captain, mother,' I said to change the subject.

'I assume you're in hiding, Marchamont,' she said with a frown. 'I suppose that's why we've seen nothing of you.'

I explained I'd been staying in Minster Lovell with Peter Heylyn and his brother for the past few weeks. Why, in that case, had I left it so long to call in at the parsonage? Parliament had issued a warrant for my arrest. I told my mother I'd added a new chapter to the "King's Book". I handed her a copy and drew her attention to passages written by Princess Elizabeth about her last meeting with her father. These had been smuggled out of her prison on the Isle of Wight and I added them to the book produced secretly by John Gauden, Bishop of Worcester, a friend of Washington's. It turned the King into a Protestant saint and Christian martyr.

I read a little to my mother but it soon reduced her to tears. 'Oh the poor child, oh the poor little girl,' she sobbed. 'Oh those terrible people.'

'She's in Carisbrook Castle,' I told her. 'They refuse to let her go to her mother in France.'

My mother looked at the picture on the front of the "King's Book" showing Charles kneeling with a crown of thorns in one hand and his eyes on a heavenly crown. She kneeled, held it to her lips and kissed it.

'For God's sake, mother, do you want to get arrested? What if one of the soldiers saw you? What if one of the servants did? Come inside at once. I'll get rid of the book. I'm sorry I gave it to you.'

I led her away from prying eyes into the parlour where, despite the warm weather, a fire was burning. I took care to reduce the "King's Book" to charcoal. All the while, mother was weeping and protesting about the devils who killed the King.

When I was about to go, she dried her tears, looked at me with her most disconcerting glare and asked, quietly, with a smile and a menacing voice, 'Have you seen your wife yet, Marchamont?'

'Lucy?' I said, somewhat startled by the question.

'How many wives have you got?' mother asked sarcastically. 'Of course Lucy. She misses you, poor girl.'

'I know,' I said, trying to adopt a suitably hang-dog expression.

'Well?'

'No, mother, it's the first place they would look.'

'Marchamont, your wife lives just up the road. If Cromwell's men come looking for you there, don't you think they won't come here too? How can you ignore the poor girl?'

'I will pay my respects tomorrow, mother, I promise.'

'Pay your respects? To your wife? Marchamont, really…' My mother threw her hands in the air.

Making my way back to The George, I took a detour via the church. Dozens of soldiers were milling around but there was no sign of my step-father. A couple of men were throwing large stones at the stained-glass. Each hit was greeted with a cheer as the depiction of Saint John baptising Christ gradually disintegrated. I heard the noise of further destruction from inside. A great crash suggested they were smashing the statues of Christ and Mary which stood either side of the altar.

I didn't hang around. These men were wild. Was it religious fervour,

I wondered, or criminal recklessness? By the time I reached The George, weaving my way around aimless groups of men milling about in the twilight, a meeting was under way in the main hall. It seemed the Levellers did have an officer or two.

I sneaked a look. One of them, more like a chaplain than a soldier, was banging a fist on the table and declaring, 'It's as if the Generals owe a man £20 and promise to pay him just £5 and then only on condition he puts his life at risk all over again. Why must we go to Ireland before we get paid? Why should it be decided by lots? Why not ask for volunteers? Many men would sign up for a foreign war if they were only paid what they were owed.'

'It's not a foreign war,' retorted a man who was plainly a senior officer. I squinted through the door and realised it was Francis White, brother of my printer Robert. I shrank into the shadows. White was Cromwell's man, a Major. He came from Witney, just down the highway. We had met before; he would know me. I crept past the hall towards the back stairs, aiming to retreat to Big Susie's room. But I couldn't resist eavesdropping.

The chaplain continued, 'All we ask is fair and honest treatment. The Army Council must hear our complaints.'

'If King Cromwell will permit it,' said another voice.

White laughed, 'King Cromwell, is it? No, the Lieutenant General has given me his personal pledge, on his honour. He will not follow you with force at your heels. We must come to an agreement, gentlemen, tonight or tomorrow at the latest.'

'We have been fighting for seven years and what's our reward? No free parliament, no free elections, where is our God-given English freedom?' It was the chaplain's voice again, quivering into a high-pitched whine.

A more educated voice took up the cause. 'It is true, Major. Widows are promised half a crown a week – a pittance – yet they don't even get that. Cripples might get five shillings, hardly enough for a pair of crutches. And we're told we must now murder the people of Ireland who have done us no harm. Must we wade further into the crimson stream of Christian blood?'

White chuckled again. 'This is getting us nowhere. We must draw up a reasonable request to the Generals, something they will accept, which will be of benefit to you all. You don't want to be branded mutineers, do you?'

'Mutineers?' A voice I had not heard before slammed a fist on the table, stamped his foot and shouted, 'How dare you, sir?' His footsteps seemed to be coming my way so I scampered up the back stairs to Big Susie's room.

I stayed there, dozing and listening to the noises around town, waiting for my friend to finish work. Susie finally returned around midnight, tired and smelling of ale, as the small army settled down for the night.

'Couldn't keep away then?' she laughed. 'If you think there's second helpings, think again. I've been rushed off my feet all day. And them soldiers with not a shilling between them. Richard's been taking Parliament tokens, more fool him. Worthless bits of paper. Still, I suppose it's better than being raped and having the food stolen.'

That's what I admired about Susie. Her ability to look on the bright side.

I made a space for myself on the floor – Susie's bed was far too small for two people to lie side by side rather than one on top of the other – drew my cloak around me, wished her goodnight and was on the verge of sleep when there was a loud report.

A gunshot.

A second gunshot.

A third. Some shouting. A scream of pain. Horses' hooves. Some, several, many horses. A troop.

We rushed to the window. Men carrying torches were riding down the hill. Others were coming from over the river. Those lodged at The George and other houses along the street were firing on the new arrivals wildly and indiscriminately.

'Oh my God, it's Cromwell,' I said. 'Look, you can see his standard.'

'You have to hide,' Susie commanded. 'If Cromwell catches you...'

'I'm a dead man, I know,' I said.

'Quick, the priest hole.'

We both knew about the priest hole, where they once hid Catholic priests after Guido Fawkes's Gunpowder Plot. Under the great hall, accessible through a panel in the corridor outside which led into a small room which, itself, led into the standing-room-only hole under the floor.

Big Susie shoved me into my coffin and quietly shut the lid.

I crouched and waited, too uncomfortable to sleep, too tired to think straight, a little too drunk to think at all. Luckily Susie gave me a pot to piss in.

If they dragged me out, I was pretty sure they could identify me. I was quite well-known, even before I became a wanted man. And I'd never gone for the Puritan look. Damned if I was going around in a pudding-bowl haircut, dressed all in black, clutching a Bible and staring piously at the ground with a solemn frown. I preferred to look a little more debonair, a little more, dare I say it, cavalier? The Chosen Ones were always suspicious of me. I never trusted them either. Some positively disliked me. I could not get their latest attack on me out of my head. One of my enemies had written:

Thus with the times he turn'd, next turn I hope
Will up the Ladder be, and down the Rope.

This little ditty played on my mind. I deplored its doggerel. 'Will up the ladder be' indeed. Why not, 'Will be up the ladder'? Did this semi-literate clown think he was Ben Jonson? The sentiment was clear, though, and no amount of literary criticism could detract from the point.

That's the trouble with invective, it's easier to dish it out than it is to take. I'd mocked so many people I couldn't begrudge my enemies giving me a good kicking now I was down. There's nothing low-born, ill-educated Grub-street hacks like better than coming down the hill after the battle is over and bayoneting the wounded. I speak from experience.

If the soldiers found me, Cromwell would march me off to prison and I'd have to go through the tedious and expensive process of getting myself out. Again.

I wasn't really afraid of a judicial execution. My death was more likely to be a murder than a hanging. A ranting hot-head, a zealous 'Saint', a maddened Leveller or a crazed Royalist – any one of them might take a pot shot at yours truly or whip out a knife in a back-alley, and finish me off. But trial and beheading or even, God forbid, hanging, drawing and quartering? I reckoned I should be able to talk myself out of that but I wasn't planning to put it to the test.

I've been accused of lacking any principle except greed. But as I used to tell poor, blind, idiotic Milton, no man but a blockhead ever wrote except for money.

Stuck in my cell, unable to sleep, I found myself thinking about Milton who, by the way, got most of his best ideas from me. Especially that stuff about Satan. He was inspired by me when he wrote about the devil. Satan has charm and glamour compared with dour, dreary old God. Milton knew it, he just wouldn't admit it. Everyone loves a villain.

There was a positive side to my incarceration. I heard everything said in the great hall. The George became temporary headquarters for Lieutenant General Oliver Cromwell and his supposed superior, General Sir Thomas Fairfax.

An odd man, Fairfax. Fought for Parliament but didn't want to kill the King. Won a lot of battles and created the New Model Army but allowed his wife to denounce Charles's trial. The King called Fairfax a man of his word but, as I squatted in my hidey-hole, I heard Fairfax, as well as Cromwell, explaining to Major White why the mutiny had to be put down with force.

'You promised you would not follow them with force at their heels – your very words,' White complained.

'This is mutiny, sir,' said Cromwell. His words were slow but deliberate, as if he were delivering a sermon, 'Against God as well as Parliament. Treason and blasphemy.'

'They are being rounded up now, Major, and will be locked in the church. Tomorrow we shall decimate them,' said Fairfax. I knew it was him by his Yorkshire accent, something not heard much in these parts.

'Decimation?' the major exclaimed. 'But there are close to a thousand men. You surely do not intend to kill one hundred of them.'

'We shall do as God wills,' said Cromwell, 'They were threatening the country with further bloodshed just when we have imposed God's peace on England and Scotland and as we prepare to impose God's peace on the Irish.'

'We must send a detachment to Banbury,' Fairfax added. 'The mutineers are at Banbury as well. They also need to be put down.'

'I have a letter for you from the Levellers, General,' I could hear Major White saying. 'They're asking for a General Council of the army to hear their grievances. Two officers and two men from each regiment.'

'Sounds dangerously like democracy to me,' said Cromwell.

'Listen to this,' said Fairfax, 'In their letter they have the gall to complain I "kept not my covenant with them". Bloody people, what do they expect? We are trying to restore order and they start demanding God knows what. Major, you're still wearing slippers.'

'I know, General, I was asleep when you arrived and sought to prevent bloodshed.'

'You did well enough, White. Though it seems three or four men have been slain and a few others hurt. We will reconvene in the morning. I'm going to bed,' said Fairfax.

Gradually the hall was vacated except for half a dozen guards. Richard Veysey, the landlord, came and went, fussing and complaining. Gradually silence descended on the inn.

In my pit of blackness, I guessed it was almost dawn.

CHAPTER 26

When pay day comes
the Souldier drinks
and sings

May 1649

I could hear a cockerel as Susie tapped on the trap door, let in a sliver of light and whispered that I should come out.

I'd never been more pleased to see the dear girl. My knees were numb, my back ached like the plague, my shoulders were crushed. As a medical man, I knew acute muscular ague when I felt it and it was all I could do to unfold myself from my confines without groaning so much I woke Cromwell's snoring guards.

Sensible Susie made enough noise for both of us, banging around to indicate she was starting work. This allowed me to struggle up towards the light unheard. When I was finally free of my coffin, I sank into a dark corner where Susie handed me bread and cheese which I ate greedily before giving her a quick peck on the lips and slipping outside to greet the dawn.

Where to go? Perhaps I should call on my wife Lucy just up the road. She would probably be saying her morning prayers. It wouldn't be safe. She was known. Cromwell and Fairfax weren't in Burford looking for me; even so they might send a trooper or two in search of me.

I could have retreated to Peter's house in Minster Lovell. It was only five miles and I knew how to get out of Burford undetected. But I wanted to see what happened to the Levellers.

A couple of young men were busy with the horses. Not the usual stable lads. Probably in the generals' entourage. I marched briskly across the yard at the back of The George, out under the archway and onto the high street without a word. Look official and most people assume you are official. Especially if they're busy mucking out stables at the time.

The sun was coming up and a sharp light slanted into my eyes. There were guards posted up and down the hill. Disciplined troops, properly armed and equipped. Probably fully paid as well.

'Who are you? What are you doing here?' demanded one under-nourished young man with a pale, sickly complexion and a scar on his cheek.

'I'm a doctor,' I announced. 'I am told there are some wounded men. Where are they?'

He accepted my assertion without question. I knew he would. It's my natural air of authority. I was born to command respect. And I wasn't lying. Doctoring is a useful profession. People assume doctors are kind and caring. It pays to maintain the illusion.

The soldier directed me to the church. The nearby school had been thrown open and further inquiry led me into the big classroom adapted for treating the wounded. There were six men lying on blankets on the wooden floor while a couple of orderlies came and went. Two women I didn't recognise were helping out. I was pleased to note neither William Lenthall's wife Elizabeth nor, indeed, my own wife was ministering to the dead and dying. Either might have greeted me by name without realising the danger.

My relief was short-lived. Standing at the far end of the room was a man I knew. John French, an old friend from Oxford. French and I studied anatomy together, as well as Latin and Greek. We also enjoyed the more dubious delights of the city – gambling, cards, horse-racing, cock-fighting, hunting, drinking and whoring, that sort of thing. Oxford was a paragon of modern civilisation.

French recognised me straight away. 'You shouldn't be here, Monty,' he said with a grin, clapping me on the back and leading me to a side room which was sometimes used as an office by my step-father.

'How are your patients?' I asked, as conversationally as I could.

'Most will live. One of the Levellers won't. Badly burned when a pistol went off in his face. Lost half of it. Sooner he goes the better. Not much I can do to relieve him of his pain. No great loss though, these Levellers. Anyway, Monty, what are you doing here?'

'I live here, John.'

'So you do, I'd forgotten. Cromwell won't be pleased to see you. Can't say I'm all that pleased either, tell you the truth. You're a turncoat, Monty, a traitor. You know they want to hang you, I suppose?' He laughed.

'Some people, maybe,' I grinned uneasily. 'You?'

'Me, Monty? Come on, I know better than to take your rantings seriously. Even if you do get a little wild at times. What was it you called Cromwell? The "pure Holy goblin", "Saint Nol the King-killer" and then – what was it? – "therefore, Snout look about thee, for if thou be catched we'll put thy neck (instead of thy nose) in a noose". Funny, I grant you. But not tactful, Monty. Not inclined to appeal to the new regime.'

'You know me, Frenchy, never short of an opinion or two. Still, I'm glad you're buying my newsbook.'

'Reading, maybe, not buying. I wouldn't waste sixpence on one of your rags, Monty.'

'Sixpence? They only cost a penny.'

Frenchy, who had been up all night tending the sick, leaned back against the bare stone wall and sighed. He was a tall, lithe man with cropped Roundhead hair but with a sense of humour rare among those folk. This morning, he looked tired. Not just tired from lack of sleep but, perhaps, exhausted from all the sights he'd been forced to deal with since signing on in Cromwell's army.

'It seems like a lifetime ago,' he said, 'When we were up at Oxford.'

'That it does,' I agreed. 'And how are they all at Broughton?'

'Well, you know it's in a terrible state still, don't you?'

'I haven't seen it for a while but it was a sorry sight last time I went that way.'

French's father was steward of Broughton Castle, near Banbury.

'That trial in Saint Alban's – you saved Nat Fiennes's life,' said Frenchie.

'Maybe,' I said modestly. 'No, actually, yes, I did.'

'Maybe,' said Frenchie. He paused for thought. 'Anyway,' he resumed, 'Broughton's a wreck. My father does his best but, you know, there's a war on. Did no-one mention it?'

'Surely it's over now you've killed the King,' I said with false cheerfulness. 'Good to see so much unity among the victors.'

'This business? Bloody ridiculous. Cromwell's right to put them down.

This is mutiny, revolution.'

'Revolution? Fancy that,' I couldn't entirely keep the sarcasm out of my voice but thought I'd better change the subject before Frenchie started going on about which side I was on. 'Where are they now?'

'Locked in your father's church, those that didn't escape. Most of them fled over the fields without their horses.'

'There's talk of decimation.'

'Is there? That'll teach 'em.'

'Frenchie? Seriously?'

'These people need to know their place. There has to be order, Monty. They claim they don't want everything made equal and brought down to the same level. But that's bound to happen if you give every man a vote.'

'Not servants or Papists,' I couldn't resist pointing out to my Puritan friend.

'Even so. Every butcher, baker and candlestick-maker. Where would we be then?'

'They just want to get paid and go home, Frenchie. Most of them have no interest in politics.'

'All the more reason to keep 'em in their place. And what about you, Monty? Where do you stand these days?'

'Must one stand anywhere? I prefer to look on from the sidelines and observe.'

'You can never simply observe, Marchamont. You're too argumentative and too ready with a handy insult.'

'Frenchie,' I said with some earnestness, 'Saint Nol wants me arrested. I don't want to go back to prison again. But I want to see what happens here. You won't betray me, will you?'

John French, surgeon to Oliver Cromwell's army, sighed deeply and looked out of the window where soldiers were forming up in the road. An expression came over him which seemed to lift ten years from his age and made him look as he had done when we were at university. He smiled, took off the bloody apron he was wearing and threw it at me. 'Here, put this on. You might as well be my assistant. Though I warn you, Monty, your services will be called for if this decimation really does take place. Come on, hang back behind me and keep a low profile.'

As we strolled into the sunlight, John told me he'd signed up to join Cromwell's war in Ireland. 'You get a chance to learn about the best treatments,' he was saying, 'How to stop infection spreading from a wound. Which pain reliefs work and which do not. Fascinating to have live bodies to work on. Not many successes but that's the nature of war and if we learn something to advance the science of medicine, it will be worthwhile.'

'You should write a book about it, Frenchie,' I said.

'I shall, Marchamont. You must know how to get it published for me.'

'I do, Frenchie, I most certainly do.'

We stopped chattering as Cromwell's personal guard clattered into the precincts of the church, which were lined with his soldiers. Cromwell remained on horseback as he dispatched an officer and two dozen men into the church and, as we watched, about 350 prisoners were ushered outside. 'Where's Fairfax?' I whispered to French.

'Doesn't have the stomach for it, I heard,' he said. 'Gone on to Oxford.'

An officer drew up a squad of ten men armed with muskets opposite a plain stone wall. Cromwell waited patiently, face turned towards the warming sun, eyes closed as if in prayer, while the prisoners were shoved into position.

After much shuffling of feet, a deep silence descended. A colonel stepped forward and marched towards where Cromwell waited, apparently indifferent to what was going on. This man bowed low and, with face averted from the great man towering above him on horseback, offered a rolled piece of paper to the Lieutenant General.

'Sire,' he said ('Sire?', I thought: a sure sign, if ever there was one, that people were already treating Cromwell as some sort of King), 'Sire,' he said, 'Here is a humble address signed by all of those rightfully incarcerated within this church for our act of presumption. We are very sensible of the odious wickedness of our act, how liable it renders us to the wrath and displeasure of God and we cannot but acknowledge the sentence of death passed upon us by your Excellency and the Council of War is very just and equal.'

Obviously, he went on to beg for mercy. At length. French said this man was called Lieutenant William Eyre. His men were the only ones to put up much of a fight last night. They actually killed one of Cromwell's troopers and wounded two others quite badly. 'Had to take one man's arm off,' French whispered as Eyre went on pleading.

Eventually Eyre handed over his document and, as Cromwell perused it, I noticed my step-father, Christopher Glynn, peering out from the church. His services would be required if the threat of decimation was carried out and Cromwell executed 35 men.

Cromwell called one of his officers over, leaned down from his saddle for a private word and the man marched back to the prisoners. He called out four names: Denne, Thompson, Perkins, Church and told the rest of the Levellers to go back inside the church and climb up onto the roof.

'The General wishes every man to have a clear view of the consequences of his behaviour,' the officer declared as his men began pushing and shoving their way back into the church. My step-father stood aside to let them pass.

This took time. Meanwhile the four named Levellers were marched into the open. One of them, the chaplain Henry Denne, carried his own winding-sheet and prayed, loudly and in tears, stumbling and collapsing as he went. He was calling wildly on the Lord for forgiveness and on Cromwell for mercy. His was the whining voice I'd heard in The George the night before.

The other three stood a little apart from this theatrical display. French whispered, 'I think Denne was working for Cromwell.'

One after another, the men were called forward, told to confirm their names and led to a spot where they should stand to be shot.

It was difficult to know why these four were singled out for death. The first and most obvious, perhaps, was Cornet James Thompson. He readily admitted he was the younger brother of Captain William Thompson who was, at that moment, leading the revolt in Banbury. Thompson closed his eyes in private prayer but made no sound as he was shot dead.

French certified he was dead and two orderlies carried away the body. Next to die was Corporal John Church, a burly fellow who had obviously seen a few battles. He stood defiantly staring at Cromwell as the squad was brought to order and he was killed. Private Will Perkins, a young, thin lad, ripped open his shirt and cried out, 'Come on boys, do your duty.'

After three executions, Chaplain Denne continued to wail until Cromwell told him to be silent. Cromwell said justice had been done, Denne would be spared on condition he returned to the church and preached a sermon to his fellow Levellers on how they had strayed from God's ways like lost sheep, or some such nonsense.

Denne and his winding-sheet made their way back into church as some of the Levellers hissed and whispered 'Judas'.

Cromwell, too, delivered a sermon extolling the virtue of service in Ireland and complaining the Levellers were raising their sea-green standard in York, Oxford, Bristol and Gloucester. He warned there were agitators in every regiment and issued warrants for the arrest of those Levellers who fled Burford overnight.

As my step-father was supervising a burial party, I melted into the background, slipping away towards the high street.

I hid for most of the day in Big Susie's garret. Eventually Cromwell's New Model Army, supported by contrite former Levellers, made its way towards Oxford where the spurious brats of my old Oxford college, All Souls, were conferring honorary degrees on King Crum and his hangers-on.

In the late afternoon, I slipped out of The George, leaving a thank-you note and ten shillings on Susie's pillow (a decent sum but not, I hoped, something she might regard as payment for services rendered) and walked very slowly the couple of hundred yards up hill to my wife's house.

The mellow sunlight reflected the mellow stones of the town's buildings. Burford looked as smug as usual, as if nothing dramatic ever happened there. It was chilly, though. Lucy would have lit a fire and be sitting beside it reading her Bible.

I knocked on the cottage door. Lucy sat by the hearth. The big Bible was open on a table before her. It was Old Testament, of course. No love and peace for her and her brethren; they preferred Hell-fire and damnation, vengeance, the end of the world and all the rest of it.

'Here thou art,' she said in a matter-of-fact tone, looking up but not smiling. 'Whither came'st thou, Marchamont?'

'I've been here all day, wife. In fact, I arrived yesterday but it wasn't safe to visit. You know the town's been invaded, I suppose.'

'The Saints have triumphed over the apostates,' she said. She looked into the feeble flames from the fireplace. I threw on a log and the embers sparked briefly. The room was dark and depressing. A cat slept in the chair opposite my wife. I thought of turfing it off but I knew this would only antagonise her.

'Are you well, wife?'

'Indeed, husband, tolerably well.' She did not look up, she did not smile, she clearly did not wish for the pleasure of my company. 'I have been parted from my husband these many months,' she said, as if by way of explanation.

'Lucy, why so frosty? Are you not pleased to see your husband?'

At last, she looked up. She was a little uninspiring to behold with the white coif on her head, her hair, the golden colour of Cotswold stone, all tucked up inside it, in her dull black dress. There was some sign of life in her eyes but, if they glistened with tears, it would be tears of anger which promised no good for Marchamont Nedham.

'Why, Mr Nedham, should I be pleased to see my husband? Hast thou not sold thine soul to Beelzebub? Hast thou not committed blasphemy and committed adultery with the Whore of Babylon?'

'Hang on a minute, Lucy, that's going a bit far.' I was hot with embarrassment.

'The King and court. Papists, all of them. Hast thou not taken the King's shilling?'

'More than a shilling, my dear,' I laughed and pushed the cat off the chair. Now she was in full flow, I needed the stool of repentance as they have in Scotland.

'Marchamont, the brethren are much perturbed by thine activities.'

'Are they indeed, Lucy? And what of yourself, my dear? Are you also much perturbed?'

'Thou art an apostate, Marchamont,' she sighed and looked at me with her glistening dark green eyes and I remembered why I'd loved her. 'You don't believe in anything, do you? You just sit and jeer at the world. What of your soul, Marchamont? Your immortal soul?'

She went on in this vein for some time allowing me to scrape mud from under my fingernails with the knife I keep inside my cloak. She offered no refreshment and, indeed, there was no sign of any in the house. Lucy sermonised about God's willingness to rejoice in souls saved and how she wished mine might be among them. Then she asked if I was prepared to repent.

'I thought only Papists confessed their sins,' I joked. It did not go down well. Apparently, there is a difference between confessing a sin and repenting. Oddly, though, if you are among the Chosen, like Lucy, you can sin as much as you like and it doesn't matter because you're destined for Heaven whatever you get up to on earth. At least that would seem to be the argument. Lucy was not impressed when I said as much.

Eventually she lost patience. 'What are you doing here, Marchamont?' she demanded with a sigh.

'Just paying my respects, my dear. Seeing if you are well. My mother...'

'Your mother? You visit your mother before your wife?' Now she really was angry. 'You know your step-father is not likely to last at St John's much longer, I suppose?' she said vindictively. 'The brethren will have him out now we have a Godly Government. And as for allowing him to teach children...'

I stood. I wasn't prepared to listen to this any longer. 'Lucy,' I said, 'I risked my neck to visit here – you know there's a warrant out for my arrest, I suppose – and I hoped for a friendly reception. I'm sorry my presence causes you pain. I shall leave. I do not know when I shall be able to return.'

'Thou shalt not be welcome within this house until ye repent thine allegiance to false Gods and reject the ways of the Royalists, Papists and Laudians and follow the true path, Marchamont. It is for the saving of your soul that I say this, no matter what my personal opinion might be.'

She gave me a wan smile as I stood in the doorway and looked at my wife. The cat crept up onto the chair I'd just vacated.

As I set off to walk back to Minster Lovell in the dying light, I reflected that at least I'd got some good copy for the next edition of my newsbook. The rebels were at each other's throats. I decided 'the Turks and the cannibals' would be a good phrase to use to describe the conflict between the Levellers and the ruling junta.

There was a spring in my step. You had to laugh; you really did.

CHAPTER 27

Now Nol have at thy nose,
I have shot nothing but
paper bullets
all this while.

June 1649

I devoted an entire edition of "Prag" to the outrageous slaughter. I exposed Henry Denne as a traitorous Cromwellian spy and commiserated with the surviving Levellers who had no choice but to risk their lives in Ireland if they hoped ever to be allowed home, with or without the money they were owed.

That spring was Leveller-hunting season. Their little revolution was put down in Burford and in Northampton, where 16 men were shot dead. John Lilburne was still alive but locked up in the Tower awaiting trial for treason. Their military commander Thomas Rainsborough, Cromwell's most popular rival, had been 'accidentally' murdered a couple of months before the King was executed. This crime was supposedly committed by a gang of Royalists in a kidnapping-gone-wrong but you couldn't rule out the possibility it was arranged by Cromwell to eliminate his most radical opponent.

Nobody believed his denials, anyway.

Now the army had to deal with a monstrous regiment of women. Hundreds of them besieged the rump of MPs in Parliament demanding the release of Lilburne and his associates. The women were driven off at gunpoint but returned in greater numbers the next day and the day after that. Parliament told them to stop meddling in things women didn't understand, go home and do some cooking instead.

By the time I sneaked back into London in late May, 10,000 women had signed a petition claiming, among other outlandish things, equal rights with their menfolk. It was bad enough the Levellers demanding equal rights for all men (except Catholics and servants, of course). But equal rights for women? No wonder their cause was losing support among right-thinking people everywhere.

Their leader, a harridan from Shropshire called Kath Chidley, ranted, 'Have we not an equal interest with the men of this Nation, in those liberties and securities contained in the Petition of Right, and the other good laws of the land? Are any of our lives, limbs, liberties or goods to be taken from us more than from men, but by due process of law and conviction of twelve sworn men of the neighbourhood?'

It might have been one of the Leveller women who betrayed me. Several of them earned a living selling "Prag" and the other newsbooks. Why would they bite the hand that fed them? Surely making a living was more important than some political principle that wouldn't get them anywhere anyway.

I didn't know it would be the last edition of "Prag" when it was secretly put to bed by a printer using an elderly press hidden some way outside the city walls. As far as I was concerned, it was just another edition of my much-admired penmanship. I'd concocted some nice insults for the King-Killer-in-Chief, Old Nol, and pointed out one of his arts was to 'hatch factions then crush them for the advance of his reputation'. I called the new, wooden Great Seal of State a Dutch butter-pat. I said the Saints were using yokels to impose 'bumpkin-justice'. I had a go at most of Cromwell's partners-in-crime. One of them was 'a baron for hanging and quartering' while four of the Peers on the new Council of State were 'Salisbury the stout, Pembroke the witty, Denbigh the chaste and Mulgrave the pretty'.

I may also have provoked them by highlighting the ridiculous decision to drive off a few demented Diggers from some waste land where the poor beggars were trying to scratch a living growing turnips. I said that, having nigh-starved the nation, the Saints sent 'troops of Janissaries prancing into Surrey to make a Conquest over those feeble souls and empty bellies' and added that the best defence against state tyranny was a just Monarch.

Yes, I was in hiding, living in the secret studio where I'd been writing for some time. Yes, I was alone – my wife still in Burford, my other wife somewhere in Holland. Yes, I was short of money though I had hopes of Washington. Yes, I was in disguise – no beard, no ear-rings, a nicely-cut black suit and Puritanical hat when I went abroad. And yes, I was avoiding old friends like Milton and Bradshaw. Even so, I wasn't unhappy. "Prag" was selling better than ever, though the army was trying to close it down, persecute the printer and arrest the writer. I was happy to be back at the centre of things and have an impact on the opinion of the people.

They agreed with me, otherwise they wouldn't queue to buy "Prag" when everyone knew it was an illegal publication. If the Levellers got their way and gave us democracy, they would be astonished to discover Royalists would win the election, form the Government, bring in the King and put an end to their nonsense.

There was satisfaction to be had from influencing public opinion. "Prag" had become indispensable and Marchamont Nedham, its only begetter, was equally indispensable.

Or so it seemed.

I am still not sure who betrayed me. It might have been a Leveller woman.

It might have been Milton, especially now he had won the Government job he'd been angling for all along. He was Foreign Secretary. Extraordinary, really, for a man who was almost blind and preferred talking in Latin. How, I wondered, would he manage his private intellectual development and enjoy the rural life if he was dealing with hostile Spanish and French ambassadors or declaring war on the Dutch?

I don't think it was Milton. For a start, he didn't know for sure what I was up to let alone where I was.

I'm pretty sure it wasn't Bradshaw either. I hadn't seen him since that day he was fumbling about in his sham court putting the King on trial. He'd been nicely rewarded for his pains – they'd appointed him President of the Council of State which made him, in name at least, the most senior man in the country, the Head of State. And they put Bradshaw in charge of new laws to tame the press. They passed an Act which meant anyone involved in unlicensed printing could be fined or jailed.

Bradshaw was taking it all very personally; maybe I shouldn't have likened him to Pontius Pilate presiding over the trial of Jesus Christ. The State was cracking down. Censorship and closure were the orders of the day.

Bradshaw was ultimately responsible for the warrant issued for my arrest. That was unnerving. Surely my old friend wouldn't want to press home his advantage quite that drastically. Or would he? After all, a man capable of condemning his King to death was capable of anything. Even so – and I had a lot of time to think this through – I doubted if Bradshaw knew anything about it.

Could it have been the Heylyns, with whom I had been hiding out at Minster Lovell, or someone from Burford? Uncle Judge John Glynn? Mr Speaker Lenthall? My parents? I doubted it, though the Judge had been restored to favour and was now on the Council of State and the Speaker was well in with the new Government. I thought the Judge would have more family loyalty, especially after I helped him escape imprisonment in Pride's Purge. Lenthall had been a source of news while I was working on "Prag". He disapproved of the King's execution. He was sympathetic to what I had been doing. No. It wasn't him.

Maybe it was the cavalryman Nat Rich, my former employer Nat Fiennes, or even Sir Henry Vane. Rich had tipped me off about Pride's Purge, so I had evidence he was well-disposed towards me. Fiennes was a friend and he was opposed to the Monarch's murder. Even Sir Henry, increasingly unpredictable though he was, studiously avoided the King-killing.

Could it have been Captain Tom Audley? I hadn't seen him for months and he was definitely involved in nefarious activities of some sort or another. Possibly.

My wife (the one in Burford)? Perhaps. She was certainly not happy with me. Would she go so far as to secure my arrest and, perhaps, my execution. Did she know about Lucy Lighthorne? If she did, that might have given her an added incentive. I was careful to make sure she did not know of my other life. She might be sufficiently vindictive to take drastic action if she did find out but I couldn't imagine how she might discover anything. With women, you never knew for sure.

My real suspicion fell on fellow news-men. It might well have been John Crouch or Sam Sheppard or even the two of them working together. There is nothing more treacherous than a fellow reporter, especially such vastly inferior imitators. No doubt they were desperate to clear the way so they might rise up from the midden in which they floundered.

Sheppard, the ex-vicar, once called me a 'counterfeit silly cur' and warned he would expose me unless I stopped 'scribbling'. I took this badly, especially as he worked with me on "Prag" for a while and I'd helped him produce his own newsbooks.

Another possibility was that idiot John Crouch, an ill-educated buffoon responsible for a pamphlet – you couldn't dignify it by calling it a newsbook – of jokes and scurrility called "The Man in the Moon". Crouch was one of those terrible writers who thought he was funny and just to prove it wrote 'Ha! Ha! Ha!' after his supposed jokes in a desperate attempt to persuade the reader it was humorous.

It might have been any of the other newsbook writers desperate to destroy competition and silence the true voice of King Charles II. Dozens of rags were being produced with increasingly absurd titles – "Mercurius Anti-Pragmaticus", for instance, and even one called "Mercurius Brittanicus" with two Ts.

I had many enemies.

I should have stayed in my rooms, scribbling away and smuggling out the copy to a trusted friend who would relay my words of wisdom to a printer. It was safe enough. I didn't know my neighbours and they didn't know me. I was short of money but I would have survived. Then word came from Washington inviting me to dine with a few Royalist friends in a private room at The George, near St Michael's Church in Cornhill.

A decent meal, wine, good company, payment for the work I'd been doing – how could I resist?

The meal was fine – ox tongue soup, leg of lamb with artichoke heart, kidneys topped with raspberries and redcurrant, herring pie and stewed prawns with cheesecake and syllabub to finish. I didn't much notice what it tasted like. I was too busy discussing the prospects of the new King regaining his throne.

I suspect I was noisier than I should have been. The spiced wine was plentiful and Washington had greetings for me from Edward Hyde. I'd been supplying private information to the King's adviser in exile and Washington coolly told me, 'Sir Edward sends his compliments and assures you of his goodwill once His Majesty is restored to his Throne.'

I didn't know then just how valuable an assurance that would one day be but almost as soon as Washington had spoken, we heard heavy boots clattering up the stairs and the small, low-ceilinged, candle-lit room was filled with Cromwell's redcoats.

They arrested me, hand-cuffed me and bundled me out of the room. I did not resist. It would have been ungentlemanly to put up a fight. Besides, they would have thought nothing of smashing a mailed fist into my face.

This time it wasn't the relative comfort of the gatehouse at Westminster or the liberties of the Fleet. This time it was Newgate where they jailed real criminals and, sometimes, forgot about them altogether.

CHAPTER 28

By reason of the foetid and corrupt atmosphere
that is in the heinous gaol
of Newgate many persons are now
dead who would be alive.

Summer 1649

Newgate was disgusting. Thank God it burned down in the Great Fire.

It was built for 150 prisoners but there must have been 400 people incarcerated there. A few were Royalists, though most of the King's men were jailed in churches and abandoned castles. The prisoners were felons of every sort – murderers, rapists, beggars, thieves, prostitutes, sodomites, Papists, foreigners of various descriptions, not to mention one or two other men of letters.

The place was a vile cess pit of putrefaction and corruption where even to be rid of the heavy chains fastened round my ankles required me to pay a turnkey's fee.

The dreadful crew of warders cast those who refused to succumb to their blackmail to the darkest, deepest dungeons which had been dripping in damp and cold since the reign of Edward III. Corpses were left to rot there.

That first night was the worst of my life. Before I could even bribe anyone to remove my chains, I was thrown – literally, discarded like a filthy rag – into a large, unlit room filled with filth, noise and stink. As my eyes adjusted to the gloom, it seemed I was in with a collection of the most loathsome men and women in London. It was nightmarish. They poked and prodded me. They rifled my pockets, stealing the money Washington paid me and anything else of any value besides. They demanded food, which I did not have. They would have ripped the clothes from my back had it not been impossible to do so because of the chains.

It was June but the walls were damp, the air chill. Some distance away a single torch flickered in the darkness. I was apathetic, without energy, too shocked to protest. I suppose I'd always known something like this might befall me but it was a fate I put out of my mind. I was invulnerable. I was Marchamont Nedham. How could they do this to me? To me of all people? To me?

I curled up against a clammy wall and hoped the human maggots of London would crawl away and leave me alone. I wondered if this was what death might be like. One minute you're laughing and joking, enjoying good food and sweet wine; the next, you're annihilated, reduced to nothing. Consigned to Hell. The Hell all those priests keep ranting about. Could the real one be worse?

Newgate. I'd seen it a thousand times. It was the gate you rode through on your way to Burford. I never ventured into the jail, not even to laugh at lunatics or commiserate with Levellers. It was best ignored, passed by on the other side. Now there I was, slumped and desperate.

Things improved.

Money was the key and Washington sent a youth called God to my aid. God was the grandson of an earl, apparently, and excited to be plotting the downfall of the Government by bringing supplies to the notorious Marchamont Nedham. He was called Godfrey Butler so I called him God, which God thought blasphemous.

Still, God was a God-send.

The money paid for the removal of my shackles, bought me out of the common cells and into the Press Yard. I chuckled at the irony of the name, though it wasn't much of a laughing matter. The Press Yard was where they sent the nobility, political prisoners, people whose only real crime was disagreeing with the junta. We could receive visitors. We had open doors and rooms, not cells. We had freedom, not chains. We had food, not starvation. God brought me paper, quills and ink. I wrote to my wife in Burford and to the other one, who was due back from Holland any day. I purchased new clothes.

Better still, it turned out there were no doctors willing to tend the sick and dying of Newgate Prison. I couldn't blame them. The place was noxious and calculated to kill. Open sewers flowed through the common yard. Flies and mosquitos buzzed about. The rats were fearless. Injuries from cruelty were frequent, often fatal. Disease was rife.

A physician could make a decent living in Newgate; a decent living until he died of disease, anyway.

Once it became known I was a doctor, queues formed outside my room. I was a sought-after man. The jailers, as well as the prisoners, wanted to consult me. I had no medicines but they sought my advice and paid good money for the consolation of a kindly word and a knowledgeable but worried frown.

This was all very well but what I wanted was to get out of there as soon as possible.

Blonde Lucy, my wife in Burford, wrote to say she thought a short prison term was a Godly thing. It would make me think on my sins, repent my evil ways and come back onto the side of Cromwell and the Saints. She would endeavour to visit toward the end of the summer but I was not to expect her before late September at the earliest. She sent me a tract called 'The Lawfulness of Obeying the Present Government'. She said I should learn from it.

Dark Lucy, my Catholic wife, returned from Holland in mid-July. I had been in jail for three weeks and there was no sign of a prosecution, a trial or even any official questioning. Several other prisoners had been less than reassuring. The jailers let it be known Marchamont Nedham was slated for the gallows. One of them told me so himself when I diagnosed a fatal growth in his stomach.

'I shall still live longer than thee, Doctor Nedham,' he growled.

I was beginning to think that might be true. When Catholic Lucy was finally able to bribe her way into the prison, we quickly concluded the best option was escape.

It wasn't hard to get out of Newgate, for all its formidable reputation and tall, black walls. None of the jailers refused a bribe. It was just a question of picking the right man and pitching the incentive at the right level – it wouldn't do to pay too much. Bribes were costly and it was in nobody's interests to raise the price above what was absolutely necessary. There was almost a tariff for bribes – ease of chains, one halfpenny from thick chains to lighter chains, and one penny from lighter chains to no chains; one shilling for removal from the cells on the common side to the slightly-less-hideous master's side; two shillings and sixpence for removal to the Press Yard. A pound for a single cell with table, truckle bed and chair. A penny a day for candles. Two pennies for pen, ink and three quills which would only last a day. More for food. It went on and on.

To look the other way, a prison officer would require two whole crowns, ten shillings. An outrageous sum.

It took Lucy a few days to come up with the money and a plan. We would leave the prison, after the usually-haphazard morning roll call, through the side entrance where deliveries were made. Our chosen jailer, Thomas Pettigrew, would look the other way for ten minutes between 7.15am and 7.25. Lucy would wait down Newgate Street with two horses and we would ride off together into the sunrise.

Pettigrew was as good as his word and made himself scarce at the appointed hour. The gate was unlocked. I slipped out, into the narrow street, met Lucy and off we went.

'It was so exciting, Marchamont,' she declared later as we lay in each other's arms in a tavern the other side of Windsor.

'There'll be a hue and cry,' I said,

'Of course. The great Marchamont Nedham fled and gone. The outlaw Nedham, the pirate Nedham, the highwayman.' She was kissing me as she said this, my dusky beauty.

The excitement quickly wore off. There was no escape from the army. It had spies in every town and village. Informers were everywhere. People were so desperate they would sell their own mothers to a Parliament man for a few shillings. Lucy and I, two strangers passing through, aroused curiosity. If you weren't an official of Parliament or a soldier in uniform, you were not to be trusted and someone would start to question your whys and wherefores.

Our only option was to make for the coast and escape to Holland. It was a well-trodden route now with a series of staging posts all requiring bribes. Lucy had money and I had a small sum from Washington via God. We made slow progress from tavern to tavern, heading for Folkestone in Kent. It wasn't far. It shouldn't have taken long but there were soldiers everywhere. Even now, the army did not trust the people of Kent who had started the last uprising in protest at the suppression of Christmas. Folkestone itself may have been a small fishing village but it was so close to France, and the threat of a Royalist invasion was so real, it was teeming with Redcoats.

Lucy and I agreed to enter the village separately. It would be safer. There were guards on the main road and soldiers patrolling the area round about. We agreed to meet near the fish market beside the quay where we hoped to find a sympathetic sailor to ferry us across the Channel. We would make our way to The Hague and offer our services to the King. Lucy had contacts there; so did I thanks to my letters to Sir Edward Hyde.

I was to follow Lucy about an hour after she arrived in Folkestone. I looked out for a group of merchants to join, thus reducing my chances of being stopped and questioned. I had no papers. I would have to talk my way past the guard-post.

At the top of the hill into Folkestone, we kissed passionately. I stroked away tears from her soft, vulnerable face. We parted, promising to be together again within the hour. I watched Lucy ride down the sunken lane. I saw her stop and talk to the soldiers. I saw her raise her head and laugh and the two men laugh in return, wish her well and wave her through.

It was the last I should ever see her.

CHAPTER 29

Those bitter Arrowes shot out of mens Mouthes,
and Pulpits being my selfe brought
under the Lash, and persecuted

Autumn-Winter 1649

Half an hour after my wife disappeared from view, I made my attempt on
the checkpoint. A group of merchants, their horses pulling carts of woollen cloth, was making its slow way into Folkestone. They were moaning
about the decline in trade and blaming the war. I attached myself to them
and tried to make myself agreeable. The guards were unfortunately dil-
igent, itself a rarity, and demanded to see everyone's papers. When my
turn came, alas I had none.

One of the Redcoats asked my name while another searched my sad-
dlebag, extracting pen and paper as if these were contraband and proved
I must be guilty of something. Who was I? A good question. I decided
to name myself Sam Pecke after the editor of "A Perfect Diurnall". Pecke
had been around some time, keeping his nose clean and producing a
newsbook which, while never reaching the heights of "Prag", was worth
a glance occasionally.

Sadly for me, Pecke was on a list of wanted men. Parliament was clos-
ing down all the newsbooks and arresting all the editors, not just Marchamont Nedham, and the two men on the checkpoint were alert enough
to realise the name I gave them was one of those they were supposed to
be looking out for. Given the illiteracy of the average Ironside, it was especially bad luck to fall into the hands of a pair of relatively well-educated
members of the New Model who had not had the misfortune to be sent
off to Ireland.

I tried to persuade them to take a message to my wife waiting on the quay. They thought they might be able to do something but, even with a crown of my fast-dwindling stock of money in their pockets, they could not guarantee the message would get through. I fretted about poor Lucy, standing at the water's edge wondering whether to escape or stay in England and seek me out again. I knew she had messages for Charles II's court. It was unlikely she would linger.

I was arrested as Sam Pecke and as Sam Pecke I was taken the ten miles to Dover Castle and locked up alone in a cell for three days. Eventually, I confessed my real identity and was transported back to Newgate where my old cell was occupied and I had to start buying my way back into relative comfort bribe by bribe only this time with less hope for the future.

There was no word from Lucy.

Prison was worse this time. More gruelling and, without lovely Lucy, with less hope. Worse than anything was the feeling, a real, palpable creeping of the flesh, that I had to take my plight seriously. It was possible, likely even, the junta would want to make an example of me. They might string me up. I assumed, and didn't want to think about it, but I did assume they wouldn't do anything worse than that. Only witches got burned these days, I told myself, and as for hanging, drawing and quartering, that was only for out-and-out traitors. They could hardly call me one of those. Could they? I tried not to think about it. Of course I thought of little else.

I wrote again to Lucy in Burford asking for help. I wrote to my mother, my uncle Judge John, and my one-time friends Mr Speaker Lenthall, Foreign Secretary Milton and President of the Council Bradshaw. But the first person to visit me in my misery was Andrew Marvell, the student I hadn't seen for years. He did not like being in Newgate, that much was obvious. He was able to lend me some coins to keep me in food and out of serious harm but he had no good news.

'It's the times, Ned,' he said.

'Need as in feed, not Ned as in bed, Marvel. How often must I tell you?'

It was our little joke. We both smiled wanly.

'You look terrible,' he said.

'You don't look so good yourself, but at least I've got an excuse. Anyway I thought you were in Italy, Marvel.'

'I was, Neeeeeed-ham, but now the war's over it seemed safe to come home. I've been back for months. Since before the King's execution. Only just heard about your arrest though. From Milton.'

'From Milton?'

'Milton's been given the job of examining "Mercurius Pragmaticus" and reporting back on it to the House.'

'Milton? Examining my newsbook?'

'Indeed.'

'So, my fate is in his hands?'

'It may be,' said Marvell solemnly. He paused, changed the subject, became animated again. 'He's found me a job tutoring Lord Fairfax's daughter. You know Fairfax has retired from the army?'

'Forced out by Cromwell and the junta,' I corrected him.

'And I have become a poet,' Marvell announced with a smug grin. He held out a slim volume.

'It's all Greek and Latin,' I protested. 'I can see you're under the influence of Milton.'

'The next one will be in English,' he promised. 'But now, Marchamont, how are we going to get you out of here?'

'A good question. I suppose I'll have to give an undertaking not to do any more writing.'

'Like you did last time?'

'Ah, well, that's a point. But as I don't know what I am accused of it's difficult to know how to defend myself.'

'You know what you've done wrong, Monty, of course you do. You have upset King Oliver and his ministers. You call them the junta and accuse them of tyranny. You're a malignant. What did you expect, especially as Parliament's cracking down on all the newsbooks – even the pro-army ones? Gil Mabbott's got the army at his beck and call as well as 50 spies appointed to hunt out writers and printers and break up their presses. Parliament's voted him £5,000 a year for the work.'

'Mabbott's a maggot,' I said. 'They make him chief censor so he closes down "The Moderate Intelligencer", gets the editor jailed, then takes over the title and produces it himself. Even awards himself a licence. If anyone's malignant, it's Gil bloody Mabbott.'

'Of course he is but that doesn't help, Marchamont, does it? That's what you're up against. I have advice, from Milton. He says, "Repent. Repent in writing".'

Lenthall wrote telling me to repent in writing. Bradshaw wrote that I should issue a pamphlet in support of the new regime. My mother said she couldn't leave Burford but she sent a clean suit of clothes, a pie that was very stale by the time it reached me and arranged for money to be got to me. Milton himself visited, very briefly. He had to be led into the jail and stumbled over the stones as he was brought to my cell. 'As my eyesight gets worse my sense of smell is improving,' he said. 'I cannot stay here. My advice, Nedham, is to write an apology and ask for clemency. I know they are discussing what to do with you. No decision has been made yet. You have a few weeks. Get scribbling, is my best advice. Write in defence of this Government. Why we all owe it our obedience. Make a plea for reconciliation.'

'Even though they have seized power by the sword only?'

'Even though…' said Milton. 'You want to live, don't you?'

What else could I do but grovel?

How strong are your principles when you are locked in jail afraid for your life?

Was I to become a Royalist martyr or, even worse, a martyr to some nebulous cause like 'free speech' – that thing Milton once championed?

I didn't think so. And when my blonde Puritan Lucy finally reached London from Burford, she was adamant I should not sacrifice my life. 'No, Marchamont, no. As the Lord says, "For I desired mercy, and not sacrifice; and the knowledge of God more than burnt offerings".'

I definitely opposed the idea of becoming a burnt offering.

I was still left alone by the authorities. Nobody questioned me or took evidence. Was I to be tried? If so, when? For what offence? Would I simply wake up one morning to discover it was my last on earth and I was to be executed by decree, without even the smokescreen of a trial? A Bill of Attainder in the Commons? It happened often enough.

Was I simply to be forgotten about? Was Newgate a modern oubliette? I grovelled.

I sat down in my cell with quills and paper – extortionate at two sheets for a penny – and, in a couple of days, wrote the most appalling drivel of my whole career. It was in the form of a letter to the Council of State. I thought at least Bradshaw would look at it. Maybe even Cromwell.

In my years of writing, I have discovered you can never under-estimate the intelligence of your audience. The more exalted it is, the more willing it is to swallow any praiseful guff you care to throw their way. The high and mighty are desperate for flattery and assurance of their wisdom, statesmanship, beneficence and mercy.

They swallowed it all lock, stock and barrel. I shall not quote much because it's all rather embarrassing.

Basically, I argued any new regime needed as many friends as it could get and the best way of winning friends and influencing people was to be kind and loving. It's a strange notion for a Government created after so much slaughter – and we had yet to learn of the massacre of the Irish at Cromwell's hands – but we all love to be loved, even dictators.

I said the people of Republican Rome cherished the indulgence, prudence and easy Government of the Senate and grew to be zealous in its defence. I don't know if this is true but nor did anyone else so it didn't matter. It's always worthwhile quoting the classical era, it adds weight to every argument. Luckily, I acquired a book by some German about the classical world which I plagiarised wholesale. This allowed me to provide a classical backdrop and give my assertions added gravitas. For instance, I pointed out Caesar Augustus endeared himself to the people 'with large immunities, ease, plenty, pleasure, sports, pageants and open theatres'. That might be going a bit too far for the high priests of self-denial but they might get the gist of it.

'Love,' I wrote, 'Is the surest guard of States and Princes; which is no way to be obtained but by gentleness & mercy, whereas severity sows the first seeds of Sedition & Enmity.'

I'm not proud of myself. It was humiliating to sit at a single candle in the midst of the stews of Newgate and scrawl this specious claptrap as a way of pleading for my liberty. It was bad enough having my newsbooks 'examined' by Milton; it was worse to be reduced to special pleading like a slave begging his master for mercy.

I showed Puritan Lucy the first few pages of my begging letter to Parliament. She was not impressed. 'Thy heart is not right in the sight of God,' she said. 'Repent therefore of this thy wickedness and pray. I perceive that thou art in the gall of bitterness, and in the bond of iniquity.'

I really wanted an argument. I wanted to tell her to stop quoting the Bible at me and think for herself. I thought of dismissing her and telling her never to return. I thought better of it, though, because I needed all the friends I could get. At least she had made the journey from Burford. She was willing to give me the time of day even though we had spent so long apart and despite my working for a King and a cause she despised. I think she saw me as her Christian duty, a burden to shoulder, a cause for which despair was forbidden no matter how lost it seemed.

Lucy charmed the turnkeys and warders with her piety, downcast eyes and wistful smile. She wished at all times to remain stern, scrupulous and modest but occasionally her natural gaiety broke through and I remembered why I once loved her.

It seemed a long time ago when Lucy was a happy, friendly, cheerful young woman. I had another wife now. My first Lucy was something of a stranger to me. My second Lucy was silent. When I wasn't worrying about my own fate, I dwelt on what might have become of Lucy Lighthorne. Where was she? Was she in Holland? Would she return and search me out? Would she leave me to my fate or see if some sort of rescue could be arranged?

My worst fear was that she might think I had deliberately abandoned her, that I had accompanied her to Folkestone and then turned for home rather than go abroad with her. Had I broken her heart?

I had no way of telling and I couldn't even write to her. I did wonder about getting a message to Edward Hyde, who would be with Charles II wherever that might be. Washington could probably arrange it. But it wouldn't be a wise move. Washington was one of the cavaliers at dinner with me when I was arrested. If he hadn't been under suspicion before, he would be now. He was almost certainly being spied on by John Thurloe's network of thugs.

Everyone knew Thurloe – another Oxfordshire and Lincoln's Inn man – was Cromwell's spymaster. No doubt Thurloe was behind my arrest. He was probably working with Bradshaw to close the popular press.

I got my little pamphlet printed and sent copies to everyone I could think of who might be able to help me – Bradshaw, Milton, Lenthall, Sir Henry Vane, Lord Saye and Sele, Nat Fiennes. I sent one to Cromwell in Ireland. Everyone who was anyone – and, indeed, several nobodies who thought they were someone. Even the title was grovelling. I called it: "Certain considerations tendered in all humility to an honorable member of the councell of state concerning the discontents of the people."

It worked.

In November, I was a free man. Or free enough, anyway.

CHAPTER 30

Vpon so sandy a Foundation, the man in the moon's
Dogge would run it down with his tayle,
or, holding up his legge against it,
pisse it into a confused chaos

November 14, 1649

'So you think "secret whisperers" are crooked and untrustworthy?'

I had just stepped out of the noxious stink of Newgate into the relatively fresher air of the Ludgate, carrying my few possessions in a bag over my shoulder. It was a crisp, bright November morning and my spirits were soaring – I was free. No explanation was given. A warder simply opened my cell at dawn and told me I had twenty minutes to quit the place. I needed no second bidding; it's not as if I had many goodbyes to say. I was delighted to see the back of the scrawny, stinking, toothless lot of them. They would be sorry to see me go. It's not every day they have a cheap physician at their beck and call though I can't say my ministrations made much difference. The poisonous atmosphere in Newgate jail was enough to kill most people, given time. Clearer air, cleaner water and better food would have been the best remedy.

Still, sixpence or a shilling per consultation covered my prison expenses and left me with a little cash in hand as I made my way towards a decent tavern for a breakfast of ale and pies before going home to my wife.

I was marching briskly up Ludgate Hill when a hand clasped my shoulder from behind and a voice I recognised asked about "secret whisperers". In my grovelling apology, I had mentioned how terrible it was for new regimes to employ informers and spies. Now, it seemed, one of them was at my neck.

I turned and exclaimed, 'Audley.'

'Nedham,' he gave me a slightly sinister grin. 'Got yourself into a spot of bother, didn't you? Come with me.'

We ducked into the nearest tavern – few were open at that time of day but a couple catered for the fishmen, sailors and merchants who were up and about first thing. It was quiet. Captain Tom ordered food and drink, led the way to a quiet corner, slumped heavily into a large seat and gazed at me with a quizzical look.

I dare say I looked quizzical as well.

Captain Tom was dressed Puritanically under one of those broad-brimmed hats. He looked like an itinerant priest, of the kind who made a living warning of the dangers of hellfire and damnation. 'You've lost weight, Nedham,' he said. 'It suits you. You were becoming a little tubby. Short and fat, I'd say. Still short; less fat. An improvement. Your hair's getting thin, though. You need a wig.'

'Got one, thank you Audley, but what are you doing here?'

'You think you are a free man, don't you Nedham?' Audley looked serious, his eyes darkened, the scar on his cheek seemed to burn.

'Am I not?'

'Of course you are. Free as a bird. Under certain circumstances.'

I was beginning to dislike this conversation.

'Do you remember John Thurloe, Marchamont?' he asked.

'Yes. Taciturn creature. Sits in the dark, like a spider feeding on flies.'

'You are now caught in his web.'

'What?'

'If Thurloe is a spider, you, Nedham, are a fly.'

'Audley,' I said, sitting up and leaning towards him to emphasise how unhappy I was with this turn in our conversation. 'I have no idea what you are talking about but I have no intention of being anybody's fly, not Thurloe's, not yours.'

'Not Cromwell's?' he asked. 'Your future has been cast for you, Nedham. You are being conscripted. You are too valuable to languish in prison and too irritating to be allowed to flaunt your tomfoolery will-he, nil-he. In future, your pen is at the service of the Commonwealth. Mr Thurloe decrees it.'

'Thurloe? That jumped-up lawyer?'

'One of the most powerful men in the country, Marchamont. My employer and now, yours too.'

'I am a free man. Look. Here I am. Free as air.' I waved my arms about and laughed. Uneasily, I admit.

Audley also laughed but not with much humour. 'None of us is free, Nedham, least of all a man who spent the last three years working for the King. You called General Cromwell all the names under the sun. You damned your old friend John Bradshaw a cut-throat and a monster. You described Charles's trial as "the most absolute stage of tyranny and injustice that ever was in the world". You are lucky to be alive.'

'And how have you been since we last met, Tom my old friend?' I asked casually.

'Pleading for your life, for one thing,' he said.

That shut me up. 'Really?' I asked.

'Yes, Nedham, really. Bradshaw put in a good word, so did William Lenthall. The Council of State was not convinced. It was going to wait for Cromwell to come back from Ireland but eventually, well, they decided against prosecuting you for treason.'

'Treason?'

'Of course, treason. Fighting the Commonwealth. "For King Charles II" as I think you named "Pragmaticus" after his father was executed.'

'I've never fought. I have not taken up arms against anybody.'

'Paper bullets, Captain Nedham. Isn't that what you call yourself? Captain?'

'Doctor.'

Audley laughed, this time mirthfully. 'Ah yes, Doctor Nedham. Cures all sicknesses. Guaranteed protection against ague and the plague.' Audley finished off his beer and ordered another. Foam attached itself to his upper lip. It distracted me. I did not like this conversation. I was not used to being mocked. Mockery was my job.

'Very well,' I said, displaying my irritation. 'I need to get home to my wife.'

'You know adultery's going to be punishable by death, don't you, Monty?'

'So they tell me.' I chuckled uneasily.

Audley leaned forward and whispered with what I felt was an unnecessarily malicious smile, 'Going home to your wife? Which wife is that,

Monty? The Protestant one or that sweet little Catholic?'

'What do you want from me?'

'Oh nothing much, Nedham. Just your pen. And don't worry, it's our little secret.'

The King's cause would not allow me to turn an honest penny. Worse, it was plainly dangerous to be a Royalist. Speaking out against the army, Parliament, Cromwell, and the rest was asking for trouble. There was no possibility of using my pen in the Royalist cause any longer. I had no wish to return to jail or spend my days skipping from one rat-infested hidey-hole to another one step ahead of the beagles of the State.

This was a brutal regime. We'd just had the news from Ireland. Cromwell had massacred thousands of men, women and children, Royalists, Protestants and Catholics. Retaliation for the massacre of Protestants nine years earlier but even so – Cromwell put prisoners to the sword after they surrendered on the promise of clemency. Three thousand corpses in one town.

The man was a monster, not that Lucy thought so. I arrived as she was about to attend some prayer meeting or another but she graciously agreed to stay at home and find her husband some food and wine. To my surprise, Lucy was pleased to see me. Her eyes shone, she smiled, there was a spring in her step. All this from a Puritanical, God-fearing woman. I couldn't understand it.

'God hath wrought his justice,' she declared, waving "The Moderate Intelligencer" under my nose. The "Mod" was a pretty unreliable rag but even Sam Pecke could more or less manage to transcribe a letter from the General. 'Look,' declared Lucy, 'He says this is a righteous judgement of God on these barbarous wretches.'

I decided not to argue. Who, indeed, were the barbarous wretches, the Catholics or the Royalists? And why, I wondered yet again, was Cromwell so certain he was administering God's justice?

Lucy was skipping round the room with enthusiasm. 'Now, at last, I will rejoice in Jerusalem, and joy in my people: and the voice of weeping shall be no more heard in her, nor the voice of crying.'

I did wonder how I was going to put up with this. Lucy's enthusiasm for God, Cromwell, massacring Catholics and the New Jerusalem were likely to become very waring very quickly. But it turned out she was in the mood to celebrate my homecoming as a proper wife should. As a result, I wasn't inclined to debate politics and religion with her; we had better things to do.

I was free and I wasn't.

First off, I had to take the 'oath of loyalty', some concoction of words everyone was supposed to swear, promising allegiance to the Commonwealth. It didn't matter really. I swore, 'I do declare and promise, that I will be true and faithful to the Commonwealth of England, as it is now established, without a King or House of Lords.' I suppose it depended how much you believed God would strike you down if you uttered a word in support of the King Across The Water. I doubted if the Lord would be interested, though Lucy, of course, was convinced of its importance.

Audley sent me to Milton. The nearly-blind Foreign Secretary told me to report to the President of the Council, John Bradshaw. Bradshaw told me the Commonwealth needed a writer to promote its cause and further its interests. Bradshaw had seen some of the things I'd written about him in "Prag".

'You hurt me, Marchamont,' he said.

'Not as much as you hurt the King,' I said. Was I being brave or foolish to banter with the King-killer-in-chief? It's not as if Charles was his only victim; Bradshaw recently condemned to death the Duke of Hamilton, Lord Capel and the Earl of Holland in one fell swoop.

He smiled ruefully. 'Charles Stuart left us with no choice, no option.'

'Well, well,' I said. 'No use crying over spilt milk anyhow.'

'Indeed,' Bradshaw said. 'We have a chance to create a new world, Marchamont. A new Jerusalem.'

'So my wife tells me.'

'Listen to her,' said Bradshaw. 'Women sometimes have greater wisdom than we give them credit for. My own wife Mary reminds me daily we are about God's work. That is why I forgive you your libels, Nedham.'

I think Bradshaw forgave me for supporting the King because he hoped I would therefore forgive him his regicide.

In a sense, I did. I said the average citizen had no choice but to bend the knee to the army. The law of the sword was the only law that mattered. The sword cut through anything devised by man; the threat of immediate death was enough to exact compliance from all but the most stubborn or idiotic.

Bradshaw said he was still trying to shut down the newsbooks and waved a copy of "The Man in the Moon" at me.

'Look at this, Nedham,' he said. 'He calls Fairfax "Tom-Arse Fairfucks", Oliver is "Nose Almighty", "Snout", "His Noseship" and "God Nose".'

I kept very quiet.

'He says, and I quote, "A Government, may stand for a while; but so ticklish, and upon so sandy and unstable a foundation, that the Man in the Moon's Dog would run it down with his tale, or but holding up his leg against it, piss it into a confused chaos." Is it any wonder we have to close them down, these rags? Especially when we've got Lilburne's Levellers to contend with as well?'

'Canons to the left of them, canons to the right of them,' I said.

'That's very good, Nedham. Very good.'

'Into the valley of death rode the rump of the Parliament.'

Bradshaw frowned.

'What we need,' he said, tapping his desk with his fingers, 'Is no news at all. No news is good news, a symptom of a placid and quiet state of affairs. What we need from you, though, is a manifesto.'

'A manifesto?'

'An explanation. Why people must support their new Government. That pamphlet you wrote in Newgate, only more so. Expanded. Expounded. We like the classical allusions.'

'We?'

'The Council of State. Write us a manifesto, Nedham. Explain why dissent and disagreement are fruitless and why we would do well to support our new Commonwealth.'

'And will the Commonwealth decree all wealth must be held in common?' I asked.

Bradshaw laughed. For the first time in our interview, his serious and anxiety-ravaged face broke into genuine and wholehearted mirth.

'It's what the Levellers want,' I added.

Bradshaw laughed even harder. 'We're not democrats,' he spluttered, 'And we're certainly not commune-ists.'

CHAPTER 31

The power of the sword is,
and ever hath been,
the foundation of all titles to government

Spring 1650

Protestant Lucy greeted me one evening early in the New Year with a scowl. What had I done wrong now? Had I said something ungodly? Had I accidentally taken the Lord's name in vain? All I'd been doing was writing my book. What could be the trouble this time?

In retrospect, I suppose, the scowl was because she assumed I would be angry. I have no idea why. Lucy declared, frowning, 'For this child I prayed; and the Lord hath given me my petition which I asked of him.'

I hugged her tightly then suddenly let go – hugging might harm the baby. This was her third pregnancy; surely there must be a chance of success this time?

It took me several months to write my rehabilitation book. This was partly because I had to make a good job of it – Milton promised it would lead to better things. It was also because I spent as much time as I could quietly visiting the dingier parts of London in search of Royalists who might have information about Lucy Lighthorne, my Papist wife.

In April, a letter reached me at my writing room, which I kept on and used as often as I could. It was short and to the point. Lucy said she left England on the ebb tide that day in Folkestone and discovered later that I had been sent back to Newgate. She heard I was now free and even knew I had been interviewed by Bradshaw. How she knew all this she did not say, though I suppose if Cromwell and Thurloe had spies all over London no doubt so did Charles II and Charles Hyde.

This was all very interesting but then came Lucy's big announcement: she was with child. It was due in the summer. She expected to be in Paris. She hoped I could join her for the birth. She sent me her love. She added she was running short of money, as were all the Royalists in exile, and if I could not come myself then, at the very least, I should send her some money.

This was all rather awkward.

What was I to do? I could hardly abandon Lucy in London for Lucy in Paris. Even if I could escape England, I was low on funds. Imprisonment and the loss of "Prag" devastated my finances. It was all I could do to maintain our living standards by a return to doctoring. It kept me busy, leaving little time to write.

The book was my priority. But I wanted to raise money for Lucy in Paris. I wrote explaining I could not join her for the time being and promising to deliver funds as quickly as possible. I couldn't borrow, however, because that would require me to explain what it was for and there was nobody I could confide in who would be both sympathetic enough and rich enough to help.

So I ploughed on with my book and worried about my two wives.

The book wasn't all that difficult to write. I'd said most of it already, in my get-out-of-jail plea. This time, I just larded on the classical quotations and references even more thickly: Cicero, Aristotle, Tacitus, Juvenal, you name it, I quoted it.

My erudition impressed people. When the book came out, I was praised for my classical scholarship and my facility at turning obscure Latin quotations into readable English. In later years, people often asked which of the authors I quoted so extensively I was most fond of. I never told them it was Arnold Clapmar, a German professor whose work was translated into Dutch and then into English. If my enemies – I knew I had some, though I could never say why – but if my enemies accused me of cribbing my classicism from an obscure German academic, nobody would have given them the time of day. The book cemented my reputation as a scholar. That alone was enough to refute even the most persistent critic. And where would such a fool get his exposé published anyway?

My case was simple: you can't argue with a sword so you might as well live under it. I suppose my favourite source was the Italian Niccolò di Bernardo dei Machiavelli. He knew what he was talking about: 'All armed Prophets have been victorious, and all unarmed Prophets have been destroyed.'

If we look at it aright, it's obvious the affairs of State are of no concern to ordinary men and women. We should reconcile ourselves to usurpers because there was nothing we could do about it other than die fighting them (Cromwell was now hammering the Scots as he destroyed the Irish). We might as well get used to the idea of Government by the army because all the other possibilities were as dead as a Catholic in Drogheda.

We all had to live. The only good martyr's a dead martyr.

My book was printed in May (and, I should add, re-printed later in the year because it was so successful) to great acclaim. Milton, who had it read to him in draft and gave it his seal of approval, was the first to congratulate me. I was summoned to a meeting.

Bradshaw and Milton, President of the Council and Foreign Secretary. Theoretically, two of the most powerful men in the land. Neither had real power and they knew it. Nobody dared to take real decisions unless they knew the army would agree and only one member of the army really mattered – Oliver Cromwell. Fairfax had retreated to Yorkshire with Marvell in tow. Henry Ireton was stuck in Ireland. There was no military man to challenge Cromwell's authority.

Bradshaw and Milton gave me dinner. Stewed carp, roast chicken, and hot salmon, neats' tongues, cheese and tansy sweetmeats for the digestion. I concentrated on the Madeira as Bradshaw took a long time to get to the point. It was his lawyerly way, I suppose, but he did insist on putting everything into context – the revolution, the regicide, the threats from within and without, the illegal pamphleteering, the late King's book, the image of Charles as a martyred, Christ-figure. Milton nodded and listened studiously. I ate, drank and waited for Bradshaw to get to the point.

Eventually he said, 'Now look here Nedham. The Commonwealth needs friends. Your book will help. But, try as we may, we don't seem able to destroy all the Royalist presses.'

'You know, Nedham, like "Pragmaticus",' interrupted Milton.

A jest? From Milton? Extraordinary.

'Anyway,' Bradshaw continued, 'We need you to start a new weekly publication. To tell the truth for once. The free-for-all we've got has to end – how can you expect to have proper discussion and make wise decisions when every Tom, Dick and Harry knows all about your deliberations? – but the appetite for news has to be satisfied. If we don't satisfy it ourselves, with the truth, there will be others seeking to satisfy it with lies, distortions and half-truths. We can't have that. We need a strong, robust, fearless voice speaking for the Commonwealth.'

'And that voice is yours, Marchamont,' Milton added.

'You will be licensed by John,' Bradshaw said, nodding in Milton's direction, 'And you will have to liaise regularly with me and, when he's about, with Oliver.'

'And, for the sake of Parliament, Marchamont, we need you to write a document explaining how you will go about this task.'

I was flattered, I can't deny it. But was I ready to switch sides again? I know I had already moved in that direction but my Royalist friends would not take kindly to my working in support of the King-killers. Did I believe my own arguments? If the choice was to be a martyr and die or live and compromise my principles, I had to choose to live – especially as I was about to become a father twice over.

There was one question, though. 'I hate to raise the matter of money,' I said, 'But are you expecting me to give up being a physician? Is this to be a full-time occupation?'

'Ah yes, money,' sighed Bradshaw, as if this was something vulgar and beside the point when I was well aware he had spent the last few years lining his own pockets.

'And how is Somerhill House, John?' I asked Bradshaw.

'Almost seven thousand acres,' he said enthusiastically. I'm not sure he realised I was making a point at his expense. Milton smiled.

'Money,' Bradshaw said. 'Well, I think we can let you have £50 on account for the work you have done already and then it will be £200 a year.'

I tried hard to look as if this was the least they could do to tempt me. I doubt if I succeeded. It was all I could do not to leap up and start dancing on the table. Money. At last. A lot more than the £30 a year I'd been getting on "Britanicus" or the subsistence money I'd gleaned off the Royalists doing "Prag".

'I'll write a plan for Parliament,' I promised.

CHAPTER 32

'Tis incredible what influence it has upon
numbers of unconsidering persons
who have that strange presumption
that all must needs be true that is in Print.

Summer 1650

Elizabeth was born in Paris in May. Her mother's letter didn't reach me
in London until July 10. Lucy in Paris said she named the child after her
own mother and hoped I would not mind if the baby was christened in
my absence. Lucy thanked me for the £20 I sent her, hoped we could be
re-united soon and pledged her enduring love.

Her letter arrived the day my other Lucy gave birth to a baby which
she decided should be called Elizabeth after Cromwell's wife.

I was delighted she'd finally given birth to a healthy child. I really
did not want two daughters both called Elizabeth but I could think
of no good reason to object. I did say I wasn't sure she looked like an
Elizabeth but Lucy stared scornfully at me and asked what an Elizabeth
was supposed to look like. I suggested Mary ('What? Are we Catholics,'
Lucy demanded), Jane (too plain), Marjory ('That's your mother's name.');
Henrietta Maria (Lucy slapped me); or even Mercy (Lucy decided that
might work as a middle name but she wanted Elizabeth, Beth, Lizzy,
Tess, Betty, Bess).

Elizabeth was christened at St Andrew's in Holborn. I wanted a party
but Lucy said, 'Let us walk honestly, as in the day; not in rioting and
drunkenness, not in chambering and wantonness, not in strife and envy-
ing.' I took that as a no.

I wrote to Paris with my love and joy at Catholic Lucy's news but
getting correspondence to France was a slow business. My letter of July
12 might not arrive until mid-September or later. I worried about my little

Lucy. Mind you, I admit I was not unhappy she was out of the country when she had our baby and that it was impossible for me to travel abroad.

I was glad I had just one Lucy and one baby Elizabeth to worry about. I was not concerned Tom Audley would denounce me as an adulterer though the law had changed and it was now a crime punishable by death.

In any case I was busy setting up my new newsbook. The official journal of the new Commonwealth. The authorised version.

I did wonder if I should be ashamed producing something so thoroughly approved of by the new regime. Was I betraying the liberty we all fought and died for? No, I had no real qualms. For a start, most of the junta were lawyers and who is more likely to turn out arguments in favour of whatever cause paid the most money than a lawyer? If lawyers can twist and turn to earn a fat fee, why shouldn't a reporter?

Then there was the appetite for news. More than ever, people wanted to know what was going on. Who better to satisfy their desire for news than the leading newsman of the era? That's why the Commonwealth wanted me. Even Milton was my inferior when it came to writing for the common man.

I gave the Council of State a prospectus. I told them the new publication would be called "Mercurius Politicus", the "Political Mercury". It would run to 16 pages instead of the usual eight, and we would charge tuppence instead of the usual one penny. It would be published every Wednesday. It would be a best-seller not just because the opposition was being systematically suppressed by Milton and his censors but because of its own merits.

It would be written in a jocular way, I told them, because humour was more likely to attract the attention of the vulgar. It would be written in defence of the Commonwealth but I made it clear I would need the most up-to-date information about what the Council was doing if "Politicus" was to succeed.

It said I would establish correspondents in Scotland, France and Holland to supply foreign news. I undertook not just to carry news of the State's affairs but news of interest to ordinary people – crimes committed and executions carried out; witchcraft and hauntings; unnatural weather and the abominable exploits of foreigners.

All human life is here, I assured my readers. They queued up to buy all the news that fits the print.

Soon after Elizabeth was born in London, Lucy left for Burford with the baby and a servant. I headed for Banbury for Nat Fiennes's wedding at Broughton Castle. I thought it might make a paragraph in my new paper and, anyway, I needed to rebuild contacts with the ruling party now I was their most notable spokesman.

Nat was doing remarkably in rebuilding Broughton after it was all-but destroyed by Prince Rupert. He said it cost a fortune but his father persuaded Parliament to pay for it. Broughton was no Windsor. It was small for a castle, built of honey-coloured stone, hidden in an Oxfordshire valley. It boasted a moat, a couple of towers and battlements but it was more of a home than a military fortification.

The builders were doing a decent enough job though it was costing almost twice original estimate. It still wasn't finished, three months after the promised completion date. The foreman said he couldn't get the men – demand soared after the end of the civil war. Building repairs were going on throughout the country, many workmen had been lost to the wars and foreign labourers were reluctant to move to England because it was too dangerous.

The wedding itself was austere – no flowers, no rings, not even any vows before God. It was merely a civil contract. The bride, Frances Whitehead, was suitably submissive, curtseying to her husband, her new father-in-law the Viscount, her brothers-in-law, her step-brothers, as well as her father Richard and her own three brothers.

Frances was a good 20 years younger than Nat, the youngest of eight sisters. She was a quiet girl which doubtless suited Nat's increasingly pious religiosity.

Most of the guests were members of these large families. I wondered why I'd been invited, even if I had once saved the bridegroom's life. The brief ceremony, short service and interminable sermon were finally followed by a modest breakfast. I was placed next to another Elizabeth, this one the wife of Captain James Thompson. He was a strong, out-doorsy-looking fellow recently discharged from the army. James told me he was put in charge of rebuilding Broughton Castle when he came back from the wars. His father had taken over from my old Oxford friend French's father as estate manager. James had recently married Elizabeth Fiennes, one of the Viscount's nieces. He turned out to be a friend of Henry Oxinden who I also knew from university. I'm sorry to say we had a laugh at Henry's expense.

'Did you read his "Dismal Summons?",' Thompson asked.

'Dismal indeed,' I agreed. 'Poor fellow reckons himself a poet but I'm not sure anybody else does.'

'More of a drinker if memory serves,' said Thompson.

Elizabeth looked nice. Didn't say much but she seemed jolly. Dimples and a pretty smile. I quite liked the Thompsons.

Strolling beside the moat as the sun was descending in the valley, the Viscount, who had not acknowledged my presence at Broughton until that moment, hobbled towards me and, without preamble, declared, 'You seem unreasonably vicious towards the Scottish, Nedham.'

I'd been thinking about my wives and their babies. It took a moment to focus on the old man's words. 'The Scottish?'

'Yes. Good Presbyterians, the Scottish,' the Viscount said, 'God-fearing people.'

'Some of them, maybe,' I conceded grudgingly. 'But if they are so marvellous, why have they declared Charles their King and why is Cromwell heading north to sort them out? It is a perfidious and hypocritical nation.'

'They did sell the old King to Cromwell,' the Viscount conceded. We strolled on, the Viscount shuffling slowly at my side. He must have been 70. It's a wonder he was still alive. 'They tell me you have a new job, Nedham,' he said at last.

'I do, my lord.'

'I wanted to talk to you about it. We are in a new world. A new world.

Nothing is as it was. These Levellers now. They won't just go away. We need to make it clear the world is not being turned upside-down. The rule of the people – what they call "democracy" – can only lead to the tyranny of the hot-headed rabble. Suppose they got their way and we had elections to Parliament every year – imagine the turmoil. It would bring in the lowest of the people and Parliament would be at the mercy of their most frenetic humours. It would lead the country down the bloody road of licentiousness, mischief and mere anarchy.'

I was inclined to point out the folly of executing the King if he wasn't expecting any change but, in fairness, the Viscount had always been against the killing. So I just said, 'The Levellers have had their day, my lord.'

'What we need is a distraction, Nedham. Draw attention away from the travails of Parliament and the Commonwealth. Look elsewhere, man, look abroad.'

The Viscount was right. People needed a distraction from their sorrows. In Lancashire, thousands were dying of starvation. In London, the MP Thomas Hoyle committed suicide on the anniversary of the King's death and another regicide, Rowland Wilson, made mad by what he had done, expired of melancholy and guilt. I reported these events but they didn't look good for the Commonwealth. We needed a new enemy. Who better than the filthy French?

The French King, Louis XIV, was facing the same fate as Charles I – a rebellion provoked by his attempt to raise taxes. I wrote, 'The French, those monkeys of mankind, are very busy at Tennis, and they bandy Bullets instead of Balls. Now the game begins indeed, and the Crown is at hazard.'

It was fun. I pointed out the corruption and depravity of the French aristocracy. The Duke of Orleans, the King's uncle, was notorious: a walking bordello. It was well-known, I said, that when he talked to even the most civil ladies, he 'faces them tossing his pike, with his hands in his cod-piece'.

I didn't have it all my own way. There were still rival newsbooks. One published by an obnoxious, round-faced, red-haired Puritan ironmonger called Henry Walker. Then there was the itinerant Cambridge man John Cleveland, who called himself a poet. He issued a rag accusing me of scandalising both sexes and three parties (I assume he meant Parliament, Royalists and Puritans). He declared me to be 'the public enemy of mankind'. He complained, 'It is not fit that we should be at the mercy of a tavern, and the drunkenness of an arbitrary pen. It mads us to be reproached by such a one as him; for there is no such torment to a Christian as to be tyrannized over by a renegade. So insatiable is his appetite of speaking ill that there is no person so intimate to him, or so deserving; nothing so secret or religious which he abuseth not; he is neither to be tolerated in society nor policy, neither in conversation nor a state; but, rather, as a public parricide, to be thrown into the sea in a sack, with a cock, and ape, and a serpent, the right emblems of his politic tri-plicity.'

'Tri-plicity?' What kind of a word is that?

I was summoned to see Milton. 'We can't have this, Marchamont, we really can't,' said the Foreign Secretary and censor-in-chief.

'Why not?' I asked. 'In fairness, if I dish it out, I've got to be able to take it as well.'

'This is not about you. We're talking about the reputation of the Commonwealth. We can't have its servants traduced like this.'

'Then silence the critics,' I said, though I rather wish I hadn't. It was not for me to advocate the arrest of writers who took a different view of things from me. I wasn't bothered by Cleveland's attack. He was of no consequence. His pamphlet was scarcely seen.

'If there's one thing worse than being talked about,' I told Milton, 'It is not being talked about. Besides, this is just the feeble moaning of a disgruntled Royalist, of no consequence at all.'

Yet the Council of State was so sensitive to criticism it was even prepared to sacrifice its leading writer rather than endure an attack by a man of no importance. Milton told me I had to work with his new protegee, some Gray's Inn child of 21 called John Hall.

'It's Hall or Marvell,' Milton told me. 'You need some restraint, Marchamont.'

This whole episode made no sense and I said so. If I were to be substituted every time my newsbook came in for criticism, I told Milton, I might as well go back to medicine. Anyway, as long as I was there to be vilified, it would deflect attention from the real targets, Cromwell and the Council of State. I was blamed for supporting the decisions of a Government which had very little public support. The more they attacked me, the less attention they paid to the real offenders.

I pointed out that, in his role as censor, Milton knew every word that went into "Politicus" anyway and, so far, I'd written nothing that wasn't in support of the Council of State.

In the end, I agreed to take Hall on as an assistant as long as the Council of State paid his wages. This inexperienced youth was supposed to keep me under control. I soon put him straight on that score and set Hall the task of covering crime news.

In November I received a letter from Paris. It was unsigned. It said, simply, 'Sir, I regret to inform you your wife Lucy Nedham, nee Lighthorne, succumbed to an illness caused by the strains of childbirth and departed this life on Friday, September 14, in the year of our Lord 1650. She is survived by her, and your, daughter Elizabeth Mary Nedham, who has been taken into the care of the Sisters at the Convent of Our Lady of Calvary in this city. Your wife has been buried in the Cemetery of the Innocents near St Eustache Church in Paris. I regret the need to pass on this news and that it is necessary for me to remain, though your obedient servant, an anonymous informant.'

Could this be true? How could I find out? What proof was there? Why was this correspondent anonymous? What did he want from me? Who was he? Was this some sort of blackmail attempt? What was I to do?

I went to see Audley.

'Washington,' he said firmly.

'Really? How can you know?'

'I've already read this letter, Nedham,' he said with an infuriating smirk. 'It was in a package of correspondence we intercepted on its way from Dover a few weeks ago. There were other things as well. Nothing to concern you, though. I thought we might as well let this one reach its destination.'

Audley and I were walking towards Westminster wharf, where the river was busy with boats. The day was cool, a breeze stirring up the grey-green water and a fitful sun going in and out of the clouds.

'I'm sorry about your Catholic wife,' Audley said. He didn't sound sorry. 'What will you do about the baby?'

'What can I do?'

'I doubt if there's anything you can do. We have friends in Paris who can ascertain the truth for us but the Sisters won't let the baby out of the convent, especially if they think she will be brought up in the Protestant faith.'

CHAPTER 33

This seems to be the setting of the young King's glory

Summer-Autumn 1651

Bradshaw suggested it to Cromwell. The Captain General passed word to Milton. The Foreign Secretary raised the idea with me. I didn't have much choice.

We were in Milton's back garden looking out onto the countryside. It was a warm late summer evening. The day was slowly melting away in the last rays of the descending sun. God was in his heaven then Milton said, 'You need to join the army, Marchamont.'

This was not what I expected. 'Join the army? What on earth do you mean?'

'Cromwell is stalking Charles Stuart and his Scottish army. They're heading south and they will have to be finished off at some point. You ought to be with them. In at the death, so to speak.'

'"In at the death" is not an appealing expression,' I replied. Milton smiled his cherubic smile, as if he was uttering the most innocent of thoughts. It made me wonder a little if he was planning to see off a competitor – if John Milton got Marchamont Nedham sent to his doom, he would have no rival. As it was, I represented a perpetual humiliation for the poor man. He was so studious, so careful, so laboured, so slow. I, on the other hand, was prolific, witty, sharp, in touch with the common man. It would do John Milton's literary prospects no harm to see his famous contemporary taken out altogether.

That was an ungenerous thought. I tried to dismiss it and focus on the proposition – that I should attach myself to Cromwell's army as it followed the supposed King Charles II on his march south from Scotland towards the inevitable battle which would settle the Commonwealth's future.

If the King were to gain a victory over Cromwell, Milton and I were as good as dead. We therefore had a very personal interest in Cromwell's success. More to the point, always assuming the General emerged the victor, it would be valuable copy "Politicus" – a first-hand account of the battle.

As a career move, reporting from the battlefield would do me no harm at all. If the King were to die in the battle or be captured and tried like his father, the crown would be Cromwell's. The battle was for the throne. The victor would be as powerful as Henry Tudor when he vanquished Richard III. As half the English nobility knew very well, it paid to be on the winning side. And it paid better to be seen to be on the winning side.

Even though attending a pitched battle in person was not something to be relished, I saw the benefits. At least I could say I'd seen action – assuming I survived, of course.

I set off two days later, leaving baby-faced John Hall in charge of compiling the next edition of "Politicus". I gave clear instructions about what to use and what to discard. I told him to start serialising my new best-seller "The Case of the Commonwealth". It deserved an even wider readership than it had enjoyed so far. It would reinforce my reputation as a political thinker and shaper of the Commonwealth.

I was given a military escort. Bradshaw ordered half a dozen men to accompany me and sent messengers on ahead to contact Cromwell, inform him of my plans and arrange a rendezvous.

I visited Burford on the way. The guards camped in the fields while I stayed under my mother-in-law's roof and enjoyed a happy reunion with my wife and baby Elizabeth. Lucy was as pleased to see me as I might have hoped. She was even, touchingly, if a little unnervingly, concerned for my safety. She was proud of my bravery and willingness to spread the good news of the General's Godly campaign. Charles the Pretender was the anti-Christ. She hoped he would meet his doom. 'Take hold of shield and buckler,' she said, 'Draw out also the spear and stop the way. Let them be confounded. Let them be as chaff before the wind and let the angel of the Lord chase them.'

I said I'd do my best.

We contacted Cromwell's army at Evesham on August 28. Evesham was a small town on a bend in the River Avon with three churches, the ruins of an abbey and a bell-tower that must have been the last one built before Henry VIII closed all the monasteries 100 years earlier.

The Scottish were at Worcester, 20 miles away. Charles was expecting to recruit locals to his cause. Royalist Worcester was the last city to surrender before the execution of Charles I, when Henry Washington was its governor. The city spread across the River Severn and once had sturdy walls and bastions to defend it. These were in a poor state after so much action, though they were now being hastily reinforced.

Captain General Cromwell was already on the way to Worcester by the time my little troop reached Evesham but I found my old friend John French, the army doctor. We'd last met at Burford where he had to certify dead the three Levellers Cromwell executed. This time he was not busy. 'We will be,' he said.

'You look surprisingly cheerful about the idea,' I said.

'I am. After all this experience, I'm writing a book about my medical theories. I'll tell you one thing, Marchamont. The need for rehabilitation. If you don't die, it can take a long time for men's wounds to heal. They need treatment to improve their muscles and limbs. One of these treatments is taking the waters.'

'Taking the waters?'

'Aye. There's something special in some waters. In Harrogate, for instance. I discovered it when we were campaigning up there. The spaw waters.'

'Spaw waters?'

'Aye, spaw. That's what they call it up there in Yorkshire.'

'I think they must mean "spa", Frenchie.'

'No, definitely spaw. Anyway I'm writing a book about it, "The Yorkshire Spaw".'

'Let me know when it's printed. I'll give it publicity in "Politicus". And what about the war closer to home. Who are that lot?' I pointed at a troop of infantry setting off in the direction of Worcester.

'Fleetwood's men,' said French airily and went on, 'The pretender's difficulty is, even the Royalists in Worcestershire won't join an army full of Scotch Presbyterians.'

'We don't need to worry, then?'

'I've been with Cromwell for years and, truly, God is on his side. His successes in the field are the mark of divine favour. Besides, we've got 28,000 men; Charles has half that. Worcester's hard to defend because it's seen so much action and very little rebuilding.'

'Talking of rebuilding, have you been to Broughton recently?' I asked. French's father had been steward there and the doctor was brought up with the Fiennes family.

'I have. They've done a good job. Nat's living there isn't he?'

'Just got married. I went to the wedding. Met James Thompson and his new wife.'

'Elizabeth? Known her since we were children. Lovely girl.'

We gossiped on like a couple of old women while French led me to his tent and ordered up roast chicken and wine. We ate well. It was another bright, hot evening. We debated various medical opinions. French believed in observation rather than ancient texts. He said the wars had given him an opportunity to try out different ways of caring for patients – not just those injured but those struck down by camp fever and the flux. Crushed leaves or bark from oak or blackthorn trees in a stew helped settle the stomach, he said. So did salt and oatmeal or powdered clay.

It was all very interesting and kept my mind off the fact that I was due to go into battle in the morning.

I did get to smell gunpowder. Smoke drifted towards us, where we were stationed on a small hill overlooking Worcester. Smoke swirled in eddies as the breeze took it this way and that and as explosions of cannon-fire added to the haze. It smelt like a bonfire of horse manure. The smell was, happily, as close as I came to the fighting though I did feel the ground beneath me tremble from time to time. I did not smell the iron of blood, though enough of it was shed, nor did I taste the bitter gall of defeat.

I had no idea what was going on. It was strange to see the spires of the cathedral and a couple of churches rising out of the smoke and standing unmoved by the commotion. They gave an air of normality to a scene that was anything but normal. There was a great deal of shouting. Pikemen scurried in one direction in little troops, running at the double, cavalry trotted in another. Messengers came and went. Occasionally I heard a trumpet; sometimes, a piercing scream.

Cromwell watched through a telescope. I saw him lean to one side and speak briefly to his escort before riding off at the trot.

'General, going into battle,' French said. I was not invited to follow, though I had been supplied with a sword which I clutched frequently for reassurance. I was mounted on a grey mare which was obviously used to the sight and sound of battle as she stood in docile contentment while I craned forward for a better look.

It was September 3, exactly one year after Cromwell crushed the Scots at Dunbar. This time he came face to face with the pretender Charles Stuart, tackled the Royalists head on and, in no time, they were spurring their horses in pell-mell retreat.

It wasn't much of a battle to be honest. It started in the afternoon and lasted into the twilight. The Scots made a few sorties south of the city but pretty soon they ran away and the Ironsides were cantering after them without much opposition. The Royalists left the city gates wide open – as Cromwell's troopers rode in from the south, Charles's men crushed each other in their haste to escape to the north.

There were few reprisals and not many executions. This wasn't Drogheda. The city wasn't even sacked badly. There wasn't much left to loot. It was also an acknowledgement that even a Royalist stronghold like Worcester wasn't prepared to support a bunch of wild Scotsmen.

Unlike other newsbook writers, I was there to give a first-hand account of the action. Better still, as soon as he was free, the victorious General explained to me personally the nature of his victory.

Cromwell took off his helmet to reveal his lumpy, sweaty face. He removed a gauntlet and ran his hand across his high forehead, through his long brown hair. It was twilight; flares flickered around us as we rode slowly through the town. Cromwell's men were bringing in prisoners and flushing out the last of the resistance. Smoke hung in the air. Occasionally we heard a gunshot.

'It is all thanks to the Lord,' he said. I looked at him to see if he was being sincere. There was a light in his eyes, almost of ecstasy. He was grim but somehow humble and sat in the saddle with his hands on his chest as if in prayer. I really do think he meant it when he said, 'The dimensions of this mercy are above my thoughts. It is, for aught I know, a crowning mercy.'

I wrote down his remarks and sent post-haste to the printer in London.

Once again, Marchamont Nedham stole a march on his rivals. I broke the news of the great victory ahead of lesser rivals and I carried an exclusive interview with Cromwell himself.

I wrote, at Cromwell's urging, that the victory was thanks to 'the magnificent appearance of God', that it was due to 'the many wondrous and mighty dispensations of His mercy' and the battle seemed to be 'the setting of the young King's glory'.

How was I to know there would be a triumphant second coming?

Talking of triumphant second comings, my return to Burford found me garlanded in the laurels of a victor. I'd seen battle, I'd faced the enemy, I received a hero's welcome. My mother cried, as mothers do. My step-father shook my hand and said he was glad to see me back again. Even my brother smiled.

Lucy was pleased to see me though her joy was not unconfined. She agreed with Cromwell the victory was entirely God's work which is why I had been spared and why the Lord was to be praised. I got no credit for courageously facing the enemy though she was interested in my descriptions of the action and made intelligent observations about the army's dispositions, the way it successfully crossed the river unchecked and about the gallantry of Cromwell in leading the charge through the city gates.

I may inadvertently have given Lucy the impression I was following close behind the Captain General during this assault. I was rewarded with a brief acknowledgement from my wife that even Marchamont Nedham must have conducted himself with a modicum of bravery. It was something, I suppose.

Oh and I do remember Big Susie was very pleased to see me.

CHAPTER 34

The Rump's Trumpeter,
being he that first found
the way to make a fart
sound in paper

Winter 1651

It took weeks before we were certain Charles Stuart had fled the country. At one stage, he allegedly hid up a tree while soldiers searched for him in the forest below. I used to think this was a Royalist myth until years later Edward Hyde assured me it really happened.

Parliament put up a £1,000 reward for his capture and made it high treason to harbour the fugitive. Audley explained, 'We have to be seen to want to capture him but the truth is Thurloe and Cromwell want him to escape. What would we do if he was caught? Imprison him? Execute him like his father? Put him on the Throne? However you look at it, the Commonwealth and the country are better off with Charles Stuart elsewhere. If we caught him, life would be even more complicated than it already is. I'm not sure we could get away with another Royal beheading.'

I went searching the stews south of the river, looking for John Crouch, the man responsible for the Royalist rag "The Man in the Moon". I found him down a back street at the Brown Bear in Southwark. It was a dreadful dive. There was a foul stink which may have come from the Thames but probably just emanated from the open drain outside and the ramshackle huts round about. We'd had days of incessant rain and there was mud everywhere.

Crouch was eating a dish of eels and listening to a group of thieves and cut-throats debate the merits of various women of ill-repute. They had a copy of "The Man in the Moon" and were reading out Crouch's reviews of the city's brothels. They did not know the author was listening.

He was a runt of a man in threadbare clothes, with long hair and a film of sweat across his forehead. He frowned when he saw me, looked back at his food, took a swig of ale, smacked his lips, looked behind me to see, I imagine, if I had a troop of soldiers with me to arrest him. Then he smirked.

'Fuck me sideways,' he growled and chuckled, 'If it isn't four-eyes Milton's Chief Secretary of Grub Street his very self. What you want, you cunny?'

'Good evening to you, Crouch,' I said as politely as I knew how. 'May I buy you a drink?'

'Good gunpowder ale only, cunny,' he growled, indicating I might take the stool opposite. 'How d'yer find me, whatcher wan?'

I called for ale and appraised the man. My fellow professional. 'I have not come to shut you down,' I assured him.

He laughed at this, exposing an almost-toothless mouth. 'Ha! You close me down? More like I'll get you shut down. I know they've got a watchdog on your shoulder. Hall, isn't he? And Milton? Nobody trusts you, Nedham. You're their useful idiot.'

'You won't provoke me, Crouch,' I said calmly. 'I am well-rewarded for my work. Does "The Man in the Moon" make much money?'

'Enough,' he said defensively.

'So I see,' I said, looking round at the low-lives he consorted with.

'No king-killers here,' he said.

'Nor am I,' I pointed out.

'Ha!' he exclaimed and spat on the floor contemptuously before draining his mug, slamming it down on the table and calling for more. 'He's paying,' he told the maid. 'He's got the chink, I ain't.' Then he turned his attention to me. His eyes betrayed an intelligence not initially apparent in this shambling man. 'What is it you want, Nedham? You don't come south of the river just to see little old me without a purpose, now do you? Looking for your old friend Washington? He's in France now, by the way.'

'I know,
' I said. This man knew more than was good for me.

'They won't forget, you know.'

'Forget what?'

'The King's man jumping ship. Again. Rats do it. Marchamont Nedham does it too. There'll be a reckoning one day, mark my words.'

I wasn't going to rise to the bait. 'I need your help,' I told Crouch.

This shook him. 'You, the great Marchamont Nedham, need the help of the poor "Man in the Moon"? You must think I'm a dull widgeon. You must think I was born yesterday.'

'Not at all, Crouch. I know you are an Englishman. We have that in common.'

'Oh we do, do we?' he scoffed. But he sat up and leaned forward. 'Go on then, I'm listening. It better be good.'

'I shall be brief. John Thurloe, Oliver St John and Walter Strickland are even now at The Hague talking to William of Orange and the States General.'

'So?'

'They are talking about creating a new Protestant country – Great Britain and the Netherlands combined. A mighty Protestant power in Northern Europe. A single nation under one God.'

'What's that to me?'

'I know you're more interested in London brothels and who is tupping whom. Fair enough. It's amusing. I don't even mind you having a go at me. But this is real news. It's important. It needs to be got out there. They're talking about a Protestant Crusade. People should know.'

'They wouldn't like it. They'd want to put a stop to it.'

'Precisely.'

'So why not use "Politicus"? You're always boasting how important and influential the damned thing is. Why come sneaking to me with this tale?'

'I can't use it, can I? It's official policy of the Council of State. Thurloe is Cromwell's spymaster, St John's Chief Justice and Strickland's been thick with the clog-wearers for years – even speaks their language. It wouldn't do for "Politicus" to report this. The censors wouldn't let me.'

'Milton, you mean?'

'Milton and others.'

'So you want me to put the story in "The Moon". Nobody would believe it.'

'They would, you know. People take all your tales of witches and goblins and orgies in Lambeth as Gospel.'

'I know,' Crouch grinned. 'And they're all true.'

'Of course,' I agreed.

As I stood to leave, I said, 'By the way, my wife would prefer it if you stopped slandering me.'

He laughed heartily until he started to cough. He swigged his ale then looked at me with a malicious half-smile. 'We are not friends, Nedham,' he said. 'Nobody will forget. Nothing lasts for ever. When the King's restored to his Throne and Cromwell and his crew are cast down, I wouldn't want to be Marchamont Nedham, no matter how much chink you make in the meantime.'

I offered to shake his hand. 'We are not friends, Nedham,' he said again.

A few days later, when the next edition of "The Man in the Moon" hit the streets, there was a fairly prominent piece in it attacking Oliver St John for marrying Cromwell's cousin and then, supposedly, slaughtering her in the days before the Captain General amounted to anything. Now, Crouch said, St John was Cromwell's messenger-boy sent to plead for peace with the Hollanders and determined to give the country away to clog-wearing, tulip-loving, dyke-digging cowards who didn't even know if they were a republic or a monarchy. How, Crouch asked, would this monstrous nation be managed? Would we be ruled from The Hague or Amsterdam? What would the merchants of London have to say about the idea?

It wasn't much but it was enough.

'Well done,' said Audley when we met next. 'Exactly what was wanted. The army is very unhappy. MPs are having to think again. The whole scheme will now be abandoned.'

'I still don't understand why you wanted this. Thurloe was one of the ambassadors.'

'He was but an alliance with Holland is the last thing he wants and the last thing Cromwell wants. It was the rump's idea, not theirs. They just couldn't publicly oppose a Protestant alliance. Now, though, the way is clear and this is your next job.'

'Clear for what? What's my next job?'

'You need to translate and up-date this book.'

He handed me a tome by some elderly lawyer called John Selden. I flicked through it. 'Four hundred pages and all in Latin,' I protested.

'I know,' said Audley, with one of his untrustworthy smiles. 'And we need it bringing up to date.'

'"Of the Dominion or Ownership of the Sea",' I said, translating the title.

'Exactly,' said Audley. 'The Dutch think the sea is free for everyone to use. We must prove the waters round our coast belong to us. And that includes the English Channel.'

'The Channel? But if we own the Straits of Dover with the French, how would Dutch traders get their ships through?'

'How indeed?' said Audley with satisfaction.

CHAPTER 35

What is Democracy
but a toss'd ship

Spring and Summer 1652

I turned the book into English. It was about the sacredness of British territorial waters. I added a few trenchant observations of my own and was duly rewarded by Parliament – £50 was reasonable for all that extra work. It sold well, especially among commanders in the army. And it made good copy for "Politicus".

I knew I was being used by Cromwell's Government to soften up public opinion for the coming war but I had no objection. It paid well and if I didn't do it, some poverty-stricken hack would be employed and the whole nation would be the worse for their stumbling, semi-literate ramblings.

It made commercial sense for England to wrest command of the seas from the Dutch, though it was a pity our closest rivals were also Protestants. This did make the impending conflict a little controversial with the more fanatical extremists – people like Fifth Monarchists, Quakers or a ridiculous bunch of pacificists who called themselves Muggletonians.

'Here,' said Audley, placing five gold sovereigns on the table. I looked round quickly then remembered, we were in Thurloe's private quarters in the Palace of Westminster not the usual low tavern. 'The boss is pleased.'

'You're looking very prosperous for a Puritan,' I told Audley, 'What with your newly-coiffured hair and your shaven face. Is that a note of sandalwood I detect?' I laughed. The big man scowled. 'Is there a lady, Audley?'

'There's going to be war, Nedham,' he said, sitting up straight and pouring boiling water over some leaves in a small cup. 'It's about tea,' he said, indicating the beverage he was preparing, 'And lace and spices. Carpets, silk. Stuff like that.'

'War against our co-religionists?' I asked, a little cynically.

'A pity, I know,' said Audley, 'But if you've invested in the East India Company…'

'I haven't.'

'Just as well. Cromwell plans to break their monopoly. It'll cut prices and create more competition. Anyway, the real competition is with the Hollanders so that means war.'

'Can we win?'

'We're building more ships, we have able generals and we have God on our side.'

'Do we indeed? That's very decent of Him. Even against His faithful clog-wearers?'

Now it was Audley's turn to look over his shoulder before whispering, 'I wouldn't talk like that, Monty, not even in jest. Walls have ears.'

'Even with God on our side, the Dutch have the wealth,' I said. 'They must have 200 ships and thousands of people. We've got what? A base in Bengal and one in Madras.'

'Bombay castle,' Audley added, as if this made all the difference. 'Actually we've got 23 trading factories all over the East Indies.'

'And how's this war to be paid for, Audley? When the King tried to raise Ship Money to pay for his fleet, he got his head cut off. Here we are and it's still all about taxes.'

Audley shrugged. 'Money will be raised, Nedham,' he said, 'And taxes are how you raise it.'

I couldn't help chuckling. 'So we're imposing new taxes, higher even than King Charles, and we are going to war – over nutmegs, cloves and tea?'

Audley shrugged. 'It's about money, Marchamont. And we all know you'll do anything for money.' He grinned and sipped his tea, smiling maliciously over the rim of his cup. Audley inhaled the steam, took a sip, gasped and said, 'What do you think of this tea, then?'

'It's alright I suppose but I wouldn't invest in the East India Company on the back of it. I mean, who on earth will want to risk scalding his mouth by sipping boiled leaves from a small beaker? There's no alcohol and no medicinal value in it so what's the point? I won't be investing my money, that's for sure.'

'It's the latest thing,' said Audley. 'There are plans to ship it over here and start to sell it. Everyone drinks it in China, so they say.'

'It'll never catch on here,' I said decisively.

'Little do you know,' Audley laughed. 'In Rotterdam, leaves of tea from China and Japan are being bought and sold for twice their weight in silver.'

Milton moved again. This time to Petty France, just down the road from the Palace of Westminster itself. A pretty little garden house overlooking the park. I was sorry for our great propagandist. He'd been forced to give up his job as Foreign Secretary because he was now completely blind. Then his wife Mary died. At one time he wanted to divorce her so badly he wrote two books about it. But they'd become reconciled enough for her to present him two daughters and a son before giving birth to a fourth child, Deborah, which killed her.

Their boy John died within a month of his mother. I tried to save him but fever burnt him up. I think keeping him warm and hoping he would sweat it out may not have been the right thing to do but nobody had any better ideas. The poor child spent his last day crying, and then whimpering, for his mother. His father preferred not to enter the sick room.

'They also serve who only stand and wait,' I explained as sympathetically as I could to Anne, Milton's six-year-old, trying to excuse her father's apparent indifference. She scowled and went to fetch some broth.

It was all very difficult for me. The day Mary Milton died – while I was at his house trying to save her life – my own wife was at home round the corner giving birth to our first son. We called him Marchamont. I did wonder if it was unnecessarily ostentatious to call your first-born (second if you include the girl, I suppose, but first-born male) by your own name. My father had been called Marchamont as well, so it was a tradition. At least that's what I told Lucy, who was too exhausted to express an opinion. Two days after the baby was born, the day after Anne Milton died in childbirth, we had Marchamont named at our local church, St Margaret's in Westminster.

Oh I didn't mention, Lucy and I had moved to Westminster, just round the corner from Milton. We bought one of the modern three-storey town houses in the Church Yard of the abbey's Great Sanctuary. Lucy was delighted. We had six servants, including a nurse for little Elizabeth, a groom who also did a little gardening, a cook, two maids and a housekeeper. Alas we even had room to accommodate Lucy's elderly mother on her increasingly-frequent visits.

The house was brick-built, only 30 or 40 years old. It was put up early in King James's reign and – like most houses in the area – once belonged to one of the late King Charles's supporters. This delinquent family was dispossessed some time ago and the place fell into disrepair. It was used as barracks for some time and had the scars to prove it. The walls were battered, the doors did not fit, the floor planks were cracked and creaking, plaster fell from the ceilings, sconces had been ripped from walls, the furniture was dilapidated. But it did have its own piped water supply, which was not something many places could boast.

The house cost £185, a bargain but that's war for you. Half London's population fled with Charles and were only creeping back in ones and twos, tails between their legs, hoping to resume their old lives and thinking nobody would notice they'd taken up arms against peace, liberty and the people of England. Unfortunately for them, the world had moved on.

Luckily, we could afford the house though we ended up employing unreliable builders and Lucy insisted on new furniture and wall-hangings. Happily, there was plenty to be had at low prices – some called it loot or the spoils of war but the dealers who specialised in handling items taken from the castles and mansions of Royalists described it as recompense for their sins. Besides, many of the former owners were dead.

I did wonder about profiting from other people's misfortune but Lucy announced, 'Treasures of wickedness profit nothing: but righteousness delivereth from death.'

This didn't make much sense but I decided it would be best not to question her wisdom on the point.

The house was situated conveniently for my work – getting to Parliament, meeting Thurloe, Bradshaw, Lenthall and Milton, wining and dining in Hell, Purgatory, Heaven and the other taverns. It was at the centre of things – our neighbours included several members of the rump Parliament, a few judges, including uncle Judge John Glynn, one or two prosperous preachers, three or four merchants and various City money-men. Cromwell, his dowdy wife and their entourage were installed in the palace at Whitehall down the road and William Lenthall found me an office in the Palace of Westminster where I did most of my writing.

The move did mean getting a ferry down river to the printers in the City but the benefits outweighed the disadvantage. I could have made them come to me I suppose. I was responsible for the country's most successful newsbook ever. I even employed a man to deal with the demand for advertisements. We were carrying at least a full page of them in every issue, sometimes two pages. At five shillings a time, this was a lucrative side of the business.

We were making money and the printer, fat little Tom Newcomb, and his two teenage assistants, were doing very nicely. But I couldn't trust Newcomb to do the job without supervision – all printers spend most of their time drinking beer and smoking pipes. They do not pay enough attention to the words they are setting in type, their spelling is atrocious and sometimes they transpose whole paragraphs, claim they cannot read my handwriting, misinterpret my instructions or simply add whole sentences of their own devising. It is not safe to let a newsbook appear on the streets without a thorough examination requiring many, many corrections most of which would be unnecessary if the printer did his job properly. It meant regular visits to Newcomb's workshop off Thames Street, over against Baynards Castle.

I also needed to keep an eye on John Hall, my assistant. I was never sure his news sense was reliable. He was obsessed with criminals executed in Scotland as if, for some reason, Scottish criminals were more interesting than our own. He had a Scottish correspondent who assiduously provided news of every man strangled to death for buggery, each woman hanged for adultery and the madmen executed for blasphemy. Hall was responsible for reading through the letters submitted for publication by our correspondents but I didn't trust his judgment and had to read them myself to make sure they were worth including. Sometimes he wanted to print the most awful nonsense. He got excited by some story about whales in the Firth of Forth and a coven of witches meeting in Dunbar. I told him he needed greater scepticism. Some stories might do for "The Man in the Moon" or even the long-winded "Perfect Passages of Every Daies Intelligence" but not for a newsbook with a reputation for honesty and integrity like "Politicus".

Keeping an eye on Hall and the printers meant close proximity to the Thames ferry steps was as important in choosing a house as close proximity to Westminster. I told Lucy when we were looking, 'Location is the be-all and end-all, my dear.'

My critics complained I acquired wealth without effort. This was not true. I was always working. Admittedly I was prospering. And there wasn't much I would rather do than be at the centre of affairs as the constitution of the nation was being moulded into a new shape. But I was working constantly.

Thurloe was a slippery customer. He knew what was happening before it happened. He had an army of informers. He wove a huge spider's web trapping information. Nothing escaped him.

'You must stop writing to Edward Hyde,' he told me. I'd been summoned to his quarters, where he leaned back from his empty desk in the semi-gloom of a cloudy June day without any candles to lighten his darkness. He looked at me with sharp, sceptical eyes.

'I haven't written to Hyde for years,' I said, 'Not since I was working for the last King.'

'The last King?' Thurloe sat up.

'Charles. The first. The last. The very last.'

'The last of that line, anyway,' said Thurloe dismissively, making me wonder about Cromwell.

'No,' continued Thurloe, 'But you have been in correspondence with Washington, have you not?'

'I have always been aware my communications with Washington would be read by you, Thurloe. As you will know, if you've read my letters, I have told him nothing I would not say in public. Really all I have done is post him copies of "Politicus". Even Royalists have a right to know what's going on in their country, I suppose.'

'I know you, Nedham,' said Thurloe.

I did my best to look perplexed.

Thurloe explained, 'Washington works for Hyde; Hyde works for Charles Stewart. Marchamont Nedham likes to keep his options open. Is that not right?'

'I have done nothing to be ashamed of, nothing you can accuse me of.'

'Enough to hold you while we make further inquiries,' said Thurloe slowly. 'And those inquiries might take time. Another spell in the Fleet, Marchamont?'

Was he seriously threatening me? Was I in danger of imprisonment again? I suppose it was dangerous to have contact with the King's party but don't they say 'Know your enemy'?

'You must stop, Nedham. And remember, now John Milton is sadly incapacitated, you have a new licenser – me. And I take my work seriously.'

Thurloe waved a dismissive hand towards the door. As I was opening it to leave, he coughed to attract my attention. I turned. He stood behind his desk and indicated the state rooms at the far end of the building. 'Cromwell wants to see you. Now.'

I suppose that was why I'd been summoned in the first place. The lecture was just to keep me on my toes.

I marched down a long, echoing corridor lined with guards. I crossed a courtyard, entered a side door, turned left, climbed a short flight of steps, down some more, across another courtyard and in through a wide portal to a great hall still lined with the old King's tapestries. I was surprised they'd survived the Roundheads' destruction.

There were several flunkies behaving as if they were guarding access to a reigning monarch, rather than just a lucky soldier. I felt nervous, excited and, at the same time, a little angry – I was not prepared to be intimidated by this man and his regime. I might owe my livelihood to Oliver Cromwell and depend on his patronage for my prosperity but he needed me too.

Eventually I was summoned into 'the presence'. The room contained a large seat one step above the table before it. This was a meeting room but the highest chair was almost a throne. I was surprised the servants – in a crimson livery the colour of the New Model Army's uniform – I was surprised they didn't back out bowing and scraping as they went.

Cromwell wouldn't have noticed even if they had. He was sitting on his throne deep in thought, a hand grasping one arm of the chair as if it were a sword, the other rubbing his head, suggesting it ached.

'Nedham,' he growled. 'Sit.'

'Your highness,' I found myself saying. 'Your highness?' I thought, astonished.

The servant who announced me said, 'Marchamont Nedham, your highness' and, without thinking, I emulated him. Cromwell was now 'Your highness'. Did he notice? I suspect he did and took it for granted. People were already talking of him as the new King. He had the powers of a King – no, he had greater power than the last King, anyway, because he commanded the army and, therefore, he commanded Parliament. He had supreme power.

'You did well with that book about the sea. They've rewarded you?'

'They have, my lord.'

He looked up. Should I have said, 'Your Highness'? 'Good,' said Cromwell. 'We need to publicise it. We need the people on our side if we're going to war with the Dutch.'

'Indeed.'

'The Presbyterians won't like it, Nedham. Nor, I suspect, will the rump. We can't rely entirely on Milton. His eyes, you know. And his wife.'

'Yes,' I said, head down, mournfully. What else could I say?

'The pen militant, Nedham, the pen militant has been as sharp as any sword. You may now stop calling this Government a "junta". You may now stop calling the Council "grandees". We are doing the Lord's work, Nedham. We would not be running the country if the Lord had not willed it. This is not for our own gratification. We are looking through the glass darkly but soon we will see God's designs.'

'Parliament, your highness?' I sort-of asked.

'Parliament?' He laughed bitterly. 'Rump they call it and rump it is.

Ripe for a good kicking on the backside.'

'Elections?' I asked. 'Democracy?'

Cromwell laughed again and banged his fist hard on the arm of his throne. 'Democracy? Don't talk like a Leveller, Nedham. How can the ignorant masses choose their rulers? How would that ever work in the country's best interests? It would end in universal bedlam. We will find a way. More importantly, we must deal with these Dutch pirates. Your readers must understand the importance of this. If England is to prosper, the Dutch must be made to understand.'

I thought it best not to ask what exactly it was the Dutch should understand but, as so often with Cromwell, their understanding would be established in the mouth of the cannon.

CHAPTER 36

Solemn expressions
of affection to
his highness

Spring 1653

Sometimes I marvel at my genius but it frightens me as well.

My genius allows me to see every aspect of a problem. It lets me understand everything and everyone. This remarkable ability leaves me unsettled. I do not have any of the answers yet, as a newsman, I must give my readers the answers. So I argue a case as best I can while sympathising with those who take a different view. Sometimes it's only by writing an article that I discover what I think about a subject.

An obvious example: I could see why Oliver Cromwell was a great man, why God was on his side, why the Commonwealth could not be constructed, let alone survive, without his firm grip on the offices of State. And I could see why he was a dictator, why the Devil drove him, why his Republic was in chaos and why, without a dictator, we would abandon this blood-soaked experiment and go back to the tried-and-tested unhappiness of a Monarchy.

As a newsman, I argued for Cromwell. I was paid to. Before they killed him, I argued for the martyred King. Once or twice — not often, I confess — I lay awake at night wondering which side I was really on and concluding the weight of evidence was insufficient to convince me completely of either cause, republicanism or Monarchy.

In those days, there were long arguments about the Levellers and their demands for "democracy". I could see why it was fair to give all men the vote (except Catholics and servants, obviously). I could also see why doing so would lead to collapse and ruin as one Government and one set of laws was replaced by a different Government and a different set of laws at the whim of ignorant, ill-educated voters.

It's like affection, I suppose. I had affection for both my wives at the same time. Little Lucy from Burford, my first wife, will always have a special place in my heart. We grew up together, we shared the same history, we had the same home. She was becoming more fanatically religious but when I looked at her, especially when she didn't see me doing so and allowed the furious furrows in her forehead to relax a little, I still saw the young, cheerful, loving girl she used to be. She was, moreover, mother to my children.

Yet when I thought of my other little Elizabeth, hidden away in her Paris nunnery, I felt a lurch of regret and panic which could be called sorrow. I was wretched – I still am – thinking of her poor mother, my Catholic Lucy. She was a brave and noble young woman whose boldness and humour I admired. To think I shall never see her again fills me with profound melancholy. What was I to do about our little daughter? I didn't know but I carried the burden with me every day and tried to avoid examining it too closely, afraid of what it would tell me about myself.

In any case, we were at war and war is good for selling newsbooks. Nobody cared much whether the rump Parliament was any use or who should be running the country when there was a good war to be enjoyed. Better still, this one was taking place at sea so everyone felt safe enough to read all about it without worrying they might be murdered in their beds. The General-at-Sea, Robert Blake, became a national hero thanks to the newsbooks. The appetite for news of his exploits on the high seas was insatiable.

Inevitably some extremists were unhappy England was making war on one of the few Protestant nations in Europe when the rest of the continent was in the hands of Papists. Still, it made a nice change from fighting among ourselves.

In September, the Dutch escaped our fleet off the Kent coast, disappearing like a flock of sheep fleeing a pack of wolves. This compensated for our defeat at Plymouth but wasn't enough to settle things. The cloggies didn't give up easily – which was all to the good for the news-vendors of St Paul's even if we did have to report another defeat in early December. For a few weeks the Dutch had control of the Straits of Dover but it's not called the English Channel for nothing; after fighting near Portland in Dorset over three bone-chilling days in February, whatever we'd lost, we regained.

The war didn't do Cromwell any harm. Even before Portland, he was hailed the nation's saviour by the moneymen in the City of London who would benefit most from its success. They gave him a lavish reception.

'Music, drums and trumpets. Fit for a King. On Ash Wednesday as well.' John Bradshaw spat. He was livid. His face had turned red. I feared for his health. He was sitting in Milton's parlour reading my account in "Politicus". 'You even say, "this famous City has, by these solemn expressions of affection to his highness, given a good example to the rest of the Nation, being sensible of the great benefits they are like to enjoy under his Protection and Government". Cromwell isn't the entire Government, you know. We are not all under his "protection", Nedham. How can you write this nonsense?' Bradshaw screwed the paper into a ball and tossed it into the fire.

'He does have a point,' said Milton.

'I am just reporting the news. It's not my fault if the Lord Mayor fawns over Cromwell and everyone calls him your highness, is it?'

'We need a new Parliament,' said Milton.

'Of course we do. Sir Thomas thinks…' ventured Andrew Marvell, who was staying with Milton for a few weeks.

'What does Sir Thomas Fairfax think, Marvell?' asked Bradshaw sarcastically. 'Your employer, skulking somewhere in Yorkshire, far from the fray? What does the great General think, now he has run away?'

'He thinks things have gone too far. He thinks we need more stability. A new constitution.'

'A new King?' asked Bradshaw.

'If necessary, yes,' said Marvell.

'So why did we get rid of the old one then?' demanded Bradshaw angrily. 'I sat in a court and condemned him to death as a tyrant. And now…'

'Now,' said Milton, 'The brave new world we were all hoping for is disappearing before our eyes.'

'Paradise lost, you could say,' I answered. 'And you, Marvel?' It was an old joke but he took the bait and it lightened the atmosphere a little as we sat in the gloom of a single candle sipping some of Milton's unacceptably sour sherry before the meagre flames of a stuttering fire.

'Mar-vell. Mar-vell, as in Bell. As you know Ned.'

'Need. Need-ham. As you know very well.' We both laughed a little. 'Anyway, your ode to Cromwell. Very ambiguous.'

Marvell looked shocked. 'Ambiguous? It's in praise of the great warrior.'

'So why say the King did "nothing uncommon or mean" at his execution? And why conclude by saying Cromwell will only stay in power as long as he doesn't give up the sword?'

'It doesn't say that,' said Marvell, blushing crimson.

'More or less, it does,' I said. 'Milton, have you read it?'

'I have, or at least it has been read to me. More than once. There is a certain ambivalence, you know, Marvell.'

I reminded the young poet, 'You do say he can only stay in power by force.'

Bradshaw frowned. 'Truth is, Marvell's right,' he said. 'Oliver can't control the Commons. He's only in power thanks to the army. If he lost the army…'

'He won't lose the army,' said Milton, 'As long as they get paid.'

'The navy mutinied over money,' I point out.

'Not for long,' said Milton. 'And we do still have a parliament.'

'At His Majesty's pleasure,' said Bradshaw dismissively.

A messenger. A note. Cromwell wanted to see me. Immediately. For 30 seconds I considered staying in bed. Lucy was at her prayers though dawn was only just breaking. Should I stir this early even for his highness? I should.

It was a week after Easter, which we had recognised in the usual half-hearted way, acknowledging its importance while avoiding any sign of ceremony or idolatry. The sun was looking sharp, rising vigorously over the already-stinking river. A mild breeze blew, birds chirruped, you would never have known the country was in a permanent state of crisis.

I hurried across Westminster to Cromwell's palace in the company of a taciturn flunkey who did nothing but frown and grunt. He seemed to think I was not being quick enough responding to Cromwell's summons.

The Captain General was at his usual place, in his meeting room, sitting on his big chair-which-was-not-a-throne admiring a sword laid across the table in front of him.

'Been presented with it,' he explained. 'No bloody use in a battle.'

I looked at the weapon. Its blade was sharp enough but its hilt was gold, encrusted with diamonds. 'No, it looks a little too precious for that,' I agreed.

'Need your help,' Cromwell said, putting the sword to one side and placing both palms flat on the arms of his throne. 'I need words. A speech. Something to say.'

'Your highness?'

'Today I am going to dissolve Parliament.'

'Boot out the rump?'

'Indeed. They're planning to pass a bill giving themselves the right to sit for ever. These whoremasters and drunkards cannot be allowed to continue.'

'Indeed, your majesty. And what do you need from me?'

'An explanation, Nedham. Sit there. Write something.'

'May I ask what you propose to replace the rump with, your majesty? I can quite see most people would support your decision to get rid of these people. I mean, how many of them even turn up for a debate these days? Sixty or seventy?'

'They all claim their allowances,' Cromwell growled.

'I'm sure they do. But they are hardly a legitimate assembly. They were first elected, what, 13 years ago?'

'Most of the original members are either dead or Royalists or both,' complained Cromwell. He looked more tired than angry. He was putting on weight. It was all those banquets. He sighed.

'And a replacement for the rump, your majesty?' I persisted. I could hardly write a speech for Cromwell without being able to offer something better in place of the thing he was getting rid of.

'A new venture altogether – an Assembly of Divines,' he announced with a certainty his expression belied. 'Milton thinks it's a good idea, so do my spiritual advisers and, indeed, my wife.'

'I'm sure it must be,' I said, trying not to sound as sceptical as I felt.

'So there you are then, Nedham. Get to work. I'll be back in an hour.'

It wasn't difficult. Cromwell was a poor speech-maker. He was gruff, often inaudible, he disliked debate and was prone to mangle words while declaring they were the word of God. He preferred to order people rather than persuade them. Good in a general, maybe; poor in a politician. In Cromwell's case, the general was turning dictator so persuasion was not necessary.

I made a few notes for him in big, bold handwriting so he could read it easily. It included the immortal words, 'The nation loathes your sitting. You have sat here too long for any good you have been doing. Depart, I say, and let us have done with you. In the name of God, go.'

There was more but it's the little phrases a speech-writer comes up with that stick in the mind and make an address successful. Credit where it's due, Cromwell himself made up the line 'take away that bauble' when he was asked what to do with the Parliamentary mace. Even so, it's galling these words will always be thought of as Cromwell's when they were really Nedham's but that's the speechwriter's curse.

According to William Lenthall, it wasn't a pretty sight. Cromwell and my old master Sir Henry Vane – once such close allies – clashed in the House as the troops moved in. Sir Henry had been Lord President of the Council of State only a year earlier, in theory, the most important man in the country, Head of State. Now he stood and shouted Cromwell's own words at him, crying, 'This is not honest, this is not honest.'

Cromwell had worked himself up into the sort of fury he displayed in battle. He shouted back, 'Oh Sir Henry Vane, Oh Sir Henry Vane; the Lord deliver me from Sir Henry Vane.'

Lenthall was forced out of the Speaker's chair. 'Not quite dragged,' he told me, 'But I would have been, I would have been, if I hadn't moved.'

I visited him that evening at the Speaker's House, which he had been ordered to vacate by the end of the week. He was very upset. 'Humiliated,' he said more than once, muttering resentfully. 'I, who stood firm against King Charles when he invaded the House of Commons, am humiliated by this Cromwell. Humiliated. Has the man no recollection of those he owes it all to?'

A few days later, Thurloe's messenger-boy Tom Audley said Cromwell wanted to mend his fences with Sir Henry. It was my job to win him over. I was sent to talk to him. Since the King's execution, Sir Henry – though he didn't sign the Death Warrant – had been at the centre of Government affairs, reforming the navy, passing the Navigation Act which led to war with the Dutch, taking responsibility for domestic and foreign trade. When Cromwell dismissed the rump, Sir Henry Vane had been trying to abolish the 'rotten boroughs' which returned members to Parliament even when nobody lived in these ancient places any longer. In many respects, my old master had been the prime minister in the Commonwealth Government. I hadn't seen him for some time and I'd always been slightly wary of Sir Henry. Audley warned me, 'He's not the man he used to be, Marchamont.'

The five-mile ride to Vane's Hampstead home was pleasant enough in the early summer. I set off in the morning when the chances of being robbed were modest (I carried a sword and a knife in case) but Sir Henry was not in the mood to receive visitors.

He would only see me on the lawns outside his rather dull, square, red-brick mansion. It was plain and unadorned, in keeping, I suppose, with Sir Henry's austere outlook. The house did command a respectable view down the hill and over the fields towards London. I could see from the Tower in the East to the abbey in the West, the spires of churches, the turrets of mansions and the masts of ships. I had to enjoy the view because I wasn't offered any refreshment and I wasn't given much chance to speak.

Sir Henry, once reserved and polite, was now humourless, stern, perpetually angry, his face lined and creased with frowns. His hair was thin and grey. He walked with a slight limp. He was 40 but looked two decades older.

I told him Cromwell was putting together a new Council of State and wanted him to be one of its members.

'Seven generals and five civilians,' said Sir Henry contemptuously. Then I had to listen to a sermon. 'Who is this man, this Oliver Cromwell, to demand my presence? He is nothing. A thug. A soldier with a soldier's manners and a soldier's intellect. He says God is on his side. He is guilty, guilty mark you, guilty, of aspiring to be God. The springing up of this spirit in man was that which cast him down from his excellency and gave him his fall.' Sir Henry paused. Looked out across the heath towards the city. It was a bright day with high clouds scudding westwards in a brisk breeze.

'It is a noble view,' I said, thinking I should say something.

It seemed to remind him I was there. He resumed, 'Self-interest. Self-interest. The whole world seems to be governed by self-interest. It is the Devil's powerful bait which bribes the conscience and, by degrees, draws off the heart from God. When I was governor of Massachusetts, we saw clearly the corrupting spirit of man. Now, again, God's true riches are trodden underfoot. We must all bow and do homage to Master Cromwell or become objects of his fierce wrath and displeasure.'

There was much more in this vein. The gist of it was Sir Henry would not take an oath of loyalty to Cromwell and had no intention of providing the military dictatorship with a fig-leaf of legitimacy.

His last word on the subject was, 'Power belongs to the people, Nedham, and don't you forget that.'

There were many debates in those days about the best way to govern. One of the troubles with printing was that it had become so cheap and easy any semi-literate lunatic with an axe to grind could put out a pamphlet. There was no effective regulation. They could say the first thing that came into their heads and some people would believe it – a lot of readers seem to think if it's in print it must be true. I didn't understand why the Government tolerated this fashion for freedom of opinion. It was dangerous.

'Mark my words,' I told Milton and Bradshaw one afternoon when we were debating – for the umpteenth time – the needs of the nation, 'If it were not for the printing press there would have been no English Bible, no chance for self-appointed holy men to interpret it in ways that run contrary to God's word and no revolution at all. A little knowledge is a dangerous thing. Giving people the ability to read scurrilous libel-sheets at a penny a time is asking for trouble. Mind you, Sir Henry Vane thinks power belongs to the people...'

Bradshaw couldn't contain his mirth. 'The people? That's typical Harry Vane. The common people are of a loose disposition. If they can enjoy a kind of dissolute liberty, they like the Government whatsoever it be. The people are ignorant and stupid and it is best for everyone – including them – if they remain so. All the people want is bread and circuses. Leave the rest up to those of us who know what we're doing.'

It was a hot June day. We were in the garden behind my house in Westminster having returned from the naming ceremony at St Margaret's Church for my latest child, our daughter Mary. Lucy was looking tired and a little unwell. Her mother was fussing over the sweetmeats in the parlour. My own parents were unable to make the journey from Burford. Little Elizabeth was toddling around getting under the feet of the guests; her brother Marchamont was in the nursery while baby Mary was in a crib in the shade.

'We can't have another election,' Milton asserted. 'We could never be sure of the outcome. Exclude Royalists by all means but what about the merchants who are still upset by the treatment of Charles Stewart? You could never trust them to support the republic. That's why an assembly of the Godly is the only answer.'

'Rather like we used to have Bishops in the House of Lords,' I laughed though nobody found it funny except me.

CHAPTER 37

Had the Devil himself
been in his news office,
he could not
have exceeded him

1654-5

It never pays to let people know what I do for a living. When I work as a doctor, I avoid telling casual acquaintances because I'm immediately subjected to a litany of aches and pains. As a newsman, I was constantly told other people's opinions and advised to take up their causes. Religious fanatics were the worst. 'Thou shouldst warn thy poor benighted readers of the imminent Second Coming' or 'The evils of the Devil are in thy newsbook' or 'Thou and thy kind art an abomination' or 'Beware 1666 – the year of the beast, the end of carnal humanity's rule. Warn thy readers, repent, repent…'

It wasn't just God. Politics was a topic everyone had an opinion on. High taxes, war with the Dutch, abolition of the Lords, the Parliaments Cromwell called and dismissed, the army and its generals. The state of trade was a constant topic, as if I could do anything about it. I couldn't take a simple boat trip from Westminster to the City without a ferryman trying to get publicity. The only subject nobody mentioned was Monarchy. It was far too dangerous.

I remember one such monologue: 'I had that Nol Cromwell in this ferry, you know. Years ago now when nobody'd ever heard of him. How do I know it was him? You never forget a nose like that. Plus, the bugger never give me a tip. Just paid his fare and left. Not even a thank-you-kindly for my pains. Thank you very much, your honour, I thought to myself. Miserable Puritan. Puritans, they're all like that – stuck-up and tight with money. One of them once told me, 'My tip to you, sir, is to avoid the evils of swearing, drinking and fornication'. Bloody cheek. I ask you. Well now, sir, what's your line of business?'

The endless stream of chatter came to a brief pause as he waited for my answer. Foolishly, I told him, 'I write.'

'A writer, eh? Anything I've ever read?'

So you can read, I thought. This was a surprise. '"Mercurius Politicus",' I said.

'"Politicus"? What you mean the Government rag?'

'It's not the Government's,' I said, bridling. 'Nor is it a rag.'

'Well, Government or not, we need you to put something in your next edition.' The ferryman leaned in towards me so I could smell his foul breath and see holes where his teeth used to be. He took out a paper from somewhere inside his thick woollen jacket and thrust it in my face. 'A petition. We're gathering signatures. Here, look.'

I skimmed over his document. Stripped of the usual verbiage, it was a plea for Parliament to scrap plans for a bridge across the Thames at Battersea.

'So you don't want another bridge across the river?' I said with a half-smile.

'We got one, ain't that enough? Look, there's three thousand ferrymen earning a living on this water. Family men, God-fearing men. Build another bridge, you destroy half their jobs. Build a third, you kill off half of what's left. Build more, you've destroyed the livelihood of London's rivermen. What then? One bridge more – it's the thin end of the wedge. Besides, ferries are quick, convenient. Build another bridge, it'll get as jammed up congested as London Bridge is now.'

'Surely it would provide much-needed relief by creating a second thoroughfare, especially for wagons.'

'Nah, you don't understand. Traffic expands – build more bridges, you just get more traffic. Bible, innit? "Whosoever hath, to him shall be given, and he shall have more abundance: but whosoever hath not, from him shall be taken away even that he hath." The little us poor ferrymen have, even that will be taken away. And it's not just ferrymen, it's the whole city – congested from Westminster to Limehouse. Now, here we are, St Paul's steps. That'll be two pence, thank you sir. And don't forget, I expect to see something in next week's "Politicus". Save our services, save our ferrymen, ban the abomination of a bridge at Battersea.'

'I'll see what I can do,' I said, having no intention of obliging, but I did give him a farthing tip. Wouldn't want him criticising me to all-comers like he did the Lord Protector.

Cromwell said, 'I don't know why I bother. The ingratitude, it's staggering. I devote my life to the well-being of the Commonwealth. I risk my all to create our republic. I give up my peace of mind, my family life, my devotional duties, I jeopardise my very soul. What do I get in return? Calumny. Insults and accusations. Contempt.

'Through the Grace of God, I give them triumph after triumph. I defeat the old King, I see off his son. I conquer Ireland and Scotland. I beat back the Dutch and assert our trading rights. I uphold true religion and give a liberty of worship unknown anywhere else in Christendom. What more do these people want? I ask you, what more?

'And who are they anyway? Pettifoggers, innkeepers, millwrights, stocking-mongers – such a rabble as never had hopes to be known as our nation's grand jury? Look at Praise-God Barebone? A ridiculous fellow – a leather-seller sets himself up as a preacher and saver-of-souls, thinks he can rescue the whole country if only we prepare for the Second Coming. The Second Coming.' Cromwell spat out these last words contemptuously.

I nodded agreement. Our leading general was pacing a wooden floor, every tread resounding through the palace. I now knew Cromwell could carry on like this for perhaps two hours without ceasing. No orator and yet, without knowing it, a ranter. His Parliament of 140 religious leaders from all over the country had broken down in chaos. Turned out Cromwell's supporters were in a minority. They ended up pleading with him to dissolve the assembly. He ordered the army to clear out the building and pack these clergymen off home.

That wasn't enough to stop him raging about the ungodly behaviour of that Godly crew. The fools demanded a rule of law that excluded anything not specifically mentioned in the Bible. 'All the decent people have gone home anyway,' he was saying, 'Sick of the idiotic fanatics and their prophecies. The world is not going to end tomorrow or the next day or in 1666.'

Yet Cromwell and his Generals craved legitimacy. Lucy couldn't understand it. She said Cromwell's power 'belongeth unto God'. As far as she was concerned, whatever method he chose was good enough because Cromwell was God's instrument and could not be questioned. Cromwell's will was God's will; Cromwell's rule was God's rule.

The man himself was less confident in the Lord's all-seeing power.

For such a bull of a man, Cromwell was surprisingly sensitive to criticism. I had to publish another book in his defence. This one was called "A True State of the Commonwealth". We used it as the basis for most of Cromwell's speeches for a year or so. We had it re-printed and handed to every member of the next new Parliament. It talked about the importance of checks and balances in the constitution so power was not all in the hands of Parliament, or the judges, or the administration responsible for putting things into action.

Yet again I had a best-seller on my hands. The book had to be re-printed for the public and again for MPs. I also plagiarised my own work, spinning it out over several months in "Politicus", thus saving me time later on.

I needed to save time. I was busier than ever. Cromwell kept wanting me to write speeches for him and debate the management of the country. This was flattering and I know Tom Audley was put out to see me by-pass him and his boss Thurloe time after time. Oliver was afraid his rebellion might not succeed. He felt unappreciated and couldn't understand why so many religious factions were adamantly opposed to him.

'You want freedom of worship,' I told him, 'But freedom's like a virgin that everyone seeks to deflower.'

The next new Parliament first sat on Oliver's lucky day, September 3, anniversary of the battles of Dunbar and Worcester. William Lenthall was back as Speaker, Uncle John Glynn returned as MP for Caernarvonshire, Nat Fiennes as MP for Oxfordshire. But this Parliament was as much of a disaster as the last. Cromwell wanted it to pass 84 Bills into law and ratify a new national constitution, "The Instrument of Government", drawn up by his generals. By January '55, they had failed to back the constitution or pass even one of the 84 Bills. Oliver was sick of his new Parliament. It wouldn't do what he wanted. In fact, it wouldn't do anything at all. He dissolved it.

In fairness, Oliver was sick of just about everything. He'd taken up residence in the King's palace with his wife and family. It was beginning to look like a regal court. He even played bowls, one of King Charles's favourite pastimes. He still wasn't happy, though, and one of the things keeping him awake at night was what was being written in the newsbooks.

Several authorised or semi-authorised pamphlets were coming out every week along with some which were definitely not authorised. The standard of writing varied from the competent to the obscene. "The Weekly Post", "The Moderate Intelligencer", "The Faithfull Scout", "Severall Proceedings of State Affairs", "Mercurius Philo-Monarchicus for King Charles II" not to mention "The Man in the Moon" and "The Smoking Nocturnall" – they appeared, they disappeared, they re-appeared, they were re-named and re-printed. They all cost a penny each. The saleswomen and the bookshops around St Paul's were kept busy with the comings and goings of these rags. Preachers were kept busy denouncing them. The public was kept busy reading them. There were dozens issued by catch-penny printers and penniless hacks in an increasingly desperate attempt to cash in on the demand for news. They were unreliable, often unreadable, largely unprofessional – some were a disgrace to the trade.

I'm not sure what finally provoked Oliver into reacting against this proliferation of pettifogging propaganda. It may have been revulsion at some of Crouch's stuff, like his poem in praise of rape, his story about naked witches or references to the lewd shape of a Maypole. It may have been the story about a peeping Tom who claimed Jonah was swallowed by a quail. Perhaps it was the guide to the brothels of London or – closer to home – the way newsbooks identified the crooks, hypocrites, pimps, whores, usurers and misers within the Government. It may have been the vilification meted out to Oliver's close supporter Henry Marten who was regularly described as a debauched, drunken whoremaster. This was nothing but the truth yet Oliver somehow overlooked Marten's sins and objected strongly when they were pointed out by the newsbooks.

Then, one August afternoon we were standing around watching another game of bowls on the lawns behind the palace when Bradshaw took me aside to say, 'Opportunity, Nedham. You can make a bit of money.' He chuckled and rubbed his finger and thumb together to indicate receiving coins. 'Cromwell has decreed.'

'Decreed what?' I asked.

'He wants the press silenced.'

It was my turn to chuckle. 'I know.'

Bradshaw looked at me with his pale eyes – even on a bright summer day, he looked pallid, as if he was recovering from a serious illness. 'You know?' He couldn't keep the surprise out of his voice.

'I may have helped Oliver come to his decision.'

'Helped him?'

'Well, he was moaning about something in the "Moderate Intelligencer" again – you know the "Mod", the Levellers' rag, all about one man, one vote and that. I said, "You could put a stop to all this, you know" and he said, "How?" So I told him.'

'You told him?'

'About your review. What you did in '49, your Licensing Act.' I didn't remind Bradshaw why he had been so keen on the Act – that he was sick of being called a 'scarlet cut-throat' and likened (by me, in "Pragmaticus") to Pontius Pilate presiding over the trial of Jesus.

'Yes, it's on the statute books,' he said. 'Nobody bothers to enforce it.'

'I think you'll find they will now,' I told him.

The Act said anyone found involved in unlicensed printing could be fined, or imprisoned if they could not pay the fine: £10 for authors, £5 for printers and £2 for booksellers. Even the buyers of unlicensed newsbooks could be fined £1. Printers also faced confiscation of their presses and had to enter a bond of £300 and print the name of the relevant licenser on all of their publications. Now Oliver Cromwell called in the Lieutenant of the Tower of London to crack down on unlicensed newsbooks.

Within a month, they disappeared from the streets of London.

Only one publication remained. "Mercurius Politicus", editor Marchamont Nedham.

CHAPTER 38

It is pity the people of England, being born free, should bow under the ignoble pressures of an Arbitrary Tyranny

1655-1657

I told Lucy about Cromwell's ban on all my rival newsbooks on the day our new baby girl Margery was christened at St Margaret's in Westminster.

'I'm thinking of starting a second newsbook,' I told her, 'We should make a fortune. Imagine, one on Tuesdays and another on Fridays. No rivals. We'll clean up.'

'Do not rub thine hands thus, Marchamont. The love of money is the root of all evil: which while some coveted after, they have erred from the faith, and pierced themselves through with many sorrows. Is it not written, "A good name is rather to be chosen than great riches, and loving favour rather than silver and gold"?'

Lucy's lack of enthusiasm was entirely predictable. It was her ingratitude I couldn't abide. Who was it that provided her with an elegant house full of servants, horses, clothes, food, everything she could wish for? Did she appreciate any of it? Did she ever say thank you or show any gratitude? She took it for granted, as if my hard work counted for nothing beside her pious Scriptures. I wanted to remonstrate but could hardly do so in front of our visitors.

'Remember, husband, he that hasteth to be rich hath an evil eye, and considereth not that poverty shall come upon him,' she said with a smile before turning away to speak to our guests.

It was a beautiful July afternoon and we were in the garden with several of Lucy's religious cronies as well as one or two of my friends, including Milton and Marvell. Judge Glynn was there, looking tired. He was debating with Bradshaw the need for another new Parliament. Thurloe turned down my invitation to join us. Audley, uninvited, arrived in his place.

Lucy was looking pleasantly sprightly now the trial of giving birth was behind her. She had put on weight, it is true, but the birth of Margery left her happier and more tranquil than in the past. Happier and more tranquil but no less willing to judge me and find me wanting.

My mother, after whom the baby was named, made the journey to London to be with us though my step-father Christopher had to stay in Burford where there was strife between the church and local religious sects.

'Your father has to hold the fort,' my mother told me before carrying off baby Margery and cooing to the child in that strange, high-pitched voice women use when they talk to children and animals.

Audley cornered me as we were about to go in for dinner. 'This ban,' he said, 'You know you have a monopoly now, don't you Monty?'

'That much seems obvious,' I said. Audley was considerably taller than me and as we stood looking out towards Tuttle Fields I felt there was something intimidating in his presence. The scar on his cheek was inflamed, his eyes seemed a little red, his hair was wild. I wasn't sure I liked what I saw.

'You're not off the hook, you know.'

'Off the hook?' I said innocently.

'Thurloe and Cromwell. Quid pro quo.'

'Quid pro quo?'

'The field is clear for you, Nedham. You have conquered all before you. But never forget to whom you owe this privilege.'

'Of course not,' I said quickly.

'There's something more.' He paused, looked across the garden to where Lucy, my mother, her mother and several other women were fussing over the baby. 'Your wife.'

'Lucy? What about her?'

'Her friends. These preachers. We need to know what they are saying. It's not enough to close down scandalous news-sheets. There are preachers attacking the Lord Protector. We need to know what they're saying. We need to silence them if necessary. Your wife is one of their followers.

What could be more natural than for her husband to accompany her to their meetings?'

'You want me to spy on my own wife?' I was aghast.

'Not at all,' said Audley, laying a calming – or threatening – hand on my shoulder. 'Not at all. We're not interested in the wife of Marchamont Nedham. Nobody would question her loyalty for a moment. But the men she associates with? They are a different proposition. We know they're stirring up trouble. We need to know more. Now, let me say hello to your lovely new child. And this little fellow over here, this is the young Marchamont, is he not?'

We became a military dictatorship. Bradshaw was livid. Oliver appointed ten major-generals to govern the counties of England, with one each for Ireland and Scotland as well. The major-generals rooted out Royalist malignants and imposed a decimation tax on them to pay for the army. But it was their campaign to make the country more Godly which everybody hated. The idle were put to work. Any remaining celebrations of Christmas were banned – even mince pies were outlawed – along with horse-racing, stage plays, cock-fighting and bear-baiting. They imposed fines for drunkenness. Hundreds of alehouses were closed. Dancing, music and fairs were banned. Anyone, man or woman, caught having sex outside marriage could be executed. I was glad to be happily married, my past sins washed away by the great tide of time.

Most people hated military rule and despised not just the generals but the collaborators who made their petty dictatorships possible. Me, I was quite happy.

My income reached £5000 a year. I'd never been wealthier. I was already charging two pennies for "Mercurius Politicus". Now I started a second newsbook called "The Publick Intelligencer" coming out every Monday and moved the publication day for "Politicus" to Fridays. To save time, trouble and expense, I reprinted half the contents of each Friday's "Politicus" in the following "Intelligencer" and vice-versa. It meant if you bought both papers, you were not getting completely new information every time but that hardly mattered. Readers were hungry for news and half a newsbook full of fresh information was better than no newsbook at all. Sales of both publications boomed.

I won an allowance of £100 a year from Cromwell for my assistant John Hall to keep him happy as I piled more work on him. Several newsmen who had worked for rival publications were keen to contribute. We paid them a few pennies a time for anything we used. We had a strong network of correspondents at home and abroad so we were never short of copy.

My policy was to support Oliver but not too obviously. Besides, news is not just about what our political masters are up to. It's about the madness of the world: The squire who values his valet more highly than his wife; the highland laird who pays a ransom for the restoration of his cook; the dockers in Newcastle who withdraw their labour demanding higher wages; the running battle in Fowey, Cornwell, between churchmen and Quakers.

Some tales ran for weeks. The ridiculous Quaker James Nayler, who entered Bristol on a donkey one October day, in imitation of Christ, was good for several editions. The stupid man was flogged and jailed for blasphemy on orders from Parliament. This was not to Cromwell's liking. He said, if MPs could be judge and jury over one fanatic, they could do the same for any man in England. I didn't point out they had already done so many times, most notably in the case of King Charles. Cromwell started talking about the need for a second House of Parliament to act as a check or balance on the Commons.

Our coverage included the case of the Quaker leader George Fox, who was jailed by my uncle, Judge John Glynn, for refusing to take his hat off in court and demanding to know where in the Bible it said a man should remove his headgear.

Much of my time was taken up accompanying Lucy to religious meetings. She was pleased with this, thinking I was at last showing some piety. She thought her lectures against avarice were bearing fruit and I was repenting of my ways. I couldn't tell her the truth that Audley and, later, Oliver himself told me to provide first-hand accounts of what was being said at these meetings.

Only two years ago, the Fifth Monarchists said Cromwell was a second Moses leading England to the Promised Land. But by '56 they had lost faith in him. I told Oliver one of their preachers in Blackfriars said he was 'the graciousest and most gallant man in war but, when he came home to Government, the worst'. Another called Oliver 'the most dissembling and perjured villain in the world'. These two were jailed.

A meeting in Allhallows was packed and, as I wrote to Oliver, 'the humours boiling, and as much scum comes off as ever'. One preacher declared the time was at hand when they should feed on the flesh of Kings and great men. They were all keen supporters of the ludicrous Hannah Trapnell, who looked like she must be a witch. She was given to prophesying the downfall of priests, lawyers, landlords and Oliver Cromwell.

Lucy was wrapped up and carried away by these people. It wasn't worth trying to talk her out of her increasingly deranged opinions but I didn't feel in the least guilty reporting to Thurloe and Oliver on the activities of her fellow fantasists. Nor did I feel guilty when various Fifth Monarchists were arrested or when Trapnell was whipped in public. It seemed to me only reasonable, though sometimes it reduced Lucy to tears of indignation.

Her view of Oliver Cromwell was changing but then, to some extent, so was mine.

Sir Henry Vane's father died and the younger Sir Henry quit London for the family castle in County Durham. Sir Henry, who refused Cromwell's invitation to join the Council of State, wrote a couple of incomprehensible religious tracts. Perhaps because they were so obscure, he became the focus of religious dissent – Quakers, Anabaptists and Fifth Monarchists were all accused of plotting with Sir Henry to undermine, even depose, Cromwell.

Sir Henry was arrested. He refused to put up a bond of £5,000 to guarantee he would not disturb the peace and was jailed in Carisbrook Castle, the place he once helped to send King Charles to.

It seemed the good old cause I worked for in the '40s was dying. How could Sir Henry fall out with Oliver Cromwell? I went to see Nat Fiennes, now back on the Council of State and lobbying for another election and a new Parliament.

'How can you talk of liberty, Nedham, when you have denied so many people the freedom to speak their minds in the newsbooks?' Nat asked. He was mocking me but there was an underlying note of dismay. Nat had come up to London, abandoning his new wife in Broughton, to sit on Cromwell's Council of State but, like Sir Henry, he was not happy.

'Cromwell wants to be King,' Nat said. We were in my gloomy little office in the Palace of Westminster. It had little natural light. The window looked out onto a stone wall. I had a couple of chairs, a desk, some shelves and piles of reports, newsbooks and letters on the bare boards of the floor. Few people visited but even the privacy of my cubby-hole was limited. Nat and I both knew what was said could be reported to Thurloe. No conversation was secret. No expression was free.

'What's the alternative?' I asked. My hands were covered in ink. I'd scribbled out today's news from the fleet. The sheets of paper were waiting to be taken to the printer Tom Newcomb. Three quills lay on my table, cut and cut again. My six ink pots were lined up. Two were empty. I had blank sheets of paper on my right, recent correspondence on the left – letters from across this country and across Europe. I had to sift through this material and decide what was worth printing. Audley, or occasionally Thurloe, called in irregularly to check I wasn't hiding something.

Every time I asked, 'Why would I do that?'

Every time they ignored the question and flicked through the correspondence to make sure there wasn't something from a Royalist or a Catholic or some other undesirable.

I pointed out, 'If I was receiving secret information – which I am not – do you really think I am stupid enough to leave it lying around on my desk?'

They ignored that as well. I suppose the aim was to intimidate me a little and remind me which side my bread was buttered.

I was determined to speak freely to Nat Fiennes, whether or not the walls had ears. I told him I was writing a new treatise to be called "The Excellencie of a Free-State; or, The Right Constitution of a Commonwealth."

'A Republic,' I said. 'That's what we need. That's what the good old cause was about. It's what Sir Henry said all along.'

'Look where that's got him,' said Nat with a bitter laugh.

'He won't be in jail for ever and the cause is good. This book of mine,' I went on, 'This is my proper philosophical statement. It's all well and good publishing thousands of words in newsbooks but nobody remembers today's paper tomorrow. Everyone will remember Milton.'

'They will,' Nat agreed, 'For all the good it does him. And you want to be remembered too?' Nat laughed, genuinely amused by the idea. 'Marchamont Nedham wants to be recalled by posterity? Oh dear.'

'The world is changing,' I said defensively, 'And I want to play a part in creating that change.'

'And your free-state book is the answer to all our prayers?'

'It might be. Bradshaw thinks so.'

Bradshaw had lost his place on the Council of State. He had been elected to Parliament but barred from taking his seat because he refused to swear an oath of loyalty to Cromwell. He spent most of his time out of town now, at his country mansion or even in Cheshire. He and Milton were more encouraging. They said Cromwell was in danger of ruling alone when the good old cause was rule by Parliament, an elected body of right-thinking men with a legitimate interest in the Government of their country. We discussed Venice, Holland, ancient Rome, ancient Greece and ancient Sparta. It was not illegal to speculate.

'The supreme power of the nation rests with the people's representatives in Parliament,' Bradshaw said.

I agreed. 'Nothing else will satisfy for all the blood and treasure spilt and spent these last years.'

Tom Newcomb refused to print my treatise saying he was too busy with my newsbooks. In reality he was afraid we'd get closed down because it was too radical. I went to Tom Brewster at The Three Bibles in Creed Lane near the West end of St Paul's. Brewster had been official printer to the Commonwealth for a while but lost the job and was struggling. He'd invested too much money into a Welsh edition of the Bible. He couldn't sell it for the obvious reason that the only Welshmen who spoke that unholy tongue were men who could not read. Your civilised Welshman spoke English and didn't need Brewster's translation. Brewster needed the money and was happy to print a new book by best-selling author Marchamont Nedham.

Cromwell didn't bother to read it but Thurloe told him the gist of it. I considered denying authorship, given that it was printed as being by 'M. N.' I could have said 'M. N.' was not Marchamont Nedham but it wouldn't have taken a genius to uncover the truth.

We were discussing Oliver's plan to call yet another new Parliament when he stopped in mid-sentence, turned and looked me straight in the eyes. His face close to mine, so I could see the moles and warts clearly as well as the worry lines about his eyes and the hairs sprouting here and there on his clean-shaven face. 'Your latest diatribe,' he said.

'Ah yes,' I said. 'My book on liberty.'

'Liberty, is that it?'

'A free state, my lord,' I said, 'A freely elected Parliament. Power to the people.'

'It's what we all want.'

'Indeed,' I said.

'But not what we can achieve overnight, Nedham. You know that. You know we can't rely on a Parliament to do God's work. You know we have many enemies – not just the Cavaliers but Presbyterians and Calvinists. You know freedom has to be earned.'

'I do, my lord.'

'Well then?' said Oliver, as if that proved his point. He never mentioned the book again though it did achieve a certain notoriety over the following months as the Lord Protector called a new Parliament and excluded 100 of the elected MPs who couldn't be trusted to do as they were told. Bradshaw was one of them.

You could say I got away with it when "The Excellencie of a Free-State" came out. I didn't reject completely the idea of a Government ruled by both a Parliament and a Head of State. You can have freedom and still have a ruler. Kings did not have to be tyrants. The difficulty was that, if they stayed in power for any length of time, they were in danger of being corrupted.

Milton and Bradshaw thought Cromwell had been in power too long. Cromwell disagreed.

The new Parliament quickly came to two conclusions – the rule of the Major Generals had to end and the nation needed a new Monarch. Parliament offered Oliver Cromwell the Crown. Arise King Oliver I.

Bradshaw and Milton explained. Lenthall said so. Judge John Glynn was adamant. Nat Fiennes said neither his father the Viscount nor Sir Henry Vane would stand for it. They all told me I had to tell Oliver.

It was a dirty job but someone had to do it.

'No, your highness,' I said, 'This will not do. You cannot accept the Crown. You cannot become King.'

I like to think I changed the course of history.

CHAPTER 39

Good against all malignant and Pestilent diseases,
French pox, Small Pox, Measles,
Plague, Pestilence, malignant or Scarlet Fevers,
and good against Melancholy.

1657-1658

John Hall died. Ague. 27. His wife was most distressed.

Damn me but it was inconvenient. I don't wish to sound callous but Hall's death was very bad timing. We'd never been busier. Then my deputy editor ups and dies. I know I should have been sorry and obviously I grew a long face for the funeral. I spoke an eloquent eulogy praising not just his news work but his poetry, which he thought would seal his immortality. Not many people turned up.

Suddenly I was without an assistant. With two newsbooks on the go, not to mention my other interests – reporting on the Fifth Monarchists for Thurloe and writing another book, at Cromwell's request, attacking that ridiculous old preacher, John Goodwin. How was I to manage?

I tried Audley. Asked if he fancied a return to writing. He laughed in my face and said he had better things to do. I tried Marvell. He was always short of money. But he was off to France with Will Dutton, Cromwell's ward, to visit the Huguenots. I even asked John Rushworth, though he was now a Member of Parliament. He said he had bigger fish to fry. I wondered if Nat Fiennes fancied a little work because I thought he might find it amusing but he'd just been appointed Keeper of the Great Seal which was used on every order issued by the Lord Protector. Nat took his role very seriously, said he had been called upon by God to place his services at Cromwell's disposal and regretted he would not have the time to assist me in my endeavours. I hadn't realised he'd grown so pompous.

In despair I asked my printer Tom Newcomb for help. All I needed was a keen young apprentice who could edit news letters sent in by correspondents at home and abroad and gather the latest information about hangings, rapes, highway robberies and the like. The printer suggested a friend. I should have known the man was a knave.

Henry Muddiman was 29, son of a shopkeeper on the Strand. He'd been to Cambridge and worked as a teacher in the choir school at St Clement Danes. We had teaching in common and quickly agreed children were evil and the pay was derisory. He was on £40 a year. I offered him £75. He almost bit my hand off. I wasn't sure about him but I was desperate. We shook hands and got on with the job of bringing out our two newsbooks.

Several years later my acquaintance Sam Pepys told me he'd always known Muddiman was an arch rogue. One look at his crooked, self-satisfied grin and I should have realised this man wouldn't be content as my deputy for long. Slippery, he was, and sly. Untrustworthy. A usurper. He never told me the whole truth about himself. I found out the hard way.

One reason I needed a new assistant was because Tom Newcomb had the idea of producing a third newsbook.

Newcomb may have been short and round but he was still hungry – for success. At 30, he was seven years my junior and I treated him as little more than a child. Even so, his idea wasn't bad.

'We need a new publication, Monty,' he said one day as we were checking the proofs of the "Intelligencer" (I was suggesting England should set up colony in Bengal to civilise India). 'Look at all these.'

He indicated the advertisements which now covered three and a half pages of the newsbook's 16. As well as the usual announcements of the latest book – this week, the fifth folio of a Bible in nine different languages, none of them Welsh – there were several involving missing persons, missing horses, missing servants, even a missing Van Dyke painting. We had one for a new fire extinguisher, one promoting an improved bed for the sick and something about the sale of stock in the East India Company.

This wasn't unusual. We were inundated with advertisements. In some cases, such as the sale of patent medicines like the Countess of

Kent's remedial powder (a quack remedy claiming to be 'good against all malignant and Pestilent diseases, French pox, Small Pox, Measles, Plague, Pestilence, malignant or Scarlet Fevers, (and) good against Melancholy'), one ad could consume two and a half or three pages. We had to discard news to accommodate these announcements. We could hardly refuse as they were worth a lot of money. A book ad was five shillings for four insertions; a medical ad cost ten shillings for four. Lost and found ads brought in two shillings and sixpence each. We even had some pompous MP take out a notice to complain people were referring to him as Thomas Barnardiston Esq when he should be Sir Thomas Banardiston Knight. This caused much hilarity in the printer's office especially as we charged him an extra shilling before we agreed to carry his announcement.

Anyway, demand was so great Newcomb had to take on two men to handle advertisements. He came up with the idea of a third paper devoted entirely to advertisements without any news at all except, perhaps, a little astrology because that had been popular in some of the lesser, now-banned, newsbooks.

I was all for it. We called it the "Public Adviser" and set up half a dozen offices across London to allow people to book their advertisements easily. We sold the "Adviser" for a penny a copy. Sales were good from the outset and it had no impact on the sales of "Politicus" or the "Intelligencer".

While Cromwell was reluctantly turning down Parliament's request to become King Oliver, we were developing our most lucrative business yet.

Or so we thought.

When the law is whatever your boss, Lord Protector Oliver Cromwell, wants it to be and enforcing it is down to your uncle, Lord Chief Justice John Glynn, you'd think it was impossible to fall foul of it. Turns out some laws can't be got around even when they are utterly ridiculous and shouldn't be law in the first place.

The "Adviser" was carrying notices about a lost mute, a vanished child, abandoned infants and runaway girls, a barber in need of an apprentice and a young man wanting work at sea. Other ads offered peace of mind through tea and coffee. But we'd only been going a few weeks when a nasty little clerk from Lincoln's Inn poked his head round the door and handed Newcomb a writ ordering us to cease and desist immediately from publishing the paper and demanding damages.

It came from lawyers working for a character called Oliver Williams. I made it my business to find out more about this Oliver. He was Welsh, from somewhere near Cardiff. Been in London several years. Gun-maker by trade. In his 30s. Not married. Living in a pitiful apartment round the back of St Paul's. Regular drinker at the Mitre in Chancery Lane with all the clerks, hawkers and crooks. Had money from gun-making, however. He'd even made a couple of rifles for Cromwell. Not rich but well-off and on the make.

Williams had bought a patent from the widow of a Captain Robert Innes, who had been granted a patent by Charles I in 1637 to create an "Office of Intelligence". This was supposed to be a place where people with goods for sale, and people looking to buy things, could meet and make deals. It never happened but somehow the Welshman Williams found out about the Scotsman Innes's patent, bought it for a pittance and thought he could turn a profit.

He claimed our "Adviser" was performing the role his Office of Intelligence should be doing. We were usurping his patent. We had to stop.

'I've never heard anything more ridiculous in my life,' I told my uncle, Judge Glynn, when I sought him out for a bit of free legal advice.

He studied a copy of the patent document that I'd demanded from Williams and eventually responded, 'Ah well now Marchamont I am not so sure it is all that ridiculous. You have to bear in mind precedent. Just because the patent was issued by the tyrant King does not in itself invalidate the agreement. We have maintained the laws since Charles's time, you know. Mind you, it seems Williams is not allowed to charge any money for deals done at his office, all he can hope for is that the two parties agree to pay him a fee.'

'So he can't make any money out of it anyway?'

'That would seem to be the case, yes. And there is no mention of any publication. So it boils down to the question of whether your "Adviser" amounts to an Office of Information along the lines envisaged in the patent. Is a "publication" an "office"? It's an interesting point of law. I fear this will take some time to resolve.'

'And expense.'

'Lawyers are entitled to a fair remuneration for their services, Marchamont. I'm sure, as a Lincoln's Inn man, you would agree.'

'But he's trying to stop us interfering with a business he doesn't even have. Nobody in their right mind could say a publication is an office or an office is a publication.'

'Now there, I am afraid, we must beg to differ, my boy,' said the Judge. 'After all, what is the office of a publication? It is to offer information to the public. Thus it is providing information in the office of a publication or, to be more concise, it is an office of information, is it not? If one were to use one's good offices to supply information then it is questionable how those informations might be provided but merely to preclude a publication from the office of supplying information does not imply the office itself is invalid especially when an office is not necessarily a physical object such as a room or a shop or even a table in a tavern but might, instead, be an activity instead. It seems quite clear to me.'

'Though not to me, uncle,' I complained, baffled. 'Nor, I might add, does it make sense even if it were clear. The patent was issued by a tyrant whose rule has been repudiated.'

'Yes but we have not abolished the law, Marchamont. How could we when we only deposed the King because he himself had broken the fundamental laws of the nation? We were upholding the law by executing Charles, not repudiating it.'

I was deflated. 'So there's nothing we can do?'

'You can challenge this man's rights. It is what the courts are for, is it not? But in my opinion, and it is not my case nor will it ever come before me so I cannot be certain, but in my learned opinion, you may retain the right to your publication, your "Adviser", but this man Williams retains the right to bring together purchasers and vendors in his offices. His patent still holds good.'

'But it's never even been put to use.'

'Irrelevant, I'm afraid. His patent lasts 41 years from 1637. Bring back your "Adviser" in 1678 and you should be in the clear.'

The Judge leaned back in his high judgmental chair and smiled benignly. I looked at him and realised I was looking at an elderly gentleman.

Uncle John had grown portly. His cheeks were pink and chubby, his hair was thin and grey, his eyes were bulging and awash with rheum but he looked particularly pleased with himself. He clearly wanted me to ask how he was but after the advice he'd given me, I decided not to give him the satisfaction.

'How is my aunt?' I asked instead but that was enough.

'Delighted at the news,' he said and, when I looked inquiringly at him, he went on, 'About the new House of Lords.'

'Oh yes,' I said. That's one of the difficulties with being a reporter. People expect you to know the news ahead of anybody else but I was not aware of any 'new House of Lords' even though I'd heard Oliver grumble about the powers the Commons assumed and how there was a need to rein it in.

'I have been asked to serve,' the judge said with a satisfied grin.

'Congratulations,' I forced myself to say, as enthusiastically as I could in the circumstances, which wasn't very. 'Lord John Glynn of Westminster. It has a certain ring to it.'

'Indeed it does,' he said.

It turned out this upper house was not to be called the House of Lords and ended up as nothing more than 'the Other House' because nobody could agree on a better name. And most of the people nominated to sit in it never bothered to turn up.

But my uncle did take his seat, so did Nat Fiennes which, considering Parliament once tried to have him executed, was quite an achievement. I visited Nat, also Milton, Bradshaw and even dropped a couple of hints to Cromwell himself. It all fell on stony ground. Nobody seemed willing to give Marchamont Nedham a seat in the House of Lords, no matter how important he was to the preservation of the Protectorate.

'You have to understand,' Bradshaw told me, 'You and your journals have their uses but it's a grubby trade, Marchamont. Don't take this personally. I, for one, am well aware of your good nature, sound qualities, pious good sense and righteousness. But nobody likes a scandalmonger no matter how loyal to the cause. Too many people think you grub about in a dunghill. They think the stench will cling to you even in ermine.'

Bradshaw delivered this damning verdict just hours after a court delivered another one – we had to stop publishing the "Adviser".

We went to the Court of Common Pleas. It didn't take long. Williams had some Presbyterian counsel; I represented Newcomb and me. I won the point that Williams had no right to publish anything in print so he was ordered to stop issuing an advertisement sheet called "The Weekly Information from the Office of Intelligence" – a badly-printed, badly-designed, abominable catchpenny rag if ever there was one. However, Judge Edward Atkyns declared our "Adviser" was an Office of Intelligence and therefore breached Williams's patent. We were ordered to shut it down after just four months in business.

Still, some of the advertisements it generated found their way into "Politicus" and the "Intelligencer" instead so we probably made more money in the end because we increased our revenue without adding to our costs.

And we weren't ordered to pay any damages to the Welshman or pay his costs so he must have ended up worse off than when he started which caused me some satisfaction.

The episode was annoying, all the same.

In that period, everything was annoying.

Lucy became pregnant and I had to rack my brains to remember how that happened. We were rarely close, partly because I was so busy, partly because she was committed to her religious nutcases. Eventually I remembered we'd been close after one of the "meetings" I reported on to Oliver. For a while she seemed to think I might be a convert to her peculiar religion with its warnings of the end of the world.

The child, a boy we called John, did not live long enough to be baptised. It was just as well because Lucy announced baptism was heretical.

'God commands all men to repent,' she told me one morning. 'He does not require infants to be instructed into the faith. These are times of repentance, weeping and mourning. These are dying days.'

They certainly were for poor baby John.

A year later we lost another boy, Robert, soon after his birth. Lucy just said, 'Jesus called them unto him, and said, suffer little children to come unto me, and forbid them not: for of such is the kingdom of God.'

I was the one who cried but I did so in private. My wife offered no consolation nor, it seemed, did she require any other than that offered by the God she was so drawn to.

I found myself haunted by the ghost of my other Lucy and the fate of our daughter Elizabeth.

There was plenty of news to keep me occupied. We gave over a whole page to the death of 'free-born' John Lilburne, leader of the Levellers. His cause had died some years earlier and he was dismissed by most as a quarrelsome, cantankerous, unforgiving, stupidly stubborn man but he'd some interesting ideas.

There was yet another plot on Cromwell's life. Thurloe knew all about it and let it run on until he could haul in the guilty parties. It was surprising how little deterrent being hung, drawn and quartered could be.

Major General John Lambert, one of army's most-loved commanders, refused to take the oath of allegiance to his close friend and comrade-in-arms Oliver Cromwell. He was paid off with a pension of £2,000 a year and retired to Wimbledon. If I had not been working for Oliver, I would have speculated in print about the reasons behind Lambert's fall from grace and what the implications might be for the protectorate. It was enough just to hint at questions over the succession.

Several real Lords refused to sit in Oliver's new Other House, including the Viscount, who declined to sit beside his son Nat. Cromwell did appoint his sons-in-law Robert Rich, Earl of Warwick, and Lord Fauconberg, even though Fauconberg was an open Royalist.

I was still gnashing my teeth at being overlooked but it didn't matter much – the new Lords didn't last long and Cromwell dissolved another Parliament.

He was ruling alone and the question nobody wanted to address was what would happen when Oliver was called to a higher purpose. It was an important question but not one we could ask in print. It was almost impossible to discuss anywhere, in a tavern, a print-room, among friends, even with people like Bradshaw and Milton. It mattered, though, because what would happen to the country, the cause of freedom, the relative tolerance in matters of religion, the hard-won peace and modestly improving economic conditions when the Head of State was cut off?

The question was becoming urgent. Something was wrong. Cromwell could hardly sign his name. Once, his signature was strong and purposeful; now it was uncertain, the letters half-formed and wobbling as the pen shook in a palsied hand.

When he was not on the battlefield, Oliver had always been indecisive. Now he was vague, uncertain, irresolute. I visited him early in August and was not admitted into his presence – his daughter Elizabeth was gravely ill. I offered to go to her when it became apparent her physicians had no idea what was the matter with her other than melancholy over the recent death of her young son Oliver. I was sent packing. A week later I was writing her obituary in "Politicus". She was only 29 and, according to gossip, she was a Royalist at heart and berated her father on her deathbed about the blood on his hands.

She'd been Cromwell's favourite daughter. Her death was a mortal blow.

I saw him on August 20 at Hampton Court. I'd gone to discuss how he wanted me to report the capture of Dunkirk, an English city after it was seized in our war with the Spanish. He showed little interest. He looked crushed. His face was grey with the pallor of death on it, his voice was quiet and hesitant, he had no energy. I was ushered from his presence after only a couple of minutes by his wife Elizabeth and a couple of servants.

What would happen when Cromwell died? We were about to find out.

CHAPTER 40

Thundering, Lightning, and Tempestous Winds tore up Trees to the Terror and Amazement of the Inhabitants

Autumn 1658

The storm started gently enough. A few rags and papers tumbling down a street and round a corner. I saw water ripple in a bucket. A window rattled. A candle-flame flickered, guttered, flinched, came back to life. A door slammed shut with the bang of a gun being fired.

Lucy and I were in the parlour. As twilight approached, the wind was getting up. It was a welcome breath of fresh air after the stale city atmosphere of another stifling August day.

The first raindrops were fat and pattered down onto the street as if a servant had been sent to dampen the dust. I stood in the doorway and watched as people stepped up their pace walking towards the sprawling buildings of the Palace of Westminster. The drops grew in frequency and intensity. Soon they were shafts of water sending passers-by scurrying for shelter, laughing in surprise.

The light airs became a strong breeze then

a storm, a gale which turned the rain through almost 90 degrees so it was plunging straight into the face of anyone foolish enough to brave the inclemency.

This was just the start. The setting sun was blotted from view and dark clouds loured over London bringing the crash and rumble of thunder and the brief, startling brightness of lightning. Dogs whined and howled, horses kicked their stables and shook their halters, children wailed.

The rain fell all night. Puddles became pools, pools turned to lakes, which linked with one another as water poured down streets and round corners, encountering other new brooks and streams between houses. These waters carried away market stalls, litter and debris, early-fallen leaves, plants in pots, temporary gravestones, wooden scaffolding, horse dung and excrement and poured in through the doors of low-lying houses. High tide on the Thames brought another wave of water lapping at thresholds, first trickling, then pouring through doors, windows, and ill-fitting joints.

The wind threw London into chaos and confusion, toppling steeples, ripping tiles from some buildings, whole roofs from others. The wind blew away temporary shanty-towns and rickety structures erected in haste and hope by the poor, the dispossessed, wounded Royalist soldiers, the despairing and desperate. The wind blew devastation as rain inundated streets.

Thunderclaps exploded as if the Battle of Naseby had come to our doorstep. Lucy was exultant. 'The time approacheth,' she kept saying as the house shook and a door slammed shut. It was all I could do to stop her running out into the rain. 'This is God's judgment,' she declared. I admit I did wonder for a while whether she had a point.

Was the Lord God angry with his chosen people? Had we betrayed the hope of a New Jerusalem? Was this truly the end of days? It certainly felt like it as the storm raged. Lucy and I sheltered in the parlour. We started by comforting the children and trying to persuade them there was nothing to be afraid of. Later we sent Elizabeth, Marchamont, Mary and Margery down into the cellar with the servants. It was dry there and the bellowing of the storm was not so loud.

Our candles blew out at about half past one in the morning but we sat on by the light of a fire, smouldering and starting in the grate. It was dangerous to have it burn brightly, sparks could fly anywhere if they were caught by a draught. We kept the fire burning low. This was August; we shouldn't need a fire. It was alight for the dubious comfort it gave rather than for warmth.

I slept a little. Fitfully. Lucy did too. At about half past four we poured ourselves two large glasses of Madeira, realised we would sleep no more and waited for dawn. As we waited, we comforted each other. Lucy was still very excited. It was the last time she and I lay in each other's arms.

Three days later, as London was mopping up from the devastation of the storm, Oliver Cromwell, Lord Protector, died of kidney disease and ague. He was 59.

The date was Oliver's superstitiously lucky day, September 3.

CHAPTER 41

Give me Elbow room
in these
tottering times

1659-1660

It was chaos after Cromwell was gone. Of course it was. It took three months just to stage his funeral.

Puritans refused to allow praying or singing because they would not benefit the dead and were hurtful to the living. It presented Richard Cromwell, Oliver's son, the new Lord Protector, with a dilemma. They solved it with a quick burial and decided to spend an astonishing £60,000 marking Cromwell's departure to a better life.

A coffin not containing the body was placed in state at the centre of a suite of rooms in Somerset House, off the Strand. The rooms were completely hung with black velvet. There was a wax effigy of Cromwell in a velvet suit with gold lace and ermine. There was a gold and diamond-encrusted sword, various coats of arms, the Imperial crown, a golden orb and golden sceptre, eight five-foot-high candlesticks, banners, taffeta, coats of arms and guards in black uniforms. This went on for weeks. Thousands filed past but, by the end of November, mourners had dwindled to a trickle of old soldiers paying last respects to their commander.

Then we had what, at other times, would be called a state funeral fit for a King – they even followed the rituals used when King James died 33 years earlier.

There was a great procession of grandees and worthies from Somerset House to Westminster. It took all day. It was late November. There was no food and no facilities despite the cost. The day was dark and bitterly cold. At one point I had to slip through the cordon of redcoats lining the streets and find a privy. I wasn't the only one. We shuffled along for hours and when we finally reached the abbey there was no service, no reception, no refreshments, nothing acknowledging that we had devoted interminable hours to our dear departed dictator.

Milton was there, hanging on the arm of his German friend Sam Hartlib. Bradshaw was prominent – Richard Cromwell had recalled him and made him Chancellor of the Duchy of Lancaster. Nat Fiennes and John Glynn were there. I couldn't see Sir Henry Vane. He was already campaigning against the new regime. He wanted a republic and claimed making Richard Cromwell Lord Protector was as bad as making him King. Mind you, Richard didn't seem inspired by his task. He didn't even lead the procession. That honour went to Oliver's son-in-law Charles Fleetwood, a cruel man with a long nose. Close by were Major Generals John Lambert and George Monck.

I watched them from a distance. All in their finery, three Major Generals, each with a sense of his own importance. They were polite, pious and grave. Monck stood aside a little from the other two. Lambert had come out of retirement, scenting opportunity. Fleetwood, sacked as Lord Lieutenant of Ireland only a couple of years ago, had appointed himself chief mourner ahead of his rivals. It was not difficult to believe Fleetwood was preparing a coup.

Monck, on the other hand, was a professional soldier; he'd fought for Charles I before turning his coat. He looked accustomed to command. Even in the procession, he had a couple of lackeys dancing attendance. I saw him talk to one of them and watched the man slip through the crowds on a mission from his master.

I wasn't to know then who Monck was communicating with, nor why it would be of such significance.

After Cromwell died, it was every man for himself. Richard Cromwell was no Oliver. He commanded neither army nor Parliament. Another bitter winter, after a dreadful harvest, did nothing to lighten the mood. People were still dying of hunger.

I carried on writing my newsbooks. They continued to sell, attract advertising and make money but caution was my watchword. Now was not the time to argue forcefully for one form of Government or another. As weeks dragged on into months, we kept waiting for something to happen. All we got was manoeuvring.

There was talk in favour of a restoration of the monarchy. There were sporadic uprisings in Charles Stuart's support. I stopped referring to him as 'the young Tarquin' in print and stopped making fun of everything he did. These things would be remembered. It was prudent to antagonise the Royalists no further. I could see which way the wind was blowing. My newsbooks devoted more space than ever to criminal matters and foreign affairs. We mentioned politics as little as we decently could, the waters were too murky.

I deemed it prudent to re-open lines of communication with Royalists I'd once worked for. I wrote to my friend Peter Heylyn, who sheltered me at his brother's house in Minster Lovell when I was hiding from Cromwell's troops after the King's execution. Peter was in Abingdon, completely blind though he said he could still recognise each of his 11 children by their footsteps alone. His wife Laetitia wrote back. She said he was as argumentative as ever and warned me, 'You are in danger of incurring the wrath of the King's party. You must do what you can to ease his restoration. It will go hard on those who resist the restoration of the rightful heir to the throne of England.'

I wrote to Henry Washington, who was with Charles Stuart in Holland. It took weeks to get a reply and, when it arrived, it was not promising. 'Above all,' he wrote, 'The King values loyalty. This is not something Marchamont Nedham is noted for, whatever his other qualities.' Washington also said he was short of money and suggested I might forward a little. I did. No less than £50. It seemed like an investment.

I even wrote to Edward Hyde, who'd become Lord Chancellor of Charles's court in exile. It was clear from tavern gossip that Hyde's agents were out looking for allies and offering deals. Hyde thanked me for previous services and said if he needed further assistance, he would doubtless ask for it. It was a brush-off.

'That hasn't gone terribly well, has it?' Audley mocked me.

He was an old man now. The past 20 years had aged him. His joints were stiff. When he walked, he dragged one leg. His hair was grey, his eyes had lost their lustre. His clothes were shabby and stained once more. He was drinking too much. But he was still a big man, and menacing when he chose, but today he was jovial.

I tried to look as if I had no idea what he was talking about.

'Our information network is intact,' he said. 'We see everything, Monty, even letters to your friends at court. Not that they seem very friendly towards you, do they?'

I grinned ruefully. 'I admit their replies were disappointing.'

'Thurloe says never forget where your loyalties lie. Or at least, where your interests lie.'

'I am well aware of where my interests lie. My difficulty is what happens next. Let's face it, Audley, you and I can't look forward to a restoration with equanimity.'

'Speak for yourself,' he laughed, supping his ale.

'At least my work has been all out in the open, clean, honest, straightforward,' I said.

'A lot of people think otherwise, Marchamont,' he said, leaning across the tavern table and looking earnestly at me. 'It's fine for the likes of me. I operate in the shadows, nobody knows my name, what I do or who I work for. You, on the other hand, everyone knows you. The great Marchamont Nedham, court jester and scribbler-in-chief. The man with the poison pen. What is it? Ah yes, "The Rump's trumpeter being he that first found the way to make a Fart sound in paper." You are hated, Marchamont, truly hated.'

'I don't think so, Audley,' I said, with a show of bravado I did not feel. 'How could they possibly hate me? Most of them don't even know me.'

'They see what you write, Marchamont. Twice a week, they see it. Not to mention all your pamphlets.'

'That's my writing,' I said. 'My writing isn't me.'

'Isn't it?' Audley gave a sceptical grimace. 'I see.'

For the past few years, I was safe. I had important friends. Now, Cromwell was dead, Bradshaw was sick, Milton was blind and out of politics, writing some new epic. Nat Fiennes was still around and so was Sir Henry Vane but Sir Henry was at war with the Major Generals and Nat was close only to God.

There was Judge Glynn, of course, and Speaker Lenthall. They would be preparing their own lifeboats; they may not have room for a jobbing wordsmith. I thought about what Audley was saying. 'Hated, is it? Among the more ignorant sort, you may be right, I suppose,' I said quietly.

'Thurloe says he'll be safe whatever happens. He knows where the bodies are buried. He says he will protect his friends. Even so, I am ready to pack up and leave. Massachusetts Bay. The colony is a Godly place. Ship to Holland, Holland to America. You must be ready, you and your wife and children.'

'I'm not travelling half way round the world to fall into the clutches of a band of humourless Puritans,' I said. I sounded brave and determined. I felt no such thing.

'See how you feel in a few months' time,' said Audley. 'You know these things always take longer than they should.'

He was right. Progress was desperately slow. Richard Cromwell dismissed Parliament; the army dismissed Richard Cromwell. Pensioned him off. Called back the old rump Parliament, the one which first started sitting almost 20 years earlier. Old men now, some of them. Many faces had changed because of bi-elections. Even so, it was the smallest, most unrepresentative collection of representatives since Thomas Pride purged it back in '48. Happily, Pride himself had been purged by the Grim Reaper.

William Lenthall was restored as Speaker and a new Committee of Safety set up. That, in turn, established a 'Secret Committee' with Sir Henry Vane, John Bradshaw and Major Generals Fleetwood and Lambert. It was never going to last.

Meanwhile Lucy lost another baby, after seven months. We would have called her Francis. This time, my wife withdrew, took her brood and left for Burford. There was nothing I could say.

I did follow a month later. I had money and thought it would be as well to buy a house out of town in case it was necessary to leave London for any length of time. I put Henry Muddiman in charge of both newsbooks for two long weeks. It was a big mistake.

At home in Burford I paid my respects to my parents. It was Mayblossom-time. The birds were singing, the trees were coming into leaf, the sky was blue and full of puffy white clouds. It was a glorious day. My mother, in the garden in her apron, was planting vegetable seeds. Her knees creaked as she rose to her feet. Her face was pale, her hair straggly, she looked old and tired.

'You do look old and tired,' she told me.

'Thank you, mother.'

'You do, Marchamont. What have you been doing? Working too hard, I don't doubt. Lucy has been in Burford these past six weeks and she has hardly said good-day. We saw Lizzy and Monty yesterday, though. What lovely children, Marchamont, I swear they are two of the cleverest little things I've ever come across. Much brighter than the tykes your father has to deal with in school. We made sugar cake.'

'I'm surprised you could lay your hands on the sugar.'

'This is the countryside, Marchamont. You forget. We have resources you city-dwellers do not possess.'

'City dweller, maybe, mother, but I have plans. I am here to buy a suitable house for Lucy and the family. Somewhere we can live.'

'Oh Marchamont, are you going to leave that terrible place and come home at last? You look as if you need a rest, my child.' Mother placed one of her bony hands on my cheek, smiled at me and declared, 'My boy does look a little pale and tired. Come in and have something to eat.'

My step-father, Christopher Glynn, the vicar, was more interested in the political situation. 'It has been very difficult for me here,' he said. He looked worn out. 'If it weren't for the Lenthalls I am not sure if I would still be in possession of my living. There have been incessant demands for changes to the liturgy just as there have been ridiculous demands for me to change the curriculum at school. It's all we can do to teach the boys to read and write yet some parents demand religious teachings we cannot possibly provide without offending some other group of non-conformists or Presbyterians. I have tried to maintain a middle course between the old forms of worship and the new – if people don't want any ritual at their baptisms, their marriages or their funerals, then I don't force it on them. But if they do...'

My little brother Robert was a grown man. He, too, wanted to discuss the political situation. Over supper he told us how important it was to bring back a Monarch, how Charles Stuart was the only man who could restore order and how the murder of his martyred father was a sin against God himself.

'Is that what they are teaching you at Oxford these days?' I asked.

Robert smiled. 'You know that is not what they're saying. But I can tell you it's what a lot of people are thinking.'

'Especially me,' said my mother emphatically as she was ladling out her special lamb potage with thyme, parsley, marigolds, violet-leaves, borage, sorrel, sage and pennyroyal mint. 'It is time this nonsense was over. Too much fighting, too many deaths. All those poor boys.'

I visited the George in search of Big Susie. I saw the landlord, my distant cousin Dick Veysey, dodgy son of a crooked father. 'Charity?' he said when I asked, casually, after the woman who used to work there. 'Oh, she died three winters past. Some sort of fever. Why? Did you know her?'

It was a blow. I was fond of Big Susie. She was a friend. She was kind and affectionate and made no demands on me. I liked knowing she was always there, to offer me consolation and shelter me from my enemies. I hadn't seen her since the Battle of Worcester seven years ago, so I had no right to mourn her passing three years after the event. But mourn it I did. It felt as if I were mourning a part of me – we'd been close since we were children.

I couldn't bring myself to call on my wife, her mother and my children straight after receiving Veysey's news so, instead, I took a long walk along the banks of the River Windrush, down the valley to Minster Lovell to visit Edward Heylyn. His son Henry was in possession because, it turned out, Edward, too, had died. Some sort of infection, Henry said, though he was vague about it. The place was in a tumbledown state which Henry blamed on the war, the shortage of labour and the fines imposed on Royalists by the Commonwealth.

'We hate the major generals round here,' he told me as he was tying up a fence to try to keep in the sheep which had spotted a gap and, apparently, made for it at irregular intervals. 'Can't afford many farmhands these days,' Henry complained, 'Can't even keep the fences mended.'

At Lucy's mother's, my wife greeted me with indifference. It was as if I were a stranger. My children eyed me with suspicion, even little Lizzie who I liked to think I had some kind of a rapport with. She was eight or nine, growing up and learning her letters (I was one of those fathers who believed in the education of women, not that Lizzie or her mother appreciated the fact).

'Your mother told my mother you were here,' said Lucy. 'Nice of you to pay us a visit.'

'I had to pay my respects at the Vicarage,' I said in my defence.

'And leave thine horse there and take dinner there and spend the night there and wait the whole of the next day before calling on thine own wife and family?

'Hello Lizzie, are you pleased to see me? Come to your father, child.'

She continued clinging to her mother's skirts while Lucy scowled as she prepared food for the little toddler Margery. She looked like some mad preacher as she turned on me, pointed an accusing finger and declared, 'O faithless and perverse man, how long shall I be with you, and suffer you?'

Lizzie did not come to me. Marchamont crouched under the table. Little Mary came shyly to me and held onto my leg. I picked her up and kissed her. She smelt of rosemary. 'Mother doesn't like you,' she said in a matter-of-fact voice.

'I know, my child,' I said, 'Though I am not sure why.'

Lucy made a contemptuous noise like a growl. 'Thou art a murderer of truth, there is no truth in thee. When thou speaketh a lie, thou speaketh of thine own: for thou art a liar, and the father of lies.'

What had I done to provoke this? Did Lucy particularly dislike something I'd written? Had I been guilty of a sin closer to home – surely she cannot have learned about dear, dead, departed Lucy Lighthorne?

I think the death of three children in a row, sorrow over Oliver Cromwell, confusion over the state of the nation and my constant absence all combined to upset my wife's equilibrium. Part of me wanted to take her in my arms and console her but I knew any attempt to do so would just make matters worse. 'Lucy,' I said, but I did not know what to add.

She screamed. It was a piercing noise, shrill, full of anger and violence. It startled the older children, provoked screaming in the infant and encouraged me to leave. 'For it is written,' I said in the tone of one of her pious preachers as I strode past her to the door, 'It is better to dwell in the wilderness, than with a contentious and an angry woman.'

I never even got the chance to tell her I'd bought a house three miles out of town with a large garden for the children, paddocks and fields, twelve rooms, half a dozen servants or more – everything she always said she wanted.

Bradshaw was pale, short of breath, incapable of standing. Milton and I visited him on his sickbed at his Westminster house. He was pleased to see us and, in between fits of coughing, he wanted to talk politics. He blamed the army for not knowing its place. He said Parliament had to cut the army down to size, pay off the officers and generals, and send the men home. It had to raise money to make up the arrears in pay but the army had to recognise the supremacy of Parliament. 'What did we fight for if not that?' he gasped.

Milton was less convinced. 'The army provides stability,' he said. 'The Commons can't be trusted. Too many Presbyterians, too many closet Royalists. There is a real danger the Commonwealth may be coming to an end.'

I told them I thought it was much more than a danger, I thought it was almost a certainty. 'What I can't understand is why people don't realise the dire consequences of a restoration. We'll all be massacred,' I said.

'I won't live long enough to see if that's true,' Bradshaw said with a half-smile and another coughing fit. His physician came to let more blood – a completely useless procedure which would hurt the patient, leave him even weaker and lead to no improvement in his health.

I thought, but didn't say because it would not be in very good taste, that at least Bradshaw would have a natural death. Milton and I had hanging, drawing and quartering to think about. I'd only seen it once but once was enough. It's quite a spectacle. The crowds enjoy the gore and the victim's screams. They like the excruciating agony the traitor, Catholic or murderer is put through. No condemned man can endure it with dignity. It is intended to deter and, while it's all very well watching this terrible torture inflicted on someone else, those with half an imagination put ourselves in the same position and that's enough to make the strongest man weak with sickness.

At no point in my newsbook career had I ever thought there was a danger I'd end up on the scaffold; not even when I was in Newgate after the King was executed did I seriously contemplate being condemned to death as a traitor. Now, though, with momentum building for the restoration of the Stuart monarchy, I was wondering what punishments they would inflict on the people – hundreds of them, if not thousands, let's not forget, not just Marchamont Nedham, John Milton and a couple of other poets – who turned out to be on the wrong side after all.

They couldn't execute us all. Could they?

CHAPTER 42

To old Margarett five markes,
to Mr. Marcham't. Nedham tenne pounds,
and to Mr. Iohn Milton tenne poundes.

1659-60

Talk about guilt by association.

Bradshaw died and left me £10 in his will and £10 for Milton. Very nice, I suppose, to be remembered by the dear departed but wills are public documents and Bradshaw was rich and famous. At a time when regicide might well be suicide, being seen publicly as such a close friend of the King-killer-in-chief that he leaves you money in his will, is not a good look. Bradshaw's little legacy felt like the kiss of death.

The State marked his passing with another grand procession. There were far fewer mourners than for Cromwell. I found I was really very busy that morning, a press day, bringing out the latest edition of "Politicus" and couldn't spare the time traipsing after an empty coffin on another bitingly cold November day.

I ploughed on with the newsbooks and squirrelled away as much money as I could, sending packages to Burford, entrusting it to my mother, not my wife. But even the news business was getting tougher.

Those remnants of the Rump Parliament, giving its cloak of legitimacy to military rule, decided, in their idiocy, to lift all the restrictions on the printing of newsbooks. Suddenly it was a free-for-all. New titles sprang up every day. Some of those second-rate hacks who had been around for years, struggling to survive, had a new lease of life. Printers who had been limited to authorised religious tracts and books about cookery were back in the business of running off eight-page rags. The Mercury-women were delighted – suddenly there was at least one new title to shout about every day instead of just the "Intelligencer" on Mondays and "Politicus" on Fridays.

That Welshman Williams started his own rag "from the Office of Intelligence" which he called "A Particular Advice". "The Loyall Scout" returned along with "The Weekly Post", Crouch revived "The Man in the Moon" and added "Mercurius Fumigosis" but even he couldn't match "The Wandering Whore" which devoted its first edition to the delights of Priss Fotheringham, 'the second-best whore in the city' and her Six Windmills brothel in Moorgate. It didn't say who the best whore was.

We held onto much of our advertising, though we had to cut our prices because of the competition. We had a reputation, a strong distribution system, a reliable readership and we were still the best-informed newsbook on the market. Even so, sales were on the slide. So was our income.

In May, the generals had the effrontery to withdraw my licence. My licence. The licence of Marchamont Nedham, the man whose work sustained the Commonwealth all these years. I was replaced as the editor of my two newsbooks by a pious little nobody called John Canne, a Fifth Monarchist of all things. Muddiman made the most of this. While Canne was nominally in charge, Muddy took control of the publications for May, June and into July.

I went to see Sir Henry Vane in Hampstead. This time I was admitted into his parlour where he sat in an armchair beside an empty fireplace, in a sea of books and papers.

'Ah Nedham,' he said, as if he were continuing a conversation we broke off only a minutes earlier. 'There's something I need you to do. You need to warn people of the coming apocalypse.'

'The apocalypse? As in, the four horsemen?'

'That, too. But sooner. Beware…' Sir Henry was wearing a white shirt open at the neck, black trousers and black leather boots. He looked a little unhinged. He jumped to his feet and began striding up and down the room quoting the Bible. '"And they went up on the breadth of the earth, and compassed the camp of the saints about, and the beloved city: and fire came down from God out of heaven, and devoured them." That is what awaits us, that is what we have to fear. You, Nedham, with your writing skill, must warn the world of impending doom.'

He said he'd pay me. I wasn't going to argue. I spend the next couple of weeks working up a warning to all and sundry of the dangers of letting the Cavaliers back into power. It was not in anybody's interests, I said, but the Papists'. Charles Stuart was a secret Papist. His mother was a Papist. His brother James was a Papist. How could Charles not be a Papist? And who would benefit from a return to Monarchy? Certainly no Protestant Christian of any sect. Not the Cavaliers who had become reconciled to the Commonwealth. Not even the Cavaliers who would return from exile to find their estates in other people's hands and their property re-distributed, sold on, destroyed, abroad, untraceable. As for the City of London, its merchants and traders, they were the very people King Charles blamed for starting the Civil War in the first place. They would certainly not be allowed to prosper under his son's Government – always assuming Charles Stuart let them live.

By the time my treatise "Interest does not lie" came out, I'd got that piffling priest Canne ousted with Sir Henry's help and I was back in charge of my two newsbooks with little harm done.

Even so, I was worried by the press free-for-all. As the year turned, a pamphlet came out directly attacking me. "A New-Year's Gift for Mercurius Politicus" called me 'a many-headed beast, a pimp for every interest, a juggling damned imposter' and predicted I would be executed. 'Expect no mercy or reprieve,' it said. I was feeling particularly friendless and bereft.

Then I discovered what Muddiman had been doing behind my back.

CHAPTER 43

A thought of mercy
more hateful
is than Hell

Spring 1660

It was war. And I don't mean that war.

In that war, Major General Lambert was marching north to face Major General Monck while Major General Fleetwood secured London for the army.

My war started in the print office where junior reporter Henry Muddiman was scribbling away.

Usually, I left him to get on with it, assuming he was writing up crime stories: the man in Norwich who took a shit on the communion table; the arrest of various frantic quakers in Leicester; the 60 Scotsmen and women accused of adultery, incest and fornication. This time I peered over his shoulder and saw he was writing a letter. Before he clutched it guiltily to his chest, I read, 'My Noble Lord, Major General Monck...'

'What's this?' I demanded. 'Are you writing to Monck? Monck is the enemy.'

'It is none of your business.'

'It is my business. You're supposed to be writing up crime stories for the "Intelligencer" but here you are, writing letters. Show me.'

He refused. I demanded. He refused. I called Newcomb over. 'Tom, what's this? What's your friend up to, writing to Monck?'

'Is he?' Newcomb feigned ignorance.

'He is, though he won't admit it.'

Muddiman and Newcomb looked hard at each other for a moment. Something passed between them, some sort of understanding. Muddiman said, 'If you must know, yes, I am writing to the General.'

'And?' I said.

'Nothing more to be said.'

'Let me see.'

'No.'

'Newcomb?'

'Marchamont? Mr Nedham?' he replied.

'What are you going to do about this? He's your friend.'

'He is also the General's friend, Monty.'

'Are you telling me this man, your friend, is also a friend of the man who is, even now, leading an army into England to meet Lambert in battle? Is Muddiman a friend of the man who wants to betray the revolution, cancel the Commonwealth and bring back the Monarchy? Is he?'

'I'm not sure Monck's gone quite that far, Marchamont, but anyway I suppose that's about the size of it.' Newcomb had the good grace to look shifty.

'Muddiman?'

He stood and, speaking quietly but with a venom I had no idea he was capable of, he hissed, 'Your trouble, Nedham, is you've always backed the wrong horse. You are a naïve fool who cannot see what is blindingly obvious. You think you're so clever writing about the constitution and what happened in ancient Rome. You might have a way with words but what you write is usually nonsense. Time after time, you get it wrong.'

He contemptuously flicked some copies of the last edition of "Politicus" onto the stone floor and went on, 'You're campaigning against the restoration just as you campaigned against the execution of King Charles. You got it wrong then; you've got it wrong now. Monck is the future – Lambert, Fleetwood and your precious Sir Henry – yesterday's men. They're the past. They're gone. Or they soon will be. You are the past, Nedham. It's all coming apart and you are on the wrong side of history. Again.'

He laughed, flung on his coat and announced, 'Thank you for teaching me the newsbook business, Nedham, I shall now pursue the profession for myself. Enjoy it while you can. There isn't long now. The old order changeth, yielding place to new.'

After he'd gone, Newcomb enlightened me. Muddiman – or 'bloody

Muddy' as I now thought of him – knew the general's wife Anne. 'When Monck was a Royalist, a prisoner in the Tower of London,' Newcomb explained, 'He met widow Anne. She took in sewing and mending for the prisoners. Anyway, they liked one another well enough and married. Now, Anne has a brother, Thomas, a physician. Thomas is in awe of Monck, according to Muddiman. Anyway, this Thomas gives up his work to become Monck's assistant. You know the general can hardly read or write – he's from Devon?'

'Oh well that explains everything.'

'Anyway, a few weeks ago the general decided he needed support in the city. He wanted someone to write him up, back his cause, that sort of thing.'

'What cause?'

'The King,' said Newcomb flatly. 'Anyway, Monck asked Thomas, his wife's brother, to find someone and Thomas suggested Muddiman. He's the son of a family friend, see. A neighbour's son. Anyway, educated, bright, willing. Anyway, Monck took him on.'

'And you knew all this?' I was irritated he hadn't told me and equally irritated because he kept saying 'anyway'.

'Does no harm to have a foot in both camps, Marchamont. Does no harm. Anyway, what if Monck prevails? What if the King is restored? Makes sense to have a friend at court.'

'Might make sense for you, Tom. Not sure it will do me much good.'

I felt as if I'd been slapped in the face.

Within a week, Muddiman produced "The Kingdomes Intelligencer" (the title of an old publication which he shamelessly stole) then the un-grateful wretch started a second paper called "Mercurius Publicus". They followed exactly the same format as "Politicus" and the "Intelligencer", carrying some new items in each edition and reproducing some news from the previous one. Thanks to me, he had the contacts, he had the names of regular advertisers, he knew the times and dates of mail posts to other cities, he'd made friends with some of the Mercury-women round St Paul's. He even had the audacity to use Tom Newcomb as his printer.

I'd taught him my business and now he was out to ruin me.

My own position at the pinnacle of the trade was growing more precarious by the day. Readers were prepared to buy Muddiman's newsbooks even though they were fawningly unctuous in their grovelling to the illiterate Devonian mercenary George Monck and his Monarchist desires. It was all 'graciously' this and 'His Excellency' that. Readers lapped it up. They positively wanted Charles Stuart on the Throne.

I first felt a fist and then a kick. I fell into the mud of The Strand and curled into a ball. I felt the impact of more feet on my back. The filth in the street, combined with the pain of the assault, made me wish for unconsciousness but I was not so lucky.

The assault didn't last long. I looked up as one of the two men attacking me leaned down with his face close to mine and suffered the glutinous taste of wine and tobacco on his breath. I couldn't see him clearly, nor the man standing behind him. He hissed, 'You filthy traitor, Nedham. You filthy scandal-monger. You whore. You'll get what's coming to you, scum.' He spat a healthy gobbet into my face, straightened up, kicked me half-heartedly, laughed with his comrade and marched off whistling. I grovelled in pain and struggled to stand.

Nobody rushed to my aid. In those days, you couldn't risk being a Good Samaritan. It was too dangerous.

Despite the frozen winter, Monck's regiment of foot marched south from the Scottish border at Coldstream and Lambert's army – unpaid, disillusioned and disliking the prospect of battling it out with their own comrades – dissolved into the mist. Thomas Fairfax emerged from retirement to lead a troop of Yorkshiremen to help Monck on his way. Fairfax's name alone was enough to deter further military opposition. Back in London, the army declared its loyalty to Parliament and appointed Speaker Lenthall commander in chief. Lenthall started taking salutes as regiments marched past Westminster to demonstrate their devotion to our unelected, antiquated, incompetent Parliament.

I sought an audience with my old friend. A snooty servant told me Mr Speaker was too busy to see me and turned me away.

I called on Milton who said, 'It is the end. It is a judgment. We are all sinners. We were vouchsafed a vision of the new Jerusalem but we erred. Now is the second coming.'

'The second coming of Christ?'

'Of the Stuarts, and we shall be consigned to Hell. This is the time of trial and tribulation.' Milton sounded as if he quite liked the idea. 'Men of high renown, admired for their value and heroic virtue, are more rightly called destroyers and plagues of men.'

I rode out to Hampstead to see Sir Henry Vane. 'We cannot stand by and let God's blessed land give up its seed to the infidel,' he said. I was none the wiser.

I walked to the Great Piazza in Covent Garden where Nat Fiennes was living with his new wife. All he said was, 'We shall all be executed.' It didn't seem to bother him. He wanted to be closer to God and execution would presumably expedite matters.

I dropped in on my uncle, John Glynn, who said, 'If the rule of the Rump was unlawful, it follows that all the legislation passed since its inception in '48 must also be unlawful. It is a nice point of jurisprudence.' This did not help.

The Commonwealth was falling apart and my friends were powerless to stop it.

Lambert tried to rally his troops at Edgehill, failed and was imprisoned in the Tower. Fleetwood was in disgrace. The Rump re-admitted the elderly members excluded by Pride in '48 and then dissolved itself. A new election brought in a Royalist assembly.

Charles Stuart, knowing his time was at hand, paved the way for the restoration by publishing a declaration. He promised a general pardon and amnesty for all who had taken up arms against him and his father. The sins of the past would stay in the past. There would be no reprisals or recriminations – except for the people who took an active part in the trial and execution of the King. What about everyone else who may have crossed the Stuarts or antagonised the Cavaliers?

It was obvious to me the restoration would not take place without the settling of old scores.

I published a last warning. "Newes from Brussels" came out as a letter from a cavalier to a friend in England making it clear what would happen next. He said, 'Thinkest thou that we can breathe in peace, while we see a little finger left alive that hath been dipped in Royal blood? A thought of mercy more hateful is than Hell. He's an Oaf that thinks an Oath can tame a Prince beyond his pleasure.'

Parliament put up £20 reward for the author of this tract to be named and arrested. Then Major General Monck issued a decree banning the publication of "Mercurius Politicus" and "The Publick Intelligencer". And, damn me, not only did he ban almost every other publication as well, he handed a licence to publish not one but two newspapers to his personal assistant's best friend's son, bloody Muddy, Henry Muddiman.

CHAPTER 44

Fallen on evil days
and evil tongues
and with dangers compassed round

Spring-Summer 1660

There was only one course left open to me – flight. I had to get out of the country before the Cavaliers got in.

In late January, I summoned my wife to London. It took until late February for her to reply and she did not make the trip from Burford until the end of April. She finally arrived with her brood of children and servants on the day King Charles's dubious declaration of clemency was made public.

Lucy was in no better temper than when I'd last seen her almost a year ago. 'This country is lost. We are leaving,' she announced as soon as the baggage had been brought in, the children settled and we were alone in the parlour.

'We? Leaving?'

'The children and I. Soon. They are bringing back the King, a filthy Papist. Since Oliver betrayed the nation, there is no hope. We are leaving for Massachusetts Bay.'

I laughed. 'Have you been talking to Audley? That's his plan too.'

'No, I've been talking to Hannah Allen, the bookseller. She says it is a God-fearing place and far from this den of iniquity.'

'Lucy, we must certainly leave the country for a while. But not to sail across the ocean. We'll just go to Holland. You'll like it there – they're all God-fearing Protestants.'

'It is a foreign country. I cannot bring the children up speaking a foreign language. No, I am resolved. We must follow other pilgrims to the new world, the promised land.'

'Lucy, wife, sit down and listen,' I told her, looking at a worn and weary woman. God, I think, took more of a toll on her than all the children she cared for and all the children she lost put together. If we'd had time and leisure, I might have wanted to console her but we didn't. Instead, I said, 'Lucy, we must leave tomorrow morning. We will go to Folkestone and find a boat to carry us into Holland. We have little time. Charles will be here any day and, when he does, all those assurances of clemency and indemnity and no reprisals and all the rest of it will count for nothing. There will be a bloody retribution and I do not intend that we should remain here to witness it.'

'The Catholics are coming?' she asked.

'Indeed, Lucy, the Catholics are coming and they may very well be coming for your husband. We must escape while there is still time. Agreed?'

Lucy looked regretful, stared into a flickering candle-flame, whispered, 'How shall thee escape, husband, if thou neglect the Lord's great salvation which, at the first, began to be spoken by the Lord and was confirmed unto us by them that heard him?'

I took that to be a yes.

Getting out of England was not easy. There was a high demand for decent boats. Those guilty of causing the martyrdom of King Charles, especially those who signed his death warrant, led him to the scaffold or chopped off his head, were in fear of their lives. Oddly, some were determined to stay put.

Sir Henry, for instance. He had not signed the warrant and had not witnessed the execution. He was working in the Admiralty that day. He did not believe he had blood on his hands. William Lenthall decided he was safe because he only ever did as instructed by Parliament. Uncle John Glynn said it was always necessary for the judiciary to enforce the law and that was all he'd been doing these long years. Milton wouldn't go either because, he said, he didn't believe in running away. Nat Fiennes went down to Broughton Castle and then to a manor house in Wiltshire but he was not prepared to travel further afield.

Folkestone was busy and there were few rooms to be had. I managed to persuade a widow woman to let us spend two nights under her roof, Lucy and I sharing one room with four children, a servant and too many bags. We had with us just one maid, Faith. She was close to the children and shared Lucy's strange beliefs.

We'd left our other servants in Westminster with instructions to keep the house ready for our return. I, for one, intended to be back as soon as things settled down.

The weather was mild with a gentle breeze blowing up the English Channel. The price of a passage across the water had shot up since the day, so long ago, when I tried and failed to board a boat with Lucy Lighthorne and head for France. Now, I paced the shoreline looking for someone prepared to embark for Holland – or Belgium or even France – and met only surly looks or unconcealed aggression. 'Afraid of something?' taunted one fisherman, spitting onto a stone.

I was offered a flat-bottomed barge anchored in the bay and used for transporting goods a few miles up or down the coast in calm seas. This I rejected. I was told of a small boat called, apparently, a pinnace, that could supposedly be had down the coast at Dymchurch. I was given the chance to buy a skiff and sail it myself but I was pretty sure it would have thrown us into the water in even a mild breeze and none of us could swim.

There was a two-masted boat in the bay. It was being made ready for departure, with rowing boats coming and going as supplies were lifted on board. I sidled up to one of the men on the shore and inquired as casually as I could about its circumstances. He was not forthcoming. I waited, sitting on a rock and watching the activity. Plainly they were awaiting someone important. This was not somebody departing in secret, taking flight at the last minute. I wondered whether I could talk my way on board, buy a passage or even stow away. But for three adults and four children that seemed unlikely. I was beginning to despair of finding a way out of England, at least from this fish-stinking little village.

The to and fro of rowing boats looked as if it was coming to a conclusion. The boat seemed ready for the off when I felt a heavy arm grab my shoulder and a voice growl, 'I knew you'd be stranded.'

It was Tom Audley.

'By God, what are you doing here?' I demanded.

'Taking you and your family to Holland, Monty, that's what I'm doing here.'

'But how did you know?'

'No time for that now. Go and get Lucy and the children and be back here in 20 minutes. The tide is on the turn according to the captain.' Audley nodded towards a gnarled and weather-beaten man supervising two sailors lowering something into the hold.

We were under way three-quarters of an hour later. Lucy, Faith and the children were stowed below in the one decent cabin while I skulked on deck trying not to worry about being afloat as land faded into the distance, darkness fell, the wind got up and clouds threatened rain.

Audley joined me as I grew chillier and chillier and sought what shelter there was from the rising wind. He offered me brandy. 'It'll settle your stomach,' he said. I didn't need persuading. It seemed the best way to cope with this ordeal would be with as much alcohol in me as possible.

'Dutch courage,' I said holding his flask up before emptying its contents.

'Don't worry, I have more,' Audley laughed, 'I came prepared.'

'But how, Audley? Tell me.'

'How did I know you'd be here? How do you think? I followed you.'

'Followed me?'

'Yes, Monty. Thurloe says he owes you. In fact, he says he owes both of us, so a few weeks ago he told me to arrange this.'

'But how could you know I'd be there? I could have gone anywhere. On any day, at any time.'

'You wrote to your mother?'

'Yes,' I admitted. Obviously they were still reading my letters. In a sense, I knew they were but, as the restoration became more and more likely, I thought there was nothing to fear from Thurloe so it didn't matter if he was reading my letters. 'I'd have thought Thurloe had better things to do,' I said.

'He delegated,' said Audley. 'It was my job. We watched your preparations. We saw your family arrive from Burford. We knew as soon as your children did. If not sooner.'

'But Folkestone? Today?'

'You told your servants and, anyway, you've been there before, Monty, remember? It was obvious it would be your first port of call. If you'd gone somewhere else, you'd have been diverted back this way.'

'Well, I suppose I'm glad to see you, Audley. Tell me your plans.'

We reached Amsterdam in the early afternoon. There was a big sky with wispy clouds and a warm sun on our backs as our brig manoeuvred into the little harbour with water slapping at our sides and the town looking brighter and more welcoming than I expected. Lizzie and Marchamont were getting in the way of the crew as they ran around the deck. Mary was sitting beside Faith, the servant, playing with a toy while Margery, no longer a baby, was trying to persuade Tom Audley to bounce her up and down. Lucy sat wrapped in blankets scowling.

This was a family adventure, I thought to myself. We need not be parted. We can make the most of this exile, enjoy life in a different country, learn new things, I could practice medicine here for a while. We could set up home. Amsterdam wasn't as stern and austere as I feared. Too many sailors passing through, I supposed, for the full impact of Puritanism to take hold.

Audley had already found a tall, narrow house overlooking a canal for us all to rent. We had the top three floors of the newly-built five-storey building in an area called Herengeracht. The lower two levels were devoted to trade – warehouses with sack upon sack of pepper, ginger, nutmeg, cinnamon, saffron, cumin and cloves. The spices gave the whole building a curious aroma. One day, cloves predominated, on another, nutmeg. Whenever I sneezed, I thought pepper had the upper hand. It was always interesting.

It was strange spending time with the children. I'd never done so before. They were growing up. Lizzie was the image of her mother before Lucy was overwhelmed by piety. She was fair-haired, lively, cheeky and full of enthusiasm for our new town and the people in it. Marchamont was much more cautious. He said he hated the smoked fish and curious stews, supposedly containing meat, which we ate most of the time. He disliked being dragged to the old kirk twice a day by his mother but Lucy was determined not to spare him and she repaired to the church for company. She would drag Mary along as well, which left me to walk the city with little Margery – Lucy decreed she was too young to benefit from the services and might disrupt proceedings.

Margery and I would find a coffee shop and try to discover news from England. There were frequent visitors to Amsterdam, traders, officials of the new regime and others on the run from it, and it was possible to glean much about affairs under the new King.

Tom Audley was looking for a passage to the new world but the only destination for ships from Holland was New Amsterdam. 'A man can make money there,' Audley said.

'Aren't you a bit old to start again, Tom? You must be past 50,' I said as we enjoyed Dutch gin in one of the many taverns round the docks.

'Nothing else for it,' he said. 'Religious toleration, trade, land, natural resources. It is a land for the future.'

'Even under the Dutch?'

'Certainly. A republic, an empire, a power in the world and prepared to let people follow the Lord in their own way.'

'Won't you miss England?'

'Not now they have a King again, Monty, no,' he said firmly. 'But about your wife and children…'

Lucy was determined to sail with Audley. I forbade her. She said she would be taking the children. I said the children stayed with me, they did not deserve to be dragged half way round the world to a strange settlement where people spoke a foreign language just because their mother was a religious fanatic.

I thought about locking Lucy out of the house, sending her away and keeping the children with me. I had money, I could hire servants and a tutor. It wouldn't be difficult. Or, at least, not too difficult. Audley, on the other hand, was keen for my family to accompany him to New

Amsterdam. He tried to persuade me to go too.

'I am her husband and command her to remain here when you depart,' I told him. 'You cannot kidnap my whole family.'

He smiled condescendingly. I looked at him in the gloom of the pub as he said, 'Kidnap? I'll be saving them. Have you seen this?'

He slapped two pamphlets on the table. They were yet more attacks on me but these were the worst yet. I read them squinting in the light of a single guttering candle and felt a rush of fear course through me. It was a physical sensation, like taking a large gulp of geneva, the Dutch gin they lace themselves with in Amsterdam. The first was called "An Hue and Cry after Mercurius Politicus" and announced I was in Amsterdam, which was a worry because some Commonwealthmen had been murdered abroad or kidnapped and taken home. It described me as hawked-nosed, with rings in my ears, a slender body, being about 40 – all pretty accurate and in verse, too. Flatteringly, it said I had a tongue 'with a grace becoming no such traitor's face' but the nastiest bit was the last verse which said:

In case you send him home;
He shall be hang'd upon a Tree,
Cut down alive, and then you'le see
His Quarters have their Doom.

That wasn't the worst of it. Another pamphlet with a suspiciously similar title called "A Rope for Pol. Or, A Hue and Cry after Marchamont Nedham" called for me to be tortured to death and devoted no fewer than 44 pages to a collection of every insult and joke I had ever written at the expense of King Charles II. This was not likely to win me a pardon.

I flicked through this catalogue of insults and I must admit I couldn't repress the occasional smile, despite the terror it caused me. Who would have gone to such lengths to read through every old edition of "Politicus" and note down all the wit and wisdom it contained? I had no idea but the damage was there for all to see. If King Charles read this, there was no way back.

The insults came thick and fast: 'That Trifle called Charles the second... The Scotch Baby King of England... His Baby Majesty... Strip Tarquin out of all his Titles and pretty Trinkets of Majesty... The Thing of Scotland... the dapper Giant of the Jockies Interest... Charles Tarquin being already a Catholick, swore he would turn Turk too, but he would be revenged upon the English; James Tarquin is to be a Cardinal, and Rupert Tarquin is as good as the best in the Bunch, having been a Thief in two Elements… our Brethren of London have little confidence in a Cause that admits of a combination with that wretched Family… It is very possible, young Tarquin may lick up again the late vomit of the sins of his Family…'

It went on and on, page after page. I couldn't help being pleased with my turns of phrase. It is quite an achievement, I thought, to offer up such a variety of invective. What pleased me was how jocular it all was. Surely the Cavaliers had a sense of humour, did they not?

I looked at Audley. He looked grim.

Perhaps not.

It was difficult communicating with England. Audley had some way to reach Thurloe who, as predicted, knew so much about so many he was invaluable to the new regime and in no danger. One or two of my supposed friends had ingratiated themselves already – Nat Fiennes was now a King's man and so was my uncle, Judge John Glynn. To my utter astonishment, Lord Saye and Sele, Nat's father, the old Viscount, was made a member of the King's Privy Council.

The most important question was what made someone a 'King-killer'? Surely writing for the Government after the King was executed could not reasonably be called regicide. Being hated for writing on behalf of Oliver Cromwell was not the same thing as supporting the execution – indeed, I spent two years writing against that very thing. That must count for something.

Parliament was preparing a list of people lined up for the chop. Surprisingly, several of those likely to be hung, drawn and quartered were not even trying to save themselves. Perhaps they thought nothing would come of it; perhaps they didn't want to live any longer; perhaps they thought they were immune and could not believe such a fate was in store for them.

Worryingly, William Lenthall and Sir Henry Vane were both made exceptions to the general pardon.

My mother wrote from Burford. She said William was living there quietly with his wife Elizabeth and his son. She said the ex-Speaker had been excluded from the Act of Oblivion and briefly feared for his life. In the end he faced nothing worse than a ban on holding any public office. For a wealthy man of 69 that wasn't much of a punishment. She said William was much subdued, though, and scarcely emerged from the Abbey house, spending time instead with his collection of paintings and dwelling on the past. She added – and this was useful intelligence – that Lenthall had given the King £3,000.

Sir Henry, by contrast, was thrown in the Tower of London and, though the King decided he should not be executed, he stayed there.

By midsummer, arrests were being made, even as Parliament was still debating an Act of Oblivion. This said all crimes against the Monarchy would be forgotten – except for people actively involved in killing the last King.

Disturbingly, the bodies of Cromwell, Bradshaw and Ireton were prised from their graves, carried to Tyburn and hanged, their heads put on spikes in Westminster Hall. Ireton had been dead nine years but that didn't stop them. This was disgusting enough but worse was Charles Stuart's order that Milton's books should be burned by the public hangman – copies of his books were piled up and set alight outside the Old Bailey for three Mondays in a row. They were burned at Oxford University as well. No wonder the blind poet kept his head down. Milton was in hiding according to Marvell, who wrote to say that, as an MP in the Parliament which restored the King, he was safe.

'You can forget all about it, Lucy. You are not leaving Amsterdam with Tom Audley and you are certainly not taking the children.'

We were in our bedroom in the house by the canal. I spoke in a low voice because everyone else was, supposedly, asleep. I was firm and forceful.

She did not argue. I had expected a terrible row. I assumed Lucy would defy me, spit in my face, condemn me as the antichrist or, at the very least, say she could not go home and would not stay in Amsterdam so what would I have her do. Instead, she lowered her eyes and said meekly, 'I am a wife and wives must submit unto their own husbands, as unto the Lord.'

I should have realised.

CHAPTER 45

Having made the French
language and humors
universal, I cannot but look on it as a
sad omen of universal slavery

Summer 1660

Lucy and Audley slunk away in the night taking Faith and the four children with them. The Captain and I had been to one of the local herbergs drinking geneva all evening – at least I thought Audley had been drinking all evening but maybe not. I confess I was drunk and fell fast asleep in a comfortable leather armchair as soon as we got back home. Even so, it still astonishes me I wasn't woken by the clatter of three adults and four children descending the steep stairs of our house in Herengeracht. I am surprised Lizzy didn't want to say goodbye but maybe she was told not to disturb me. I shall never know.

I didn't come-to until the middle of the following morning. I could hear the usual sounds of workmen coming up from the canal-side, the shouts of stevedores, the cries of boatmen, an occasional thud as some large container was lowered onto a wooden floor. But the house itself was discouragingly quiet. I listened for the children; there was nothing, not a sound. Usually, Lizzy and Monty would be having a fight or Marjorie would be whining. Today they were silent. I groaned out a call for Lucy – my head ached – but she did not appear. I summoned Faith and demanded water and answer came there none.

The house was empty.

I struggled to my feet and, clinging onto pieces of furniture or wall hangings, made my way from room to room. Tucked into the frame of the mirror in our bedroom, I found a note in Audley's hand. He said he was taking Lucy and the children with him on a boat called "De Trouw", captain Jan Jansz Bestevaer, bound for New Amsterdam, to start a new life with the Godly people there. He said he would care for them and write again when they were settled. He said he had taken half the money I hid in a trunk in my room but what he left should be enough for the time being.

I was dumbstruck.

I ran out into the street and tried asking the men in the warehouse next door where the "De Trouw" might be moored and whether she had set sail. I had no Dutch, they had little English or Latin, so it took time. They indicated the direction in which moorings for large sailing ships might be found but it turned out to be another part of the canal system where you might hire a rowing boat to take supplies out to the bigger vessels offshore, at anchor in the Zuider Zee. It took most of the day to discover the "De Trouw" left for the new world at about half past six that morning when the tide was at its height.

While I was frantically running around from one friendly, incomprehensible Dutchman to another trying to understand what they were saying, I didn't have to think about what had happened. When I eventually understood the ship had sailed and there wouldn't be another heading for the new world for weeks, if not months, I crept back to the Herengeracht and wondered what to do next.

I took stock. It didn't take long and it wasn't enjoyable. I'd lost my wife and children. I'd lost my job, my living, my reputation, my country and I was in danger of losing my life. I had some money but it wouldn't last for ever. I was in a foreign country where I understood nobody and there was not a single soul in the entire city who cared about me unless one or two Royalists had arrived intending to murder me. They'd done such things before and there was nobody to protect, advise or guide me.

I should have felt lonely, in despair, vulnerable, endangered. The truth, which I feel a little ashamed to confess, is I felt a sort of exhilaration, a sense of freedom, a new hope.

I went out for a dinner of smoked fish, Rhenish wine and coffee, I hired a servant, a tall, thin, quite good-looking young man called Jan van Something-or-other (all Dutchmen are called Jan van Something-or-other) and, two days later, I set off for Paris.

I was on the Continent, alone. I should see the world and I should make contact with my child, Elizabeth, the other Elizabeth, the orphan in the convent in the custody of Catholic nuns. I should save her for the Protestant cause and return her to her rightful home, with me, in England. Being deprived of my four children, who I was only just getting to know, left me surprisingly bereft. I can't say I missed their mother but the children were a loss. I was their father. How dare my wife disappear with the entire brood in the custody of a man who was supposed to be my friend and mentor?

I thought of appealing for help to the authorities in Holland. Perhaps they could force my wife to return from New Amsterdam. But why should the Dutch Government care? Worse still, if I made myself known, there was a danger they would lock me up and send me back home for the King to deal with as he thought fit. After all, the States General of Holland had pledged their support and love to the King as they waved him off on his voyage home. They would be keen to round up any refugees from justice on his behalf.

And there were refugees – Parliament was publishing lists of 'conspirators' responsible for the execution of Charles I. These people were being hunted down to be put on trial and, in all probability, put to death. The likelihood was that they would not enjoy a clean kill at the hands of an axeman, a swordsman or a hangman. They would be executed painfully, slowly, grotesquely and the whole process could take an agonisingly long time. The sort of death the Cavaliers had in mind for the King-killers did not bear thinking about.

I could think of little else.

It took three weeks to ride from Amsterdam to Paris with the help of Jan van Something-or-other who spoke some English, a little Flemish and some French as well. It was high summer, the way was dusty and dry. The countryside was flat and stretched away for miles in every direction. Only a year earlier the Low Countries were filled with warring troops in a quarrel between the French and the Spanish – the war which won us Dunkirk – and signs of siege and devastation were all around. People lived beside the highway in hovels, food was expensive and we saw the bodies of several children who had apparently starved to death.

Jan van, only 17 himself, was much moved by the sight of these emaciated corpses. He wanted to bury them and say prayers over their bodies. I had to point out that was not what I was paying him for and if he wanted to become a priest, he needed to look elsewhere but not while he was helping me on my journey.

It was the farthest I'd ever travelled by many miles. The longest ride I'd made, I realised, was from London to Worcester, less than half the distance we were going.

The accommodation was grim. Filthy auberges with nothing to recommend them except that they were close to the main track – it would be wrong to describe those pitted, rutted, crowded, dangerous, neglected routes as 'roads'. Bridges were rickety or non-existent. We would have to detour miles upstream to find a way across, wade through shallow water or, on one occasion, trust a ferryman who made us abandon our horses with one ostler and hire two more on the far bank.

Eventually we reached Paris and found much of it to be a vast development site with huge new buildings in various stages of construction. This activity was intended to proclaim the might of the French King, we were told. The Monarch in question was Louis XIV, another boring Louis. You might think French mothers could come up with a more original Christian name but apparently not.

The centre of the town had been cleared for re-development but elsewhere within its walls, the city was a warren of backstreets stinking of excrement, manure and garlic and filled with the cacophony of the French tongue. This language is a corruption of Latin mixed with the Druidic gargling of the uncivilised Celt. Frenchmen, it turned out, are short people but fat. It is as if they were fed on truffles, like pigs, and denied the chance to breathe fresh air. Their women are hairy and sour-faced, scowling and angry all the time. They talk so fast it is impossible to decipher their gibberish. Their children are snivelling, ragged and crushed.

What a terrible place; what a terrible race.

Yet there I was, seeking out my daughter Elizabeth, trying to find her mother's grave and wondering how to get back home. I found the Convent of Our Lady of Calvary easily enough, about a mile north of the river not far from the great fortress of the Bastille. The nuns had a tall, impressive chapel and three stories of cloisters but I was not allowed beyond the main gate.

I'd left Jan van-Whatever at our auberge while I went to negotiate with the nuns but I didn't get further than the porter who spoke rapidly, in low tones, using strange, guttural sounds which may have been French or may have been something entirely of his own invention. I did not see him, only an eye and its socket, a piece of nose and some grey hair as he peered through a hole in the door. I tried Latin to no avail. He was not the most educated of men. I tried asking if he would take a letter to the Mother Superior. I decided he might respond if I spoke loudly enough. 'Une lettre pour la maman superior,' I bellowed and included a few sous. Now that, the garlic-breathing Catholic did understand. His hand appeared at the aperture and his filthy thumb rubbed his encrusted palm suggesting a few sous might not be enough.

Eventually, after two further visits to the convent, during which the porter and I became quite familiar with one another, a nun was dispatched to meet me at the gate though she, too, would not grant me admission nor would she show me her face. Our interview took place with me standing in the shadows of the building while the nun, whose name was never revealed to me, remained firmly on the inside where she repeated the word 'non' often enough for even someone who spoke no French to get the general gist of what she was saying.

We did make ourselves understood by speaking in Latin, though her French accent was enough to distort the classical elegance of the language into a rustic travesty. I told her I'd come for my daughter Elizabeth Light-horne, 'Veni ad filiam meam.'

'Exite, hic non receperint, nullas filia hic, Omnes filiae Christi sumus,' she said, 'Go away, you're not welcome here, you have no daughter. We are all daughters of Christ.'

The debate lasted most of the morning before this adamantine Saint Joan announced she had to attend sext or nones or terce or some other Catholic rite. She would not even acknowledge the convent contained an English child called Elizabeth whose mother died shortly after her birth ten years earlier though there was, apparently, a Sister Benedicta who may have come close to fitting the description. The net result was that my ten-year-old daughter would remain a stranger to me and she would never know her father had done all he could to find her. But what was I to do, in a strange city, knowing nobody of any influence?

I also visited the Cemetery of the Innocents in the naïve belief I might find a gravestone for my Catholic wife, the novice Elizabeth's mother Lucy. The place was disgusting, an open-air charnel house with mass graves which were not filled in until enough corpses had been dumped to justify the labour. It stank and the vile smell infected all the streets in the district. A handkerchief to the nose and even lavender in a pomander were no match for the odour of the cemetery.

One glance made it clear there was no chance of finding where poor Lucy might be buried. Alas, her beautiful body must long ago have been forced to mingle with those of hundreds of Frenchmen and women interred indiscriminately in this vision of Hell.

I fled as if pursued by demons.

I had to get home.

CHAPTER 46

Then let us chear,
this merry New Year
For CHARLES
shall wear the Crown

Autumn 1660

I spent much of my time in Paris teaching English to Jan van-Whatever and picking up a little French with the help of a local girl called Madeleine. I met her at the theatre. This was a novel experience after the ban on such entertainments at home. It was all very juvenile and unsophisticated but what can you expect, this was France? The great innovation was that they allowed women, as well as men, to act. It wasn't a bad thing. It turned out not all French women were ugly. Some were remarkably attractive and most actresses were happy to appear scantily-clad on stage then sell their favours to selected admirers. This increased the popularity of otherwise unfunny productions. As I tried to explain to Jan van, not so much treading the boards, then, as treading the bawds. He looked blank. A wasted witticism.

After paying a whole franc for one of Muddy's rags, I gathered Parliament passed its Act of Oblivion. Those excluded from the legislation, a dozen or so fools who hadn't had the sense to flee, were being put on trial.

I wrote to Thurloe, who was now advising Edward Hyde, the Lord Chancellor. I urged Thurloe to secure me a pardon. I wrote to Hyde pointing out my previous services to the King-martyr.

I wrote to Peter Heylyn, appealing to my old friend, who was sure to be back at court now.

I wrote to Judge John Glynn, who had been elected to the new Parliament.

I wrote to my mother telling her my wife and children had done a midnight flit.

I wrote to Henry Washington – he would be with the King seeking reward for his loyalty. He might be in a position to help.

I also wrote to an old friend, Henry Oxinden.

Oxinden was a sad case. He advertised himself as a Royalist clergyman and poet. He was seeking a living from the King to repair the family fortunes. I became reacquainted with him via Nat Fiennes. I'd written to Nat congratulating him on his father's elevation to the Privy Council and Nat replied with a long letter which mentioned Oxinden was a mourner at the funeral of James Thompson, the man in charge of rebuilding Broughton Castle. I'd met him and his wife Elizabeth at Nat's wedding, he reminded me. As Oxinden was short of money, I wrote asking for his help.

Thurloe didn't reply, nor did Hyde, now Earl of Clarendon. I did get a letter from my uncle, Judge John Glynn, mainly to inform me he'd received a Knighthood and I should in future address him as Sir John. He did say there were many impecunious Cavaliers in London and my best course, should I wish to return in safety, was to seek the assistance of one of them to obtain a pardon from the King. What was needed, said my uncle, was a piece of paper with the King's seal on it proclaiming my loyalty and forgiving me for any crimes I might have committed during the Commonwealth. He said he knew of several people who had received such a pardon. It was a standard document. He didn't know how much it cost.

Henry Washington did though. As I'd already provided him with a decent sum of money, he was, to a small extent, under an obligation to me. He replied surprisingly quickly to my letter, saying he understood why I might be afraid to return. I should be safe because I had not been excluded from the Act of Oblivion but if I felt the need for a pardon under the King's seal, he thought it could be arranged. It would, of course, be a costly business. He would be obliged to go to considerable trouble to secure the indulgence of members of the Privy Council and – he put it more delicately than this – their services did not come cheap.

Washington did not put a price on it, exactly, but he referred to the £50 I'd sent him some time ago and said this time he would probably need fifty times as much. I'd been expecting to pay £3,000, the same as William Lenthall, so £2,500 was almost a bargain. I did have that much money, plus a little more, stowed away in Burford so I wrote to Henry

Oxinden again, offering him a fee to ride to Burford, collect a package from my mother and take it to Washington in Whitehall. He would then need to be ready to come to me in Paris. I told Washington he would get half the money now and the other half when I had the pardon in my hand and I was safely back in London. I wrote to my mother explaining what was happening.

It all took time. I was impatient to return but it wasn't safe without the pardon – the Government had started killing its enemies. In November, Muddiman's "Intelligencer" reached Paris with an eye-witness description of the first execution.

The victim was Major General Thomas Harrison, one of the 59 'commissioners' who signed Charles I's death warrant. Harrison was strapped to a hurdle and dragged by horses to where Charing Cross stood before it was torn down during the rebellion. He was hanged by the neck but not until he was dead. He was cut down so he could watch as his private parts were cut off and his entrails torn out of his body and burnt. Only then was his head cut off. The King was there to witness the revenge, along with a huge crowd, which cheered on the bloody work. There would be more executions.

Milton had been found and jailed in the Tower. His books hadn't escaped the hangman; maybe he wouldn't either. I was happy to stay in Paris until I held a King's pardon in my hands.

Oxinden reached my lodgings before dawn one late-November day. He'd been in Paris for two days trying to find his way around but, not speaking the language, he found it difficult to grasp the little help offered by reluctant Frenchmen. They would shrug, spit and turn away, he said. I understood, having had much the same experience.

I had not seen Oxinden since we were at university what seemed like a lifetime ago. We had a lot of catching-up to do. He was as poor as a church mouse, with a wife and three children. He wanted the King to give him a church living or two. 'Everybody wants one, Marchamont,' he said, 'Clarendon says the King had no idea he had so many friends. If he'd known during his years in exile, he would have returned sooner.'

'It was a joke, Henry,' I said.

'Oh, really? Do you think so?'

'Clarendon was mocking you,' I explained.

'Oh, really?' Oxinden looked crestfallen. 'I thought he really did think the King should have come back sooner.'

'Henry,' I said, 'Without wanting to go through the events of the last ten years – and without mentioning the Battle of Worcester – do you really think the King could have just walked back into England any time he liked?'

'That's what Clarendon said.'

'Oh dear, Henry,' I said, 'He was joking. Obviously joking.'

'Oh, joking. I see.' Oxinden rubbed his unshaven chin with his hand and contemplated this. 'A joke,' he said, slowly, 'I see. Hmmm.'

Henry Oxinden was not especially endowed with intellectual capacity but he was a decent enough fellow. Thin, through years of poor food and penury; badly-dressed; with the constantly harried look of a man who expects the worst to happen at any moment, he was still surprisingly cheerful. I liked him at university for his optimism which hadn't been beaten out of him even though he was a prematurely old man whose prospects were constantly dashed.

Now he withdrew from an inside pocket of his riding cloak a piece of parchment with the seal of King Charles II. The seal was a red wax image of the King sitting on a canopied Throne wearing a crown and holding a sceptre and orb. The words announced, 'Now know ye, that We, in consideration of circumstances humbly represented unto Us, are Graciously pleased to extend Our Grace and Mercy unto the said Marchamont Nedham and to grant him Our Free Pardon for offences committed during the late detestable long and great Troubles Discords and Warrs that have for many Yeares past beene in this Kingdome.'

It did not specify the nature of these offences, which was just as well because, as far as I was concerned, I had not committed any. Writing the news, and commenting on it, could not reasonably be described as treason as far as I was concerned. What had we been fighting for if not freedom? Still, I suppose we had lost. Or won. Depending on which side you were on. Like many others, I was on both. And neither.

I kissed little Madeleine goodbye. I may have told her I would send for her in due course but I'm fairly sure she knew I didn't mean it. She made a pretty speech of farewell and went back to the theatre. As for Jan van, I paid him off and sent him back to Holland with my thanks and a promise to look him up if I were ever to find myself exiled there again.

It was odd. In the space of a few months, I experienced the rich, self-righteous Presbyterianism of the Amsterdam merchants and the chaos of Catholic courtesans in Paris. Each had its merits but the more time I spent in these cities, the more I longed for the filth and stink of a good old London street.

I was angry at the way Audley betrayed me and my wife abandoned me. I was surprisingly disappointed not to meet my daughter Elizabeth in her French nunnery and outraged at the so-called grave provided for her dear dead mother.

Yet I could not keep a spring out of my step as I finally set foot on English soil at Dunkirk and found a coal-carrying brig called "Brotherly Love" to take me home to Dover. It was a rough, uncomfortable crossing with a winter gale perishing the bones and sending the "Brotherly Love" flying across the choppy waves but it was mercifully short.

Three days later I was back at home in Westminster wondering what I would do now.

I had a pardon but I still had enemies. The pamphlets calling for my execution, not to mention the beating-up on the Strand, required some sort of response. It was time I got back into publishing even if I was banned from newsbooks. My first answer was obvious – a history of the civil war, now called the rebellion, of course. It was the very first published history. In my own words. As it happened. In verse. From the King's perspective.

It was an impressive effort, though say it myself. No fewer than 263 four-line verses describing the destruction of King Charles as it happened, from the pen of the leading news-writer of the day and published at very end of 1660, the last lines reading:

> *Then let us chear, this merry New-year;*
> *For CHARLES shall wear the Crown:*
> *'Tis a damn'd Cause, that damns the Laws,*
> *And turns all up-side down.*

I visited Burford for Christmas – we were at last allowed to celebrate the festival without fear. My mother said, 'You weren't always such an enthusiastic Royalist, Marchamont.'

I admitted as much but added that one learns from experience and, anyway, as one grows older one becomes less fanatical about changing the world. I was now forty, I pointed out.

'How are you going to get my grandchildren back, Marchamont?' she demanded. She was very unhappy about their disappearance and cursed my wife for a bigoted and disobedient woman. I couldn't disagree.

My mother was upset about many things. My step-father Christopher was ailing. His health had always been robust but now, when he should be enjoying his King-given freedom, he was slow, his mind wandered and his duties were largely undertaken by his son, my brother Robert, who was waiting for a parish of his own. Lucy's mother, Lucy, died in the summer, of plague, apparently. I don't suppose her daughter, my wife, even knew of it. The Lenthalls were at home but keeping close – William was ageing and humbled, according to mother. His wife Elizabeth felt humiliated and was subjected to vicious words and accusations whenever she ventured out. The Lenthalls employed ex-soldiers as bodyguards to protect them.

'The King's pardon is all well and good,' my brother Robert told me, 'But there are many Royalists looking for revenge, Monty. I'd keep my head down if I were you.'

'Bit late for that,' I said, waving a copy of my new book in his face. Robert groaned. 'It's selling well,' I told him.

Milton, when he was released from the Tower and before he retreated to the countryside, was dismissive. He said, 'That doggerel. Really Marchamont, is that the best you can do?'

CHAPTER 47

There is no pleasure
in the memory
of the past

1661-1662

I had to go a-doctoring. What the French call a 'journal-ist' without a journal is like a horseman without a horse, a boatman without a boat or, indeed, a King without a crown. The chronicling of the events and personalities of the moment was denied me by Government decree – indeed, it was denied everybody except that traitor Muddiman and his new best friend, Sir Roger L'Estrange, an unpleasant, vilifying bully without a single redeeming feature.

It was a dying season and even modern medical science – what little science there is in medicine – was not capable of curing the plague, the ague or old age let alone the executioner's sword, noose, knife and axe.

I spent two years mending limbs hacked about and festering from the wars; assisting ladies with unmentionable maladies (I had warm, dry hands, which they particularly relished); and wondering why the medical profession devoted itself to nostrums prescribed by ancient Greeks when there must be a more scientific way of curing people. Superstition, suspicion, witchery and hokum confounded even the most intelligent physician. Old wives' tales and nonsensical remedies involving toads' hearts and wood-lice not to mention bleeding the patient at every opportunity were as likely to be prescribed as poultices, clean water or fresh air. I still believed the safest remedy for most illnesses was to do as little as possible and let nature effect a cure. It was often successful and patients were eternally grateful not merely for being restored to health but for being spared the humiliation and agony usually prescribed by the quacks of my profession.

Alas, it was impossible not to be aware of the world beyond the sick room. It was a sad world. The King-killers were being done away with in batches and then Sir Henry Vane was brought back from prison on the Isle of Wight to face trial for treason.

And counsel for the prosecution? None other than my own uncle, Sir Henry's old friend, Judge Sir John Glynn.

I couldn't bring myself to visit my uncle. How could he turn his coat so easily and so completely that he would prosecute an old colleague for treason? He was trying to secure the death penalty for a man with whom he had shared responsibility during the Protectorate. Sir John and Sir Henry had been friends. Now, my relative was helping to impose judicial assassination on a troublesome nobleman. Maybe Sir John was trying to conceal his embarrassment and complicity. I was appalled.

A year earlier, on St George's Day 1661, King Charles II was finally crowned in a glorious ceremony. London was in its pomp. The fountains, by Royal decree, flowed with wine. I was watching in the crowds when Sir John was thrown from a horse which spooked at an explosion of a can-on-fire. The horse rolled on top of him, breaking several ribs. It looked like he might die but I strapped him up tightly with bandages, required him to lie still and prescribed regular doses of opium for the pain.

He recovered from the injury though not from the humiliation of being laughed at by the whole of London. Had I known one consequence of his recovery would be that he prosecuted Sir Henry, I would have offered the job to some incompetent sawbones and avoided visiting my uncle. He was an old man of 59 and would never have survived.

Sir Henry was passionately religious. Most of his pronunciations were too obscure to understand though the main theme was awakening us all to the approaching end of the world. Sir Henry had always been a quietly determined man with little sense of humour and a profound sense of his own importance but even his enemies would admit his trial was a farce. The King originally pardoned him because Sir Henry had deliberately avoided taking part in the trial or execution of Charles I. Yet, because Henry was a republican and remained a republican even after the restoration, Parliament decreed he was too dangerous to be allowed to live.

I tried to see him during his trial, when he was incarcerated in the

Tower, but I was told he would see no-one.

In April '62, the Viscount died. Age caught up with him. He'd lived no fewer than 80 years, born at the time of Queen Elizabeth.

I went to his memorial service in Oxford, the city he and his army occupied at the start of the rebellion. Was that really 20 years ago? I asked myself, as we filed out of St Mary's Church into a gentle rain. I found myself beside Elizabeth Thompson and commiserated with her on the death of her husband James, who I'd met and liked when we sat together at Nat Fiennes's wedding.

She was a comely woman though getting on a little – 30, I reckoned. She had most of her teeth and her hair was still brown. Her black mourning clothes did her pale complexion no favours but she was almost as tall as me and capable-looking. I offered her my arm as we walked towards New College where we were to take wine and refreshments.

'You know, my uncle was called Old Subtlety, don't you?' said Mrs Thompson.

'Your uncle?'

'The Viscount. Old Subtlety.'

'Was he? Why?'

'Because he used the twists and turns of the law for his own benefit.'

'I wish he were here now to help Sir Henry,' I said.

Nat Fiennes joined us. 'I was just saying, Nat, we need your father's skills to rescue Sir Henry.'

'We need your propaganda,' Nat said. 'It helped me when Parliament wanted my head. Might help Henry now.'

'Alas, I don't have a newsbook any more, Nat. And this Government is much better at enforcing the law than the old one was.'

'Is there nothing you can do?' asked Elizabeth and I saw a look of trust and expectation I had not seen in a woman's eyes for many years.

'I could write a pamphlet,' I said, 'But it wouldn't save him. The trial's already under way and when we were fighting for Nat, we were only taking on that fool William Prynne. This time it would be the King himself and, at present, the King can do no wrong.'

'That won't last,' said Nat.

'Maybe not but it will last longer than Sir Henry's life, I'm afraid. Everybody knows when a case like that goes to trial there can only be one verdict.'

'My uncle, your father,' she turned to Nat, 'Would have said it was time to forgive and forget.'

'He would,' said Nat. 'He's ordered some Latin to be inscribed in the porch at Broughton. It says, "There is no pleasure in the memory of the past". I'm inclined to agree with him.'

In May, blind priest Peter Heylyn died. I went to his funeral in Westminster Abbey. He'd been restored to fame and fortune by Charles II and was given a magnificent send-off in the high church manner he loved.

A memorial service was also held for Peter at St Mary's in Oxford and, as I was in Burford at the time straightening out my new house, I thought I should attend, if only out of gratitude for the way he and his brother sheltered me from Cromwell's troops back in '49. It was a long and tedious service with lengthy sermons on loyalty and honour, both of which Peter possessed along with a filthy temper and an argumentative nature so in tune with the times.

As I emerged, hoping to meet Elizabeth – we were to dine together that evening – I was suddenly set upon by a gang of thugs. They punched me in the face and ribs, kneed me most cruelly between the legs, kicked me to the ground and rained blows down on me. Nobody stopped them. It was worse than the beating I took on The Strand a few years earlier and this time they didn't run off but hauled me to my feet, dragged me along the cobblestones and announced they were taking me to a magistrate.

'We'll have you hanged for a traitor, Nedham,' one of them drawled in the unmistakable accent of a foolish, ignorant cavalier.

'Drawn and quartered as well,' laughed another.

'Guts spilling out all over the stage,' mocked the third.

I was dragged towards the castle while two of these cavaliers ran ahead to summon a constable and a magistrate. I tried reasoning with them and was awarded with another punch in the face and a rag tied across my mouth. I was in pain, tattered and bleeding. My captors yelled out to various surprised passers-by, 'Look. We have him. Nedham the scribbler. Nedham the traitor. Nedham the poison-penman. This man out-slanders Satan.'

At last we reached the castle gates where the two cavaliers were waiting with a gentleman I took to be a magistrate. Four guards were drawn up to one side. The cavaliers, so young they were babes in arms when the rebellion first broke out, were sobering up in the face of a figure of authority.

One of them, with long hair, a thin face and a drawl only the wealthiest affect, declared to the magistrate, 'Sir, we present you with the living corpse of "Mercurius Politicus", Oliver Cromwell's loathsome creature. Sir, we urge you to dispatch him with the utmost celerity before he commits further crimes against our beloved monarch.'

The magistrate, a middle-aged merchant, did not look amused at being hauled away from his other occupations – dinner, perhaps – by these rowdies. He asked me, 'You sir. Identify yourself and be quick about it.'

I shook off the hands holding my arms, removed the gag from my mouth and bowed to this figure of authority. 'Your worship, allow me to present myself. Doctor Marchamont Nedham, gentleman, at your service. And allow me to offer you this document for your perusal.'

For I had in my possession, in case of just such an occasion, the document with the King's seal granting me a pardon. The magistrate took it, opened it, gazed at it with a long look which made me wonder if he were truly capable of reading, handed it to my main accuser without a word, waited while it was read again, demanded its return, handed it back to me and, looking at my captors, said, 'Release this man immediately. I will thank you not to take the law into your own hands. You owe Doctor Nedham an apology. Whatever offences you think he may be guilty of are irrelevant. He has a pardon under the King's own seal.'

'Forgery,' said the leading cavalier but not convincingly.

'If you can prove that, sir,' said the magistrate, 'Then perhaps we might re-open this case but in the meantime you will apologise to Dr Nedham at once.'

The students were forced to beg my pardon and the magistrate dismissed me with a wave of his hand, leaving me bloodied and bedraggled outside the castle with no help.

I staggered away towards Queen's Lane where I was to meet Mrs Thompson and her two companions but I was so late I despaired they would stay for me. I arrived, entered by the front door into the warm atmosphere of Jobson's coffee shop when the heat, pain, exhaustion and smell off the coffee overwhelmed me and I fell down in a dead faint.

Mrs Thompson ordered up a coach and horses and insisted on accompanying me back to Westwell, a couple of miles outside Burford, where I was trying to make my country home habitable. It was a modest place, built a little over 100 years earlier, near the village pond, with fine views over open fields and made of that charming golden or honey-coloured stone which is a feature of that part of England.

Mrs Thompson took command of the servants, ordered them to prepare me a warm broth and bring brandy, stoke up the fires and put me to bed. She said she would remain overnight provided Mrs Green, the housekeeper, stayed with her to ensure the proprieties were seen to.

Mrs Thompson sent word to my mother, who apparently turned up while I was asleep, discussed my condition with my new-found saviour and withdrew knowing I was in safe hands.

I did tell Mrs Thompson not to summon a physician and asked her to supply me with laudanum for the pain. She insisted on administering thick doses of honey on the worst bruising on my ribs, legs, face and arms. This was an intimate procedure which I found myself delighting in as Mrs Thompson's natural fragrances, her delicate breath and her light fingers, overwhelmed my senses.

Had I felt a little stronger, I would have taken her in my arms there and then.

Sir Henry Vane was executed in June. I was still recovering from my beating and did not see the terrible sight. I felt I should have been there to show moral support or gratitude for the opportunities he gave me but I was not fit enough. He wouldn't have noticed. Sir Henry was not of sound mind. It seems he made a noble exit and at least he was spared the torture and indignity set aside for the king-killers. He enjoyed an aristocrat's death – one accurate blow with a sharp sword parting his head from his body in an instant. For that blessing, at least, I felt we should be grateful.

My mother was not helpful. She wanted me to move into the rectory to be cared for and then she wanted me to sail to New Amsterdam to find my wife and children. I was unwilling to do either, especially as Elizabeth Thompson appointed herself my nurse for the next few weeks and moved into the servants' quarters of Westwell Manor.

She said she had no commitments. She was living with her mother-in-law in a cottage on the Broughton estate and she would far rather do something useful with her time than listen to the old woman muttering about her dead husband and her dead son.

Once I was fit again, I wanted to return to London and resume my medical practice. I could not afford to be absent for long or my best patients – that is to say, those who were unwell but wealthy and unlikely to die of their illnesses – would seek out alternative physicians or rely on the bogus medicaments peddled by the semi-literate apothecaries whose concoctions contain everything from rat droppings to arsenic. If I cared for the lives of my patients, I had to be there to protect them from medical mountebanks.

Before taking my leave of Burford, I visited William Lenthall. He was a broken man. At 71, he was old, not as old as the Viscount, but more decrepit. He had lost weight. He was ghostly thin, the skin drawn down his face, his eyes large, bloodshot and half-unseeing, his clothes stained and shabby despite his wealth and his wife's best efforts. His voice was as shaky as his hands. He had little conversation but stared through the large windows of the big, cold great hall of the priory house at the summer rain.

He did say, 'I am a worm, Nedham, I am a worm. I should never have done what I have done. Defy the King. Give evidence against his killers. Command the army. Take money. Sell favours. None of it. That shall be my epitaph, *vermis sum*, I am a worm.'

CHAPTER 48

It mattered not from
whence the plague came but
all agreed it was come into
Holland again.

November 1662

'My Dear Nedham,' began the letter, written several months earlier. In familiar hand-writing, it went on, 'It is with great regret I write to inform you of the death of your wife Mrs Lucy Nedham, who took sick not long after our arrival in New Amsterdam and did not truly recover but became gradually weaker and weaker. We sought out the best medical assistance to no avail. Her disease, which I believe may have been caused by the conditions on board the "De Trouw" and may be described perhaps as a recurrence of the plague which has visited these shores as it has the shores of Europe, was not confined to your wife. I regret to inform you your children Elizabeth, Mary, Marchamont and Marjorie also contracted the illness and died within days of each other. For the wages of sin is death; but the gift of God is eternal life through Jesus Christ our Lord, Amen.'

It was signed Thomas Audley.

CHAPTER 49

Valuing money rather than conscience,
friendship, or love to his prince,
many can not endure
to hear him spoken of.

1662-1663

I presented Audley's letter to my mother and there was much wailing and gnashing of teeth, particularly as my step-father Christopher was going blind and her life with him was increasingly difficult. She was devastated by the news. Her grandchildren didn't even have graves she could visit. There was no chance she would ever venture to New Amsterdam or anywhere else in the new world.

I was in mourning for months. My patients were sympathetic. Mrs Thompson was solicitous and kind. I preferred not to talk about this tragedy. 'It is the times we live in,' I would say quietly and people would nod in understanding. It was devastating. I threw myself into my work and visited my mother more often now the roads were free of soldiers (though the highwaymen problem was becoming worse now most of the army had been paid off and discharged). My brother, the Rev Rob, was still in Burford to help his parents but it was all a little dismal.

After receiving Audley's letter, I broke out in a hot, fiery impetigo. It was an unsightly illness which I was reluctant for Mrs Thompson to witness. The rash ran through my beard like a red half-moon from one ear to the other. I went to the apothecary's and tried all manner of unguents, waters and lotions. Eventually I devised a purifying liquor infused with mercurial powder. By administering it with the tip of my finger twice a day, it quickly cured me and I have been using the infusion on my own patients ever since. Its success was one of the reasons I wrote my best-selling book on medicines and the medical profession.

Mainly, I wrote it because I needed something to absorb me after the news from New Amsterdam and because it would promote my medical qualifications and bring in more patients. There was satisfaction to be gained from taking on the medical establishment, the pompous practitioners of ancient Greek medicine. This might not be as rewarding as attacking politicians but it was satisfying enough. My book "Medala Medicinae" became compulsory reading for anyone engaged in the constant struggle to improve the health of the nation. It was another triumph.

Milton said, 'It's all very well, Marchamont, but curing people's health is a task for God. You should be trying to cure their souls.'

Milton had moved house again and acquired another new wife. Elizabeth was 31 years his junior. He was 55, she was a mere 24. Mrs Elizabeth Thompson, my new Elizabeth, was only ten years my junior. It seemed a more respectable age gap. I assumed Milton's relationship was that of a wise, blind sage and his willing pupil and amanuensis and certainly there were no children though, on one of my increasingly rare visits, he did say under his breath, 'There's no reason why we shouldn't have children you know.' I tried not to look surprised even though he couldn't see me.

Milton was busy revising a very long poem whenever I visited him. It was a hard task because Elizabeth, his young wife, would have to read each passage to him while he thought about whether this was as he wanted it, before asking her to read on. She read me a couple of excerpts. It was impressive but I did wonder if he wasn't writing about the civil war all over again. God was, presumably, the republic but Satan was an attractive character and very hard-done-by. 'Are you sure you don't really prefer the Devil?' I asked him.

'Satan has to be attractive otherwise the temptations of the Devil would not be temptations at all,' Milton countered.

Mrs Elizabeth Thompson became Mrs Elizabeth Nedham in a quiet ceremony at St Bride's Church in Fleet Street on April 19, 1663. There were few witnesses – just my brother Robert and Nat Fiennes and his wife. Elizabeth looked younger than her 32 years; I looked all my 43.

A year later almost to the day, our daughter Temple was born. She was some compensation for my great loss.

CHAPTER 50

*I owe thee nothing,
reader and look for
no favour at thy hands*

June 1667

The King was presented with his three saddles costing £21 – I had to contribute ten shillings as one of the welcoming party at The George in Burford – and we all enjoyed the sight of his pretty little mistress Nell Gwynne. She flounced from her carriage with lightness and grace, all red, green and pink frills and furbelows, a gleam in her eye and a charming smile for everyone. She was the leading actress of the London stage. I'd seen her several times myself.

The King, his brother the Duke of York and pretty, witty Nell were in Burford for the races. They were notorious affairs which took place up on the downs a ten-minute ride from the town. Their notoriety had little to do with the horses – in the past 30 years, there had been three murders during race week, two of them at The George itself.

The family hotel was given over to the King and his entourage for a week.

As he walked from the presentation into the hotel, the King took the time to talk briefly to members of the welcoming party. He was accompanied by Edward Hyde, the Earl of Clarendon, and the town mayor. My step-father should have been there but he was too unwell. Instead, my brother Robert took his place and shuffled along in the King's wake as Charles made his way down the line of local dignitaries smiling, laughing and joshing in high good humour.

They reached Marchamont Nedham. I bowed deeply and looked up at my King.

Clarendon tried to move the King swiftly on but Charles waved him away impatiently. I'm not sure how I felt at that moment. I recalled bowing and kissing the hand of his martyred father and reminded myself I had campaigned on that unfortunate monarch's behalf in the two years before they chopped off his head. I could not forget, however, the insults, taunts and mockery I had thrown in the direction of his son in the years of his exile.

A writer can be embarrassed by coming face to face with a victim of his satire but I was a different man now; older and wiser. The commonwealth and all that talk of republicanism, of the vote, of democracy and government of the people, by the people and for the people had faded away. The only dispute these days was whether the Catholic Duke of York could become King – but that day was far off and everyone knew Charles was more than capable of fathering sons so it wasn't something anyone worried about.

We'd survived the great plague of '65 and the great fire of '66. What we wanted more than anything was entertainment, gaiety, enjoyment, a release from the cares and scares of the past 25 years.

Even so, I rather missed the old days. I missed being at the centre of things. Doctoring was all well and good but it didn't compare with the excitement of being engaged at the heart of the nation's affairs or the thrill of feeling you were able to influence the course of history.

All this flew through my mind as the King approached, as I bowed, caught Clarendon's eye, watched Charles move away and then return.

'Nedham? The Nedham? "Politicus" and all that, hey?" he said.

'Your Majesty,' I said, bowing once again.

'Clarendon,' the King said, turning to his Lord Chancellor, 'Marchamont Nedham. The notorious Marchamont Nedham.' The King smiled, turned back to me and said, 'We may have work for you, Nedham.'

We have been all ill us'd, by this day's poet.
'Tis our ioint' cause
I know you in your hearts
hate serious plays

Marchamont Nedham went on to write at least four propaganda books on behalf of King Charles II. He was paid £500 by Thomas Osborne, first Duke of Leeds, for the first of his attacks on the King's political opponent Anthony Ashley-Cooper, the Earl of Shaftesbury, founder of the Whig political party.

The last of Marchamont Nedham's books was a call for England to go to war with France. The radical republican had become a confirmed Tory.

A century later, his writings on republicanism influenced American revolutionaries Josiah Quincey and John Adams, the second US President. They sometimes signed their own articles 'Marchamont Nedham'.

Nedham died a wealthy man, in December 1678 at the age of 58. It was a sudden death, probably a heart attack. He was in the Grecian Coffee House in Devereux Court, off Fleet Street, at the time. He was buried at St Clement Danes Church on The Strand.

Elizabeth Nedham died in their London home in 1683. The fate of her daughter Temple, and that of his daughter, the French nun Elizabeth, are unknown.

His first wife, Lucy Nedham, died in London in 1679. Their son Marchamont married Mary Grault in London in 1684. Their daughter Elizabeth died in England in 1697. The fate of their other two daughters, Mary and Margery, is unknown.

Acknowledgements

Many thanks to:

Bethany Jones,
Matt Madden,
Aly Hartley
not to mention Fiona Hastilow.

The chapter headings in this book are all culled from publications of the Civil War era. For the sources of these titles and also to see a list of books and publications which I have used, abused and plagiarised, please see www.themanwhoinventedthe.news

Printed in Great Britain
by Amazon